I0612048

IN THE MIRROR

Welcome To My World

1

KRYSTAL CYRUS

Publishing & Media

IN THE MIRROR

Published by OOTW Publishing & Media

Canada

Edited by Le Shaundra Muhammad

Requests for permission to make copies of any part of this work should be e-mailed to info@ootwonline.com or mailed to the following address: Krystal Paterson-Cyrus, OOTW Publishing and Media, 132 Commerce Park Drive- Unit K Suite 203, Barrie, ON L4N 0Z7. Canada.

www.ootwonline.com

Library of Congress Control Number: 2017914585
ISBN: 978-0-9959819-0-4

To my mother,
for being the angel on my right shoulder.

Also by Krystal Cyrus
The Enigmatics

Acknowledgments

There are quite a few people I'd like to thank for helping me get this book going. Firstly, I'd like to thank my mother for always providing unfiltered, uncensored, and sometimes unsolicited advice. She was usually right. Secondly, I'd like to acknowledge my high school friends- the fun stars. Though we've been separated and hardly talk anymore, this story began with them. I'd also like to thank Gerald Harris and Lena Lalsee for not ignoring me when I messaged them with ideas at three in the morning. Jucil Phillip, I could always count on her to send three full pages and a voice note whenever I hit a plot wall. For that I am forever grateful. And finally, I'd like to thank Atiya from I Am Network for taking the time to walk me through every single step I took in the publishing and business launching process. I could not have made it this far without her wisdom.

Preface

In The Mirror was a story years in the making; it spent most of its life brewing in my mind. I often found myself wondering if there was another world within mirrors. I imagined our reflections were other versions of ourselves trying to keep us out of a bad dimension. It was difficult finding a plot to surround my obsession with the idea of a world within a mirror at first. I had many, but it felt like I'd either be running with scissors or running into a brick wall if I tried to pursue them. One day while writing another story I was having a hard time tying all the back stories together. In time, I grew more interested in the backstory rather than the main story itself. Eventually I branched off writing the backstory as a whole other book because, in my mind, it deserved more than a fleeting mention. From there the ideas kept flowing and thus In The Mirror was born.

This was a very difficult story to write. It's one thing to imagine something and another to find the right descriptive words to bring it to life. The story surrounds Giselle Thomas; a young curious girl who has found herself in a peculiar situation. Everyone has had a bit of Giselle in their heart at some point. It's that point in life where you know who you are, but you still feel a bit lost. Throughout this writing and publishing process I'd like to think I've moved, even if only by five steps, away from that point. Publishing 'The Enigmatics' was a monumental moment in my life that I will always remember and cherish. I have to say though, publishing 'In The Mirror' has been one of the greatest experiences I've ever had. Not only have I completed my second book, but I also self-published it through my own company.

My mother always said, "you are your own enemy." I know she says it so I won't be so hard on myself. Sometimes it is ridiculous how thin I spread myself. I like to look at it as a positive thing though; I am my own tough critic. We should all be our own tough critic. We won't change and be great because someone else wants us to. We can fake it, but how long will it last? We can only change and be great when we truly want it for ourselves. I hope that my journey to find myself and accomplish my childhood dreams inspire you, my readers, to do great things. Don't be afraid to be great! One day, someday, depends on today!

Krystal Cyrus

TABLE OF CONTENTS

CHAPTER ONE..1

CHAPTER TWO 11

CHAPTER THREE 43

CHAPTER FOUR..69

CHAPTER FIVE 99

CHAPTER SIX 117

CHAPTER SEVEN 143

CHAPTER EIGHT 183

CHAPTER NINE...225

CHAPTER TEN...265

CHAPTER ELEVEN 289

CHAPTER TWELVE..337

CHAPTER THIRTEEN 355

CHAPTER FOURTEEN...377

CHAPTER FIFTEEN 395

CHAPTER SIXTEEN...427

CHAPTER SEVENTEEN 445

CHAPTER EIGHTEEN 471

CHAPTER NINETEEN.......................................487

CHAPTER TWENTY......................................513

CHAPTER TWENTY-ONE...............................537

CHAPTER TWENTY-TWO 547

CHAPTER TWENTY-THREE........................573

I believe that sometimes the bad times in our life put us on a direct path to the very best times in our life.

~Unknown

CHAPTER ONE

MEMORIES

SHE DIDN'T GO straight home that day. She didn't know why, but she felt a strong need to visit her grandmother. Weekdays, she usually went straight home, weekends she would spend with her grandmother. Today, for some reason, she had to go to her, to see her. She lived in Good Hope, her grandmother in Madigrass, which meant that whether she took a bus going straight to Madigrass or Pedmontempts she would still get there; all roads had a way of connecting at some point. One way was just longer than the other. Madigrass busses were so hard to get. First of all, there were only four of them. Compared to the million and two busses there were for everywhere else in Grenada, that wasn't a lot. Because the busses were so few and the distance they need travel was so far, they didn't come out on the stands as frequent as the other busses so whenever they did, there was a rush. She couldn't deal with the rush, so she hopped the first Pedmontempts bus that arrived and headed to her grandmother's house.

The drive was long and not at all quiet. She could hear the squeak of the bus she was in as if it had a self-made sound system. This wasn't one of those high roofed busses that everyone her age ran for. And it wasn't one of those 'pound-road' low roofed busses that disregarded speed limits and passenger safety. This was one of the old school, no tint, *fig-truck* busses. If she was seen in this her friends would never let her live it down. Never expect much from a fig-truck. This thing could break down at any moment and the driver would have to flag down another bus to take you the rest of the way. The radio was in and out of static. One minute you could hear the station host talking about what Mr. Killa, Tallpree and the other Soca artists were planning for carnival, the next a *'crsshhh'* sound.

At the back of the bus this tall, old guy was sitting by the window refusing to give his lips and her ears a break. You always found one of those people on the bus. Those that never shut up and never had anything to say that made sense. If you didn't have at least one annoying person on the bus, then you were in the wrong country. Believe it or not, the normal people on the streets were sometimes more disruptive than the ones they had committed to the Mt. Gay Mental Hospital. That was one thing Giselle Thomas of Good Hope knew too well.

After a long time of catching bolters behind her neck she finally reached her stop. Now she had to climb the long, dreaded hill that led to her grandmother's house. Just standing and looking at it wouldn't get her there, so she started a fast climb to the top wishing, after ten steps, that she was there already. When she finally made it, her grandmother didn't seem surprised to see her at all. Giselle felt like she should be. How often does she show up on a weekday? Never.

"Aye, Gizzy," her grandmother greeted her after Giselle called her attention. "How come you pass today?"

"I jus' feel to," she said. "You good?"

"I just here holdin' on. I fightin' a little head ache, but by the grace of God it go pass," she said.

Giselle's grandmother was a very lovable woman. She was cheery and sweet. She loved children. That's why Giselle and her brothers always looked forward to visiting her, even if they had to walk to her house. She always had something interesting to say or somewhere fun to take them. She was very short and meaty with a full head of grey hair, a round face with endless smile lines and a big mole near her right eye. Giselle loved her more than any granddaughter could love her grandmother. In a way, she was like the mother they wished they had.

"You drink enough water today? Sometimes you just need water that's why you get head ache, nuh," Giselle informed.

Her dad told her that every time she got headaches. He wasn't a fan of Advil and Tylenol and those other tablets. He preferred the sleep-it-off method. Her grandmother raised a half empty Glenelg bottle shaking it to emphasize the missing content. Ok, so she did drink water.

"How you been? Why you come by today? Is just Thursday."

Her grandmother monitored every twitch in her facial expression. She was looking for signs. There was a loss in the family some months earlier, but Giselle hadn't seemed affected by it. She should be. She could tell from a mile away when Giselle wasn't feeling like herself, but this visit had her stumped.

"I good. I doh know. Somethin' jus' tell me to pass by you today." She sighed and plopped down on the chair near the dining table.

"That's God," her grandmother's rusted voice warmed up.

Her voice didn't travel far enough for Giselle to hear though. Ruby was simply relishing in God's goodness. Her head was low and she seemed as though she had something heavy weighing down on her shoulders. Something so powerful it fought to make her emotional in front of her granddaughter. That was something she had never done before and nothing she wanted to start practicing now.

"Gran'mom?" Giselle softly called to her.

As she took a moment to gaze around the room, mind deep set in upsetting thoughts, her eyes landed on Giselle's feet. Feet covered in shoes so battered and worn it was barely recognizable as school shoes. Much less would she call it black. It was so gray and washed out and the leather was peeling along the sides; certainly, a shoe that had seen better days.

4

"Why Brent have you wearin' this shoes?" She bluntly pointed at it.

"This?" Giselle scanned her feet self-consciously.

"Yes. Why he doh buy a new shoes for you?"

"I doh want him to," she responded timidly.

"Why?" Ruby rounded on her. "You doh see how this thing beat up and indecent? You walkin' on the ground."

"Is ok. I doh want a new one." Giselle's voice was stronger now.

Ruby's eyes washed over her ready for an argument she knew she could win. But after looking upon her young, strong granddaughter she held back. She understood. She more than understood. She felt what Giselle was feeling. Their family wasn't fortunate neither in wealth nor in health. In fact, it was the uncontrollable circumstances of health that had lead them to such misfortune. It was Giselle's mom that had "broke" the family. It wasn't a loathing, gold digging drain of money. As mentioned before, it couldn't be controlled. Ruby could see it on Giselle's face that it was those events that was bothering her granddaughter. That was why she would never ask her dad to buy her a new anything.

"You doh have to feel bad." Ruby succored. "He is you father. He will take care of you."

No response. Giselle sat there anxiously playing with her fingers, excessively rubbing her hands and avoiding eye contact.

"Oh ho, as I remember, I have somethin' for you." Her grandmother said trying to lift the weight that had befallen so suddenly.

Giselle walked across the living room to the one-seater couch Ruby brought herself to sit in. The house was nothing special; a two bedroom, concrete box with a no gate verandah and a water tank. It wasn't fancy. In the living room, just like in any other Caribbean woman's house, there were a bunch of ornaments, fake flowers, really old pictures of relatives Giselle didn't know and a few TV remotes with no battery in them. Typical Grenadian, they always have a bunch of useless stuff in the house. Stuff that, if you made the mistake and move it an inch out of position, they would kill you for. Gosh! She learned her lesson after breaking one of her grandmother's ornaments. She acted as though she pulled a blade on her or something. She was so attached to her stuff.

Her grandmother proceeded to lift her weak, flabby arms up to her neck and fondle with the hook of her chain. It was a sturdy, snake chain with a small hand-mirror pendant attached by the handle. It wasn't that big, but it was big enough to see your reflection in it. It was a really unique and unusual chain that she had never seen anywhere else in Grenada. Her grandmother never took it off, ever. She had always known her with that chain. Her grandmother wouldn't be her grandmother without it honestly. It took some time, but after offering some help it was off. It felt strange seeing her without it. The home of the pendant, her chest, looked so bare and not like hers. It was empty and without personality.

Giselle handed it to her, but all she did was close Giselle's fingers around it and said, "Is yours now."

"You lie," was her impulsive response.

"Is not *lie*, is *story*," she corrected her granddaughter's abrasiveness.

She never liked them to say lie. She always told them instead of saying 'you lie' say 'you tellin' stories'.

"Why you givin' me your chain?" She asked.

Sure, it would be a great honor to own something that her grandmother cherished more than life itself, but it also felt wrong. It was Ruby's.

"Cause, I want to pass it on. My mother give me and I want to give it to you," she smiled.

"But…"

"I doh have any girl children, Giselle," she said.

It was true. Her grandmother had four boys. And all of them were scattered all over the world. Uncle Andrew, the eldest, was in England. He was a business man. Uncle John was in America. He went there to study and ended up staying. Now he was married and had two children. Uncle Rohan in Canada was probably getting arrested as they spoke and then there was her father, Brent. He was a middle child. He had four children just like his mom and he almost ended up with four boys too. That was, until Giselle came along. She was the youngest of three of the most annoying boys in the world.

She thought for a moment before responding. "Th-thanks."

She couldn't think of anything to say. What she really wanted to ask again was, "why?"

"This chain been in the family for a long time." She started giving her the back story. "Is not necessarily a must that I give it to a girl in the family, but I feel like you deserve it. You remind me of myself when I was younger; curious, boisterous, troublesome, thoughtful. But you also stronger and more passionate than I could ever be."

Giselle could feel her cheeks get hot as they rose into a deep, pleased smile.

"As long as you have that everythin' go be fine, Gizzy," she smiled back at her.

"Thanks," she said again through an extremely toothy grin.

Giselle could remember that day as if it were yesterday. She remembered how jolly she was for the rest of the day after she accepted her gift. She remembered how determined her grandmother was to talk to her brothers, so much so that she called them before she left. She remembered her grandmother hugging her so tight when she was leaving that she still felt her stubby arms around her after she descended the hill. Her scent was ever present, like *blue* soap, bush tea and some other sweet aroma she could never name-the smell of an old person. She remembered everything. It was really hard to forget amazing people. Someone who touched your life in more ways than one was always hard to let go of. They always seemed to live within you. And when they died, it was like a part of you died too. It was as if you were incomplete and nothing you did would ever make you whole again. That was how she felt when she heard that her grandmother, Ruby Thomas, passed in her sleep the next day.

Giselle was lying on the couch at home thinking about all this a month after Ruby passed. She missed her grandmother so much. Her weekends were void now. To be honest, losing someone wasn't the reason why people felt so upset after a death; it was the memories. The memories were more haunting than the actual news of the loss. When they were gone, it was like everything in the past found it ideal to come flooding to the surface. Memories you hadn't visited in ages suddenly become your most prized possessions. Knowing all the memories you had were all you were ever going to have. It hurt. It was a benefit to her that school broke soon after, because she honestly couldn't think of anything else, but Ruby. She was lying there, TV running, showing some random talk show on GBN. They were talking about some ten-year-old girl that had gone missing two weeks ago. She switched the TV to Disney junior. She couldn't hear that right now. Imagination Movers was showing. It was a show for little children, but even at fourteen she still liked watching it. For some time, she couldn't even bring herself to watch TV, so this being the first thing she had seen since then was comforting. Giselle had her fingers clasped around the pendant of the gold chain on her neck as she watched the movers talk about their 'Idea Emergency'.

"As long as you have that everythin' go be fine, Gizzy," she heard Ruby in her head.

"I hope so." She thought.

CHAPTER TWO

HALLUCINATIONS

BOOM! BOOM! BOOM!

"I not stoppin'!" Amron, Giselle's older brother, was drumming on her door.

Eight o'clock Friday morning. Eight o'clock and the idiots come out to play. It was too early for this. She was so irritated with him that she didn't even care to respond.

"G-I-Z-Z-Y! Get up or I'll leave you behin'! You lazy! Yeah, yeah! You lazy!" He was singing like those bring it on cheerleaders did.

Giselle rolled her eyes. "One mornin'," she whispered. "Just one mornin' where I doh want to knock him out. That too much to ask for lord?" She looked up at her ceiling praying.

He continued excessively drumming on her door. She sat at the foot of her bed, hands clasped as she stared out the window to the back of her house now. Some song lyrics were dancing through her head. She never knew the artist of this song, or the entire song really. All she knew was, *"Them big head boys who don't have any education."* She only knew that much because she always sang just that part for Amron. She would have opened the door and sang it to him now as per usual, but she was still glum and not fully Giselle. Her vibrancy left with Ruby. She couldn't deal with anything as she usually did. Two deaths in such short space of time…

"One! Get ready to go! Two! Get… ouch!"

"Shut up, boy, shut up," Giselle heard her dad.

She giggled. Now she needed to go outside to see his shame face. When she opened the door, he was standing there rubbing the back of his head and scowling.

"You cause that," he blamed her.

"I did? I so proud of myself," she would have said before, but now she just shrugged and offered a teasing smile.

That wasn't the response he was expecting at all. What happened to his sister; the one that gave him a hard time with everything, the one that occasionally threatened to beat him up but never seriously hit him before. Where was that girl? Amron's spirit noticeably faltered before he went after her again.

"You have everythin' you need right? 'Cause after that forty hours you spend in your room I shouldn' have to hear *'I forget to take…'* ok?" He said, as he took the lead through the hall to the front door.

"Why you like to exaggerate so much?"

"Why you so ugly? I just doh know."

She rolled her eyes again, shook her head and walked out the door.

"Dad! We gone!" Amron shut the door after exiting behind her.

They were heading to the netball court in Tanteen. Amron was a snare drummer in The National Drum Corp and they had practice there. He was really good at drumming; always beating on something with his hands, sticks, pencils or pens. The house was never quiet when he was home. Giselle ended up being a part of the band when she went to watch practice one day and the teacher said, "No spectators." She played the symbols. It wasn't a big deal in her opinion, but all the drummers in the band seemed to love the symbols. Depending on the song they were playing, they'd go off when she hit it at just the right time. Giselle on the other hand found it hard to handle. Hearing it was one thing, but holding onto that heavy-ass piece of instrument and clapping it throughout a three-minute beat was hard work. The first time she played them, she wasn't aware of the "proper" way to use them, and ended up hitting herself in the lip. It bled a lot. All her brother did was laugh and pull out his phone to capture the moment. Since then, she'd been asking to play tenor, but the Major said she couldn't this time around.

She didn't start going to the practices just to follow her brother though. She would never do that. Her friend Emma was in the band and she liked hanging out with her after practice. They barely saw each other during summer vacation anyway so why not milk the opportunity? Her dad was ok with it since he wanted her to start opening up again. Giselle just wasn't Giselle without the sass.

Emma was one of the two bass players. It was really amusing to see such a skinny girl hold up that big drum and hit it with so much power. It was an amazing and scary sight. Will she fall or will she break? All jokes aside, the bass was Giselle's favorite. Without the bass there was no body to the rhythm.

"Squad!" Mr. Williams, the Major, shouted and clicked his sticks twice.

Whenever they heard that, they were supposed to form up with uniform movement. That meant sticks upright by their noses and stand at ease. That didn't happen. They were all too busy talking or showing each other a beat to realize he was ready to start, so the response was late.

"Nah, all-yuh not ready yet," he waved his stick and wrinkled his nose. "Squad!" He did it again. This time they got it right.

"Attention!" He yelled and they brought their feet together with sticks behind their backs. Giselle had to hold the symbols by her side.

"At ease!" He yelled. Every left foot took a step to the left, hands still behind backs. This time they were more in sync than the second. "Alright. Today is the last practice..."

"I thought we had tomorrow?" Raheem reminded him.

"I tell you to talk?" Mr. Williams pointed him with the stick. "But yes, I think we supposed to have tomorrow."

"Ok, so today is the last before the last," Raheem kept joking around like nobody's business.

"I want a clean run down with no mistake. Any mistake and you startin' over from the top. We not leavin' until it run smooth," Mr. Williams instructed.

He wasn't joking about that either. He could be a really chill guy as long as they did what they had to do. Today, the second to last wrap-up practice before the big carnival launch, was no day to be screwing up the beats. They should have it by now.

"Ok so is the Normal Soca, The Independence, The S&S Soca and then, em..." he was thinking hard.

"'Charge up!' Big man you forgettin'?" Amron reminded him of the last beat.

"Yeah, that. Alright! Squad! By the centre- Normal Soca-quick march!" He shouted and they began with a seven-pace roll.

Everything after that seemed to go on forever. He had them playing the Normal Soca for a long time. It was a really nice beat to play, but after playing it for about five minutes, bored wouldn't begin to describe the feeling. Or maybe it was just Giselle. She was new to this. He was walking in and around the band straightening lines, making some people stop then start and randomly asking one or two of them to solo. When he finally made the signals to move on to the next beat, a few people weren't paying attention. So half the band was still in

Normal Soca while the other half were rolling up The Independence. You could imagine the groans after having to start from the top again. When they started, it was still bright outside. When they finished, it was almost dark.

You'd think after all that, they would be tired enough to quietly put the drums away and head home, but no. They partied all the way to the store room on the other side of the court to put the stuff away. Amron truly found his place with these noisy set of people. Who was she kidding though, she loved them too! They were so funny, laid back and talented. Just the type of people she needed to help her forget the pain of losing her loved ones.

"Woi, woi!" Rayanna yelled out over the noise after they secured the drums in the room. "I have a project workin' on for TAMCC Com class. I hadda do a report on racism, so I want an interview with all of you," she said.

"And now you choose to say that, when the sun goin' down?" Cheddi spoke up.

"Hush! I reach late today so I couldn' do it before. Anyway, plant all-yuh ass on the steps and let's make this quick," she pointed.

There were a few jokes, cursing about how rude she was, but within a minute they were all sitting on the steps waiting to be questioned. She pulled out a ripped piece of crumpled paper from her side bag and straightened it. Then she turned on her phone to record.

"Ok. What is the first thing that comes to mind when you hear the word racism?" She asked.

It was then that Giselle's suspicions about the entire band being a pack of idiots were confirmed.

"White people hatin' on black people!"

"Slavery!"

"Africa!"

"Short people hatin' on tall people!"

"Shut up, Raheem!"

"You see!"

"How 'bout all-yuh raise your hand before talkin'!"

"Doh even get me started!"

Everyone was shouting over each other and having a ball of a time screwing up Rayanna's interview. She didn't seem to mind though. She was laughing hard behind the camera too. She asked a few more questions, all with responses like that, until she gave up on getting them to be serious. They weren't serious people unless they were behind the drums; even then, just barely.

"You done?" Mr. Williams asked her as she folded the piece of paper and shoved it back into her bag. She nodded. "Alright, turn the camera here."

The real comedy show began.

"Racism… is wrong! Racism was invented by… the white people!"

He started literally preaching. The entire band was in a fit of grins, laughter and claps shouting "AMEN!"

"Why? Because they do not like to see us black people succeed! Alright!" He continued breaking out in laughter as well.

Raheem shouted, "Preach brother!"

"One more thing, one more thing…" he called the wondering Rayanna's attention again.

She seemed as though she forgot it was supposed to be a legitimate interview. He suddenly got serious placing his hand on the fence next to him to hold up his weight as he spoke.

"This happened a couple weeks ago. This lady, I think she works on fox news, you guys heard of that, the fox news? This lady gon' have the audacity…"

"THE AUDACITY!" Raheem, the tall boy who liked nothing better, yelled.

"… a matter of fact, a black lady said that. She said that Santa Clause should be changed to some type of animal or somethin'. What she sayin' is that there is too much emphasis on the white. But she don' know what she sayin' because Saint Nicholas, the real Saint Nicholas, was a black man! An Jesus, my people, Jesus, was a black man!"

They laughed even harder.

"Jesus is a black man like you, you and you! Black people!" He raised a fist high in the air.

"YEAH!"

The band members were shouting and stretching out to give him hi-fives as if he was some top-notch athlete that just won his race. They exploded in excitement probably echoing through the whole area waking the residents.

"And cut." He pointed Rayanna then made his exit.

Giselle hadn't felt so weak from laughter in weeks. Before school was closed she was one of those people that made a fool of herself like that to entertain. But her grandmother's passing had changed her. Turned out band practice really was the medicine she needed. She picked up her stuff as they started flowing out of the court after Mr. Williams.

"Aye, Cheddi, Raheem, we bombin' ride!" Amron ran off and left her.

Emma and Giselle walked behind everybody on the way out and watched as they tried to flag a ride to town. No one wanted to stop for such a large group of children. They started play cussing each other again saying, "assholes, doh walk so close together, nah" and pushing each other. It wasn't her intention to join the band, but suddenly she was feeling happy that she did. Her only problem now was finding things to occupy herself when they weren't around. When it got quiet and all she had was her thoughts, she would need something to occupy her then. If she didn't she'd only end up crying again; crying about Ruby, about her family's hardship and her mother. It was a stifling sense of pain she had to endure.

"You ok?" Amron asked Giselle.

They had finally left the band behind as well as the hustle and bustle of St. George's. It had been about two minutes now since the bus had taken them to their stop. Since then they had made considerable progress down the Good Hope road in search of home. Despite their squabbles one would say Giselle and Amron were as close as brothers and sisters came. They spoke to each other way more than their father, brothers and friends were aware of, but frankly they liked it that way. It was like having a secret best friend to hold you up when the world threw you down.

"Yeah," her voice was almost a crackly whisper.

"You doh want to talk about nothin'?" He urged.

"No," she mumbled in response.

He let the words fall for some time. All they could hear was the cool night air rushing by them, owl calls and their own foot-steps bouncing off the walls of houses. There was some chirp-ing here and there from the crickets and random crackling of branches. It was a pretty normal night; just like any other. The only thing unusual about it was the lack of Giselle's loud voice waking every living thing within earshot of her. That was what Amron was missing. That was what he was seeking from her. Being loud was fun, but he'd rather not be loud alone.

"It had to happen sooner or later," he said, his voice distant.

He knew their grandmother's death was still troubling her. It was troubling him too. For heaven's sake, he had spent a lot of time with her. She took care of him like he was her own son and she always called to check up when he didn't pass by for a while. He didn't have a mother to do those things for him. Even though he never openly expressed it, he really appreciated his grandmother for everything she was and everything she did.

He wasn't one to act all mushy and express signs of hurt, but he truly missed her. She was his grandmother. What hurt him most about losing her was that he lost his sister too. She didn't want to do anything anymore. No more playful arguments or teasing or covering up his mistakes from their dad. Nothing. He wasn't about to say this out loud though. He decided to wait it out. Giselle would come around soon.

"Well I would of choose later," the bitterness in her voice was almost livid.

"You doh get to choose," was his wise response.

"I know," she groaned. "That's why mom dead too."

"Gizzy…" He called after his sulking little sister, but she was long gone. Home was only a few feet away now and she took advantage by bolting forward and letting herself inside. All Amron could do now was huff, cuss under his breath and hope to get his sister talking again.

~*~

"Gizzy," she heard a male voice whisper her name.

She rolled over in bed, eyes still closed.

"Gizzy." The voice called again.

She groaned and swatted the air around her ears. Her room went silent again, just the way she liked it. Not long after she felt something thin and fuzzy penetrate her ears, she jumped out of sleep swatting herself only stopping when she heard Amron bellowing in pure bliss on her bedroom floor.

"You can' just leave me alone for one mornin'?" She hoarsely shouted at him.

It was too early to abuse her vocals like this.

He pretended to wipe a tear. "Drum Corp practice in two hours."

He was too dedicated to getting her there for her liking. Did her dad put him up to this? Did they have some type of deal to get her out of the house because she honestly would have preferred Andre for that job. He had more, how you say, common sense. He wasn't any less annoying. He just had more smarts about his annoying behavior.

"Lord give me the strength… to knock out this boy," she dropped her head back on her pillow.

"Lord give me the strength… to stop laughin'!" He choked on air trying to talk and laugh at the same time.

The rest of the day went on just like the previous one. She went to practice with her brother where he ditched her to hang out with Raheem and Cheddi. Then she hung around with Emma who insisted on keeping Giselle talking and on her toes. They did a rundown of the beats. Half the time, Raheem drove Mr. Williams crazy. Then they did their last party across the court to the store room. As exciting as it sounded there was something almost saddening about it. This was the last practice. This was the last time they were all going to be together for the school break. Knowing this made her feel like yet another piece of herself was going to be gone. She was going to involuntarily leave part of herself with these people and most likely not hear from half of them until the next event. Wasn't that a comforting thought? School wasn't even opening next week. They still had the rest of July and all off August to go through.

"Last lap! KFC or Creole Shack?" Raheem shouted over them as they walked across the Carenage.

Since this was the last night of practice, they all wanted to have a little hang out before going home. The 'last lap' as they called it.

"You buyin' for me?" Emma asked him.

"Well you know," he wiggled his eyebrows. "After freeness comes what?" He put his hand by his ear waiting a response.

"I don' know what kinda business she think we runnin' here?" Cheddi laughed.

"Let's just get KFC and chill behind the mall with Rayanna and them," Amron picked back up the food talk.

"Always studyin' your belly," Giselle shook her head.

She was actually a little open today; more talkative. But that was because she had gotten comfortable. Too bad it was the last day; last lap.

"Who you want to study it for me?"

"Who buyin' it for you?" She smirked.

Amron never had money-ever. As opposed to Giselle who was always saving. She could guarantee he would cuss her out now then ask her to pay when he got to the front of the line. She was going to make him beg for it.

"My bro covered man!" Cheddi tapped Amron's shoulder.

Damn, she thought.

Raheem started to sing, "Like a good neighbor Cheddi is here with-some-KFC!"

Giselle couldn't resist the urge to laugh.

"I got insurance," Amron grinned and chucked his thumb in Cheddi's direction.

~*~

Today was Carnival Launch. They were dressed in their uniforms looking smart and ready for the road. The band wore black pants and white long-sleeved shirts. Giselle being who she was, had to add a little something to it to make the look her own. She had on a thin black tie that set her apart from everybody else. She wasn't going to wear it at first, but Emma made her. Emma was just like her. She had her own style. She wore a black bow tie. At first glance one would think this band was made up entirely of boys. All the girls had their hair pulled back neatly in pompoms. Then Emma and Giselle with their neck wear. That could play some mind games.

"So how you feelin'? You ready?" Emma asked while rotating her head and stretching her neck muscles.

Giselle took a deep breath before responding trying to fight the nerves from her voice. This would be her very first performance with them. She had been a member for three weeks and now it was time to prove that she belonged there. She didn't know what to expect when they marched out there and started a rendition of what they rehearsed for so long. She had never been to any of her brother's performances before, so she didn't know how the crowd usually reacted to them. She had been to drum fest once. It was a beautiful thing watching the drummers dance and get into different formations all while perfectly executing their beats. The audience seemed to enjoy it too. Even if they weren't supporters of a certain school they politely cheered while they played. Booing only came along when results were being called.

Giselle nodded while looking at Rayanna conduct a pre-performance interview. She was still trying to get that project done. Taking on the band members one by one seemed to work for her. Can't have too much stupidity in one camera lens, right?

"You know, you doesn' talk as much as you used to. We hadda fix that."

Emma made note of Giselle's lack of input in any of their recent conversations. Not that she hadn't noticed and made great effort to change it. She was just annoyed enough now to mention it out loud. Giselle just shrugged. She didn't feel like it. She had all the witty responses and sass in her head, but just wasn't in the mood to voice them yet. When she did, then she would go on like she used to. How long would that take? God alone knew.

"Ok. Is time. Squad, strap up," Mr. Williams came hollering.

It was finally time to go out there and do what she did best; clap two pieces of metal together. She went over to the side where all their stuff was stacked and picked up one of the symbols. Then she put her right hand in the leather loop and twisted it a bit to make sure it was secure. Everyone else was finding their spot in line hooking their straps to their drums. Some of them had to use brace drums. She never wanted to use one of those. The brace by itself was heavy and restricting. The drum for the brace was heavy. Put those two together- that would be deadly for the back. The one thing she liked about it, though, was the fact that the skin was tighter and tougher than the other drums so it sounded bone chillingly beautiful when someone soloed on it.

Before picking up the second symbol she lifted her chain and stared at it; it was tucked into her shirt. Contrary to what you might think, after Ruby's death she didn't wear the chain as often. She actually put it away because she couldn't bring herself to look at it. Every time she saw it, it would revive a memory of her grandmother that she was trying to suppress. After all, she had only known the chain on Ruby's neck. She even contemplated putting it in Ruby's coffin on the day of her funeral. What stopped her? She literally couldn't let go. It was a gift so she had to keep it. Only recently, as she started trying to put things behind her, could she bring herself to wear it.

As she placed her gaze on it she focused on her reflection looking back at her.

I wonder if gran'mom was still alive if I would be in drum corps?

She thought as she held onto it. Disrupted from thought by the spec of dirt on the glass drawing her focus she made motion to clean it. Only, that didn't go exactly as expected. What happened next couldn't be expected. In what universe would something like that be expected? Not hers, that's for sure. In shock, she let go of it letting it fall hard against her chest. Her heart beat on the other side hitting with twice its usual strength; it was almost pushing the pendant off her chest, resisting it. She stood baffled as she tried to process the scenario that had just gone down. Did her thumb really just…

"Giselle! Get in line!" Mr. Williams yelled at her.

"Don' mess up. And if you mess up make sure is 'cause you bust your lip again cause that was funny," Raheem said as he raced by her.

"Up high?"

He stretched out his hand to do their weird little handshake, but she didn't follow. She was still a bit shaken up.

"Maybe next year."

She couldn't even be amused by his remark. In that short space of time she had forgotten where she was. She thought she had forgotten everything she was about to go out and play as well. What type of obeah is this? She grabbed the other symbol, walked over to the last row and stood up. She couldn't hear anything around her anymore except the third bass in her chest and her mind questioning, "how?" She looked around her. A few of the boys were having trouble with their straps and so weren't ready yet. She took the opportunity, before readying her symbol, to look at the mirror again. The dirt spot had gone and it looked as normal as ever. Maybe she was seeing things. This was her first play-out. Maybe she was nervous. She took a deep breath and lifted her thumb just as she did before and swiped the mirror again. She wasn't seeing things! It happened again!

"Giselle! Why we have to wait on you?" She jumped out of her trance and pulled the leather strap around her hand.

"Ok. Squad…by the centre! Normal Soca… quick march!" Mr. Williams instructed.

They were off into the streets of the Lagoon Road following other marching parties. She was hitting the symbol on time and loud enough. Though, she wasn't doing it with the same energy and vibe as she did in practice. She couldn't. At this point her mind was far from where she was. The entire performance was a ringing blur because all she could think of was her thumb going into the mirror.

When the performance was over they had to go all the way up to the Ministry of Culture and pack the drums away. Just to be clear, that was no joke walk. It wasn't far from where they had stopped at the Carenage. What was hard was walking up the hill, signing in their names at the front desk, climbing six floors because she hated elevators, packing away the stuff and doing it all again in reverse. On top of it all, she was completely freaked by the piece of jewelry on her chest. Not once since her thumb went through it, to her getting into the botanical gardens near the ministry did it leave her mind. Not once. Things like that didn't happen every day. She was worried about what kind of witchcraft the chain might be enclosing, but because of her bond with it she couldn't bring herself to rip it off and throw it away. A few weeks ago maybe, but now she had grown to love it. Maybe she should tell somebody. She could be seeing things. There was still that possibility. Emma said it herself, she hadn't been herself lately. She should show her what she just saw and maybe she could put some logic to it.

"Raheem, take the symbols for me, nah? I doh want to walk all up there," she called to the preoccupied Raheem. His mouth never got a break.

"Jus' the symbols you have and you doh want to walk?" He questioned her.

"Girl, walk with your thing!" Amron scolded. She watched him crossed eyed as he passed them. "Emma have the big-ass bass and you doh want to hold symbols?"

"Relax and mind your business!" She snapped back.

Amron paused, taken aback by Giselle's response. Was she just irritated or was she actually returning to being his sassy sister? Then again 'irritated' was Giselle's middle name.

Raheem shook his head at their banter and stretched his hand. "Give me." He took it.

"Thanks." She said then headed back down the hill where Emma was bringing up the rear. Giselle pulled her aside to the patio at the entrance to the gardens. She had no clue why they called it gardens when ninety percent of the plants in there were a mix of grass, fencing and missed weeds. Five percent were spacey, thick trunk trees and the last five percent was the Bouganvillia; the national flower. That wasn't a botanical garden. It was more like a really big back yard. Then further up there was this random stunt, lion's head chilling in the grass minding his own business. At least the place was well kept. She had knowledge that in the past it actually used to look better. There were plants and a lovely view to wonder at and even a zoo. In recent days, however, it just wasn't like that anymore.

They were in the round patio a third ways up the hill. She wanted someplace quiet to tell Emma what she saw; somewhere far from the rest of the band. Most Grenadians weren't very accepting for things like this. They were very religious people and the second something stepped out of their religion or comfort zone they shunned it. Nothing supernatural, paranormal or unexplainable by some term in the bible should take place around them whatsoever. That was how it was. The moment something unusual happened they'd say you had a demon, or you were working obeah. They always knew who needed prayers. Then, after that, they'd do away with you for good. Strictly speaking, they were terrified of those things.

Emma was leaning against the wall, obviously annoyed that Giselle stopped her from taking the bass to the store room. Giselle's load was long gone with Raheem. Whether or not this conversation was prolonged or stalled, her work was done for the day. It was different for Emma though. None of the boys were gentlemen enough to help her so she'd have to take the bass up there herself.

Bring back what you take out,' they'd say.

They weren't even willing to trade instruments. Raheem probably only took Giselle's symbols because it was barely much to carry on top of his own stuff. At least that was what Emma said. She had been complaining since Giselle took her by the wrist and lead her to the patio. She didn't say little; she said a lot.

"Hurry up and talk, jah!" She rushed.

"Ok, so before we do the parade I was holdin' my chain and it get dirty so I try to clean it, but instead of cleanin' it this happen."

She was rushing her words so close together it was unclear whether Emma caught any of it. She didn't want Emma to walk away before she could get to the point. And her nerves were grating so close on the edge that she couldn't slow down. Things like that didn't happen often or at all as a matter a fact. So why was her chain making her see strange things? Emma's face was laced with confusion. Still Giselle proceeded to lift her chain and chuck her finger against the glass and it just sunk through again.

"Sooo…" Emma raised a brow. "You make a sweaty finger print?"

Giselle's expression was plagued with perplexity and decorated with a furrowed brow that could be read as, 'the hell?'

"My finger go in…" her voice died as she drew her hand away from the pendant.

Emma smiled the most pleased smile she could ever pull off.

"Aw, makin' up stories. The real Gizzy ready to come out?"

Irritated and slightly offended by this Giselle stood up. "No, I not lyin'. My finger... it... you didn' just see that? Emma look!"

She was trying to convince her. Seeing is believing, isn't it? That was what she always heard. So why wasn't Emma seeing her finger penetrating this glass as though it was some sort of jello? Giselle was seeing it. She couldn't be that deep into a hallucination. No way.

Emma just hauled up her bass drum and began walking.

"Right. Wait for me. I comin' back next year," She joked about the distance.

"Emma!" She called.

"Child, put your finger in your mirror and wait!" Emma laughed.

Giselle had no words.

~*~

I doh understand. I just doh understand. Why she didn' see it? Giselle thought to herself.

She was dumfumbled. This mirror earned her attention. Why couldn't Emma see it? She was right there. What was going on? That shouldn't be possible. Things like that didn't just happen. She had to be imagining it. She sat on her verandah wall breathing the cool air before going to bed. At night, it got too hot too quickly in her room, and she hated sleeping without covers. The only way to survive was to get cold so that she'd fall asleep feeling warm under the covers. Once she was knocked out nothing would wake her. Giselle and sleep had a special relationship. Tonight, sleep was pleading for her attention in the back of her head, but she couldn't help to sit and stare at the cause of her confusion. Thumbs don't just go through mirrors every day.

She had taken it off and was holding onto it in both hands over her lap. It didn't look strange. Nothing about it was magical. Her grandmother was a good woman, there was no way she would purposely give her a cursed chain. She wouldn't do something like that. Period. So there had to be some reason her eyes were playing these types of tricks on her. Maybe she just needed to go to bed. Yeah, maybe that was it. Her brain was probably worn out from cramming beats three weeks straight. Then the anxiety on top of that and her grandmother's death swimming in her brain, among other things. Maybe she was just hallucinating. She swung her leg over the wall in a half way attempt to go inside.

Maybe am hallucinatin', but what if am not?

Then she'd have to throw away the last thing she had to remind her of her grandmother. She gazed at the mirror. She was looking at a tiny version of herself; the chubby faced girl that didn't laugh as much anymore. She seemed confused and lost. She was. She felt tied up in the head. Something inside her was saying 'get over it already- live!' But she just couldn't find the incentive. There was a time, not long ago, when she could find excitement in anything. She literally sat on the step and endured ant bites just to see them work. It was fascinating. The females did all the outside work, the males stayed in and mated with the queen who just spit babies like a pipe spit water. They were so organized and together. Then she'd watch bees pollinate the flowers or play detective if she saw a dead plant or animal and try to find what caused the death. That was just her; curious Giselle. But now she'd lost her motivation to do anything. Between their financial situation and losing the lady that gave birth to her she was secretly depressed. She was only fourteen, but she already worried about her family's financial future as if she was a forty-year-old, jobless single mother. She always tried to help out where she could, but her dad said she was too young to worry about that stuff. He told her to just think about being a school kid for as long as she had left and leave that stuff to him. She couldn't though. She wished he would stop saying she was too young and just explain to her exactly what was going on. Even though she already had bits and pieces of it figured out she still wanted to have that talk.

Her mom was admitted to the Mt. Gay Mental Hospital when she was about six years old. That couldn't have been cheap. Then, in January of the current year her mother mysteriously passed away even though her mental health wasn't a threat to her physical wellbeing. That funeral definitely wasn't cheap. Since her mom wasn't around for most of it her dad had the four of them to look after; her, Amron, Andre and BJ. Now her grandmother was gone. The entire cost of that burial wasn't in her father's hands alone, but it still was a lot. She knew they were suffering. He was just one man.

Stop thinking about this!

She had to clear her mind of this tied up mess and find a new focus. She needed to get back that life she once had. Where she knew that things weren't perfect, but somehow, she managed to find joy in the little things. Playing drums was just a spark. She needed a flame.

Rubbing her fingers across the excessive designs on the mirror's edge, she was contemplating putting it in again. Just to see if it would go in once more. Now that she was home, took a bath and was rid of the pre-performance jitters maybe this time it would be different. So, she slid her finger around its perimeter one more time then plunged it in the center. Again! It went in again. Still hallucinating.

"What if this thing is magical for real?" She was intrigued as she stirred the permeable glass. Sometimes she felt like she was born into the wrong world.

It looked just like water in a cup around her thick finger. Strangely, it didn't feel wet. It was like the mirror wasn't even there. Her finger felt warmer though. She turned it around to get a better look of the back expecting to see a protruding brown digit. Nothing. She didn't even know what to think. Giselle's hands started to tremble against her will shaking the chain loose from her grip and it fell. Only, it didn't fall on the ground. No, no! Ms. Chain dropped down her wrist swallowing up half her arm. It didn't even expand. Instead, her arm was shrinking to suit. She had lost all feeling in it and before she could react, it moved all the way up by itself. And in no time, something she never thought would happen, happened. She was eaten by a mirror.

Where was she? Was this the afterlife? Couldn't be. She could still feel the hot breath leaving her nostrils rather heavily. She could still hear her heart beating its infamous rhythm in her chest only ten times faster. Her thoughts were loud, clear and terrified and she was fully aware of the fact that she was purposefully keeping her eyes closed. She was alive and she was somewhere, just afraid to know where that somewhere was. Ok, maybe she was just being stupid. She could open her eyes right now and still be on the veranda wall touching the mirror instead of penetrating it. She had to be. Or maybe she had just woken up from the deep sleep she was in and it was time to get ready for her carnival launch performance. Any minute now Amron should wake her up. She wanted to believe that was the case, but she was also fully aware that her hands were squeezed tightly into fists. Then there was the fact that she felt a lot warmer than she was a second ago. What if Giselle was in the mirror? Her finger did feel warmer when she put it in.

Slowly Giselle pulled her eye lids apart until they were just two slits. There wasn't anything to see. It was dark. She definitely needed more viewing space. At some point, after all the squinting and fighting to make out objects through cracks, her eyes were fully opened. There was nothing to fear here, but the unknown. She was in a cave. But it wasn't empty or lit by torches or full of bats or anything. No, this cave was lined along the walls with twelve brilliantly gleaming mirrors; one of which she was lying in front of. Slowly she lifted from her lying position on the hard ground to get a better look. There was nothing else there, just mirrors in a self-illuminating room and a passage leading to a white light.

Her head spun with urgency as she felt something flutter by her ear. What was that? The room was now alive with a faint flapping sound and a tiny voice singing unsettling lyrics.

Welcome to my world
Where chaos and mysteries and nightmares will follow you
If you are weak inside
Then I promise that my world isn't the place for you.

That tune was in an endless loop. Who was singing? Why was that their choice of song? Did they not see that she was in a situation right now? She didn't need to hear that! The voice was raising the hairs at the back of her neck. Soon something small and white came into her line of sight. It took a minute before she could really focus on it. Then, she wished she hadn't. Giselle had seen some scary things in her life (she had three brothers), but none like this. This little white bird was fluttering, not even sure if to say happily, in front of her. It had bulging green eyes like a human's and it was as if it were gazing into her soul, not blinking once. Adding to the horror, the tiny voice belonged to it. It was singing to her from its small orange beak.

She pulled herself up and hastily, started backing up to the wall, but it kept following her singing and not blinking. What was wrong with this thing? Why wouldn't it leave her alone? What was it anyway? Surely no bird in Grenada looked like that. The pitchy voice was getting to her. Giselle's back was against the wall and it kept coming closer and closer until it was right in her ear torturing her. Something about its voice was terrifying and draining at the same time. The more she swung her hand to get it away the more it flew around her. It felt like the singing was getting louder and more passionate; juicy even. She closed her eyes and bowed her head as she began to fling her hands harder and faster. Screaming. Fast paced footsteps were now echoing in the room. There was a thud and then she couldn't hear the bird any more. She kept still for a moment. If her heart beat any faster she feared her blood vessels would pop and kill her.

"Are you ok?" She felt a callused, large hand clamp around her wrist.

She raised her head and tugged away before the person could get a good hold. It was a reflex. Before her stood a messy, tall, gruff looking boy. He looked around eighteen. He had a thin layer of uncombed hair on his head and a buff outline. When she pulled away from him he took a step back and raised his hands surrendering to show he meant no harm.

"Sorry," he muttered. She stared at him wide eyed unable to speak. "You must be Ruby's granddaughter?"

How on earth did he know who she was? There was no formal introduction. She wasn't wearing a name tag and there was nothing in here besides her, him, the twelve mirrors and a motionless white bird on the ground. She looked at him with furrowed brows.

"Did you come through that mirror?"

He pointed the mirror she found herself lying in front of. The dust in front of it was disturbed. Giselle didn't notice it before, but there was a brass plate at the top with Ruby inscribed on it. All the mirrors had name plates. She nodded.

"K, well..." he paused and watched her with an uncertain face.

"Giselle." She said half-heartedly.

"I know your name," he said promptly. "You gonna get off the wall or...?"

His question made her realize how desperately she was clinging to the wall to keep distance from him. Giselle straightened her knees and did her last observation of him before easing off the wall. The sweat she didn't even know she was spraying out ran down her fore head from the sudden movement. He seemed ok. He did just save her from that crazy bird and he respected her space. Maybe she shouldn't be afraid of him. She finally held up her own weight.

"Marko," he said.

Her attention was now back on the bird on the ground. It was unconscious and the wings were sprawled carelessly across the ground. Seeing it near their feet she realized just how tiny it was which made the size of its eyes even more miraculous. The lids were uncomfortable to look at. They were veiny and appeared as if they were forced to cover the entire ball. Did he kill it?

"That's a songbird," he informed. "Whenever they sense an uneasy vibe they sing ballads to amplify it. They feed off your insecurities. Negative creatures. It's not dead though, not that easy. But we should leave before it wakes up."

He used both hands and gestured the passage ahead of him. Giselle walked with as much distance from him as possible along the wall to get to the passage. She didn't know him. She had to be cautious. Just because he had an accent didn't mean he was ok. She still didn't know where she was or what exactly happened or where he wanted to go. She peered down the passage only to realize it wasn't as long as she'd initially assessed. There were six doors, three on either side then an exit. The first two doors said 'Male' and 'Female'. The second two said 'Medic Room' and 'Weaponry'. Then the third 'Kitchen' and Rec. Room'. She made her way slowly through the little passage fully conscious of Marko behind her observing her every move.

"This is the headquarters of the Guardians," he said.

Guardians? Who were they and why was she in their headquarters? Soon she realized the source of the white light. It was magnificent. The colours under the gleaming sunlight, the lush vegetation, the way it all enclosed around a crystal-clear body of water forming a cove. Perfection. She had never seen a place so beautiful in her life. There was a tame rustle about the noises around her. It was like a mix of a busy city, crashing of waves and a rainforest. There was something so tantalizing about that noise that just soothed her instantly. She could tell there was so much life in this land. Giselle stood in awe observing the new world she had just walked into. Marko was standing next to her now with his hands on his hips and a stupid grin plastered on his face.

"Giselle," he called her proudly like he had known her his whole life. "Welcome to Majesty."

She couldn't help but think that this was the most beautiful hallucination she had ever had.

CHAPTER THREE

IT'S BACK

FLORESCENT ROOFS, EXTRAORDINARY houses, copper colour roads and lush green vegetation. It was hard to turn away from. All of it looked so enticing, like something out of a Japanese anime or a Korean music video. It was amazing. She never knew a place like this existed. Majesty, he called it? The air was so fresh and the atmosphere was cool; clear, sparsely clouded skies and a round yellow sun to close the deal. It was all so breathtaking. Somewhere in the moment of complete admiration and confusion she was at last, able to speak to Marko.

"What is this place?" Giselle spoke in a loud whisper.

"Not Grenada," he smirked.

She looked at him. The sun seemed to illuminate his skin giving him a flawless appearance. It almost gave his lack of grooming an attractive glow. He had short side burns that she didn't notice in the darkness of the cave and he wore a muted outfit. A simple black shirt with pants that were baggy and dull. They had about six pockets; two in the back, two in the front and two by his knees. They all seemed occupied by something. The foot of his pants was tucked into his tall, black boots. Over all, his attire seemed worn out. It was more than obvious that whatever work he did was neither clean nor easy. Maybe he was into construction like her father. He always had some concrete mix or saw dust embodying him.

She looked at him with a raised eyebrow awaiting further information.

"Majesty- home to any crazy, magical creature you can dream up," he elaborated.

So, that explained the creepy bird then.

"How…" she started up, but he cut her off.

"I'm still not fully clear on how this place exists either. They say it's been around for long time," he stooped and watched over the glowing village. "A crap load of magical creatures live here and it's our job to keep them safe. That's what they say at least. I think it's the other way around. Can't have them leaving here and going on a killing spree in the normal world," Giselle's eyes widened. "Killing spree!!!!!" He yelled out in a tone not his own and pretending he had a gun. "Pew! Pew!"

"Our?"

"Yeah. You're here, aren't you? Making it this far seals the deal that you're one of us now."

His words had her scared for her life. Did he mean she was stuck there forever? And did she hear clearly? He said there was a "crap load of magical creatures?" So there were more of those creepy-eyed birds? And who was "us"? So far he was the only one she had seen. Were the others hidden away somewhere spying on her? Maybe he was the only one nice enough to come out and help.

"So I hadda stay here… forever?"

"Oh," he chuckled surprised. "No. Sorry I should have spoken more clearly. The mirror, it can take you to and from Majesty whenever you want."

Oh. So, I am in the mirror! She thought.

She looked down expecting to be greeted by the gold chain in her neck, but it was gone! It was as if someone slammed the insta-panic button in her head. She went full lunatic mode. She was feeling all over herself trying to see if she absentmindedly tucked it in her pocket or something. When it was clear she didn't have it on her she started retracing her steps rather wildly. She couldn't lose her grandmother's chain. She didn't care what magic it had inside of it. And how was she to get out if she didn't have it. She dropped to her knees and started feeling around the floor in the dark, warm mirror room. She couldn't see clearly as her eyes were adjusting to the change in light so she had to rely on feel. She couldn't wait until her eyes were ready to adjust to the light again. This was urgent.

"Giselle!" Marko came running and pulled Giselle to her feet in one swift motion. "What's wrong?"

"I doh know where my chain is," she almost cried.

"Don't worry about it. Once you come in here the chain stays behind in a safe place so that you can get out. My mirror is in a gold watch and whenever I come in it stores itself under my bed."

Giselle tried to calm her breathing. She was putting everything on what he said right now. He seemed to have all the answers and was willing to share. Hopefully, her chain really was somewhere safe. He walked over to the mirror labeled Ruby and insisted that she follow. She did.

"These," he gestured to the mirrors. "They're actually called Sui Generis'. Each has two pieces and you must have the pair for it to work. And for you to even know that two pieces exist, it has to like you."

"Like me?" She repeated.

"Yeah," he shrugged as though that wasn't a strange thing to say at all. "They'll do anything for you. Just talk to them."

"Talkin' to them is basically talkin' to your reflection," she spoke softly.

"They are your reflection. That's why it's called a Sui Generis. It's unique to anyone that comes across it."

Her mind was clouded with nonsense. Nothing Marko said to her thus far made sense. He seemed to take her confusion as a joke too. His mannerism was leaving the impression that soon she'd be comfortable with all this and it would all become a part of everyday life. As though everything she had seen here would become one of those things she didn't know how she knew or how to explain. She would just know it and understand it for some reason. The sound of the masculine figure clearing his throat in front of her shook her out of speculating everything.

"Talk to it," he said insistently. "Ask it to show you where it's other half is."

"You do it," she shoved the task in his lap.

"I can't. It's not mine. It's yours."

This made her pause.

"I-is mine?"

"Yeah. How else would you get here? The other half of it is your chain." He smiled and shook his head still urging her to talk to the mirror.

Looking uncertainly at her reflection in the mirror Giselle began to speak.

"Show me the other half?" She asked, her voice lacking power.

One thing was for sure, her reflection wasn't her reflection. She was sure when she spoke her lips moving was a given; it was a necessity. Her reflection's lips didn't move. Instead it nodded obediently and faded out of view and a dark familiar room appeared. It was her late grandmother's house; cold and lifeless. Seeing it again after such a long time was nostalgic. That was the place she spent most of her childhood. Now it was reduced to a concrete cage full of heart wrenching memories. The house was left to her uncle Rohan. Ruby must have thought he might need a place to stay when his badly-behaved ass finally got deported. So, that was her chain's safe spot? It did make sense. After all, it did come from Ruby.

"You can use the Sui Generis to communicate too. All you have to do is talk to it. If you want to talk to me for example, because who doesn't want to talk to me, just say my name." He continued in depth with his bigheadedness.

He had a certain charisma about him that made her feel calm about the fact that she was in a completely different world. She nodded at everything he said until he was finished explaining. Apparently, each mirror led to different places; he was from Canada. And there was another mirror there that led to Jamaica. That was why this room was known as the Universal Passage. To be honest, she wasn't completely sold on anything that was going on around her. As far as she was concerned, Marko wasn't real. Majesty wasn't real, and everything he said was nonsense. Still, she stood silently and listened to him. Giselle was amused at the fact that she could supposedly travel the world just by stepping into those mirrors until he told her never to do that. The other Sui Generis' weren't meant for her and so no matter her title in Majesty, they'd never let her in. As to who the other owners were, she was about to find out. He led the way back to the door labeled rec. room and opened it making way so that she could enter first.

The noise level was at a minimum. She could hear laughter here and there, dominos knocking on a table and talking throughout, but it wasn't loud. There was a crooked bar on the side of the room with no one behind the counter. The room was a light shade of brown because of the brick walls. There were tables stationed around accompanied by arm chairs; some of which were occupied. There was a television on over the bar area, but it didn't look as though any of them were watching except for this one bandaged guy. There was a comfy, homey, feeling about it. None of the six people in there noticed them enter. Two were in a fully captivating game of dominos, another two were playing cards. One was making his way over to the bar with bread hanging from his mouth to get himself a drink. There was another guy, eyes closed, deep in his tunes with big red headphones on. Marko started clapping to get their attention while he spoke in an excited tone.

"I'm not wonder woman's jet people! Not invisible, see me!" He said while throwing his hands over random parts of his body to prove he wasn't invisible.

All their eyes lazily glanced up at him, some of them smiled and shook their heads at him and then went on with their business. All except headphone guy, that is. Then, as if they didn't notice Giselle at first, they all became alert. The guy with the bread was gaping at her, causing his food to drop to the floor. It couldn't be her they were looking at like that. Giselle turned around to see if anyone came in after them or if Marko was doing something silly. No one was there and Marko was still wearing that stupid grin.

"Yes," he put his hands on her shoulder and turned her around. "They're looking at you."

"Which mirror?" A visual tease near the domino table called.

This lady was simply stunning. It was obvious she wasn't wearing any makeup or anything. She wasn't even dressed up. Everything about her seemed natural yet she still had an eye rendering glow.

"Ruby," Marko leaned on Giselle's shoulder.

"Oh ho! Unu so small," the bread guy said. He had gauze for days wrapped around his right arm and what she could see of his left leg. "'ow old are you?"

"Fourteen," she mumbled.

Giselle found herself backing up, feeling more comfortable when it was just Marko being playful and bigheaded. They were an intimidating bunch. Especially the man in the blue shirt sitting opposite the first lady that spoke.

"Hm," the blue shirt man hummed. "Ming is no longer the newbie."

"Anyway, this is Giselle; I heard they call you Gizzy so I'll call you Gizzy. Gizzy, these are some of the members. As you can tell by their reaction, you are the youngest to ever come here after Ming and I of course. If you couldn't tell, then heads up, you are the youngest to ever come here."

Members? She looked at all the people who were way older than her. They all had a tough rugged appearance as oppose to Marko's untidy, giddiness and the lady's glow. Their outfits were similar too; well the pants were at least. They all wore the same pants and shoes, but different shirts. Maybe there was a vote because no one wanted to wear the same type of dirty black shirt as Marko. Again, except headphone guy; he wore black too. The man with the silver thermos stood up and approached her. Just to be clear, it was blue shirt man. He had short locked hair. He wore a pleased expression on his face coming toward her until Marko started to speak again.

"This is Eco-listen-to-everything-I-say-cause-I-am-law."

The room erupted in laughter. The guy punched Marko square in the chest causing him to crouch and stumble away laughing. Giselle didn't get the joke until he introduced himself.

"Am Ecoli. Chief of Majesty," he said.

It made sense now.

"I come from Grenada too," he stepped aside so she could see everyone while he spoke. "That's Marcel- my sister…"

His sister? She thought as he went on talking.

He pointed at the pretty lady he was just sitting in front of. How could that be his sister? They looked nothing alike. Whereas she had a thick alluding air about her and an inviting aroma, everything about him screamed, "run." There was just something about his whole aura that was intimidating for no reason. Maybe it was the fact that he was chief. It was common for authoritative figures to demand a humbling respect from their followers. The only thing they had in common was the locked hair and even with that it wasn't the same. Hers were thinner and neater. Together they were like a rose bush. She was the beauty that drew you in and he was the thorns that kept you at a distance.

"…Hozen, Trevor by the bar, Ming and Scout," he finished.

Everyone in the room was absolutely unique. In no way did one look like the other. She had the feeling their personalities would be as different as soap was to an oven. The majority of them made some type of sign showing they acknowledged her. They either did a slight wave, said hi or nodded. She especially made note of the hooded figure in the brown cloak; it didn't look too friendly. The girl introduced as Ming just stared at her though. She was sitting there in her common pants with a creamy-red, glittery, navel-breaker top and cards in hand. Her red nail polish had a different design on each finger. They were simple; bunny head, star, heart, skull and cross bones, polka dots and so on. She inspected Giselle with careless eyes, then back at her cards dropping one on the table. The headphone guy didn't really partake in the greeting either. Ecoli called him Scout when he tried to get his attention.

"I got this," Marko said moving from the bar area to where Scout sat. He pulled the headphone from his ears and dropped it on his lap then walked away.

"Bruhhhh," Scout dragged in a deep, lazy voice.

Ecoli shook his head. "Scout," he said again while gesturing the young man that had only now noticed her.

"So…" he tucked his thermos in his pocket and faced Giselle again.

The pocket obviously was too small for it. Yet, it seemed to disappear in there.

"Ya finally reach."

Ecoli opened the door and proceeded to walk out. She stood there bewildered until he told her to follow him. Why did they act like she was supposed to know so much about this place? Either that, or their attention was so short spanned that they kept forgetting she had no clue where she was. He went down to the weaponry room. Inside was unlike anything she had ever seen in her life. Just like the rec. room the walls were bricked giving off the vibe of some ancient, historical maze. There was something artistic about the way everything looked here. Though, the walls weren't what caught her attention. It was what was on them; cross bows, swords, guns, hunting knives, scythes, nun chucks, grenades you name it. There were tables buried in armor and guns of all types and trunks with stuff probably deadlier than what they had on display. There were humanly mannequins in king's armor stationed around the room; they didn't seem to be touched very often if at all. Instead of taking five steps back, she went forward. Her hands were itching to grab onto just one thing. She had seen most of these before on TV shows and Animes she'd peeped over An-dre's shoulder. To hold and touch them in real life, however was a surreal experience. Her first grab was the shot gun resting neatly on its post against the wall. It was heavier and smoother than she expected. Resting the recoil pad near the crease of her arm pit she pointed it at a mannequin yearning for the feeling of firing it. She observed the front and back sights along the barrel for the first time; Giselle never knew guns had little mounds at the top.

"You ever use this?" She had to ask.

What kind of stuff did they see on a daily basis in such a beautiful place that they needed such high level of security? She couldn't imagine. Then again, that bird wasn't exactly welcoming so there could be worst out there.

"Not all," he said.

Then he walked over to a section planked with swords and picked up one with a white and black stripped handle.

"This right here is my baby though." He smiled and pulled it out of its case. It was a black, sharp, venomous looking blade. "Is a Katana. I alone use it. Ming makes good use of the others."

She nodded. His love for his katana wasn't making her feel better about what was out there. It only gave hints that it absolutely had to be used and on more than one occasion if he called it his baby. She had to admit, she was flanked with excitement and the curiosity to head out there and see for herself. She was just doing a really good job of hiding it. Hearing was one thing, seeing was something else. The only thing stopping her now was the fact that she had moved on from the thought of this being a hallucination and upgraded to saying these people were mental. After he put away the Katana he went into a silver trunk and pulled out a flat piece of brass and with it, a marker. Then he directed her out of the room.

She was back where she started; in the Universal Passage eyeing the second halves of the Sui Generis'. He led her back to the one she came through, reached up and took her grandmothers name plate off of it. Something about seeing it come down made her feel somber on the inside. She tried her best to push that feeling away. That bird could be anywhere, ready to sing to her again. He handed her the stuff he took from the trunk, then he began to explain. His tone and mannerism was now less easy-going and more of an authority figure.

"The Universal Passage is the main way in and out of Majesty for guardians. Ya only use ya mirror…nobody else own."

"No exceptions at all?"

"Not that am aware, no. Ya gon be enterin' some other country illegally, and dependin' on the exit point, might cause unavoidable problems. Best just not do it." He seemed to over pronounce his words to make sure she got the point. "Anyway…"

"How you know I was comin'?" Giselle didn't intend to interrupt him, but she did.

"Before Ruby go she say she would give the chain to ya because it already chose ya."

"But how-"

"-would ya let me talk for like five minutes and then maybe ya might get the answers ya lookin' for?"

"Well, sorry," she humbled.

So what, she was curious.

"Good," he wrinkled his forehead. "First thing first, ya gotta accept the Sui Generis. They does choose the owner and once the owner figure out the passage they need to accept the other half."

The Sui Generis chooses? Accept it? How does one accept this thing? What if she didn't want to? She had a million questions she couldn't contain, but the minute the first syllable of a word flew out her mouth, he shot her a look that made her shut up and wait.

"To accept the mirror…" he paused and stared her dead in the eye.

I get the point! Ah go wait! No need to roast me like that. She thought.

"Just write ya name on this and on the back put ya safe spot. Then tuck it in the space and it officially belongs to ya."

That was it. Just write your name and screw it into the vacant spot? A whole magical world and that was all they could come up with?

Gosh, I hope what outside more impressive than this. What next? Just put cheese between two slice of bread and I own a sandwich. Talk about magic! Where was the talkin' in tongue twistin' language and shootin' light out of wands or whatever? What's up with that? I get drop off in the knock off magic world? Did I need to not know where the hell ah was, jus' a little longer to get to the real deal thing?

Everything the old Giselle wanted to say out loud was rolling through her head without pause. Sure, she was a bit intimidated by it all, but on the other hand she wanted to see something amazing. She was, just a little bit, starting to miss that bird.

Giselle exhaled loudly, making a point to not speak at all. She held the flat piece of brass in her left hand, pulled the cap off the marker with her teeth and hovered the tip over the surface. Did she want to "accept" the Sui Generis' offer? Should she? She didn't even know fully what this Guardian thing was about. On the other hand, her grandmother was the one that gave the chain to her. She told her everything was going to be ok, as long as she had it. She couldn't be talking about anything else other than this. And was she just supposed to give her life into protecting a place she didn't know existed until twenty minutes ago? Her grandmother already preapproved the place. So, technically, she'd be going against her if she didn't accept it. She glanced at Ecoli who wore a soft, understanding look. This boy needed to pick a mood and stick with it... honestly.

"No," she put the cap back on the marker.

"Wha'ya mean no?" He asked genuinely.

"I doh want to accept the mirror or whatever it is you tryna get me to do," she pushed the stuff back in his hands.

"Why not?"

"Because," she paused. "This is crazy. This place even real?"

"Ya standin' in it," his tone was slightly annoyed.

"I doh know what am gettin' myself in. I doh care what you say. This is a dream. How I goin' back home?" She shook her head and folded her arms.

Ecoli held his gaze steadily on her. His aura curled back to that intimidating pressure she felt when she first saw him. He couldn't be mad could he? What did he think? She was just going to accidentally fall into some alternate universe and become a superhero. No questions asked? If he did, that sure was stupid of him. She wasn't interested. As far as she was concerned, this wasn't real. And she was going to make sure her frame of mind about this place remained that way. She couldn't go back home and talk this crap about Majesty to even the people closest to her. No. She might end up following in her mother's footsteps.

"Ya sure ya doh want to do this?" Ecoli asked with a hard voice.

"I want to go home," she sort of ordered.

He clenched his teeth making his jaw line more defined.

"Think about it," he said.

"I want to go home," she repeated.

Ecoli exhaled and after staring at her, spoke again. "Fine. Just walk through the mirror."

"That's all?" She questioned.

He nodded, fists clenched. "Good night," his voice was even stiffer than before.

She hadn't made note of the fact that it was day time in there and about half hour ago she was preparing for bed. It just came to her, that she had stood in front of a room full of mostly males with her night outfit on. Reality hit like a flying brick. She applied ice where it hurt and her mind wondered again.

This world must be the complete opposite of everything in Grenada, she bet. She was itching to find out, but at the same time scared. What was out there? What other magical creatures were there and why was it the job of these people to protect them? Marko said this place had been in existence for a long time now. She couldn't help but wonder how many generations of people had dedicated their life to protecting this place. Look how old Ruby was. Since she was the one that gave Giselle the chain it meant that at some point it was her job to protect this place as well. She wanted to go down to that neon town and take a swing on everything it had to offer. She wanted to know what was so special about this place that it needed protection. Then again, imagine all the scary things that must be hidden down there. What if it looked good from afar, but got nasty as she got closer. She had never been so two sided about something in her entire life.

Giselle looked at Ecoli who was intent on her staying, then down the passage that led to untold adventures. Maybe running out there would be an idiot move. Ecoli was going to be pissed, no doubt. And what if leaving without an escort or permission would get her banned from there? She wanted to see Majesty again before she left, but she wanted to be alone when she did it. Her gaze then traveled to the full-length mirror beside her and the reflection that had her face, but wasn't completely her own. This thing was supposed to take her home. How? What kind of magic did it hold? Was this place actually real or not? She fully adjusted to face the, now, nameless mirror. This place was where her grandmother spent her time and now she was entrusted with her secret. Or so it seemed. How could she not be grateful for that? She couldn't describe how she felt. After taking one last glance at Ecoli she cautiously stepped through the mirror. Next thing she knew, she was sitting on her grandmother's old couch, in the living room, in the same spot Ruby sat when she gave Giselle her chain. Giselle looked at the chain that somehow appeared in her hands again. How did she end up there? She had expected to be back on the veranda wall gazing at a regular old mirror that had no magical qualities. She expected to feel herself snap out of a day dream. But no, she was in Ruby's house. Maybe this was real after all?

"Majesty is not real," she whispered to herself.

That was what she wanted to believe. It was too much to process that there was another world out there. What's worst, it was too much to process that her grandmother had a whole other life. Why did she wait to share it when she died? The bigger question, why did she only share it with Giselle? She spent the next hour convincing herself that nothing she had seen was real and she'd wake up in her room in the morning. She was also telling herself that if she found herself in Majesty again she wouldn't be timid. She wouldn't act like she did this first time. She was going to see it all herself. If she ever found her way back she was going to let the curiosity within her run free. Then maybe she could live again. Giselle slowly dozed off.

She was awakened by a chill that spread through her body. It was a fact that when sleeping you lost body heat. That was why most people found it impossible to sleep without covers. It was a way of trapping that heat to stay warm and comfortable. She didn't have a cover though. She couldn't feel the one she usually used about her. In fact, her bed didn't even feel like her bed. It was so small and tough. By the way where was Amron? The morning was too quiet; too peaceful. She wouldn't admit out loud, but it was also too lonely. He didn't wake her up. Why not? He always did. She stretched her arms and yawned out loud opening her eyes in the process. That was when everything was cut. She froze. She was in her grandmother's house folded up on the couch. How did she get there? She was supposed to be in her room. She did go home last night, didn't she? She finished off her band performance and went straight home. After that she…

Majesty…

That magical world whose existence Giselle feigned. She remembered falling into the mirror and ending up at the mercy of the strange singing bird. The memories were slow coming. Seeing as she had only now awakened. But they were there. As more memories flashed across her mind, the temptation to render it all a vivid dream was inviting. She could easily say she had made it all up. It would be easy to declare it unreal. If she did, however, how would she explain her being in Ruby's house? No way in hell did she sleep walk all the way there. That would mean she walked from deep within Good Hope all the way to the St. David's side of Madigrass while asleep. No matter how you looked at it, that was no short walk. She'd have had to cross the boundary line that separated the parishes. She would have had to climb and descend hills to get there. Not to mention walking alone at night wasn't safe. There were a lot of old folktale that surrounded the woods of Madigrass that people would rather blindly believe than prove its integrity. How did she manage it alone? No. Sleep walking wasn't the answer.

Accept the Sui Generis…

The pendant had somehow found home on her chest once more. What would happen if she did accept the mirror? What would be her role then? She groaned. Nonsense. Why was she even thinking about this? Whether or not this "Majesty" was real was none of her concern. What made them believe she was willing to protect it? She had no obligations to that world. Besides, everyone she had seen last night, if they were real, appeared normal. There was nothing too unnatural about them. Well, except for the hooded figure that had greeted her as equal. Then again, it could have been someone who liked dressing up. The explanations she could think up for this one person were boundless and so, she let its strangeness be.

Setting a light foot on the cold concrete floors, she crossed the room miserably. Her body ached from her condensed sleeping position and her fingers and toes felt like ice. What time was it anyway? How long had she been asleep? The light was dim; bright enough to recognize the things around her, but not perfect enough for clear distinction. As of now, everything was the same colour; a pale black. She had to get home before she could enjoy privileges like eating. This house would have nothing. Acknowledging this only invited a pang of pain in her chest that she didn't need right now. Giselle felt broken and on the verge of tears. She had only woke out of slumber less than five minutes ago and already she was crushed. The house was empty. One word. One ironically heavy word; empty. Empty of warmth, of love and of life. The silence inside had a bite to it. The place that was once her escape became what she was trying to escape from.

"Sorry," she spoke weakly as she freed the chain from her neck and placed it on the bare shelf closest to the door.

She couldn't have it. Her feelings for this one piece of jewelry were so conflicting. She wanted it. She wanted to own it so badly. But it instilled a fear in her that she had never known before. It made her to believe that there was a magical world somewhere, and that her grandmother was a part of it. It made her have gaps in her memory because she couldn't remember setting foot in Ruby's house of her own accord last night. Lastly, the biggest con about the chain, the reason why she couldn't keep it was because it made her memories of her grandmother intensely, bitterly, painful. That pendant didn't belong on her chest. It didn't look right. Not in the slightest. Ever since she started wearing it, she felt that way. It was pos-

Krystal Cyrus

sible to love something enough to know you didn't belong together. It was only after last night that she finally had the courage to take it off again. The best thing to do was leave it in the place that she had gotten it. Then, in a way, it would still belong to Ruby.

Walking home, her mind was crammed with thoughts like town during rush hour. She shouldn't have left the chain behind. What if Ruby was watching over her and felt disappointed or rejected because of Giselle's actions? She felt a strong need to turn around, yet she never wavered from her strenuous path home. She couldn't own it. There was something wrong with that pendant. If in fact, what she saw last night was real, she couldn't own that chain. Nothing good could come from it. So, this magical world, what if her grandmother never knew it was in there? What if it only sprang up after her death? What if it was some sort of trick to drag Giselle into unknown terrors. Growing up in Grenada she was always told not to take things from random people and be careful who she dealt with. Everything ultimately lead back to Obeah. Say you upset somebody, if something bad happened to you they'd say you were cursed. Then people would talk. They always talk. Every mouth in the island was like a personalized news media. They always had stories to tell about things they didn't witness themselves. Always gathering information as if they were trained and getting paid full time. Giselle was afraid. She couldn't have that mirror anywhere near her. This was just another con. But, Ecoli did say Ruby's name. He did say she told

64

them about her, but that was a piece of information she was willing to scrap.

"Where you come from this ungodly hour!" The familiar voice made her jump.

It was Andre standing in front of her with so much rage and concern, that she couldn't tell which he was feeling most. He had clenched fists, a tight jaw line and eyes so stony that Giselle got scared even after she realized it was only her big brother.

"I..." her soft voice trailed.

Had she walked so far already? Raising her head and taking in her surroundings she only now noticed that she was standing in Good Hope. She didn't remember descending the hill or bending any corners getting there. Had her mind been that caught up?

"Amron say you wasn' in your room," he let out a shaky breath that related more to worry. "Where you went?"

She opened her mouth to speak, but to say what? How would she explain making it all the way to Ruby's house in the dead of night? In the end, she just shook her head and shrugged.

"Dad still sleepin'."

The more Andre spoke the calmer he got. He only had one sister. As a big brother, he saw it as his job to look after her. Sometimes he took it too seriously and sometimes he was a way too intense. After all he was the goodie two-shoes of the family, having perfect grades and never braking any rules. He was always on Giselle and Amron's back to do things the right way.

Basically, he was annoying and they couldn't stand him. Over all, he really cared and wanted what was best for them. Even if that meant acting like a mad person every time something happened outside of his expectations.

"You know how he go get if he find out you leave the house without tellin' anybody," Andre warned. "What if something happen to you? Nobody know you missin'."

"You go tell'im?" She already had a clue of what his response would be.

"Yes."

There it was. He couldn't resist. He always had to do the right thing. This was why Giselle, Amron and BJ never told him anything.

"Where you went?" He asked again this time more stern.

"Gran'mom house," she responded.

She could see the hardness of his eyes soften significantly. Unlike Amron, you would always know what mood Andre was in. He could be a little too dramatic at times. He was as clear as day with all his emotions. His rage, his happiness, his sadness; it was always clearly addressed on his face. And whenever he was feeling confused or mixed up he showed that too. He did things in a way that no one ever knew how to act around him. For example, when he cried the morning he heard of Ruby's death or when he went on mute for a whole week after because every time he went to speak it would be concerning Ruby. If their mother was alive and with them, it was obvious he would be a mama's boy. They never had her though, their mother. So he was a grandma's boy.

"Go inside," he spoke quietly.

Without saying more, she strolled along the side of the road, him in tow and made her way home. A place lived in, warm and most importantly- not empty.

"Where you went?" Amron was right behind the door waiting for her. "Dre outside lookin' for you."

"I see him. He comin'."

"Oh. You ok? I won' tell dad," he offered protection, but it was too late for that.

"Dre say he go tell'im."

Amron scuffed.

"I go talk to him," his eyes searched hers. She didn't look fine to him because she wasn't. He knew her too well. "Still thinkin' about Gran'mom?"

"Why you ask?"

"Cause you holdin' the chain so close," he motioned to her neck.

"Chain?" She was confused.

What chain? She couldn't be holding any chain. The only one she had that would provide any memory of their grandmother was resting peacefully in the house afar. So maybe he meant something else when he said chain. It had to be a metaphor for something. Still, at mention of the chain she reflexively glanced at her chest. She only then realized that her arm had been laid across her chest for the longest while. Not only that, but her hand was enclosing something within it. There it was, in all its gold glory, wrapped in her stubby little fingers as if it were home- the mirror pendant chain that her grandmother had gifted to her.

"The chain!" She gasped.

Then Andre came walking in.

"Dre, you tellin' dad?" Amron bypassed Giselle and stepped up to his big brother.

"Obviously," Andre had a fake amusement about his tone as he locked the door behind him.

"You can' see something and keep quiet just once in your life?"

She didn't need to stay for their argument. It was the same every time anyway. They would argue. It would get heated and then Amron would walk away while Andre was in the middle of making a point just to annoy him. Then Andre would tell their dad whatever it is they were arguing about and most likely Amron would find himself in trouble. Same old routine in the Thomas household. Though Giselle couldn't possibly see a reason for Amron to be at fault this time around, she trusted in Andre's ability to find one.

"See, even Gizzy can' stand you right now!" She heard Amron yell as she was leaving.

"Well sit me," was Andre's smart response that echoed through the house.

Their dad was sure to wake up now.

CHAPTER FOUR

THE TRUTHFUL SPIRIT

SHUTTING THE BEDROOM door tightly behind her, she kept her eyes fastened on the chain wondering if she had even left it behind. Maybe she had meant to leave it, but in her heap of confusion and fear, left the house before she could. And maybe because she had originally gotten up to leave the chain on the shelf, was why she was convinced it was actually there. For sure, that had to be the reason. She couldn't see any other explanation. She did just stroll through Madigrass and not even realize she had made it all the way back to Good Hope. That spoke tremendous lines of her mental occupation.

No longer catering to the chain's safety, she made her way, heavy footed, to her bedroom window and slid it open. Outside wasn't as dark anymore. The sky was bluing and the green of the tree leaves were starting to blossom in her sight. Her little rabbit coup was void of life as her pets weren't yet active;

not that they ever were. Somewhere in the distance she could hear the triumphant crow of a rooster like a dreaded morning alarm. The still of morning was always so beautiful. It was hard to wake up to watch the world come to life for yet another day. Witnessing it brought a peace that no other activity could fully accomplish. Except, if burdened with frustration one would be easily blinded to the remarkable awakening. Much like Giselle was right now. All that was on her mind was putting distance between her and this *special* chain. Watching it soar through the morning air and taking refuge far in the shrubs at the back of her house was what delivered peace. Sliding the window shut she found her way back to her bed, a ghostly feeling hovering her. She really did toss her grandmother's last gift this time. Knowing that, she was subjected to all the thoughts that had accompanied her on the walk home once more.

~*~

No plans. No destination to run off to. None of her friends in close proximity to hang out with. She was finally starting to see the summer for what it really was- boring. She had an urge to watch television, but she knew it wouldn't be streaming anything new. Besides, every time she turned it on it was on the GBN channel. That was the local news channel: The Grenada Broadcasting Network. That alone melted the soul and discouraged all television watching for a day; just mere sight of that fuzzy channel. It was like poison to youth. She never watched the news unless her father was watching; there was only one television in the house. She couldn't even change the channel after he dozed off because he always jumped out of it, as if programmed, and said, "I was listenin' to that." Not once could he tell her the last thing that was said.

GBN's favorite topic of late was some ten-year-old girl that had gone amiss. They'd been covering that story forever. Not that they had anything else to report. When did anything interesting ever happen in Grenada? The country was far too small to actually have different, mind boggling events to report every day. At least, that was how Giselle felt about it. The only things she could bring herself to watch on there were the school debates, knowledge bowls, drum festival and Independence Day Parade.

It wasn't Tuesday so there was no new Awkward episode to look forward to. But it was Monday, which meant that Teen Wolf would have something to offer. In the meantime, she spent the day lying in bed. Nothing else was interesting to her. In her wake of boredom Teen Wolf seemed to take the fore front of her thoughts. Neither Scott nor Stiles believed in such a thing as werewolves. Not even after Scott was bitten. Stiles kept saying there were no wolves in California no matter how hard Scott tried to convince him that he heard howling. The idea of the supernatural prevailing was too farfetched and unrealistic, but eventually he believed. When things started to change and danger poked its head on the horizon then he believed. Eventually, the supernatural proved to exist and not only that, but there were so many things out there that until his moment of realization, were slipping by right under his nose.

Could this be what was happening to her? There was a chance the chain was her bite. Had her life become a Teen Wolf episode?

Click.

She heard the door knob. It was Amron. Not that she expected it to be anyone else. If it were someone else they'd have knocked first. Creeping into the room, he was lathered in devious intent. The disappointment that washed on his face when he saw his sister was awake was almost too satisfying for Giselle.

"Phone," he pelted it in her direction not even waiting to see if she made the catch. She didn't. It landed on the ground battery and body in two different locations.

"Idgit," she picked up the pieces and carefully reassembled them.

Less than a minute after, the phone rang.

"Hello," she answered breathlessly as she pulled herself off the ground.

"Gizzy," Emma greeted. "You home?"

"No. I in Japan," was the first thing that came to her mind, but she settled for, "Emma this is the house phone."

"Leave me alone," her chuckle had a bit of shame in it.

"What you doin'?"

Giselle took tiptoed steps around her room for no reason at all. It was just one of those weird things you did while on the phone because you were idle. It would be fruitless to try to explain it.

"I was outside with my neighbor tellin' her about the carnival launch and then I remember you never finish tellin' me what you was sayin'." She stated her purpose.

Giselle froze in the middle of a twirl causing her to stumble backward.

"O-oh"

"Yeah," Emma's tone mellowed out. "So go ahead. I listenin'."

"Is nothin'," she leaned against her wooden dresser.

Emma sucked her teeth making that squeezed sound that Caribbean people believed meant, "kiss my ass."

"Jus' tell me anyway."

"For real," Giselle's free hand found comfort playing with something around her neck.

She tried to show Emma before and she wasn't able to see the mirror the way Giselle saw it. It was like there was a barrier between them that sheltered Emma's eyes. After that, she had gone on to discover some magical world that she still wasn't sure she had actually seen. She met some people she didn't think were real and saw a bird she wished she hadn't. On top of it all, she woke up stranded in her grandmothers abandoned house. No. She wasn't confident in relating any of this to Emma anymore.

"Is ok. I was jus' jokin'," she lied through her teeth.

"Girl!" Emma sounded jokingly relieved. "You really catch a big fish. I well say maybe you had somethin' important to tell me…"

As Emma spoke Giselle threw out a fake laugh and a few unspecific responses to keep her friend engaged. While doing this her eyes dipped to see exactly what it was she was fondling with. What she saw was a gold snake-like chain with a unique mirror pendant that she was sure up until now was in the bushes behind her house. She let out a loud panicked scream dropping the phone. Just like before, it split apart. There was no question of it being damaged for good. How in God's name did the chain find its way back around her neck! It laid there as though it never left.

"What happen?" Andre bolted into the room closely followed by Amron.

The fear in her eyes was nearly livid. Seeing her in this state, Andre did a quick scan of the room still charged as if prepared for a fight. Amron took large strides in her direction taking note of the separated phone on the ground. Emma must've been calling back like mad.

"Calm down," he said in a caressing tone meant to make her relax. It wasn't going to though. Not while that thing was around her neck.

"Somebody was here?" Asked Andre hopelessly trying to figure out what had rattled her.

Amron was still in front of her muttering words of comfort, but his eyes seemed interested in searching the room too. Was he really expecting to find an intruder because, if yes, it was around her neck. Giselle was prepared to tell him everything. She was going to tell him that she had fallen into some other world and that was why she was walking home this morning. She trusted him more. She was going to confess that she got rid of the chain twice and somehow she still had it. But, her lips were involuntarily sealed. Everything she wanted to say about the chain and its return, couldn't escape her lips. It felt as though she had lost the ability to speak. Seeing her frustrated attempts at speaking, Andre thought she might have been having an asthma attack, even though she wasn't asthmatic, and ran for his old inhaler.

"Better now?" He asked after she took a hit.

"Yeah," was the only word that managed to leave her lips.

They walked her to her bed and waited until she was stable again before questioning her. They were interested in what happened and who could blame them. The whole scene seemed to unfold out of thin air. Again, when Giselle attempted to say anything about the chain, she felt choked. This earned her another pump from the inhaler.

"I good," she finally settled on saying.

It seemed the only words that would leave her mouth were those confirming her wellness.

"Forget it."

"Gizzy," Amron started.

"I good," she repeated sadly a second time.

Once this was over and realizing they were to get no information from her, Giselle's brothers unwillingly left her room leaving the door wide open. She had full knowledge that it was no mistake or absent minded motion. Hastily, she unhooked the chain from her neck and placed it on the bed rather roughly. She absolutely wanted nothing to do with it now. She knew for a fact that she hadn't put it back on. She saw it go flying out the window. So how did it get back and how long had it been on her? Why was she so comfortable with it on that she didn't even notice its return? While pondering all these questions she could hear the responsible whisper of her brother from the other room.

"Yeah, I give her the puff, but I don' know what wrong with her," he paused. "I tellin' you, she just scream out of nowhere."

No doubt Andre was talking to their dad and for some reason this made her cry. Wiping her tears in quick resolution she got up, pocketing the chain, and made her way out to the living room. Amron anxiously sat there with a basket of clean clothes their dad had demanded he tend to before he left the house. Seeing her walk by him to the front door he stood up.

"Where you goin'?"

"For a walk," she gave no more detail.

"No. What if you get an asthma attack again?" He took some steps forward.

"I doh have asthma," she said shutting the door behind her.

She made her way, all aquiver, down the asphalt road in the blazing afternoon. The sun was being a terrorist burning everything the way it was. In her miserable state, she barely acknowledged the gossip-Mrs. Maitland, bidding her good afternoon as she walked by on her way home from work. She hadn't noticed the stray dog that begged her with pleading eyes hoping she had something edible to offer. All she saw was the golden chain she had gripped once again in her hand as she made her way to the big sports flat not far away from her house. Amron and his friends played football there often and every now and then the women's cricket team would take a swing in the clearing. Giselle wasn't interested in games and luckily for her there were none in progress. She marched across the field and made her way to the wooden stands. She couldn't think clearly enough to question how the chain was back and make up possibilities. Nor was she fully molding through what she was about to do. Then, as if planned, she kneeled beneath the stands where the dirt was less compact and dug a hole as deep as she could manage, remorselessly. Once finished, she set the chain in it, covered up the hole being sure to pat the soil and compress it, then found the biggest rock she could and rolled it over the disturbed earth. No way could it get out now. That rock served as the guard that tolerated no escape. Standing up she admired her work in a sadistic way.

"Why you buryin' it?" Amron nearly made her jump out of her skin.

"How you reach here?"

"I walk," he breezed the answer. "That's not the chain gran'mom give you?" He pointed the secure prison Giselle had just made.

Feeling abashed she nodded.

"So why you buryin' it?" Enraged he attempted to walk around her and rescue the chain.

"No Amron," she blocked him with her dusty, slightly dampened, soiled hands. "Leave it."

"Why? She give you and you throwin' it away? That's disrespectful!" He made another attempt at the rock, but Giselle stood in his way.

"Why you actin' so funny today?" She made nothing of his observation. "Answer me!"

"Cause the mirror..." she held back dreading that clogged feeling again.

And as the tears fought their way to the surface and the utter disappointment in herself settled in, she left Amron hurriedly making her way back home. If he wanted to dig it up then fine! She just hoped the chain would follow him instead of her. Her chest rose and fell heavily from both the run and the overwhelming pressure inside of her. Why did he have to follow her? Her little trip would have been just as heavy hearted without him. Why did he have to show up and make it harder? Damn Amron!

~*~

"Yeah, uhm," Brent conversed on the phone taking regular pauses. He left the bathroom with the phone pressed between his ear and shoulder as he looped his belt. "So, when are you available?"

This call must have been important. He was using his professional voice. The one where he put on a twang and pretended he didn't speak dialect, yet some forms of dialect still crept through. He journeyed to the kitchen pulling together the ingredients to make warm milk in a sort of absentminded way. His eyes weren't focused on what he was doing. Seeing this was his house and he knew where everything was, it helped him to pull what he needed without looking.

"So Thursday?" He asked taking another pause. "Alright," he smiled. "Alright. Same to you. Bye."

Brent finished stirring his powdered milk into a cup of warm water and reached for the nearly empty box of corn flakes. Then he made his way to the table where he had placed a bowl and spoon. Giselle wasn't following him. She was just going into the kitchen the same time he was. The curiosity of who he was talking to flamed. If Andre or Amron were to ask, he would shame them saying they were "too fass". He always took a softer approach with her though, so should she ask? Then she noticed her dad was only wearing one sock. He must have been in the middle of putting them on when he got into his phone call.

"Mornin' dad," Andre spoke over the splashing of water and clicking of utensils as he washed up a few dishes in the sink.

"Mornin' dad," she greeted as well, pouring herself a cup of juice.

She didn't get why she felt so tired and weighed down. She did next to nothing yesterday. Well, nothing she'd like to remember.

"Mornin'," he answered. He poured some milk over the cornflakes he dropped in the bowl. "I make an appointment for you." He invited a spoon of cornflakes and milk into his mouth.

"For what?"

"It been a while," he chewed and swallowed loudly. "Just a check-up."

"But I not sick," she complained. "Yesterday was just random."

"That doh mean you doh need to go," he said.

"Yeah, it does. If that happen to Amron or Andre you would tell them is gas and give them some hot tea so why you spendin' money on a check-up?" Her voice was higher pitched than normal.

"Lower your voice," he took another spoon.

"Gizzy, dad know what he doin'. Doh argue," Andre gave his unsolicited opinion.

"Shut up! Nobody ask you!" She yelled at him.

"Make me!" He shouted back putting down the wash cloth he was wiping down the sink with and turning to face her.

"I'll bus' a slap on both of you if you doh cut it out!" They subsided at this threat. "You goin' to the doctor. End of discussion."

And it was.

"You sleep with that on?" Her dad motioned to her with his spoon.

In the midst of her frustration she bent her head to observe her clothing. She had on a simple soft, boy short that was more than likely one of her brother's wear-home-pants that ended up in her clothes by accident. With that, a big red shirt. Nothing fancy. After all, she just wore it to sleep. She didn't have to dress up for that. So when she spotted the rather dressy golden chain resting on her chest, it looked out of place indeed. In shock, she inhaled so deep, so fast it burned. Then she froze. She couldn't hyperventilate here. She couldn't have a repeat of yesterday. It would make her dad believe she was truly sick after she said she wasn't. So she held her breath and slowly set it free.

"You ok?" Brent noticed the change in her face. He put his spoon down.

When Giselle first came home with the chain he was uneasy about it, asking if Ruby just gave it to her just like that. He even made the bold move of asking her if she tried to give it back. After Ruby died, he said nothing more about the chain, but he always admired it when Giselle brought it around. She didn't mind. Ruby was his mother and the chain had belonged to her since he was only a boy.

Giselle nodded. "Um," she gulped. "Where Amron?"

"I don' know, but when I do find him is me and he today…" Brent broke out in a rant about how he told Amron to move his clothes, that he didn't finish folding, from the living room. He was in double trouble.

"I could use your phone?" She asked cutting over him.

"…because I know I tell him not to leave-why?" He said in one breath from his quarrel to addressing Giselle. "I don' see why you need my phone."

81

"I just remember somethin' I need to ask Amron," she sort of pleaded her reason to him.

Brent fished in his pocket handing his Nokia phone to her. "I don' have much credit so hurry up."

Nodding okay, she pressed down on one of the grey buttons to illuminate the screen. Then, as fast as her stubby fingers would allow her, she dialed the number and excused herself from the kitchen. She knew full well her dad would be listening if she stayed too close to him. If she moved he'd only be able to capture pieces of the conversation and most likely not understand it.

"Aye dad," Amron answered.

"Amron! You take out the chain?"

From the other end of the phone Amron sucked his teeth and it was the longest she had ever heard.

"Why you askin' if you doh want it?" He spoke roughly.

In the back-ground she could hear Raheem shouting, "Doh let it go!"

"I look stupid?" Cheddi responded annoyed and worked up. What were they doing?

Giselle exhaled loudly, "If you want to keep it then keep it. Why you give me back?"

"I never."

"Cheddi!" Raheem shouted angry now.

"We go talk when I get home," Amron closed then hung up before she could even say anything.

She was, once again, on a mission to be free of this chain. In one day, she had put it in the trash and thrown it by the side of the road for the garbage truck. Then found it on her dresser when she got back in her room. She took it to the public pool house near her home and threw it over the galvanized barricade, hoping the mirror had smashed in the process. It came back unscratched. It wasn't even chipped. Every time it came back, it made her more nervous and even more scared. That night, she spoke to Amron. He told her he had indeed dug up the chain, but he kept it to himself. He didn't intend on giving it back to her. No matter what she said to him, he refused to believe anything other than Giselle had taken back the chain. In his mind he did her a favor. He truly believed she changed her mind and she was lucky she had a brother like him to get it back for her. Giselle went to bed that night placing the chain a careful distance away from her. It wasn't going to go away. She knew that full well. No matter what she did to it. No matter how far she threw it or how deep she buried it. It wasn't going anywhere. She figured the best thing to do was keep it around, but keep it away. Whatever was making it come back to her couldn't harm her from a distance. At least she hoped so.

That night she tossed and turned but couldn't get comfortable. With the covers it was too hot and without them, chilly. Sitting up wasn't something she fancied, but sleep wasn't showing her grace. Giselle was restless. Every time she went into a state of tranquility she found her thoughts back on something spiritually rattling. It was one of those situations where she wanted to go to bed, but her brain thought it was the perfect time to reflect on life. Summer had only just begun. The down side to that was soon it would have to come to an end. For now, her dad didn't have much to worry about. He had three big kids looking after, ages fourteen, sixteen and eighteen. They could easily find ways to entertain themselves without putting their dad in expense. But summer would end soon and that meant school. Giselle's school shoe was at the end of its journey before the last school year was even over so she definitely needed a new one. Plus, she had to get new books and everything. Then there was that monster, Amron, who couldn't take care of anything. He'd more than likely need new everything. Now Andre was starting a new school so there was that to worry about too. She wished she could think up some sort of get rich quick scheme. And every so often, as those thoughts clambered though her mind, her eyes drifted to the chain on the window ledge and the magical place she had found herself in. She still couldn't explain to herself how she had ended up in her Grandmother's house Sunday morning. How did she get there? What if she did actually go to this place? What was it called again? What if that little bird was real? What if she could use it all somehow to help her father? Ruby never seemed to ever carry dept. Giselle never heard her complain once.

Slowly, and trying with everything in her to keep the noise level down, she tip-toed to the window ledge and gazed down at the chain. Her reflection was a black silhouetted outline of her frame. The light in her room was off. It was probably around the early hours of the morning. All she could see was the parts of her face the moon was kind enough to highlight. She could just faintly make out her eyes, round cheeks, and lips. Her expression was plain and strewn with deep thought. She was staring at her reflection, but not really seeing it. Her mind had already strayed. Then the smallest movement flickered at the corner of her eyes. Did her reflection just smile at her? Heart thumping loud, she ran back to her bed almost tripping on her shoes. The same shoes her dad told her not to leave all over the place. She had to get rid of that mirror. At the time, she was trying to think about ways to get money while shooting down everything that involved believing in the magical mirror. Nowhere between those circumvent thoughts did she start smiling. She had no reason to. What was with that mirror?

The next day dragged by. She mostly spent it trying to think of cruel ways to get rid of the mirror so that it wouldn't want to come back to her. She snuck into her dad's tool shed that afternoon to see what she could do. It was a small, four wall, block shed that he kept all his stuff in. There were shelves with different kinds of nails, screws, wrenches, screwdrivers, and ratchets. The heavier tools like the chain saw and such were on the ground pushed to the side. There were a few things in storage there like the old refrigerator and a few gas cylinders that had to be refilled. The first thing that caught her eyes was the hammer lying idly across the makeshift wooden table. Immediately she picked it up and spun it in her hand a bit savoring the grip. With a devious smirk, she dropped the chain on the hard ground, stooped over it and with all her might, pounded the hammer into its petite frame. Not a dent. Annoyed, she slammed it again and again and again. It still looked brand new, as though her grandmother had handed it over that second. Why wouldn't it bend? Or at least why wouldn't the mirror crack? Most of her ideas to destroy called for serious physical damage to its appearance. If it couldn't even dent then all her other plans were useless.

Tossing the hammer back in its place she gazed around the toolshed a bit longer. She needed something that would put a lot of force on it. Or something that would continuously shock it faster than it could fix itself. In a daze, still considering strategies she ran a screwdriver across the surface of the glass. It was just as she thought; it wouldn't scratch. The mirror was permeable after all; the screwdriver just went straight through. Not thinking much of it, she dropped the screwdriver into the glass and with the same speed flames burst out of it. It shot like fireworks and crackled like water flicked in hot oil. Giselle dropped the necklace.

That is what it looks like when I go in? She wondered. *Or it probably just doh like screw drivers.*

Her curiosity was getting the best of her now. Scooping the piece of gold off the sawdust heap on the ground she marched outside, eyes sharp. The vegetation around her house danced in the slight breeze with a swoosh. The sun was hidden behind a massive passing cloud and it was almost as if the trees shaking were their desperate cries for the rays to beat against their leaves once more. She could hear the thumping of her rabbits taking a hop around their home. Few birds sang and in the distance, she could hear a dog barking consistently. Right in the middle of that sweeping peace Giselle scampered around, head spinning in circles. She had a thought; a strong feeling she felt impulse to act upon. It was another one of her imaginative escapes from reality. The only difference was the mirror's power wasn't imaginary and her struggle to rid herself of it was real.

What if it only like living things inside it? Her mind raced as she scavenged the bushes around her yard. *Like, the mirror is a kinda portal and sometimes things might fall into it by accident. Maybe it does only let living things go in.*

She turned every leaf and rock she came across; every rotting piece of wood or random scraps of garbage. Her search was thorough. She was focused. This wasn't just something she could turn away from now. It was on her mind. She had to finish or she'd never sit still. Finally, she found what she had been looking for. Over by the fencing that marked the boundary of her fathers' land, just between the tiny leaves, were ladybugs. Something living. Letting one crawl onto her hand Giselle took a seat right there. It didn't matter that she sat on dirt or that she was out doors. Her house only had one floor, but the land it rested on slopped greatly so the back of her house stood on pillars. Being in her backyard was like going into some undiscovered wonder of the world. The tower of a house in front of her, the rabbit coup and tool shed on either side, the trees and shrubs and then the lush fencing caging it all in. She was covered. Holding the scampering ladybug over the mirror with a steady hand she prepared to drop it in. What was the worst that could happen; maybe Majesty needed ladybugs. They were cute. With that resolve she flicked the unsuspecting bug into the mirror. Sparks flew. There couldn't be anything left of that ladybug. Giselle was stumped. So it wouldn't allow inanimate objects and it wouldn't allow another living thing into it. But it allowed her.

Marko say the mirror have to like me to let me in, she caught herself thinking. *Huh, this boy not real.*

She laid flat back on the grass now facing the tool shed. In her head memories from that magical world flowed along with her own stern voice trying to convince her otherwise. She couldn't have this chain. Only bad things could come from it. Imagine what people would say about her and her family; imagine how they'd tarnish Ruby's name. Yet, having a chain that liked her and her alone, a chain so loyal it would destroy every and any thing that tried to penetrate its sanctuary and stand against any weapon formed against it; it was a bit intriguing. She couldn't keep it though. What if her father found out? He was saved man. He had strong beliefs and lived religiously by certain sayings. What would he say to her if he knew she had a magic mirror? Imagine all the things she could do with it. She could probably visit that weaponry again and take a swing at those katanas and guns. Mostly the guns. That was all she thought about; how heavy it was, how it must feel to pull the trigger, what the bullets must look and feel like. She bet she could hit all her targets with one shot.

With her mind so deep in thought she started tossing stones to prove herself. There was a hole in the corner of the wall of the tool shed. It wasn't broken down or anything. It was a construction error her father neither bothered or cared to fix. He just let it be. Grabbing some pebbles off the ground she aimed at the space. Then, with one fell swoop, she threw them one after the next and they went straight into the hole. She didn't miss once. Only twice the pebble had bounced off the side of a block only to find itself ricocheted inside.

When ball is life, she chuckled to herself. She'd never played a game of basketball a day in her life. She was simply a good shot.

The following day came and to her surprise the necklace wasn't on her or anywhere in sight when she woke up. She'd left it in the grass the day before expecting it to let itself in as it always did, but it didn't. The light fluffy feeling that made its home in her chest was something she cherished and hadn't felt in a while. Maybe she did make it not want to comeback. She hummed as she got dressed and made her way to the doctor. Bet they weren't going to find anything wrong. Right she was too. She went there and waited in the waiting area for about twenty-five minutes. When the receptionist called her in, Giselle, accompanied by her dad, made her way into the office.

There she was asked a series of questions that at times got awkward. Imagine answering questions about your monthly cycle in front of your dad. She had to give a summary of the symptoms she was experiencing which wasn't much since it only happened that one time. Then the doctor checked her weight. She ended up having to take most of her clothes off and put on one of those backless gowns. After some time of breathing in an out while a cold stethoscope was pressed against her chest, having light shined in her eyes, her reflexes checked and a few other things, the checkup was over. Conclusion, she was healthy.

"Thank-you doc," Brent shook her hand as he stood up to leave.

"No problem," Dr. Sheppard smiled. "Oh, and Giselle, I like your chain."

Those dreaded words. Giselle knew she left home chain free that day. Furthermore, she left the backyard chain free. So why was Dr. Sheppard complimenting her on something she should, for no reason, have. Mouth shut, face taut, Giselle nodded and exited the room staying quiet for the whole trip home. Her neck was tingling and her shoulders suddenly heavy knowing that the piece of unwanted jewelry was there. No matter what, she couldn't let out the frustrated cry within her. Not in front of her father who kept questioning whether she was ok. She got home and just as she did the night before, she placed the mirror on the window ledge and took refuge in her bed. It seemed this was the only way it wouldn't mysteriously latch itself onto her. Then she sat there, at that distance, and stared at it with raw fear. What was she to do now? It wasn't going to go away. She could see that now.

For the rest of the week it stayed that way. Where ever she went she brought it along, but left it at a safe distance from her. When she was in the living room it was on top the television. When she was in the kitchen it was on the fridge. When she went to the bathroom it was on the sink. When she went outside it was on the verandah wall. But when she forgot to take it along, it showed up around her neck. She felt this process was the best way to keep it away without throwing it away. That was until she got the smart idea to burn it. She took a pot from the kitchen and brought it to the back of the house. Carefully wrapping the chain in wads of old paper she found in her room, she set it alight in the pot. For a few seconds, all was fine. The smoke was minimum and the paper was slowly being engulfed by the flames. That was when it began. When all seemed well a loud ear piercing screech awakened the air and almost shook the pillars of the house. She was home alone and there was no one to burst around the corner to see if she was okay even if she wasn't the one screaming. Then just as abruptly as it had begun it ended and the flames were no more. The smoke that had risen slowly dwindled in the frazzled air around a panic absorbed Giselle who stumbled back in the dirt. She didn't even wait to find out the cause of the scream. Instead she just ran.

She stepped into her room and shut the door behind her clutching dearly onto her chest. Her ears burned and she felt too weak to even walk further so she leaned back on the door. What on earth was that dreadful cry? It was so close too. Almost as if it emanated from inside the very pot she was hosting her mini chain-be-gone bonfire in.

"Why do you not accept me?"

A milky female voice poured into the room. Giselle's eyes roamed crazily, her attention swiftly changing from her fears to her safety. She was as sure as the day was long that she was the only one home. Added to that she was the only female taking up residence in this house. She was the only one in there gifted to speak in such a light tone. So who did that voice belong to?

"I am not leaving."

The voice seemed to be right under her nose. It was as though she was the one speaking.

"Who is it?" She trembled and reached for something. Anything.

"I am Vrai- the truthful spirit. I am your Sui Generis."

And slowly, with wide eyes and dangerously unsteady hands she unhooked the chain from her neck. She already knew it was there. After it said Sui Generis she just knew. First, she had heard those words somewhere before. Second, it was a habit of the chain to show up where it was not wanted. This was not the time for her to act frazzled and surprised. Placing it in the palm of her hand she had no idea what she expected to see. At this point anything she saw would be beyond any expectations she could dream of having. The glass of the pendant appeared as a pool of disturbed water with her reflection as an oddly visible wave staring at her.

"You… you just say somethin'?" Giselle spoke nervously to the chain hoping that there would be no response.

"Yes," it said and in that exact moment she let it fall to the floor.

"Why do you refuse me?"

"How come you could talk?"

She countered while taking refuge on her bed to gain as much distance as possible from it. As if that were going to change anything. It was still going to talk to her.

"I was always able to talk," it responded simply. "Pick me up." It demanded.

When Giselle didn't obey, it magically found its way back to her hands again. It just appeared there. Shakily she held it away from her setting it loose on her mattress.

"What you want?"

"The question is what do you want?" It said in a wise voice.

"What?" She mumbled.

As a matter a fact she didn't even care. She could stay there and talk to this chain all day, but it wouldn't make it any less strange. Nor would it make it any more innocent. Easing backwards off the bed she vacated the room leaving it to rest on the unmade sheets. She couldn't stay in there. That chain was possessed! Her room was taken over! Needless to say, there was no escaping. By the time she stepped out of her bedroom door's proximity she was holding tightly to the chain again.

"Leave me alone!"

She screamed throwing it against the wall and running with no destination in mind. Just like before, by the time she was in the living room the chain was around her neck.

"Why do you run?" It asked forcing her to wrestle herself and wrench away the piece of jewelry again.

Once it was off she made a mad dash to the kitchen instantly regretting it. She should have run outside. Surely it wouldn't come out into broad daylight and speak. To get outside she'd have to go back the way she came. There was a back door in the kitchen, but it was one of those that didn't have steps. An incomplete project of her father's. She'd have to jump. Should she? God knows the last thing she wanted to do was have a run in with that demon accessory again.

"Why do you not answer me?" She heard the voice behind her.

There it was on the kitchen table. Resting. Everything lifeless about it except the watery glass rippling over itself. Giselle, feeling hopelessly trapped, back up against the counter and gripped tightly to it.

"Cause I don' want to!" She felt obligated to respond. "Cause I 'fraid."

"You want to know something about fear? One is not afraid of the cause. One is afraid of the consequence."

"What that s'pos to mean?" Her wobbly vocabulary sold out how truly terrified she was.

"No one is afraid of heights. They are afraid of the fall. No one is afraid to play. They are afraid to lose. No one is afraid of the dark. They are afraid of what is in it," the mirror cleverly said.

Giselle held her pose stiffly as she considered this thought. Her mind was still cloudy and her knees still weak.

"You are afraid of me, but am I hurting you? Am I threatening you in anyway?" The mirror spoke.

"No, but you might," was the snappy response.

"Aha! Consequence." It said in a winning tone. She could swear her own face was smirking at her. "I chose you. Why do you not accept me?"

Easing off the counter, but not making motion to step away Giselle spoke again.

"Why you choose me?"

"I am starting to ask myself that same question. I have had countless talented people use me willingly in the past."

It appeared all the chain spirit really wanted to do was talk. This put a false sense of ease within her. Slowly gaining courage she spoke louder.

"Then go find them and stay away from me!"

"I refuse," the chain spirit responded calmly.

"Why?"

"I watched you grow up. I have seen your happiness, sadness, strengths and weaknesses. You are noisy, nosey, annoying, absent minded and more reckless than any owner I have ever sought out to protect my world."

"So why you choose me then? If am all that?"

She asked unable to see the positives in anything the spirit had said to her. If she was really all those things, then why would it choose her? It was basically calling her a waste of time. She was starting to see why it referred to itself as the truthful spirit.

"Because you are different. As years pass by what was once considered different becomes common. So every once in a while we have to find a new different to obsess over and try to plagiarize. You are my new different."

The chain spirit's words blessed the kitchen.

"Plus, the serious ones do not seem to last. Perhaps we need feathers, people that know how to go with the motion. Marko was chosen and he appears fine. So was Scout."

Bewildered, lost, somewhat proud and a slight bit scared she approached the mirror again. Cautiously she scooped it up in her hand and gazed at it wondering if she should believe anything it said. She wanted to continue believing that the other world was a dream, but how could she when this was going on right now? Was this why her grandmother said everything would be ok as long as she had the chain. Was this the real meaning behind her words? Maybe this world didn't spring up after her death after all. Besides, if she kept running, this chain would keep haunting her. She was tired of feeling insecure about it.

"My name is Vrai- the truthful spirit," it repeated. "I am here to protect you as long as you protect my world. So, will you?"

CHAPTER FIVE

IN LOVING MEMORY

HER SECOND ENTRANCE into Majesty wasn't very different from the first one. The mirror-Vrai, was tired of waiting and took her in unwillingly. She opened her eyes to find herself, as if thrown, across the ground. She was greeted with the identifiable warm air that swarmed the room. There was no songbird attacking her, and she was grateful for that. She wasn't as shaken up as she was the last time. The first time it had been so unexpected and she didn't understand what was happening. Not this time though. She had continued to question Vrai even after the second introduction. Annoyed, she sucked Giselle in saying, "How about you go and get a taste of what you have been missing?"

"Damn chain," she was muttering curses under her breath.

"You know, I am still here," Vrai's voice made her stumble over after she'd just gotten off the ground. "Did you think I was only in your chain?" The full-length mirror said to her.

"Maybe," she dusted herself when she stood up the second time.

"See that space," Giselle's reflection made note of the removed brass plate. "I want you to put your name there."

"And then?"

"Putting your name is like signing an official contract. It binds you, me and this world together."

"I don' want that. Why I have to protect this place anyway?"

She nearly growled at Giselle. The way the glass vibrated viciously exposed the spirits rage. "I chose you! Which makes you a Guardian of Majesty! Majesty is fragile. It is toxic to itself and to the outside world. This is why it needs strong people to stand on the forefront and lead the way." She almost couldn't see herself anymore, but she faintly caught sight of her own fist being held threateningly toward her.

"And I strong?"

Her voice had that same fake amusement that Andre's had that morning she walked home. It also had a tinge of disbelief.

"You are. I see potential."

Giselle snorted. "And where the people that used to own you before? You just leave them when things get bad?"

"As I have previously stated, writing your name is like signing a contract. I am here to protect you as long as you protect

Majesty. Everything that happens while you have me is confidential."

That settled it. If Vrai was ready to set aside everything and commit to Giselle it meant that she had always done it that way. No information was going to be leaked. Not from this mirror. Still, she didn't have to stand and take this. Vrai had her turn to talk. She made her points and carried out her argument. It was meant to sway Giselle's mind, but Giselle still had the right to take her time to think about it. That was what arguments were for anyway. Both parties got everything off their chest in the heat of the moment and only after, when they were alone, did they really think about what was said. Only after, could a true decision be made no matter how things were left. She stepped up to the mirror with full intention to walk through, but she couldn't. The rippling on the mirror wasn't for show. It was icy and as sharp as a razorblade. She was suffering the consequences of carelessly throwing her hand out at it. It was a good thing she didn't just run in. Imagine what could have happened to her. Her finger looked as though she had held a razor blade the wrong way. The skin was lifted and sliced very shallow. A little more and she wouldn't have a finger print. She wasn't bleeding or anything, but if she had pushed her hand any further she knew she would be.

"You cut me," she gasped pulling her hand back.

"Go explore," Vrai simply said.

Passing down the halls for the second time was still as inviting as it had been the first time. She couldn't wait to get to the end of the tunnel and see that wonderful view again. She had no doubt it would be just as she had remembered it. A little defiant that she had no choice but to go this way, her curiosity was still getting the better of her. She felt more in charge of her actions this time. Well, somewhat in charge. She couldn't go home. Not as long as the mirror kept rippling. She wasn't trying to butcher herself. Not that she minded staying if just to satisfy her curiosity. The mirror was only pushing her to do what she was afraid to do herself.

Slowly, she made it out to the ledge and held on to the brown railing where she could look over Majesty. It was late in the afternoon back in Grenada which meant it would be the opposite here. It was windy. The nice cool air was blowing over her skin giving her a little chill. It wasn't too cold, but she wasn't feeling comfortably warm anymore. In the distance she could see the full moon hanging low over the sea with its reflection beautifully pasted in the black water. Building lights stretched as far as the eye could see, in a checkered pattern. Only where there lay forests, the light show would die down. She noticed the little town she had seen before wasn't as florescent at night as it was during the day. Still, the lights that illuminated randomly from every building was something she didn't see every day in Grenada. Everything had a unique touch to it. She especially made note of the few street lights she saw from her position. They were long poles that ended in a saucer. In it fire blazed flamboyantly as if trying to show off its glow.

The click of a door being closed alerted her. Someone was coming. Would she get in trouble for showing up unannounced? Fearing the answer to this she dipped back in the hall and raced to the universal passage. The mirror was still rippling. How was she to leave now?

"You!" She yelled in a whisper. "Mirror!" It didn't answer her. "Vrai!"

"Yes," it said cheekily.

"Stop now. I want to go back. I see everythin'," she lied.

"So fast?" Vrai took her sweet time to respond.

"Yeah," Giselle said looking over her shoulder. "Let me go back. I go think about it."

"Hmmm…" Vrai hummed.

"Ya came back," Ecoli's footsteps echoed as he walked in.

When she turned around she saw Ecoli approaching with those same common pants but with a different shirt. It was yellow this time. He seemed to have just finished up some heavy lifting. His clothes appeared to have some burns on it as if he was playing in fire and his hands and face a bit ashy. He had his Katana at his side.

"Yeah," she stated, resentfully turning around.

"When?" He fished in his pocket for his silver thermos and drank from it.

"A while ago," Giselle responded still feeling that intimidating air rising off of him.

"Ok," he sighed and wiped his mouth once he was done quenching his thirst. "Wasn' here for a few days."

Ecoli sounded exhausted.

"Where you went?"

"Guardian business," he stated, finality in his tone.

He then excused himself to the male's room. When she turned around to talk to Vrai again the mirror didn't look the same. The ripples were gone. Did she leave? When Giselle actually wanted to talk to her again she had ditched the scene.

"Vrai?" She called, but there was no answer.

Did she do this on purpose? She did throw Giselle in here and force her to stay. Then as soon as Ecoli showed up she was nowhere to be seen. Maybe she felt his strong aura too. Or maybe this was all a ploy. The chief of Majesty shows up and she makes herself scarce? She was just pushing Giselle to accept her and become a guardian. What better way to do it than with the help of the chief? That sneaky little snake! She reached out and petted the mirror testing it before attempting to dive through. It was safe. No sharps.

"You leavin'?" He asked her.

She nodded.

Ask him about this guardian thing. She thought.

If she wanted to shut Vrai up she would have to ask him. Plus, she couldn't deny her blundering interest in it as well. Now that she was here a whole load of questions were running in her mind. She was here again proving that this place was in fact real. She was cut and she felt it. If this were all a dream, at that point she should have woken up or stirred in her sleep causing the setting of her dream to change to something completely different. It was now or never. She had to speak up now about wanting to know more about this world or forever hold her peace. She knew whatever she wanted to know he would have the answers. After all, he was the chief. Giselle wasn't raised to be a shy person. She was loud, a bit obnoxious and once she got comfortable, very bossy. She just had to get back to being that person. When Ecoli presented himself once again she was ready to question him to the ends of the earth.

"Before ya leave can I show ya somethin'?" He said.

He wasn't exactly cleaned up, but he didn't look a complete mess. She was curious. What could he want to show her? This was only the second time they had come into contact. Was he waiting this whole time in hopes that she would return?

"Show me what?" She asked.

"Follow me," he gestured with a wave of the hand.

She was unsure and her face certainly told it.

"Don' worry." He smiled. "So wha' brought ya back 'ere?"

He took her out of the Universal Passage all the way down the tunnel. Along the side of the railed ledge where she had seen all of Majesty, there was a trail. It was a thin crooked path lit along the sides by smaller versions of those strange street lights. Upon closer inspection, all it was, was a small dancing fire hoisted an inch above the podium by nothing. Giselle couldn't help but stare.

"The mirror," she said distractedly.

"Ya met the spirit," he chuckled. "Heard she could be blunt, yeah?"

There was a long drawn out howl that filled the early morning air. "You hear?"

"Guardians don' exactly mingle with the other spirits," he stated not looking back at her.

"Why?" She asked walking quickly to keep up with him.

"Don' know. We just never do. We have our own." So there was a spirit for every Sui Generis then.

At first the trail went down a steep slope of a massive stone building. Once at the bottom it ran flat for a while. She knew they weren't in the town she had seen though. They might have been close to it, but by the surroundings, they hadn't made it there yet. She wondered if that was where he was taking her. One side of the path lacked footing other than bountiful bridge-like trails while there was algae building up on the wall on the other side. The smell was like wet mud and fresh rain with the air becoming moister the further on they went. Once they cleared the flat and started to ascend again, the path became a bridge with a free fall on both sides of them. Luckily, there were railings. The rock beneath Giselle's feet was starting to get quite slippery. The last thing she wanted was to fall. Beneath, ran a river flowing with sparkling water. She lost herself staring at this. This must be the cause of the gradual dampening of the area.

"So how ya feel 'bout this place so far?" Ecoli's twang kept flipping.

It was like one minute he was Grenadian and the next he was not. She couldn't identify his other accent. Plus, his speech wasn't from any country in the normal world that she was aware of. He curved his words and stressed a lot on his 'E's and completely dropped the beginning of some words. At least she could understand him and she wasn't asking him to repeat all the time.

"I feel like I don' know nothin' and I shouldn' be here," she said.

"Understandable," he nodded. "Ya go soon love it."

She didn't respond, but not because she didn't want to. The trail dissolving into the woods stuck a pin in the conversation for her. She halted.

"Somethin' wrong?" He asked when he couldn't hear her anymore.

"Where we goin'?" She spoke with uncertainty.

"Is just beyond the trees. Come now," he waved her along then continued walking.

She didn't feel comfortable going in there, but she was equally skeptical about standing alone. Was it ok to trust him? He was the chief, even though he looked about the same age as Andre. What made him good enough to be chief? She crossed over into the woods that led to a clearing introduced by a stone arch.

Majesty's Fallen
Not Forgotten

With the dim moonlight she just barely managed to read the engraving. Her eyes fell from the monument as she scoped the area. It was a bit darker since they left the enigmatic lamps behind. Everything appeared to her as silhouettes. There were lifeless protrusions erupting from the ground all around her. Ecoli confidently marched through the arch setting off some kind of reaction. The place was ignited. More of those lights were there scattered sparsely throughout. This lot was wooden instead of on a small metal poles. As for where they were, the answer became evident.

A graveyard.

Why would he bring her here? She wasn't afraid of walking through the bedroom of the dead. She merely found it odd and creepy that this was the place he wanted to take her. Or maybe they were just passing through. She shouldn't jump to conclusions. He didn't stop. He was still walking wasn't he? He better not bring up any talk about "accepting" anything else! Giselle wasn't about to accept jack-squat in the middle of a graveyard! That one thing was for sure. Wordlessly, he continued to lead her between the lumpy beds and gray headstones.

Oelreh Postale

1981 - 2004

Guardian- Emissary

Your time was short, but you made a lasting impression.

If her calculations were correct this Oelreh died at age 23. Short was a mild word to use here. His life had barely started.

Rebma Fross

1985 – 2007

Guardian- Reconnaissance

Your services will not be overlooked

This lady was only 22. Giselle continued reading as she walked along behind Ecoli. Her pulse was rising steadily with every step. Every single one of those headstones said Guardian. Even worst, more than half of them died before they reached 30. Why would he think this would boost her interest? This was actually shoving her further and further away from accepting the mirror.

In Loving Memory of

Ennoaj Raspy

1971 – 2008

Guardian – Documenter

This lady's age still gave no hope.

"So all these people accepted the mirror."

This wasn't a question. Her voice had more realization in it.

"And they provided excellent years o'service," he defended.

She said nothing. Her thoughts were falling back on how to rid herself of that mirror. It wouldn't go away easy. Not even if she buried it. Though, that wasn't exactly proven. That big head Amron dug up the chain before she even made it home.

"Ya can always tell who was born here from who migrated by the name." He observed her obsessive reading. He seemed to miss the part where she was freaking out. "Names in Majesty are more… free."

She scanned a few more headstones this time only reading the names and nothing else.

Talon Spark.

George Mc Andrew

Those names seemed normal enough. She checked out a few more.

Eénad Smock

Enomis Windy

Those must be what he meant by free. They certainly weren't names she'd heard for a person before. Why were their names so all over the place? There was even someone called Enidan. She couldn't tell the gender of some of these people with just their names. She played a game 'Local or Foreigner' for the rest of the walk. It kept her occupied and not focused on the fact that she was walking between the death beds of the people who came before her. It kept her from asking him just how many of them owned Vrai at one point.

"Here," he stopped abruptly causing her to run into his back.

Never in all her life had she felt someone with such intense body heat. Ecoli's body was so hot she actually had to pull away from him. He didn't even seem bothered by this. He was nearly roasting. Was he sick? A terrible fever that would be. He didn't look under the weather. He was fine. Damn.

"Sorry," he apologized.

Taking a few steps backward she charged her vision on what ended their journey. Finally, she was about to see what was so important that he kept it a secret the whole way there.

Ruby Thomas

1918 - 2013

Guardian – Chief

You were and still are the definition of Greatness

A memorial dedicated to Ruby. There it stood in the middle of about six others looking more sacred and cared for than any tomb she had ever laid eyes on. The concrete was so fresh and the engraving still new. This emphasized that her grandmother was with her not long ago. Now she was reduced to this. A woman that was once the light in everyone's eyes was now represented by a piece of rock. She gazed wordlessly for some time. Her emotions welled up inside of her. Her throat felt stuffed and her eyes burned. Hold it in. Don't cry here.

"Best leader Majesty ever had," Ecoli informed.

That was right; the grave did say chief didn't it? So Ruby was the chief of Majesty? That was a big deal. This was a whole country. Her grandmother was the head of a whole alternative world and she didn't even know. These people must have been grieving just as much as she was and again she had no idea. Now that she was gone, Giselle finally got to see the place. She felt a sense of betrayal seeing as she wasn't introduced to this whole-other-life Ruby must have had. She felt robbed; robbed of the opportunity to see Ruby do something great, robbed of the opportunity to see her in her prime. Feeling weighed down, she dropped to her knees. She couldn't tear her eyes away from the memorial. The anger eating away at her insides wasn't stopping the fresh pain of losing a loved one.

"I could go," Ecoli suggested.

She balled her hands into fists and pressed her lips together. Then she shook her head, her hair not budging an inch from this motion. She had curly afro like hair that she didn't care much for.

"She was chief," she mumbled. "She never tell me that."

This statement seemed to take Ecoli by surprise, but he quickly recovered. "She had good reason," he responded.

"Good reason?" She repeated.

Her eyes faltered. She was about to look at him, but for some reason she couldn't. And looking back at her grandmother's memorial once her gaze was broken, turned into a task. Now she was reduced to staring at the earth beneath her. The earth she had only now realized, as she was kneeling on it, was dry. This place wasn't as soggy and moist as the path that lead them here. How far had they traveled from the river? In the distance, she heard the rushing sound of water flowing. The air had a hard, natural scent about it. A smell she was quite fond of. Still, the beautiful noises and addicting smells wouldn't change the fact that she was kneeling in a graveyard. It wouldn't change the fact that her grandmother was no more and she was now a part of the world that Ruby ruled. It wouldn't change her conflicting rage and feelings of rejection.

He observed her.

"So what? I s'posed to just become a guardian now?" Her voice was bitter.

"Is up to ya." he said.

"Stop lyin'." She called him out. "The mirror already tell me I have to. I jus' askin' since you probably know more about my own grandmother than me. That what she want? She jus' want me wake up and take over like she wasn' keepin' this a secret the whole time?"

"Is not like that," he defended. "She was lookin' out for ya. She didn' want ya to get involved."

She thought for a moment. "And that is not what guardians do? Get involved in Majesty?"

"We protect it," he finished.

"From what?" She finally faced him and he saw that her eyes were two big pools.

The silence grew thick between the two. Ecoli buried his hands in his pockets and stayed quiet. He was giving her time to think; time to process. He might not have understood exactly what she was feeling, but he knew what it was like to feel confused. He understood the pain of believing one thing your whole life and then one day realizing it wasn't so. It was a bitter taste of reality that seemed to always show up when someone was vulnerable. As if only when they were at their lowest point did the truth find it acceptable to peek its head. Though, it was really them finally paying attention to their surroundings, it was more settling to blame pain on the universe.

"Fine," he thought he heard her say.

"Huh?"

"Fine," she said clearly. "I go accept the Sui-whatever."

"You sure?" He asked her knowing that he provided no solid argument for her to do so.

"I want the mirror spirit to leave me alone," her response made sense. After all, the only way to shut Vrai up was to accept her.

"Ok," he said. "Follow me."

So maybe she was wrong. When he had told her before that all she had to do was write on a brass plate she found it underwhelming. Maybe there was more to it than just writing with a permanent marker. If it wasn't, then this was the most incredible marker she had ever used in her life. From the moment she started forming the letters the black ink started to smoke. The path of the marker point looked fiery. She stopped after the 'I' to admire what was happening. She had expected this to be as ordinary as writing in a notebook. She underestimated this place. Giselle continued writing again after Ecoli's urging. Still, she was so focused on the burning letters being permanently engraved that she almost messed up her own name.

When she was done with that she was instructed to turn over the plate and write on it just like before, only this time Giselle had to write her safe spot. Where was her safe spot? Ruby's was her house and Marko said his was under his bed. So where would hers be? She could put it somewhere in her room, but her brothers- really just Amron- were unpredictable.

What if she wasn't there and he took it back? Then what? She couldn't imagine it being a nice little chat when she suddenly emerged from the mirror in front of their friends.

"Ecoli?" She wasn't sure what to write. "Where your safe spot is?"

"In the garage by my house," he folded his arms. "Is a real closed up place."

She hummed. So it could be anywhere then. Giselle thought for a while. She couldn't think of any quiet place she'd like to hide it. Not only to keep the whole Universal Passage thing a secret, but to make sure she never lost this chain- not that she could lose it. Eventually, after searching her brain she wrote "Ruby's House." It was already there so why not just keep it there.

"I suggest ya keep this hush from ya blood for a while," he cleared his throat.

"Why?"

"Because," he paused and thought for a while. It looked to her like he was trying to come up with a legitimate reason. "How would they react?"

Although his response was weak it was thought provoking. How would her family react? Her father was a bit eccentric and would surely try to take away the mirror. Though she might not fight much to get it back she knew the mirror would come back to her of its own accord. Especially now that her name was on the plate. Andre would be on her case and rat her out to her father every time it came back. Not to mention he would say it was demonic or something. As for Amron she couldn't exactly call a reaction for him. On one hand the chain might intrigue him to the point where he might want to go in. On the other hand, he might act like he didn't see anything or want money to cover for her. Majesty would just have to be her little secret for now. Just until she knew enough about it to explain to them; enough to convince them that it wasn't a bad place. To do that, she would first have to convince herself.

"Ok, but…"

The "don't you dare talk back to me" look on Ecoli's face gave the hint that this conversation was over. Gosh. Wasn't he a friendly guy just a second ago? He really flipped the switch quickly. Were all the guardians going to be like that?

"Anyway, s'almost night back in Greenz." his voice went back to smooth. "Look," he sighed. "If when ya get home ya decide to help, m'here every day."

With that he took his departure.

CHAPTER SIX

FLORAL COVE SQUARE

GISELLE,

I'm sorry you had to find out this way. There are a lot of things that I had to tell you; a lot of things that I should have told everyone. I just didn't know where to begin. Due to unforeseen circumstances, I can't be with you anymore. Again, I'm sorry. I wanted to tell you, but I had reason not to. I made a promise. Plus, I didn't want you to resent Majesty or see it as an evil place. It is not. I do acknowledge, however, that the lonesome trail your mother went down has everything to do with it.

By now you should know that I was chief of Majesty. Being chief had more disadvantages than benefits. Nevertheless, I still loved it. Your mother saw some things- magical things. She couldn't cope and when I tried to explain, when I told her that her children would one day be a part of this world whether she liked it or not, she chipped. She couldn't deal with it. It is just like your father to find a stick in the mud, tunnel vision woman just as himself. Sorry to say it that way, but it is what it is. She couldn't accept what she saw and it made her crazy. That didn't make me love her any less. She asked me to keep her children out of my twisted affairs and I kept my word. After she died I kept quiet out of respect. She never told me that I couldn't give you a gift.

My words to you now are to be very careful and wary of your surroundings. Now that you know of Majesty a lot of danger will present itself to you. Many strange events will take place and some will leave you confused for years to come. There is no doubt. But please, try to see the good in Majesty. Try to understand its purpose and why it exists. The people there are one of a kind and I guarantee you will find them to your liking. Please try for me.

I love you,

Ruby.

When she journeyed home this message was awaiting her on the chain. Vrai was given this message and asked to pass it on only after Giselle had accepted the mirror. Once again, Giselle was feeling conflicted and stuck. Her mother, the woman she barely knew, went mad because of Majesty. Why was she supposed to serve a place that caused her to go motherless for most of her life? She had only known her mother, Grace, for six years before she was admitted to the mental hospital. Six years! She barely knew her because of Majesty. Should she really give Majesty a chance now? Ruby clearly stated she didn't want Giselle to hate Majesty, which was kind of what she was beginning to do.

Lying back on her bed she wiped her hand down her face. This was stupid. If being chief had so many disadvantages, then why did she love it so much. What was wrong with Majesty? Just what exactly was going on there? Ecoli said the guardians had to protect it. Now Ruby was saying that danger would "present itself" to her. How was she to find good in a place so terrible?

"Will you go back?" Vrai had not stop talking ever since she revealed she could.

Giselle listened to Vrai as though she was an actual physical person in her room. Why fight it now? The chain wasn't going anywhere anytime soon. She only had one warning for it.

"Listen, doh jus' talk loud so as if me and you is friends. Okay? It have other people livin' here too and I doh want them askin' questions yet."

The night was a dead one. It was as if the universe was giving her all the conditions she needed to think about her decision. This was the first night Amron and Andre didn't have some type of squabble before bed. Her dad always had the TV on watching him while he slept on the couch, but tonight it was off. Everything was right. It was just her and her thoughts. Even if she wanted to escape them she couldn't because no matter what she did, her mind always fell back to the same place.

Should she get involved?

The next day Giselle wanted nothing more than for seven pm to arrive. From the time she woke up at six in the morning (because of Amron of course) she wanted it to be night time. He woke her up out of habit, they had no plans today. The anxiousness wouldn't let her go back to sleep. She had decided to take the trip back to Majesty, but she wanted to go there in the day. That meant waiting until it was well into the night to leave Grenada. She was going to go back to hear whatever it was Ecoli had to say and attempt to keep on the positive side of everything. She was going to try to keep an open mind and try to see what Ruby saw, for Ruby's sake. She couldn't even remember what she did that day. Her mind was dead set on one thing and everything else she set out to do paled in comparison.

Giselle spent the entire day doing and redoing her chores out of restlessness. Emma called and invited her on an outing with her family, but there was no way she would enjoy it with all the anxiousness she was feeling. The first thing that flew out of her mouth when Emma asked was "I go be home by seven, right?" Emma saying no was a deal breaker. Giselle couldn't miss her time to go in the mirror. She convinced herself that not going with Emma was a good thing.

"You realize is four o'clock?" She said to Amron who she'd just seen properly for the day. The first glimpse she had caught of him was when he woke her up that morning.

"Your point is?" He asked crossing the living room.

"Since when you home so early?" She asked him.

"I come to get something," he disappeared down the hallway then came back with a plastic bag.

"What you have in that?" Giselle asked.

Amron watched the bag then back at her. "Not this time," he said. "I can' tell you."

"Why not?"

"Jus' cause. Doh worry Gizzy," he made his way to the door. "Is nothin' bad… in my opinion," he grinned and shut the door behind him.

That, other than petting her rabbits, was the only interesting piece of entertainment she managed to muster up that day. The day seemed to drag on as if it dreaded seven pm's arrival. What could she do now? TV was boring and nothing was calling out to her. Eventually she took a nap on the couch.

Finally, the time had come.

Seven o'clock pm. She made up some silly excuse about cramps to her dad and told him she was going to bed early. That way he wouldn't come and check on her (because he always did as if she was a baby). Giselle went into her room, into her closet making sure to shut the door behind her then went off into the other world. This time the trip was less flustering and more mind boggling. She kept her eyes open hoping to see herself floating ridiculously fast through some sort of well-lit portal before dropping off into the universal passage, but all she saw was herself stepping out of a tall mirror. It was like walking through a door. When she got there Ecoli was in there as well, silver thermos in hand fixing what looked like a bullet proof vest over his chest.

"Oh!" He exclaimed once he noticed her.

"Ok so this is the deal," she didn't wait for him to say more. "I go see what this whole thing is about and then decide if I want to be a guardian or not."

He chuckled smugly.

"What?" She grumbled annoyed.

"Ya became a guardian when you put ya name up there," he pointed the brass plate with her name on it.

She scoffed, "Not in my mind."

"Guess this mean my plans for today just got canceled," he was slightly enthusiastic about that. She couldn't imagine why.

After enduring what must have been ten minutes of Ecoli warning her not to tell anyone about this they finally moved on. He was going to give her the run down on how things worked and "get her trained". She had mixed emotions about this. On his agenda they had to: see something; discuss job titles and discuss the history of Majesty. She was excited about the "something", but most likely he would be talking the whole time. He'd probably hop onboard her train of thought and start controlling things so, yeah, this could be boring.

"So, we got a few titles to go 'round here," he began as they walked out of the universal passage.

"Which are?" She urged.

"Reconnaissance, Patrol, Recruit, Documenter, Medical Unit, Emissary, Public Relations, Dispatch and Chief." He spoke. "The unit leaders responsible for they specific unit specialization and the chief makes the final decisions concerning Majesty on a whole." She let his words sink in for a moment.

"You boastin'?" Giselle questioned knowingly.

He shrugged wearing a really cocky smile, "A 'lil."

"How long this place been around? How long you been doin' this by the way? As a matter of fact, how this place even come about? Who build it? Answer that first."

Ecoli appeared to be getting annoyed with her at this point. He stopped walking right outside the kitchen door, placed his hands on the door frame an invited air into his lungs before speaking again.

"Ya the most inquisitive person that ever come in here."

"Thanks," she spoke with a sheepish grin.

It wasn't the first time she had been told this. She grew up around a few adults that didn't like to be questioned. They had the mentality that whatever they said was gospel and asking why was like going against it. They rather someone took the words straight from their mouth and not think about it. Giselle couldn't do that. She had to know the why. She lived for the why. She always questioned the what, how, when, where, who and why and if she didn't get a straight answer then she did her own research. That was just who she was.

They were in the kitchen now. A wide carved out area with a big counter and basically everything you would find in a regular kitchen. Well everything except the blue couch adjacent the door. The stuff wasn't new though. The couch had a few black patches that looked as burn marks. What appeared to be stainless steel kitchen appliances and accessories had had certainly seen better days. The cupboards were made of stained brown wood and the varnish smell suggested it had just been redone. Everything around this place seemed handmade and laden with historical value. Maybe that was a part of the training. Probably, if she built a crooked table Ecoli would stop having chronic mood swings on her. Soon Marko walked in, ignored all the walking space he had, and bumped into Ecoli on his way to the counter. She hadn't seen him since that first visit and he was acting just as comical now as he was then.

"Why are you always in my way, Eco-lingering," he shifted Ecoli.

"Why ya like to play so much?" Ecoli fanned him away. His voice wasn't harsh or threatening though.

"Ain't nobody playing, fam." Marko shoved him with his shoulder then went deeper into the kitchen. "Yoo hoo!! Ri Ri!" He hollered in a high note, tone full of kicks.

"Who is that?" Giselle asked. There was no one else in the room.

"Lead Recon-" Ecoli started.

"-and a scary cook." Marko cut him off. "Word of advice," Marko went on as though Giselle had been with them for days. "Don't touch anything in here or ask what's on the menu. You'll have a bad day if you do."

Well this "Ri Ri" person must be a peach; just lovely. Marko walked over to the cupboard, took one last look around, then grabbed the handle. The instant his hand made contact a trap door near the couch flew open and hit the ground with a loud bang. A straight-haired head popped out with squinted eyes cutting Marko like he was a piece of cheese. She didn't even acknowledge Ecoli and Giselle standing behind her. She emerged like a predator in a jacket kind of like the one Marko was wearing now; one hand on her hip, neck rotation to emphasize attitude and the other hand to point.

"Is what going on here?" She growled. "Why you interfering with things in my kitchen?"

"Is why you can't hear when I calling you?" Marko mocked her Trinidadian accent.

Giselle sniggered. Ariel turned around all attention on Giselle now. Instantly Giselle became hypnotized by the unusual sight of her intensely blue eyes.

"Who is this?" The woman asked.

"Giselle. She just reach. Was bringin' her to meet ya," Ecoli stated his purpose. Clearly it was his because Giselle had no clue she came to meet her.

"Oh ho."

Giselle observed the woman in front of her. First thing she noticed, once she got over the glowing eyes, was she wasn't wearing the same pants as everyone else. Different jobs different clothes maybe? She had on khaki short shorts and it was obvious that she wasn't wearing a shirt under her jacket, mainly because she had it unzipped exposing her cotton candy green sports bra. Somebody was a bit too proud of their defined abs. Definitely not the person to make angry; she could see it already.

"You eat already? I just make some breakfast…" she found a way to make offering food sound unkind and scary yet intriguing.

"…that's what I came for," Marko cut her off.

"Sshhhhh," she shut him up. "I en talking to you. When I talking to you I go say Marko. Nobody here say Marko."

"See this type of disrespect." Marko said in a lower note. He slammed his fist on the table when he spoke. Her neck snapped around so fast Giselle thought she might have pulled a muscle. Marko opened out his fingers and started dusting the spot muttering, "saw a fly."

When she turned back her eyes weren't blue anymore; they were solid black. Giselle wanted to ask her about it, but she noticed the lady was still awaiting her response and pretending to not hear what Marko said.

"I good. Not hungry," she told her.

The moment the words left her mouth Ecoli grabbed her shoulders and outright pushed her through the door.

"Ok we have things to do, places to be, people to see," he said and shut the door behind him. He looked at Giselle with a flushed expression. "When Ariel offer ya food jus' take it."

She nodded vigorously.

Finally, they were going into Majesty. Giselle was literally itching to set foot on the paved roads. After Ecoli took his sweet time talking to Marko in private, they went outside ready to start the day. Ecoli gave her the choice for their method of transportation. Out in the opening there was a techy looking pod that would shoot them into the heart of Majesty within a matter of seconds. Or they could take the steps and roam until they were tired. Giselle wanted more than anything to go into the tunnel, but quickly chose the steps. She hated the elevators. A faster one wasn't the solution to her dilemma. Someday she would get in it, however that day wasn't today.

They walked down the seemingly endless batch of steps into the vibrant town. She was beyond wow at that point. Everything was put together in such a unique fashion. It was seductively terrifying and wrenchingly mind gripping. The moment she got to the base she was able to see the houses clearly for what they were, instead of just their colorful roof tops. They were in a residential area. The buildings were all cylindrical. Some were terse, some were tall and all were spaced so randomly. Some of them appeared as if they had grown up out of the ground; like deadly beautiful mushrooms made of glass. Others were like mud huts that were being swallowed up by vines, but there was still a beauty about it.

"Main Street." Ecoli pointed a sign fashioned with the same material she placed on her Sui Generis.

Giselle was swelling with pride and utter disappointment at the same time. Deciding which emotion to acknowledge was harder done than said. She wanted to be happy that Ruby had a part to play in making this place what it was, but she couldn't fully accept that. This place was kept secret from her for fourteen years of her life. This place ruined her mother. How could she look past that? Still, she wanted to hear so much more of what Ruby did in here, but, the moment she began her question, Ecoli said save it for the end. He started talking about some man named Hubable and why he was important, but Giselle only caught his words faintly. She heard something about three portals and a place named Floral Cove and after that nothing. Her mind was wondering the surroundings again. She was stupidly mad at her eyes for not being able to look in two directions at one time. Sometime during Ecoli's talking, a strange someone emerged from one of the houses. She had tattoos plastering her arms and shoulders and around her ankles. The lady walked out to her home garden and was pointing to different spots and a floating bag behind her was dropping fertilizer. Then a rake was following closely behind it spreading it. Giselle couldn't turn away. Ecoli followed her gaze to see what she was looking at.

"Mrs. Gomez," he nodded in her direction.

The lady looked at both of them then slammed her door after storming inside. Ecoli's composure and tone carried on as if it hadn't happened, though his grip on his Katana hinted his unease.

"Ever wondered where folk tales, myths and fairy-tail stories come from?"

"No," she spoke honestly.

"How ya gon feel if I tell ya those stories ya grew up hearin' was 'bout you?"

"Like you talkin' crap."

He chuckled, "Well am not. The stories 'bout people doin' magic and shape shifters and such had to come from somewhere, no? I doh know if ya'll call it a good thing, I would, but ya come from the same world as them." His words were making no sense to her.

"Not possible," She shook her head.

A myth was just that- myth. Why was he trying to change its meaning?

"The fact that ya here says ya are," his eyes had a certain sparkle in it that she couldn't name. "And not only that, the fact that ya get ya own Sui Generis makes ya superior to the rest."

Now she knew for sure he was bullshitting her. Ecoli saying she was superior just sealed the deal that he had a funny side to him she didn't know about yet. Marko wasn't the only one with a funny bone after all. Superior was one thing Giselle always heard she wasn't. She was fourteen and always the youngest where ever she went. She wasn't as mentally mature as her friends as she'd been told time and time again and she was still a baby according to her dad. So Ecoli calling her superior was total rubbish.

"Yeah right," she laughed. "And now I could do magic!"

"Maybe," he spoke rather seriously.

They came upon cross roads and waited a while. The place was busy; people walking in and out of tall buildings that looked like professional work areas, cars, bikes and other unrecognizable methods of transportation taking residence on the streets.

The deeper in they went, the brighter and lighter the atmosphere became and the better structured the buildings. Most of the bigger buildings were made of stained glass that was slightly transparent.

Some type of vehicle floated to a stop in front of them. It looked like a patio with five rows of benches and some rails. The weird thing about it was that it didn't have wheels or anything to explain why it was floating. Ecoli stepped on the lift that doubled as the door for this weird vehicle and showed the driver, if it was right to call him that, a blue card. The guy took off a white sailor's hat and bowed to Ecoli with a pleasant smile. Then he turned back to the steering wheel which was really a brown ships wheel. The hostility and admiration towards Ecoli could have very well given anyone whiplash. There were four people on the shuttle, two of which scowled and the other two smiled and waved desperately for his attention. A girl even giggled and blushed when he said hi to her. Ecoli remained impassive about the whole thing. They walked to the back where one of the benches were facing behind and sat down.

"So you say you had some history to tell me," she recalled from his distant speech earlier.

"Ya wanna know right now? You doh wanna wait 'till we get where we goin'?"

"Yeah, but by the time we get where ever that is, my mind go be preoccupied I sure, so lay it out now." She didn't look at him once while saying this. Too much was going on around her. He wore this amused expression like she was some enter-taining, inattentive kindergartener.

"Ok," he chuckled. "A mass o'years before, there was this island in the north where all supernatural creatures were cre-ated. They call it The Land o'Spirits or Tlos for short. Tlos was supposed to be a winter territory, but there was a group in the settlement that altered that; they were dominant over all. Ap-pearance o'humans, but they could do extraordinary things, yeah. Magical things, like make an island strictly subjected to the cold change to suit their mood year-round. Shamans- peo-ple who have great influence in the world o'good and evil spir-its. They had control over The Land o'Spirits for mass time, yeah. Is not like Tlos was a democracy though; like, how on earth ya gon get an island full o'demonic schemers to pick one leader to narrate how to live? Not happenin'. There was mass fightin' among the different creatures for power. A really young guy, Somaki, didn' find that life style too appealin'. He was an Ersatz; a group considered as an inferior replica o'the Shamans- peaceful people, servants to the Shamans. While every other group could rise and fall from power his group was stagnant. Somaki wanted the creatures o'Tlos to unite and co-exist. He didn' think it was necessary to have a ruler. Every pack, clique, herd or wha'ever had different needs and different cultures and practices that the others would never understand. Durin' this time Somaki was the only known copycat; the most unique type o'Ersatz that could ever exist. He was only sixteen when he became the most respected man in Tlos all because he persuaded them to put away the battle plans. Things was fine for a while; reduced fights in Tlos. The Shaman's didn' like it though; they wanted control and they rather not dwell among commoners. They consider themselves almighty powers. So Somaki was murdered not long after. After that a whole new war break out because Somaki supporters had a vendetta."

"Supporters?"

"Every single group in Tlos except the Shamans," he shrugged.

She pursed her lips not knowing whether to believe his tale or not. It was all so farfetched.

"And what any of that have to do with Majesty?"

"Everything," he said. "Chaos broke out in Tlos again. Some couldn' deal with it and fled the island. Since then humans around the world been claimin' to see shape shifters, vampires, Loveland Frogs, Aswangs and Obeah men. That's how the stories began; when creatures had to run and find a new home- Majesty."

They turned onto a street that seemed to burst with life. Everywhere was flooded with things she hadn't seen, nor dreamt of seeing, in her life. She couldn't name any of them. There was a tall slender woman in a long white dress whose face she couldn't see and with every step she took there was a clunk. She could have sworn, when a light wind blew, that she saw a cow hoof. Off to her right there was this big, brute, furry animal with large, naked hands and feet having a conversation with a vendor. Above head what looked like a large bird flew by, but when it landed in front of the shop nearby she realized it wasn't. It was pitch black and had veiny wings and a thin head with a pointed nose. It straightened up on its two legs and suddenly she was staring at a woman in a large black hat, veil and cloak entering the store. Endless numbers of weird things walked along like being in the presence of each other was no big deal. It probably wasn't, but to her it was. These things, she'd heard stories about them. She'd been told they weren't real. She'd read books and saw TV show's dedicated to finding the unimaginable to no avail and now she was standing in their presence. Turns out monsters weren't under your bed or in your head; they're shopping in a city called Floral Cove.

Her heart was thudding so hard in her chest she felt it absolutely necessary to hold on to it and the shortness of breath she was experiencing was threatening to make her pass out. Giselle wasn't sure if she was heating up out of uncontrollable levels of excitement or fear; although, something in her believed it was the latter. All this stuff was real. The stories about ol'higues and all those things were real. Well, as they always say, seeing is believing. In all her contemplation about finding this place and learning more about it, seeing those weird things that were said to be myth and folk tale never crossed her mind once. It made sense though. Those stories couldn't have just flown up out of nowhere. There had to be some truth behind it, or something to spark the beginning.

Ecoli looked at her with a proud glow about his face. He had finally loosened his hold on his Katana and now had both hands on the bench. Was he waiting for her to say what she thought of this freak town, because right now words were not forth coming? She'd rather ease close to him for protection than talk at the moment. His attention floated from her slowly to admire their surroundings. The sun seemed to be giving this area special care because everything was more vibrant. The buildings here were just as the ones they passed by on the way there, but they seemed better kept and taller. There was just something very fortunate about it.

"Floral Cove Square. This is where I grow up," he summarized.

"You not Grenadian?" She caught on.

"Yeah, but I been comin' and goin' in 'ere since I was six. I get my Sui Generis when I was seventeen. M'twenty now."

The weird shuttle slowed to a stop. Someone got off.

"One thing ya should keep in mind, The Square never sleeps. S'like Vegas," he smiled. "If ya got a weak heart I suggest you stay outta town at night," he only amplified her fear.

The shuttle took them down the street which seemed to have cross roads after every four buildings, each road as busy and lively as the one they were on before. Bars, supermarkets, linen stores, a mall; it had everything. They passed by this large crowded area engulfed in pods of different sizes. Silver bottomed glass pods that lit up whenever someone went in and seemed to have its controls embedded secretly in the walls.

Above every ten there was a blue and white number floating overhead; four numbers to be exact. Ecoli said this was the Inter-city Terminal. It took you out of the city faster than journey by bus or foot. There was another one just like it some distance away called the Inter-world Terminal; it was much larger. Then next to it an area with the same set up only instead of pods there were shuttles just like the one they were on. This one was the Inner-city Terminal. They exited the terminal and started walking down the sidewalk.

"It have three cities in Majesty, yeah. Floral Cove is the Capital, Nocturn Niche and Heavenly Heights."

"I didn' realize the place was this big."

"Has to be, yeah. D'ya know the mass o'magical supernatural and mystical creatures it have in the world?" That sounded rhetorical.

Giselle still answered in a duh tone, "No."

"Well there be plenty. That is why we have three cities; to split them up. Nocturn Niche is for shape shifters. Heavenly Heights is for mystical creatures. Then Floral Cove is for Shamans and Erzats. Anything else outside that classification can stay where they want, but those three major groups need to stay separated." He rubbed the back of his neck nervously. "We can' have history repeating itself, yeah?"

Just beyond the inner-city terminal they came up on a massive cabin structure with a very crowded patio. Every table was loaded with guests, some laughing and one or two with people that seemed to be indulging in serious business. Giselle looked up at the well placed logo of the building; a very recognizable effigy of her grandmother and the words 'Rowdy Ruby'. This calmed her a bit.

"She ask me to bring ya here whenever ya show up," he said.

So this was the something, huh? She thought in admiration.

Giselle's reaction seemed to drag up some warm giggly feeling in Ecoli because he chuckled and said, "This is a change from yesterday."

"Majesty started out as a place of refuge," he spoke again. His gaze was in the sky now. "Hubable, the creator, get tired of livin' in secret so he created this place. Then he started to seek out other refugees from Tlos and bring 'em here. For some time, they live here in unity as one big cluster of magical people coming together to form a workin' society. But he knew one day he would get too old and Majesty too large and he wouldn't be able to take care of the place alone anymore. To make sure Majesty stayed safe, he got twelve o'the most loyal originals from Majesty and sealed them in the Sui Generis. Then he created the Universal Passage and left it up to the Sui Generis' to seek out strong, unique candidates to watch over Majesty and keep it alive. The guardians could be anybody no matter what they are. That way each o'the three groups in 'ere have a fair say in the runnin' of Majesty."

Strong candidates? Again, she only heard what she wanted to hear. Sure, she got the rest of it, but it went into storage. The primary concern here was that the mirror must have come to her by accident. It must have defected. She couldn't help, but feel that way. Vrai did say she chose her because she wanted something different. Strength probably wasn't part of the criteria. Giselle looked around at all the unique faces. There were animal outlines standing out, in and between. She wasn't superior enough to call the shots in a unit. Actually, Giselle knew she was capable anything, but no one else seemed to share this sentiment. Letting Ecoli know that might change his opinion of her, whatever it was. If he had a good one she didn't want to put faults in it.

"What if people doh want to come here? I mean is really the descendants of the ones who fled you lookin' for by now."

Her mind formulated a question out of habit, meanwhile her eyes were still darting around soaking in the new scenery.

"We still gotta give them the option. How'd ya like it if at some point in ya life ya find out ya have magical or supernatural abilities and a whole world was created for people like ya and ya were left out o'the loop?"

She shook her head.

"S'not necessarily a permanent livin' agreement. We not forcin' people. If ya wanna stay, then stay, and if ya wanna come and go, then do that. This is just a place to release the part of ya that ya can' show the outside world," he said then made his way into the Rowdy Ruby. "And look 'round, people wanna come."

When they walked in they caught everyone's attention. Some of them observing her and gossiping. She made sure not to wear her night clothes this time, so she couldn't imagine what that was about. Others were acting just like the people on the shuttle did. With the unease coursing through her veins she could feel the hairs raising on her skin. It was one thing to have people stare at you, she didn't care about that, but it was another when they had red cat slits for eyes. They made their way up to the unmanned counter. There was a hare sitting on the counter looking over the place. Ecoli just walked up to it as if this was a normal, everyday, occurrence. It probably was.

"Hi Ms. Lyn," he greeted.

The hare hopped off the table and suddenly an ageable woman stood up from behind the counter. She had on a long sleeve white shirt that stretched long as a dress, but it was obvious she was wearing a soft white pants beneath. She had shoulder length grey hair that was a bit untidy, but oddly in place and a friendly face. Giselle watched as the pupils and iris of her eyes morphed into a more common appearance.

"Mr. Ecoli! Chief!" She gushed.

Ecoli blushed. "Doh say that too loud."

"Why not?" She crossed her arms over her chest. "If ya got it flaunt it m'dear," she flipped her hair.

Giselle grinned. This lady spoke just like Ecoli.

"And who be this cutie?" She reached over with her ashy hand and black nails and pinched Giselle's cheeks. Great, more baby treatment.

"This is Giselle, Ruby granddaughter," he patted her shoulder.

Giselle nodded.

"Ahhh," the woman sighed with a pleasant smile clapping her hands together. "My new boss, yeah."

"Boss? I not the boss," Giselle shook her head. "Wrong person."

"Sense o'humor. I like," Ms. Lyn said. She came from behind the bar saying, "lemme grab a good look at ya. Aw, ya like a 'lil marsh mellow. I could just squeeze ya."

She tugged Giselle into a hug. Giselle couldn't ignore the fact that she had a strong herb smell.

"Ruby asked me to watch the place 'til ya old enough to take over, m'dear," she went back around the counter.

"Oh, for real?" Giselle got up on her toes and leaned on the counter. "This place is mine now?"

"Most popular spot in The Square. All yours. Everyone loves it. Floral Cove's filled with people from 'round the world and the Rowdy Ruby serves food from 'round the world," she opened her hands to gesture to the sitting room. Giselle was grinning at this point. "Go sit, have something to eat. S'on the house, although, Ecoli, ya have to pay." she looked at him under her eyes.

He stood there with a hardened expression not saying anything.

"Son, m'just joking. Come on now? Ya don't got that under control yet?"

Giselle's eyes bounced back and forth between them. Have what under control? What were they talking about? Ecoli had a lighter look on his face now. Not a full-blown smile, but there was a slight one.

"This is progress," he said. "Come Giselle, let's sit."

The name was totally ironic. The restaurant was very civil and a bit fancy. She could see the wait staff and bartender lived up to her grandmother's standards; crazy, weird, and questionable sanity. When they sat down a gnome approached them with menus in his hand and wide vacant eyes. He had a smile twisted on his thick-skinned face that looked permanent. Tiny C shaped ears rested on his broad, wort-faced head. Holding the menus to his chest while looking at them as though giddy with joy, he let out a high-pitched laugh that sounded like an owl hooting.

"Menu?" His flaky voice suited his appearance perfectly.

"Two Cheerio's please," Ecoli said while accepting the menus. Giselle stared at him uncertain. "Ya won' know much on the menu. Made mas mistakes in the past with some o'these drinks. Trust me on this."

The man's eyes flicked and rolled over him almost robotically. The way he observed him, Giselle was sure if that smile wasn't glued on his face he would be scowling just like the other people. Did people here not like Ecoli? Was it a love hate relationship he had with them?

"Watch ya back," the gnome said to her after his long trance on Ecoli.

After placing the menu's on the table, he walked away blessing them one more time with his laughter. Giselle stared at Ecoli who just shook his head and told her pay no mind to him.

"Is a Japanese drink by the way," he informed. "Choose what ya want to eat, but the drinks will throw ya. I kinda like that drink though, so I thought ya should try it."

Amron and Andre would have liked that. She thought of her brothers and how they always obsessed over Japan. They watched way too much anime. One time, she actually caught them trying to make the Ichiraku ramen like it was in Naruto. They had watched a YouTube tutorial and everything.

"Ya grand mom was the best Chief we ever had. I grow up under her and work under her. The denizens have the greatest respect for her, even the ones in Nocturn Niche. Trust me, is not easy to sway them, but she could," his voice trailed. "She mentored me last year sayin' she jus' wanted to see how I would handle. And now the job is mine completely," he did not sound happy about it.

"You doh like it?" Giselle asked.

"Is not that I doh like it…" he trailed again. "We didn' come to talk about me," he tried to kill the topic.

"But you have a lot of influence in Majesty being the chief and all so I think we should talk about you a little," she played smart.

"No," he shut down.

They stayed in the Rowdy Ruby for about an hour. Ecoli was telling Giselle about her grandmother's crazy ways and sizing her up for what lay ahead. Plainly stating, once she got over the fact that a woman next to her had claws and whiskers, she was fully captivated.

CHAPTER SEVEN

ENTER: TEGAN

THEY LEFT THE restaurant and made their way back up the street to the Inter-city Terminal. Ecoli navigated his way through the vast tubes passing each group of ten blindly. There were people in there; scanning a purple card before entering. A few people patrolled up and down the concrete paths helping travelers that looked lost and keeping a close eye on everyone that passed through. They wore long black pants with a blue stripe down the side and blue shirts. On top of that a navy-blue jacket. The jackets weren't like Marko's, which seemed to be made of a tougher, heavier material. Their material seemed softer. There was no zip or Velcro so it had to be pulled over your head; on the left pocket, there was an embroidered horse, 'Patrol' written under it. All of them saluted when Ecoli walked by.

"I thought the guardians did the guardin'," Giselle commented.

"Yeah they do. But every guardian have a team to lead. Ya don' expect the few people ya see in HQ to do everything, no?"

What could she say? She kind of did. Eventually they reached the end of the path they were strolling. There were still pods there, but they were different. Each of them were sealed off individually in a brownish cage and was anything, but approachable. There were five patrollers stationed there. None of them marking the grounds like their fellow associates. They were still and stiff as statues; chins up, feet together, and armed. Ecoli stepped up, unfazed by the patrollers, and pulled a bunch of keys that had been clipped to his side and jingling all day. Without hesitation his fingers dived into the bunch latching around the one silver piece that he needed. Soon he was fitting a key into the lock. He held the door open waiting for Giselle to go in. She didn't budge.

"I doh like elevators," she said.

"This look like an elevator?" He asked.

"Well, no, but…"

"Is ok. Just go," he urged.

They stepped into the pod. There was a melodious beeping sound and then a red dot appeared. He dragged it up the glass to his line of sight then released it. A detailed map appeared. It was too complicated to take it all in before he started to alter its appearance by zooming. She did catch sight of a massive building that housed Headquarters and cut across the land in

Floral Cove with the resemblance of a freight train. Then there was a much smaller, but still huge part of the building like an add-on, that jutted into Floral Cove even more. It was labeled Guardians sub HQ. If that were the case, then she barely saw anything today. Still, she found herself questioning the accuracy of the map. She saw jet representations. How on earth were there jets in this building? There were no openings large enough anywhere that would make it possible for there to be jets. Maybe she needed a personal map to study on her own. After he zoomed in, she was able to make out the kitchen, the rec. room and some lines she assumed symbolized the steps they had taken to get into town. On the ceiling in the pod there was a sky-blue symbol. There were four arms holding onto each other forming a square. They were smooth and all various shades of a soft blue; the third seemed translucent. It was a bit odd that all the hands were blue except for the fourth one which was harsh black.

"Ecoli," she began another question.

Ecoli was about to tap something else on the glass, but withheld. Eyes still on the spot he said, "doh hold onto me. I value my personal space."

Then he tapped and suddenly she was swallowed by darkness and a floating feeling in her stomach. The world around her had vanished. All there was, was a hollow zooming sound and the unmistakable presence of a relaxed Ecoli standing next to her. It took her a few seconds to release her breath after the abrupt change in light. What did she expect coming in here?

She attempted to raise her hands to hold onto the glass, but pressure was keeping them neatly to her side. It felt as if she were lying face down. At regular intervals there was a burst of light and for a brief moment she could see the sky through a checker board clearing. Then darkness.

"Blasted," the unnaturally still figure beside her spoke. "Gotta get that light fixed."

As blunt as the aggressive thrill ride began it ended. Now, instead of the terminal, they were at the dangerously high lookout where they had begun. Ecoli stepped out like nobody's business and made his way to the rec. room. Giselle followed him slightly out of step feeling relieved to be on steady ground again.

"How come we use the tube and not the funny lookin' bus? I thought the tube was to go in the other cities."

"Cause it faster and cause HQ is between Floral Cove and Nocturn Niche."

When he got inside he dipped his hand in his pocket and pulled out a light blue card. It was shiny and had the words Giselle Thomas- Guardian written on it. While handing it to her he said her pass code was 492 and she'd need to remember it. In the back ground the symbol from before as a watermark.

"Credit card?"

He laughed. "Remember ya not in Greenz," he shook his head. "A Point Card. To everybody else this is their life line, but is just a formality for guardians; ID."

"What you use it for?" She flipped it over. The back looked like a credit card except it had unnatural bar codes.

"Ya get points for jobs ya do in Majesty and points are like money. They go straight to the card."

"So basically, I broke." Giselle concluded.

"Guardians have privileges," he smirked. "Notice I didn' scan my card in the terminal or the shuttle. Still have to pay for certain things though. And ya still better off than any o'us."

She was lost. This was only her third time here. How on earth was she better off? "But I didn' do anything."

"But ya the granddaughter o'the former chief. Everybody gonna want to know ya. Plus, Ruby wasn' broke and guess who getting out of her points." He laid down the facts. "And ya got the Rowdy Ruby. Ya stocked for life. Ya don' even need the card."

"Wow. Went to sleep broke woke up rich. Wish I could hold the points so I could make it rain." She joked and pretended to throw up money.

"I got a feelin' ya gonna get along real well with Marko," he leaned across the bar. "Any other questions?"

She had a whole load of questions on everything she had just seen. For example: why were people scowling at him so much; when exactly would she be taking over the Rowdy Ruby; what did he mean by maybe she had magic; what did he need to get under control; what was in The Land of Spirits today? There were so many more questions she could come up with, but she honestly wanted to discover the answers by herself. She wanted time alone to discover all the mysteries of Majesty and pass her judgment. Time alone would tell her if she should accept it for all it was worth or hold a nasty grudge. She thought hard before responding.

"So, if I agree to work here I go be protectin' all the people I see today and more?"

"Yes," he nodded.

"Why they can' protect they-self?"

"Remember the story I tell ya'bout Tlos breakin' into war?" He asked her and she nodded tentatively. "If we let them protect themselves that is the only result we could be sure to get."

"Ok," she said realizing how much sense he was making.

If his story was true then leaving a magical world to run itself wasn't the solution to their problems. They had done it once before and the result sparked a new world called Majesty.

"Alright then," he drummed his fingers quickly against the counters' edge. "Ya have a few more things to do and I have to get back to work."

He led her around the unkempt bar while saying this, opened the cupboard beneath the hanging TV. There were steps in there rather than drinks or cups. He went down first and she was more than keen to follow. They ended up in a technology based room that was by far better looking than any other she'd seen thus far. Marko was there.

"I need to look into somethin' so I can' stay. Stick with Marko for a while." Ecoli told her as though he was regrettably dragging her into great misfortune.

"You say that like it's a bad thing." Marko was sitting at a desk, foot on table, hands arched behind his head and a smile playing on his lips.

"In many ways it is," Ecoli said exasperatedly as he took his leave.

She was left standing at the entrance of the room, hands at her side gazing expectantly at Marko. The first time they had met he saved her from a silly singing bird. He was the one that introduced her to Majesty and he acted as natural as any human being could act around a person; as though they were siblings raised in the same home. He had a carelessness about his whole attitude that she couldn't deny admiring. Today, with Ecoli, the sassiness that was Giselle had escaped and there was no doubt that it would only bloom more being here with Marko. Although she had only pulled out the hot head, pepper lipped, curious portion of herself in order to face Majesty head on, it didn't look like it was going to be repacked any time soon. For Amron's sake and Brent and even Giselle's sake, hopefully it stayed opened for the world to see.

"How you been?" He asked pulling his feet off the table.

"Not bad. Ecoli kinda funny," she said in a disapproving tone.

She didn't exactly mean funny as in laughter. She meant it more along the lines of strange and hard to figure out.

"Oh, Eco-leathal," he chuckled. "Don't worry about him. He has his moments."

Oh, the irony in this. How does one not worry about something that was considered lethal? At least he was true about one thing. Ecoli did have his moments. His moods flipped faster than a two-sided billboard sign. More reason to call him "funny". What she did find truly funny, however, was the fact that since she'd been there she hadn't heard Marko say Ecoli's name right once. And it was just him. Or maybe he did it to everybody and he just hadn't found the right descriptive words for her yet. One can only wait.

"So, what is this room?" Giselle asked while taking everything in.

To begin with it was huge. There were several computers set up on one side of it and a shelf with endless books. It appeared as if someone was working there recently, but they were gone now. Then there was a large strip of emptiness leading across to where Marko was. The ground wasn't too bare though. On the ground there were markings; the symbol from the ceiling off the pod and some words. The words *"It is not the smartest of the species that survives; nor the most intelligent. It is the one that is more adaptable to change- Charles Darwin."* was written beneath it. Across where Marko was seated there was a wide stretched panel with too many controls and buttons to keep count. Some of them lit up while others had solid colours. Then, just beyond him was a room sealed off by glass. On the smooth wall inside, was the same symbol like the one on the floor.

He stared at her, pride gleaming in his eyes. "Simulation Training Room."

"Neat."

"I know right." Marko grinned. "First we need to know what you can do."

"Huh?"

"Ok, I guess Eco-lazy left that part for me to explain." He spun on his chair. His attempt of a serious expression was failing him. "See, you didn't come across the mirror only because you were chosen. The magical world has a way of reclaiming its property."

"Property?"

"Each of us here has magical abilities. We just need to find out what type of magic you have and what you can do?"

"But I didn' 'come across' the mirror. My gran'mom give me. I can' do nothin'." Giselle shot down.

Marko shrugged and hooked his index finger in a very untraditional necklace he was wearing. It kind of had an island boy vibe to it being strewn with beads and a few unique shells. It wasn't a long drop or stretchy either. It seemed stiff and permanently in place as though made with wire instead of elastic string. The most particular and fascinating feature of it was the beautiful Welo Patchwork Opal sitting front and centre. It gave the impression that it was glowing.

"Point is you still have it," he said

"But, I never do one magical thing in my entire life."

She went on opposing him suggesting her magical probability. This didn't seem to bother Marko at all. In fact, he seemed to take pleasure in answering her unasked questions.

"You know how they say all babies can swim, but as they get older they forget how," he began. Giselle nodded. "Well our magic is like that. You just need to get a little practice and you'll be fine."

"Alright. If you say so," she muttered uncertainly.

Marko instructed that she step into the glass room. As she entered she couldn't help think maybe Marko wasn't right in the head. He just said that she had magical abilities. Who just says those things out of nowhere and out of the context of gaming or films? Still, more than a week ago she didn't even know Majesty existed, so why not? She was looking forward to this. He was going to help her find out what she could do so it was best to just go with the flow. For a while she thought she mistakenly ended up in there, refusing to believe Ecoli and his "superior" talk. Maybe he knew what he was saying after all. Was she really capable of doing magic? The more she thought it over in her head the better she felt about it; finally, a place where she wasn't too young for something; finally, a group of people not limiting her to her size. She fought with the smile crawling onto her face waiting for something to happen. As she did so a distasteful feeling of guilt found its way within her. Remember, this is the place your grandmother kept secret and the place that ruined your mother. She had to tell herself this to reduce the excitement growing in her. She heard a click which was probably the sound of the door locking then a static sound and soon, Marko's voice echoing all around her.

"Now, first to test if you have free magic or limited magic."

Giselle had no clue what he meant by that, but she didn't care. She carried on like she did. Suddenly a machine rotating sound filled the room and two panels opened in the floor. Then two stone pillars rose from the ground. It stopped. She looked at it, then at Marko. What was she supposed to do now?

"Go ahead. Just touch it," he said.

She approached slowly and put her hand on one. It was cold. No sign of anything out of the ordinary. She let her hand slide off it as she made her way to the other one. What was she looking for? What was he looking for? Was something amazing supposed to happen? She was thinking all this as she reached out to the second stone. When Giselle made contact she felt a jolt run through her body and her hair stood up and a wind brushed past her as the stone started folding over itself, crumbling. She jumped back a little frightened by the abruptness of the phenomenon, but then edged closer in amazement. It opened up and a bright blue light flew from the core, straight to her forehead and disappeared. Instantly she started feeling refreshed and ready to take on the world. The stone was reduced to nothing, but dust. Giselle looked up at Marko worried, but all he said was,

"Limited magic! You're an Ersatz!" He grinned. "I am too."

She felt her heart sink a little. She had only just found out about this classification and somehow hearing she was in an unimportant group kind of hurt. She was an Ersatz; inferior, a replication, useless. They can neither rise to something greater nor fall to something lesser and that in itself was something lesser. They were like a penny- you can't make change for a penny. So much for Ecoli and his whole 'superior' talk.

"Why so glum?" Marko noticed her sudden change in mood.

"Am Ersatz," she mumbled.

"Oh. You know, that means we're only capable of doing one magical task. Some are more use full than others I must say and no two Ersatz have the same power. It always skips a generation. Shamans can do anything they want. The old folks say- To be Ersatz is unfortunate, a Shaman is lucky and a Copycat is a gift. I think being Ersatz is blessed, though, I wouldn't call us magical. We're just unique beings." The talkative young man went on.

Giselle tilted the side of her lip upright pretending to be comforted by his words. "And what is a Copycat?" She asked.

"A limited magic user born of Shaman and Ersatz parents with the ability to copy the magic of any Ersatz they come across. Only one was ever known: Taunt Somaki. It's a rare power to come across. We don't really know much about it. Do you know how strong he must have been? Its legend that he copied the power of every Ersatz that existed in his time and just imagine his one true ability was to copy," he sighed. "Copycats are kind of like 'if he can dance then I can dance and if she can sing then I can sing and dance'. You get it. That's why limited magic users are amazing. You never know what to expect. In a way limited magic users are limitless."

He spoke about this with a fiery passion. Maybe, after falling into the Ersatz class, he had to find reason to accept it himself. She was going to need a little more to convince her that this was good. Marko went on to tell her that it was legend that Copycats will only be born when the Magical-supernatural world was in grave danger. He told her he thought the legend was born from the fact that Somaki, the only Copycat that ever existed, tried to save the magical-supernatural world from destroying itself. When he finished rambling he took a moment to gather his thoughts then went on.

"K, let's find out what you can do. I'm going to throw a lot of random stuff at you. All I need you to do is react. Simple shit," he smiled. "Oh yeah, you might get hurt!" He rushed his words together then started his test before she could respond.

It began. Multiple random secret doors opening around the entire room each with a different threat inside. Rats running across the room. Fire blazing overhead. Water flooding the room to the point where there was no space to shoot up for air. Sea creatures she had never seen before circling her. She swam around, but couldn't find a way out. All this seemed to last forever then suddenly she was transported to a different scene.

She was in a desert like surrounding dripping wet in the scorching sun and she couldn't even see him anymore. She went wondering around looking for what, she hadn't a clue. Maybe there was some trap door somewhere she could escape from. Maybe that's what he wanted. Then the bipolarness of the room began again; sandstorm, tornados. Flip to night and lightning was striking down all over and while she was losing her mind the floor beneath her opened up and she was falling helplessly. She heard gun shots and bombs and metal rubbing together. Something cut her on the arm and she had no clue what it was; she couldn't see. Then she hit the floor with an unusually gentle tap and saw that she was in a room full of snakes. Then as if by magic they disappeared and an army of different critters flooded through the room one type after the next. In all this chaos all she did was scream and run for her life; nothing more nothing less. Nothing happened. Not one magical thing. All she gained was a raw throat, sweaty appearance, runny eyes and the task of washing her hair when she got home. She wasn't able to pull out anything unusual.

She sighed. The room was white again and all that was left was Giselle dripping wet, covered in sand, with a shallow scrape across her right arm. The way she was breathing she felt as though she was in that room for three days even though it was probably just forty minutes. Marko leaned forward, both elbows on the panel and hands covering his face. In all her shock of the recent events she was more worried than anything else that this meant she couldn't do any magic. What if the stone breaking was just luck? What was it anyway? What was that light? Did it have any effect on her that had gone unnoticed? What if her grandmother giving her the Sui Generis was a mistake? If she was supposed to be there and be a Guardian why wasn't she able to do anything amazing? She was classed as a damn Ersatz of all things! Being there and remaining positive for the whole experience was proving to be more difficult than she had imagined.

"Marko..." She called him wanting to apologize for wasting his time.

He raised his hand as to tell her wait. "Don't flip your shit. Hold on."

Giselle held her tongue. Was he thinking in all his life he had never seen someone as untalented as Giselle? She could bet he was. If he was though, he would be wrong. As far as Giselle was concerned she could do anything; especially when it was a challenge. She never liked to back down from things. If she started she had to finish. She had a compulsive setting in her that the harder or riskier something was the more she wanted to do it. She wiped some of the sand off her cheeks in a weak attempt to clean herself up. All she did was spread it more. Soon he raised his head and took off the large black goggles that was strapped over half his face. When did he put those on? She heard a familiar click and the door to the left opened. She walked out. The moment she stepped through the door frame it was like she hadn't been through everything she did in there. She was cleaned up and dry. She didn't know how, but she was. Even the scratch on her arm had disappeared.

"So..."

"Let's take a walk," was all he said.

Giselle questioned his sudden urge to abandon his duties, but he insisted they go. Somehow that "let's take a walk" didn't sound very trust worthy. He told her they should go outside for a bit; just to get some fresh air so he could think. He wore a devious look on his face, but then again this was Marko. She hadn't known him that long, but she was certain he always had that devious look on his face. It was probably his natural expression by now. If someone were to call him out every time he wore that look they'd turn into the boy who cried wolf. They went through a different door than the one she came in. It led to this air bunker equipped with about ten jets (now the little jet representations on the map made sense). If she thought the training room was huge then she was wrong. This place was extremely spacious. Men and women were scurrying back and forth doing their do. She and Marko walked straight through to the exit which brought Floral Cove into view from a different angle. They were on another cliff. From there she could see a massive pole rising from the top of the mountain with a white flag flying proudly on it. Again the symbol was on there. So, that was Majesty's crest. It wasn't just some manufactures logo.

"Yup, fresh air," he sighed looking out into Floral Cove. He placed an uncomfortably firm hand on her shoulder. She looked up at him. The deviousness on his face had increased by a thousand and he was practically grinning now. "Good luck," was all he said before scaring the life out of her.

Marko shoved Giselle's shoulder forward, she lost her balance and the next thing she knew she was falling hopelessly off the cliff. She started to cry out as though the louder she got the more chances she would have of surviving the fall. The only thing below her was bare hard rock; smooth, flat and ready to crack her skull. What was wrong with him? She'd only known him for two days and he was already trying to kill her! She couldn't tell if it was the wind pressure beating against her wide eyes or if she was crying from fear, but there were tears walking up the side of her face into her thick hair. She hated the weightless feeling she had. It was like the extended version of the way she felt whenever she went into an elevator; like earlier that day. It also reminded her of that scary feeling she would have whenever she dreamt she was falling. Only, this was the real deal. Giselle clamped her eyes shut. She was so close to the ground now. She was about to hit rock bottom and have the lights knocked out of her- literally. She started to flail her arms and legs wildly. She bet she looked like some confused dog over a water bath or something. She kept swinging her arms more and more aggressively as if under the impression it would save her. It was an automatic reaction she couldn't quit. The more she swung the less helpless she felt; if that was the right way to put it. The tears weren't even running up her face anymore. They were running down now. She hadn't reached the ground yet… but why? The wind was still beating against her face and making the loud rushing noise in her ears. What was going on?

"Gizzy, open your eyes!" She could hear Marko shouting from a distance.

Giselle eased her eyes open carefully like she did the first time she entered Majesty. When she did she saw that she wasn't falling anymore. She was flying. She was really flying; out of control, but still flying! She was moving with such amazing speed back up to the edge of the cliff where she began her decent. Then when she got to the top she heaved in Marko's direction and landed roughly on the ground near his feet grating her elbow in the process. He looked at her approvingly.

"I knew it! I knew it! When I dropped you in the simulator you didn't fall like a normal person. You just needed a longer drop!" He clapped his hands together.

"You big idgit…" she paused to catch her breath. "…what if that ended bad?"

"I have my ways." Marko smirked and pulled her to her feet.

"I jus'…" Giselle began again knees wiggling under the re-appearing weight of her body. Forgetting her fright, two cuts and the blood on her elbow, a spring of delight exploded within her.

"I could fly… I COULD FLY!"

"You enjoyed that," he said, rather than asked.

"Yeah, I mean, I thought I was about to die, but then…" hand gestures took over as her dominant communication skill.

"Good to know," he nodded with pursed lips and another failed attempt at a serious face. He just couldn't pull it off. He grabbed her arm and started walking towards the edge again.

"Marko! Marko wait!" She protested. "I lie! I doh like it, wait- AHHHH!!" He threw her over again.

This time she was falling with confidence. The first time she thought she was a goner, but this time she knew she had something in her arsenal. But wait, how exactly was she to activate it? She started swinging her hands the way she did before, but it was ineffective. Why was this happening now? Was she not flying a while ago? Was that a fantasy of what she wished could happen and now the reality was bursting in on the show? Her eyes were bulging and no matter how much she wanted to she couldn't look away from the fast approaching rock beneath her. The wind beating against her face and eardrums amplified her discomfort. In the wee moments of crashing she came to a halt in midair and before she could even think, she was standing on the cliff next to Marko, who strangely, wasn't beaming with excitement. Why not?

"I jus'…" she said. "I could fly!"

When the words left Giselle's mouth it felt strange; unoriginal. Like she had said it before, but she just couldn't remember when. Maybe it was for something she did with her brothers. She knew she was saying it now because she just flew up the side of the cliff. That must be what the ringing, panic feeling

161

tingling in her gut was about. She looked up at Marko who looked less enthusiastic than she'd expected him to. Somehow, she felt he was supposed to be amused after she said that.

"You need to focus." He said slightly gruff. Then when he spoke again his voice was as light as she had come to know it. "I'll throw you off every cliff I could find until you can fly on command so take your pick, today or every day for the next two months?" He joked.

What he talkin' about? I didn' jus' fly? She thought this.

She shook off the nerves and prepared herself mentally to go over again. Maybe he wanted her to go again. But why was she feeling so calm about this now? There was something funny about this whole situation. She could have sworn this would only be her second time going over, but somehow it felt like more. Somehow she was feeling immune. The knowledge of her being able to glide weightlessly through the air had in-stilled new found determination. She faintly had an image of herself about to crash into the hard rock, bottom of the cliff, but she had no recollection of what happened after that. Was this another day already? No, it couldn't be. It was probably the coward at the back of her mind trying to make her back down. She stepped up to the edge about to jump off when she felt something stab the centre of her back.

"Too slow," she heard and next thing she was falling. Again.

This fall wasn't as much drenched in panic as determination. This time she was more decisive about flying again. She couldn't pin why though. She hadn't failed before, but then again, she hadn't tried flying before that first fall and even that time she wasn't trying. Maybe it was the brief moment of strictness Marko pulled on her. Down and down and down. She was trying. She couldn't seem to make it work. FLY GISELLE, FLY! She flapped her arms, kicked her legs and straightened up. It only seemed to aid in her decent. How was she supposed to do this?! Her face was edging closer to the rock bottom and in a strange swirl of déjà vous she found herself standing next to Marko again. She had the urge to yell "I could fly!", but it felt so worn out. It shouldn't be. Didn't she just fly?

"What were you thinking before you opened your eyes?" He asked with deep set interest.

"I was bein' murdered," she spoke reproachfully.

There was a lack of unsteadiness in her voice which she found out of character since she just fell off a cliff.

"Hm." He tapped his chin. Looking over the edge he said, "Expect the unexpected." Then retreated into the bunker.

All she could think was, *What the hell?*

They went back through the bunker absorbed in vivid conversation. Marko was going on about all the fun stuff he did there and how active his life had become since he found the watch (that was his Sui Generis). His mirror spirit's name was Ellis, apparently. Marko had been in there for about two years now. He met Ecoli there and, in his opinion, they hit it off right off the bat. Giselle found that funny. Since she had gotten there he was the one initiating interaction between him and

Ecoli rather than there being mutual interest. To add to that, he never addressed Ecoli correctly. Apparently, this started since day one. He went on telling her about his outside life which wasn't as exciting, but there was still a tinge of interest hearing about life in a different country. He attended Centennial College and worked at Tim Horton's; he just started both.

His summary on the two was, "I give myself two weeks to screw up one of them." He sounded rather confident in his inability to complete something. "Anyway, this is where I leave you. Tegan should be here by now." He said as they entered the training room for a second time.

Sure enough when they entered there was a lean, muscular male, rocking the chair in front the computers. He had a sleeve of tattoos on his left arm and checkered on his right. He was clicking around on an unfamiliar website and seemed deep into what he was doing. Marko stared at the stranger, who oddly didn't notice them walk in, with pleasure at the opportunity presented to him. He took a tighter grip of the door handle and slammed the door shut causing the lengthy guy to jump, falling backwards in his seat. He rushed on his knees toward the computer and closed off what he was doing before spinning around to face them. His face looked flushed. He had a tattoo on his fore head that seemed to fall from his hair line. It ended in a spiral on his right cheek. It seemed like it was battling to make him look tough when he wasn't.

"Marko!" He growled while getting to his feet. Marko was showing so much teeth that the pinkness of his gum was exposed as well. "What's wrong with you!"

He didn't appear angry, just a little shaky. The one thing that really stood out about him was his accent; just like everyone else in there. Giselle might have been taken aback if he had broken out speaking like a Grenadian. She had come to terms with the fact that everyone in there was from different parts of the world. She wanted to spark up conversations with all of them just to hear their accent and a little about where they came from.

"You have to teach her. I already did my part." Marko informed him. "Alright, well, peace!" Then he disappeared up the steps. It felt as though she was a ball in a court being passed from one hand to the next. First it was Ecoli, then Marko and now this guy. They all seemed to know what they had to do as if they had prepared and were awaiting her return.

"G'day," the guy said. His hand was outstretched. "I'm Tegan Taylor."

"Giselle. You could call me Gizzy if you want," she responded deniably smitten by his blue eyes.

"K, Gizzy," he smiled. Her stare shied away. "You're gonna be stuck with me for a while."

"How long is a while?" She regurgitated the words.

"Depends on how fast you learn," he responded.

"What you teachin'?" She narrowed her eyes and stared at him already mentally building a barrier between them. What was she to expect now? Seeing as Marko just threw her over a cliff she was a bit apprehensive about Tegan's lessons.

"Don't worry. I may not be Marko, but I can make this fun. It's not hard really. It's more like you following me around while I do all my work and getting hands on feel of everythin' before you can be trusted to go out on your own. You're a Guardian so you don't train with the denizens." He flicked his finger and the chair that had fallen over was on four legs once more. "Ok so somethin' about me. Let's see. You already know my name; Tegan Taylor. I'm from Australia. I, uh, I'm a Shaman. I'm in charge of the Recruit team and... and I've been in Floral Cove for about nine-ten years now so, uh, excuse me if I'm not as Australian as you expect me to be. Yeah, I saw that look. Marko told me that the first time we met so I dunno. Is there somethin' people from other countries expect Australian's to say?" Tegan addressed the bemused look on Giselle's face.

"Well," she mustered up some courage to talk to him, but she was mildly distracted.

Seriously, anybody in Greenz ever looked this good? Nope. I would have known. She thought.

"Whenever people try an Australian accent or English accent the first thing they say is some crap "bout shrimp on the barbie. I doh even know if that's what they say," she informed.

"Oh God," he rubbed his face. She sniggered.

She noticed Tegan had a nervous twitch about him; not something she expected from someone covered in tattoos. He couldn't stay still. After he picked up the chair he played about with his fingers a bit, then fondled with the books on the shelves and when it was clear there was absolutely no more straightening to be done, he played with the light on the computer's mouse. She couldn't tell if he was naturally this fidgety or if it was because he was stuck with a fourteen- year-old tail for a while. When he finished the brief introduction, he beamed her with his soft expectant eyes.

"Oh, me now? Ok. My name is Giselle Thomas. Am fourteen…" he broke in at this point.

"Oh yeah, I'm nineteen, sorry mate… sorry continue," he sat on the chair back. "Sorry."

She giggled and tried not to make eye contact. "Um, am Ersatz," her volume noticeably plummeted a great deal when she said that. "Born in Greenz, I mean Grenada. I'm in drum corps and I like to have fun basically."

Between the two of them it was unclear whose introduction was worst. He seemed to find it amusing that she was fumbling so much over her words and laughed at her saying 'just relax'. Where was that advice when he was uming and uhing? By the time the whole getting-to-know- you session was over, she concluded that he was naturally a nervous person. He also seemed to have a hint of the 'I like thrill' disease that Marko had. Maybe everyone in here had it. She definitely wasn't a tied down and get work done kind of girl unless it was something completely unnecessary and probably dangerous. That was probably their nature- being magical and all; they had that in common. Things in the normal world didn't satisfy them.

He gave her a copy of his schedule for the next two months since she'd be doing whatever he was doing. It was really just two calendar months stapled together; August and September. Each job he had was allotted a two-week period then switched over to another. He was currently in the middle of Patrol. Then he would take post as a medic, after that Recruit; each of his jobs had the word trainer in brackets and the time to start and end on it. Maybe Giselle was the cause of the specification in his schedule. Otherwise, it was really empty.

"Two questions."

"Shoot."

"Thought you was in charge of Recruit?" She asked taking a second look at the schedule in front of her.

"Yeah, but I still do other stuff. It doesn't change the fact that I run the Recruiting team at the end of the day. You'll understand when you start."

"Second, school openin' in September and most of your stuff says seven am," she said flatly still studying the schedule. Not that she minded skipping school though.

"Yeah but that's in MT. Don't worry, once you get a cycle going you'll be right. Right now, I can't go to bed before three am Aus. T."

"MT? Aus. T.?"

"Majesty time and Australian time," he cleared up. "You'll learn the many abbreviations too," he reassured her skeptical face.

He then pulled what looked like a thin drum stick out of his extremely visibly shallow pocket. Seeing things like this was going to take some getting used to. She almost asked how he did it before remembering he was a Shaman. He suggested that she pull a chair then materialized a new, empty desk in front of her and dropped an empty notebook on it. So class was starting now? He blew on the end of the drumstick and said his name clearly into it.

"Tegan Taylor. Theory," said Tegan.

"That supposed to be a mike or somethin' cause…" she paused.

"Oh yeah," he mumbled and fidgeted before pulling the note book open.

He was the one that gave it to her and now he was acting as though he couldn't take it without permission. He pressed a very concealed button on the shaft of the stick and a blue grey light shone from the point and spread out like a fan. He brushed the light across the page and suddenly the words 'Tegan Taylor. Theory" washed across it in computer type print.

"What is that?"

"A pen." Somehow she expected a more extravagant name.

Excuse me for thinkin' I was goin' to get one while sittin' in the trainin' room of a completely separate world from the one I was born and raised in. My bad. She thought.

Tegan then hesitantly, reached for her hand and pressed her index finger along the words in the book. Then, even though his lips weren't moving, she could hear his voice speaking again.

"Tegan Taylor. Theory." Giselle inspected her finger as though expecting to see something there.

"The correct name is gumshoe pen. It's used to pass on urgent messages in compromising situations. Everyone has their own that's unique to their style."

Giselle listened with great interest. As he spoke she observed the object in his hand. It was yellow with a simple strip of black on the end and right at the butt of it she could see 'T.T' scratched on.

"Where mine then?" She finally looked him in the eye, her butterflies only increasing.

"What's the rush?"

He pulled up a chair for himself and sat down. Well at least he was on the seat area this time, but he still had the chair turned backwards.

"You're only fourteen. You're not gonna be doing anything dangerous anytime soon. Ecoli won't allow it." This news was rather disappointing. "We are commonly known as Guardians." Tegan began talking in his pen again. "We're like, well we are, the law enforcement of Majesty; the governing body. That's why everyone was so surprised when you showed up. We expected you'd be a bit older. Imagine a fourteen-year-old parting a fight and taking someone to the slammers; hilarious thought, right?" He spoke jokingly. "Lucky for you Floral Cove and Heavenly Heights are very self-controlled places."

"And Nocturn Niche?" She inquired.

"Floral Cove and Heavenly Heights are very self-controlled places," he repeated. She got the message. "I'm sure you can handle though. I mean, you found the mirror."

"I didn' find it. My grandmother give me," she cleared up resentfully for the second time.

"Point is you never lost it." She raised an eyebrow. Didn't Marko say the same thing? "If it wasn't meant for you then you might have gone to sleep with it one night and woke up and it'd be gone forever. Never see it again. It's the spirit. Same way you can never lose it unless it wants to be lost."

"Oh."

Well that explained a lot. That was why the chain never left her. Vrai wouldn't allow it. Even if her grandmother didn't give her the chain it would have found its way into her possession somehow. This made her question whether it was really Ruby's intention to reveal Majesty to her or if she went through with it because she knew Giselle would end up there no matter what.

"Ok. Let's just talk for a while," he said after noticing her retreat in mood. Tegan put down his pen and pulled his seat closer. "You know, we practice new magic. It's like a mix of magic and technology; Magnology."

"Magnology?"

She found her tone was more harshly disapproving than she expected it to be. Tegan in a split second seemed to regret ever telling her that. His overall appearance came across as offended.

"Yeah."

He urged failing to wipe the hurt look off his face. She stared at him narrow eyed not considering at all that he seemed upset. It usually took her a while to pick up on things like that. On several occasions in the past, she spoke without thinking and only realized the damage she had done right before she fell asleep that night.

"Ok fine. We don't say Magnology, but it's cool, right? Tryna to get it to catch on." Tegan forced an extremely weak laugh.

"No, it not," she playfully shot down his attempted creativity.

This seemed to root him up from the garden of disappointment. Giselle was still oblivious to his temporary depressed state gone good.

"I bet you if Marko said it first it would be a thing by now, but I say it and everybody thinks it's stupid."

His slim face was so pleasant and his voice so innocent. His look and behavior made him off younger than nineteen in Giselle's opinion. And his tattoos were nothing, but that; tattoos. He wasn't edgy and foul as tattoos like his generally suggested. He was actually a bit timid.

"Magnology? I doubt. But I go petition it for you." Giselle joked. Tegan glowed.

"So, who do you know so far?" He asked her.

She thought for a while. "Well, Ecoli obviously and Marko and the lady in the kitchen kind of and you."

He laughed at her sentencing.

"Ok. Her name is Ariel by the way; she's a werewolf." He pulled out his pen again pressing a few buttons before talking. "I'll give you a run down. So there's the lead Recon- that's Ariel. She and her team do undercover work to ensure no one's plotting anything against any denizen of Majesty or Majesty itself. Lead Recruit- yours truly. My team and I seek out magical members in the normal world and introduce them to Majesty."

"Nice." Giselle broke in smiling. He Nodded.

"Then there's the lead Documenter- Ming. She might be young, but she's good at what she does."

Hearing him say that stung Giselle. If Ming was so 'young and good' then why couldn't they see her that way too?

"Ming's team has record of everything and everyone in Majesty to date. She might even know more about you than you know of yourself by now. She's an Ersatz."

He sounded genuine, but Giselle took it as if he was gloating.

"Right, so lead medic- Marcel. That speaks for itself. She and her team take care of us and everyone out there. Marcel's a fairy, but fairies are like the angels of Majesty so most people just call her an angel. Lead Emissary- Trevor. Shaman. They travel everywhere in here and the normal world delivering messages, packages and whatnot."

Now that sparked some interest. Did all the guardians have to be leaders of their own team or could they share? If they could, then she was ready to sign up as an emissary. He didn't say Grenada, he said the normal *world*. She would be travelling.

"So they just travel all the time to all different places?" She spoke again.

"Sounds simple, but it can be a pain mate," he shrugged.

"I think I would like that."

"So, wait I'm lost what did I say so far? Let's see, Recon, Recruit, Emissary, oh I remember. Then we have lead for Public Relations- Hozen. That speaks for itself. I know it seems kind of weird to have Hozen do public relations, but somehow it works. Hozen's a Slaugh."

Giselle's eyes widened at his choice of words. "Well damn. He might pass around, but you doh have to call him a slut."

"Oh, no I didn't say slut," Tegan quickly defended. "I said Slaugh. Huge difference."

"Which is?"

"Slaugh's are manifestations of restless dead people. They didn't get into heaven or hell so they endlessly roam the earth in search of resolve." She nodded in understanding while making a mental note to check out google later.

"Moving on we have Dispatch. It's a pretty decent team I kind of wish I was a part of sometimes." Tegan openly admitted.

"What they do?" Giselle questioned.

"They're basically the face of Majesty. People recognize the rest of us for what we do and although we are well known, the Dispatch team will always have a higher status. Whenever an emergency arises they're the first on the scene. Any fights, dirty work or mission to get your hands bloody, they do that. Only if the situation spirals out of control do me or Ecoli or any of the rest of us leave position."

"And you want to be part of it jus' to be known?" She asked.

"No," he sighed. "I just want to do more."

"Who in Dispatch now?"

"At the moment, just Marko and Scout. There's usually four of them though."

"Ok," Giselle hummed. "So where would I be if I decide I want to stay? Dispatch or Patrol cause you didn' name anybody for that one."

"You need heavy trainin' for Dispatch; that or be a prodigy at something decent. Technically speaking you could lead patrol, but the patrollers are like, uh, they're like the army. You might get overwhelmed. That's why Ecoli runs that for now." She stared at him silently. "No offence or anythin'."

"Oh really?" She spoke sarcastically.

After some long, strayed talking (due to Giselle's excessive questions during Tegan's educational take on Majesty) they ascended the steps and left through the Rec. Room. They made their way to the Female room and Giselle was starting to feel in a loop. The amount of times she had been taken back to point A. Every time she encountered someone new they always brought her back to the starting point. She was starting to wonder if there was really anything to see in Majesty now or if it was going to be packed with boring legal work. Tegan did say they were the law enforcement.

Yay, she thought unenthusiastically.

They had been outside the room labeled "Female" more than a minute when Giselle said, "Tegan, if you have to show me around today then I suggest you stop bein' so nervous."

This order was aroused by the fact that he was whispering to himself and seemed to be having a heated debate on whether he should enter the girls room or not.

"But this is the girls room," he said what she had suspected.

"And what boy doh want to go in here?" She shrugged and again, at least in Tegan's opinion, her voice was harsh.

He looked at her with a twisted lip and a deep thought expression on his face. Then he placed his hand on the door knob for what must have been the millionth time and turned it. He stepped aside and let her go in first. Giselle rolled her eyes and marched in shaking her head, but the thought, *he so cute*, was spinning in her head. The room, like the training room, was very different from anywhere else in HQ. It was painted in turquoise, had some closets built into the wall, a few blue-ish lockers, two one man beds on either side of the square room, a dresser with clutter all over it and a lot of other homey stuff. It was cozy. The first time she had been previewed to that room was with Ecoli and she remembered questioning whether they lived in there. It didn't seem like a place she would willingly leave if she was ever given the chance to get comfortable. On entering, the sight of Ming and Marcel filled her eyes. Marcel was sitting on one of the beds with a book opened in her lap inspecting her nails and Ming was in front the mirror brushing her hair and blushing at a red piece of paper. Before Giselle could voice her thoughts, Tegan started talking behind her.

"I'm sorry if anyone's changin'. Could you please get decent for a minute, please?"

His hand was clamped over his eyes and he manned his post at the closed door. Giselle shook her head feeling second hand embarrassment from him. That could never have been Amron. Her brother would have burst into that room so fast he would have gotten whiplash just because the girls were clothed.

"Tegan we decent." Marcel's apologetic smile told Giselle that they were used to Tegan's behavior.

"Huh," he slid his hand down his nose. His eyes darted from Marcel to Ming then he straightened up and stepped deeper into the room. "Ok good. I was helpin' Giselle, but since you're here…"

"I'm not." Ming said in a sour voice then left with her paper in her pocket. Giselle could have sworn she got a reproachful glare from Ming.

"Ooookayyy." Tegan dragged awkwardly. "Marcel?"

"Do what ya doing brethren," she set down her book. "By the way we didn' officially meet."

Giselle noticed a significance in the way the mature lady in front of her spoke. Ecoli said that this was his sister which meant, Giselle assumed, she was from Grenada too. She didn't fully speak Creole though, or even looked Grenadian for that matter. She was speaking like Ms. Lyn; her accent was tinged with some other cultures lingo just like Ecoli's. Her hair was locked like Ecoli's, but something about her narrow jaw, wide hips and tallness (as opposed to Ecoli's stumpiness) seemed foreign. Then again, he was in Majesty since he was six. Who knew how long she had been in there.

Marcel strolled over to Giselle and reached out her hand, not for a hand shake, not to do the awkward 'hi' wave people did when they were too nervous to talk. No. Her hand went straight up and into Giselle's poorly kept afro like hair. Grooming wasn't exactly an activity Giselle took seriously and considering, she lived with her father and brothers. Since her grandmother passed away her hair wasn't being taken care off like it used to be.

"Ya got nice hair," she pulled on it to see the length. "Ya should comb it."

"That is too much work and my hair hard." Giselle complained.

It was the first time someone addressed her hair situation other than her grandmother. This made her heart sink a little and something in her chest was getting unbearably heavy.

"Because ya not combing it." Marcel responded smartly. "I could do it if ya want," she rubbed Giselle's head playfully then pulled her fingers from the tangled mess.

"Yeah?" She was feeling deep set appreciation for the offer.

There was something about Marcel's tone. It was nothing like Ecoli's for certain.

"Just tell me when." Marcel returned to her book.

"So uniform." Tegan made his presence known again. "It's not anything official. You'll just have a certain outfit you wear for training with me. Professionalism, you know."

Giselle's eyes switched from Marcel after long staring. As if he was a malfunctioning robot, Tegan was back to his hesitant state and molding over thoughts in his head again. Marcel, peeping over her book, watched him cross the room. She watched him place a gentle hand on the closet handle before turning to speak to her.

"Do you-"

"-no Tegan," she spoke.

She was expecting him to buy time before opening the closet. Not that there was anything to be feared in there. She just had the feeling that he would question if her personal belongings were in there and so saved him wasting his breath.

"What?" Giselle asked eyes bouncing between them.

"Hopeless." Marcel was getting off the bed and rolling her eyes. "Ya know that?"

"I don't want to invade anyone's privacy."

He was moving away from the closet as if he and Marcel had some type of telepathic conversation to switch positions. Now she was opening the closet and he was sitting on the bed inspecting her book.

"Giselle, darling, do hope ya got patience," she smiled and spread all the hangered clothes. "Tegan is the worst."

"I am not!" He spoke defensively.

"Why you say that?" Giselle found it easy to settle her butt on a chair and partake in friendly conversation.

"He's so nice and sweet and sensitive…" none of these things defined "worst".

"That's not a bad thing." The book slipped out of his hand the precise moment he spoke. He hurriedly picked it up and started rushing through the pages.

"I'm sorry. I lost the page. Marcy, you remember the number? Oh no, I'll find it. I'm sorry." He apologized more than enough.

"Exhibit A." Marcel gestured to him like the lady on wheel of fortune did the board. Giselle laughed hard at this. Tegan hardly found this amusing as finding the page was near impossible. "All am saying is sometimes he can get a little tiring. Don' get mad or he'll feel guilty and apologize more." She whispered.

"You think I don't know you talking about me?" He said.

"Woah." A sarcastic, aghast gasp left Marcel's lips. "The ego on this one."

Giselle laughed some more.

Tegan huffed. "Take your stupid book." He threw it roughly on the bed. The way it landed one of the pages bent and he rushed to pick it up. "I'm sorry." he mumbled, smoothing out the pages and completely airheaded about why he threw it in the first place.

"Ya just can't help it." She shrugged and pulled open a secret compartment behind the closet. It was dark, musty and didn't contain much. Out of it Marcel pulled a tired jumper after leafing through the contents. "Stand up for me, darling." Giselle slid off the chair and stayed quiet as Marcel walked around her and measured the clothes on her back. "Ok," she sounded satisfied. She walked over to a bare patch of wall and rubbed the wall. In no time, a white door appeared. "Go in there and try it on while I deal with this one for touching the Queen's property." She rounded on Tegan. He broke out in another fit of "sorry's". This time he was grinning. Giselle found it hard to choose between going into the room that just appeared out of nowhere or watching Tegan plead to Marcel who looked as threatening as a newborn rabbit.

A broad vivacious expression stretched across her face as she crossed to the mystery room. Her grandmother was right about one thing for sure. She was indeed growing quite fond of the few people she met in there. The time she had known them wasn't long, but they were growing on her already.

CHAPTER EIGHT

THE HANDBOOK

THE DAY STARTED like any other holiday morning; quiet, peaceful and with an empty schedule. Psh! Yeah right. Giselle lay in the comfort of her sheets half awake. It was one of those mornings where everything in your brain was saying get up, but your body was too comfortable to take orders. Her sheets were warm and loosely tucked around her body and her pillow and mattress seemed to have a perfect Giselle sized sink right where she lay. Her nest was too sweet to abandon. Her windows were open letting in the refreshing, light winds, but the curtains were drawn tightly. She took deep, full breaths of the morning air. The sun was like the devil in the morning. When that curtain opened she always felt like a vampire being forcefully revealed to the sun. It was just too early for anything to be that bright and happy. She needed more time to wake up before she tasted the sun's smiling rays. In the peace of the moment she hugged her thick pillow tighter to her body and lingered in a hazy dreamy state. She saw a few crazy pictures flash across her eyelids. She saw a thriving restaurant with her grand-mother's effigy winking at her and other things she couldn't quite make out.

Out of nowhere, a loud, lawless boom exploded throughout her house causing her to jump so far out of bed her hand clutched the door knob without her knowing how she got there. The voice of the well-known soca artist, Mr. Killa, filled her room singing, *"bo'n in ah ban'! Liquor in me han'! Stink and dutty!"* She rolled her eyes and groaned in annoyance. This early morning! Who in God's name was blasting soca this early in the morning? A complete disregard for anyone else in the house when coming to his music; this had Andre written all over it. With kids like them it was understandable why Brent got extremely annoyed all the time. It even got to the point where he came up with classifications for all of them. Her eld-est brother BJ was "please-move-out-of-the-house". He was always home and always trying to be in Brent's business instead of going out and living his life. Although it wasn't common for Grenadian's to encourage their kinds to move out, Brent kind of had to with BJ or else he would never leave. Nowadays though, they hardly ever saw him. Andre was "contradiction-in-the-house". That one was inspired because he always sold out everybody for not doing the right thing and every now and then whenever he did something utterly stupid he always had a "logical" excuse. Amron was "never-in-the-house". One can't imagine what would inspire that name. Giselle was "destroy-the-house". Her name was born from the fact that she almost burned down the house twice. She was a child that had just learned how to light a match. Cut her some slack.

She pulled her door open so violently that it slammed against the wall behind it. This early morning! That was all she could think. She made her way through the hall and into the deserted living room. She pulled up on the stereo and turned the music so low that you'd have to put your ear against the speaker to hear and even then you'd be straining.

"What the hell!"

A heavy masculine voice was ringing in the now ghostly house. The air seemed to still be vibrating from the sudden blast of sound that surged it. Sure enough Andre occupied the doorway between the living room and the kitchen.

"What you doin'?"

"This early mornin' you come with this music!"

Giselle let out a frustrated groan. She really wanted to be buried in her bed undisturbed. How dare he take her away from bed? That should be a crime.

"Is after ten you lazy…" he held back his insult and bit into a slice of salami he held in his fingers gingerly.

This over confident act made her size him up and consider fighting him. Andre was about five feet ten inches tall. He was her second-oldest brother, being eighteen. He was a recent graduate of The Grenada Boys Secondary School and preparing to start T.A. Marryshow Community College at the end of summer holiday. It wasn't much of a move considering GBSS and TAMCC were basically connected being right next to each other. Still, he seemed utterly pleased about it as if he wasn't going to be taking the same bus to Tanteen and seeing the same people he bade farewell in graduation. Basically he was a book worm. So yeah, he was big but maybe fighting him wouldn't be a total loss.

Giselle looked at the set box for confirmation. There it was in green, digital numbers- ten thirty-nine.

"Well people sleepin'," she fussed.

"YOU sleepin' and is about time you get up so you're welcome."

Andre walked over to where she was, nudged her out of the way protecting his salami and turned the dial blasting the music again. Giselle defiantly turned it back down.

"Gizzy, I not playin'. Come on it too early for this," he looked down on her.

"Oh now it too early?" She faked surprised.

"Yes. It early when I say it early," he turned up the music. She turned it down again.

"Aye girl!"

"Aye boy!"

Both of them started to struggle with the stereo forcing the dial in the direction they wanted it. They were being so rough with it that the little stereo rocked on its stand. Giselle elbowed Andre in his stomach and when he moved away she shut off the radio completely. Instead of diving at the object they were fighting over he lunged at her, still holding onto his salami. Then he flicked her three times in the fore head with his index finger. Mad enough to have steam rise, Giselle committed the biggest crime she could against her brother. She swiped the salami from his hand and stuffed it in her mouth. It was like an alarm had gone off in his head that seized his whole body for a moment. He looked at his finger where residue of his late breakfast still remained and back at her, crazed. Andre loved his food. One thing you should never do was take his food without asking or being offered. He had a kind of OCD about it. If he cut three pieces of cheese and someone broke a piece out of one while he wasn't looking he lost his mind like he was robbed of a thousand dollars or something. Then he'd go and cut a new piece to look exactly like the one before. He stepped forward and Giselle prepared to run when a firm, authoritative hand clasped down on both their shoulders.

"You bigger! Set an example, nah!" Their dad's voice pounded over them.

"Dad she take my meat!" He pretended to point her when really he just wanted to get the last lash. He did. His dad smacked him.

"Meat?" He shook his head and pushed Andre off in the direction of the kitchen. Andre made a point to turn on the music again on the way. "You!" his eyes fastened on a sniggering Giselle. This wiped the smile off her face. "Stop provokin' your brother!"

"But dad, this early mornin' he come with this music!"

"I didn' ask a question! I said stop!" He was done.

He joined Andre in the kitchen. Giselle, mad that she had a taste of the discipline, followed him into the kitchen. She was already up and out of her bed for more than five minutes, if she went back now it wouldn't be as warm, peaceful and fitting as it was when she just woke up. That thought made her curse Andre's name even more in her head. Just one morning, that was all she wanted. Her stomach was making those weird cry noises to catch her attention anyway. Why not eat now? She took pleasure in turning down the music when she passed.

The kitchen was just like any standard kitchen one would see. Window over the sink and the curtains that looked like someone cut them in half hanging lazily over it. The cupboards seemed crappy now compared to the unique ones Giselle observed in Majesty. Then to the left was a two-part back door with the top open. The oven and fridge were alongside each other and the counter was laden with jars containing white sugar, brown sugar, salt, and random pasta. Seriously, one week there would be macaroni then the next it would be spaghetti then for some time a mix of different shape and size macaroni. There was a bread bin and a tray with some bananas and two mangoes. The house, considering it contained seventy-five percent men, wasn't as cluttered as one would think. Sure it got a bit messy sometimes, but Brent made an effort to pick things up here and there when the mat in the living room was no longer visible.

Brent was a strapped patterned haired man with rough hands and a dusty complexion. His children doubted he was ever completely clean once in his life. He was a construction worker. A single father trying his best to make ends meet and take care of the three children left in the house; Andre, Amron and Giselle. His eldest son BJ, Brent Junior, moved out about a year ago. They didn't see him as much anymore because of his job; he was a travel agent. He sent money to help out whenever he could. On top of that he wasn't even in the country. He had gone to visit Uncle Rohan for a few weeks.

"You sleep good, Gizzy?" Her dad asked.

"Yeah," she answered rubbing her head.

"You must go to bed early more often then," he suggested.

"Why?"

"Cause you more lively than I see you in weeks," he smiled at her.

She didn't respond with words. She merely folded her lips and shrugged knowing full well she didn't go to bed last night. In fact, at mention of her early sacking, she started to relive her time in Majesty. She found out she could fly last night, didn't she? A small smile found its way on her lips. Plus, she had fun which wasn't at all what she had expected going back in there. She expected to have a hard sit down talk with Ecoli to find out what he wanted from her. Instead, she was blessed with tales on how amazing her grandmother was. She got first-hand experience of Marcel's kindness, Tegan's quirkiness, and discovered how impossible it was not to laugh at Marko. She couldn't

189

stop reading everything Tegan had put in the notebook over and over when she got back.

"Guess that mean no more late-night walkin'?" He chuckled.

This made Giselle alert. It took a few seconds for her to realize he was talking about last week when she'd somehow found her way into Ruby's house. Andre stood sour in the corner. When he had brought up the incident to his dad he seemed angered at first, but quickly that subsided. Giselle merely escaped with a tap on the wrist and more baby treatment which she did not in the slightest fancy. There was no way Brent could be talking about last night, anyway. If he knew, it would have been the first thing he addressed this morning. She wondered if he knew anything about Majesty at all. Clearly from Ruby's message her mom knew about it. But did her dad know? Was he aware that his own mother had been entangled in a world most islanders would consider damned?

Just then her other brother cut in the kitchen breaking their "father-daughter" moment.

"I is a man that like to eat ramen! Ramen! Ramen, ramen, ramen...!"

"...as VAT come in!"

Amron came in the kitchen singing and Andre finished for him.

"Nope," his father said promptly shutting the cupboard he was rummaging through. "I eat the last one last night." Amron's whole physique hung in disappointment. "It taste good too," Brent teased.

"Yuh see this shhhh-should not happen," he was about to cuss, but caught his dad's eye. "I go start labelin' my things."

He sat down at the dining table now trying to figure out what he was going to eat for breakfast. Oh, the disappointment of making up your mind for one thing only to realize it was gone.

"You does buy things and put in the cupboard?" Brent's eyes found its target and lingered.

Something about the way Brent stared at them whenever he said stuff like that added a sting in the atmosphere. Andre stood in the corner with a big chunk of salami cutting off pieces chewing amusedly.

"No more milk." Giselle announced as she waved the empty powdered milk tin.

"Till Saturday." Brent sighed.

Giselle turned off the kettle. "No point doin' this then."

"I know. Doh worry I go get stuff soon."

"Dad, I could just get a part time job-" Andre suggested for the millionth time.

"-No. You go to school. I'm the parent," he finalized.

They had the same breakfast comfortably. Brent divided the bread and salami for the four of them. Giselle accepted her bit graciously even though she'd have preferred something else.

"I doh want this," Amron scorned.

"Then you not hungry." Brent scolded.

Amron grimaced.

"The yard have to clean." Brent directed his words to no one in particular.

Hearing this Giselle started inspecting a banana like it was the most interesting thing she had ever seen. Andre spun on the spot in the corner where he was and picked up the spaghetti jar. Amron opened the fridge and stood aimlessly in front of it for some time.

"Mr. Man, you does pay bills inside here?" Amron pulled out the juice then closed the fridge. It was clear he didn't want it. "All-yuh could play you didn' hear me all you want. Just make sure when I reach back here tonight the grass cut and rake, the steps sweep and scrub and one of all-yuh need to get vine for the rabbits. Not Gizzy." He dished out orders.

"Where you goin'?" Giselle inquired only hearing the "when I reach back" part of his list.

"And help out Mr. Griffith with some work." He told her. When he finished his breakfast, he drank some water straight from the pipe and left the kitchen. All they heard, in a warning shout, before the front door shut was, "The yard hadda clean!"

Amron put the juice back in the fridge and opened the cupboards looking earnestly for breakfast. He was just as picky as Andre about food. That never stopped him from eating like a pig, however. He was one of those people that could eat the world without gaining weight. Giselle envied him for that. Her family was generally big boned so she had to watch what she ate. Amron and BJ were the only ones that could get away with a diet like that.

"I see the wax apple tree down the road full," Amron began. "I goin' and raid it. Me and them fellas meetin' up in a while."

"I doh really business what you do as long as the rabbits get vine," Andre retorted.

"Who say I getting' vine for the rabbits? So Gizzy can' do that?" He swung his hand in her direction.

"If I could do it then you could do it," she smart mouthed.

Amron's stare stayed on Giselle a moment longer than he intended observing how chatty she was being. She hadn't said much since he entered the kitchen, but her speech sure had a clicking difference. For instance, she wasn't mute.

"Dad say not Gizzy and anyway she too small to be goin' in the bush and cut vine for she self." Andre reiterated his earlier statement.

His reasoning was the precise explanation why she liked to rebel. She was the youngest, *the baby*. Not only that she, was the youngest of three boys. Every single time something came up her brothers and father always put her in the back seat. Everything was 'she too young' for them or 'she just a little girl'. Only two people in her family treated her like she was capable of something; her uncle Rohan (she figured that was because he was the youngest of his brothers and he knew how it felt) and her brother Amron (though he usually used her to get out of work and trouble so saying she was old enough really only helped him). In her opinion Amron should have been Uncle Rohan's son; they were just alike. They both had a hot foot, hard head, were magnets for trouble and excellent negotiators. Their dad would be more shocked he forgot to pay the light bill than he would to hear Amron or Uncle Rohan got arrested.

"What so hard about cuttin' vine?" Giselle directed her annoyance to Andre now.

"Nothin'." Andre was putting what remained of the bread in the bread bin. "You just shouldn' be in the bush doin' that by yourself."

"Nothin'go happen."

"Dre." Amron sighed. "Bro, come on just let the girl cut the vine nah."

"No. And if she do that what you doin' then?"

"You deaf?" Amron pulled the Crix pan. "I say I goin' and raid the wax apple tree."

"I want some." Giselle giggled.

"Funny," said Andre.

Amron smirked, "I wasn' tryin' to be, but it happens naturally." Then he captured some crix and ate with a teasingly serious look on his face. "Gizzy, I hear Mr. Williams callin' a meetin'."

Silence.

"Sooo…"

"I doh know. I askin' you."

"Well you start up like you had a story to give me."

"I can' stand when he do that. He startin' like he have a whole book to tell you and have people waitin' in vain." Andre chimed in.

"See, all-yuh doesn' listen to me properly." Amron spoke with a full, dry mouth. "Always quick to talk."

"You need to learn how to talk properly." Giselle and her big brother spoke in unison.

"Don' do that." Amron spoke. He started to cough violently spitting out crix. He ran to the sink to get some water.

"How you go eat all that dry crix with no water?" Andre spoke to him like he was an idiot.

Giselle laughed. "You big ass."

He drank some water and took some time to regain his composure at the tune of Giselle's laughter.

"Shut up. Nobody ask your opinion. See, that is why you go clean the yard for your damn self and Giselle go get vine for she damn self." He pointed them both, then stormed out of the kitchen after quenching his thirst. Two seconds later he popped his head back into the kitchen. "Oh yeah, Gizzy, and if you want wax apple then give me a bag." Then he disappeared. They could hear him walking down the hall saying, "This early mornin' they gangin' up on a man."

The day had already shown its potential to be wasted. It was hot, windless and lifeless. Nothing quite made the cut of interest peaking. If anything, Giselle just wanted the day to be over so she could disappear into the mirror once more. A bit of Marko's antics would come in handy now. She'd appreciate if he left out the gag of throwing her over cliffs, but everything else was appealing, to say the least. In a world like that, where the people seemed so carefree, she couldn't see what she had to protect them from. She couldn't imagine what her mother might have envisioned to drive her to insanity. Whatever it was it must be long gone by now. Still, the curiosity was gnawing at her brain. How did her mother come across Majesty? Did Ruby present it to her? It was obvious why she forbade Ruby to introduce her children to such a place. In all eyes, Giselle was sure, this place would be seen as unholy, demonic and the devil's playground. Taking that into consideration, maybe running off to Majesty at night wasn't the best idea. But it wasn't as though Vrai was giving her any other options.

Marko was a part of dispatch wasn't he? If Dispatch was the group that always got their hands "bloody", according to Tegan, then why was Marko so cheerful. She guessed he hadn't seen many scary scenes in his lifetime. Conclusion, Majesty wasn't bad and it didn't need her. It wouldn't stop her from going in, but her services weren't exactly required right now.

After breakfast they all went along their own business which in no way included what their dad told them to do; well, partly. Andre was hard at work outside, but Amron was doing whatever he wanted. Giselle retreated to her bedroom to prod at her latest object of interest. As much as the curiosity was prickling under her skin to jump in, Ecoli's words were keeping her at bay.

"If you have a weak heart I suggest you stay home at night."

What happened came out night anyway, she wondered. Probably ligaroo or leshies; it was all she could come up with, though something told her whatever it was it would be more extravagant than she could ever imagine.

"Stop prodding me. I am not a toy." Vrai got loud and obnoxious.

Giselle pulled her finger back remembering what happened the last time she touched stirred glass.

"Shhh!" Spit was almost flying off her lips.

"Do not *shhh* me!" Vrai screeched.

"Well hush!" Giselle completely contradicted herself with how noisy she was being.

"Gizzy you talkin' to somebody?" Amron called from the living room. The decrease in the TV volume wasn't exactly discrete.

Giselle did not have a cell phone, nor was the house phone in her possession or anywhere within her reach. If she had said yes then it would only mean who ever she was talking to was in the house and there without her brother's knowledge.

"No," she sounded unconvincing, but all the same, Amron tamed.

Making sure to rudely shut Vrai up she relaxed on her bed studying the schedule. The first thing on there was patrol. What would they be doing? Just walking up and down like those guys in the terminal did or was there something else… something more. Tegan did say they were like the army. After staring so hard at the piece of paper that she could have bored it, she was struck with an idea. The words on her notebook spoke to her when she touched them. Would these words enunciate too? Giselle, after peeping out her room door to make certain Amron wasn't still spying, ran her fingers along the page. The sound of Ecoli's voice filled her room calling out Tegan's schedule. Hearing the voice without the face made him sound so cold and soulless like machine. Maybe he was. It would explain why people turned away from him when he greeted them and the warning she got at the restaurant. The gnome told her to watch her back. What was that supposed to mean? Was Ecoli some kind of inconsistent hard-ass or something? What did he do? Or maybe it was the common trend to hate the chief of any law enforcement because they were too strict with the laws. He did come off as a very strict by the book person. He had a very low tolerance for foolishness and an extremely short string of patience. He tended to flip the switch to his agitated side pretty easily. But there were still a few people that liked him when they were on the tour like Ms. Lyn and that girl on the shuttle. Plus he wasn't unapproachable. Well, to a certain extent and he made her laugh a few times.

"Mirror…"

"I have a name. Use it." The spirit spat and went on muttering curses. "Total disrespect. Only wants to talk when she feels like…"

"Vrai," she exhaled. "What kind of woman was grandmom?"

"Do you not understand our contract?" Vrai asked casually.

"I doh want to know what she do in Majesty." Giselle laid back on the bed placing the chain on her stomach. "Unless what I want to know is against the rules. Just tell me where you would put her; Nocturn Niche, Heavenly Heights or Floral Cove?"

For some time Vrai said nothing and Giselle was beginning to worry she was gone again. She peeked at the glass for confirmation, relieved when she saw it still rippling.

"Floral Cove," she finally said.

"So she was Ersatz too?" Giselle's voice had some finality in it.

Vrai snorted. "Not likely."

"So Shaman?"

"Gizzy," her room door swung open.

Giselle jumped to a sitting position snatching the mirror out of fear and brushing her schedule to the side.

"I goin' for wax apple now. You still want?" Good, he didn't appear as if he suspected anything.

She nodded.

Amron straightened his posture. Instead of leaning against the door frame he brought himself to stand inside of her room now.

"Doh do that," he softened.

"Do what?" She was clueless.

"You not talkin' again," he said.

"All I do was nod my head, Amron." she lifted a brow.

"Yeah, you been noddin' for a while. You was talkin' an' laughin' this mornin'. Doh start back noddin'."

The hard look on her face couldn't show any less emotion. In truth she was touched that he cared enough to address her behavior. Truly though she was only stunned that he didn't notice she was talking to jewelry.

"Oh gosh, is jus' vine Dre." Giselle was saying this for the millionth time to her brother as she left the yard.

She was only going around the back of the house. What was his deal?

"Ok, go ahead." He picked up the weed eater.

As usual, Amron wasn't doing what he was told. He went wax apple picking instead. Giselle didn't mind because she knew he would deliver. Andre didn't care because he was planning to leave the raking for Amron anyway. If anyone got in trouble it definitely wouldn't be Giselle or Andre. Giselle made her way around the house to the little coup her dad had built. Just over three weeks ago they had gotten some rabbits and a hare; they were young. Brent knew a guy that cared for many unusual animals out of love and bought some off him. It was a failed attempt to get Amron to be more responsible. He took one look at them and discarded his responsibility for it. She gathered up as much vine, twigs and bark as she could in the bushy area then trotted over to the rabbit coup. It was just five of them. They didn't need much, right? The cage had two parts. One side had the hare and a rabbit in it which were their pets.

Then the other side was, according to Amron, a future banquet. She first put some vine into the slaughter cage then went over to tend to her pets.

Something struck her mind. Back in Floral Cove when she entered the restaurant there was a hare on the counter. It didn't take much before she realized it was really Ms. Lyn, the woman in charge. What if her pets were shape shifters. Giselle dropped the vine and scoured her surroundings before rounding on the coup again. She looked at her pets that were sitting there doing what they usually did- nothing.

"Hi." She felt awkward trying to hold conversation with them. "I doh know if you could understand me. This doh even make sense, but I doh know. Jus' to be sure, I guess that is why I talkin' to you."

She felt even more stupid now than when she just said hi. Maybe she was letting this thing get to her head. Not every hare was going to suddenly change into a human. Her shame grew even longer when she remembered her chain was still in her neck which meant Vrai was with her.

"What are you doing?" Vrai asked.

"Shhhh." Giselle did this roughly.

"So I jus' figure out that not everythin' is what it seem. And, well, I jus' want to know if you, I doh know, not actually, you know. If not, I could help you." The animals just sat there as clueless and adorable as they were when she walked up with no hint they understood a word she said. "Ok. Maybe I should stop talkin' before people think I crazy."

"I already think you are crazy," Vrai sounded tired of Giselle's behavior.

"You doh count." Giselle said.

Giselle walked to the other side where she had dropped the remainder of the vine. She should just feed them and leave. That would be best before Andre found some reason why she shouldn't feed them again. When she turned her back she heard a thumping noise. Swiftly she turned around to be greeted by the brown hare that hopped to the front of the cage. It was skinnier than the others and had tall attentive ears. Giselle went back. Heart thumping.

"You hear what I say?" She whispered.

The sound of Vrai snorting annoyed her almost as much as her brothers did.

Again the animal made no sign of understanding, but it's eyes never left hers. She hesitated for a moment before unbolting the coup and reaching, cautiously to scoop it up. Her dad had warned her to pick them up by their ears, that way they couldn't scratch. She had seen what they could do when Amron completely disregarded this information and grabbed it by the stomach. He never went near them again. Still, she felt like she was hurting them when she did that.

"Don' scratch me." She said hoping the hare did really have some type of human sense.

Slowly she slid her hand around its warm, soft stomach and picked it up. And immediately it did what she told it not to; it scratched her. Though, it wasn't like the way it scratched Amron. With him it was done repeatedly and didn't stop until he threw it wildly back in the cage. With her it was more of a reflex; then it stopped. Peculiar. Giselle walked over to the area she had gotten the vine from placing the hare gently on the ground and backing up.

Waiting.

What was she waiting for? The hare just sat there and looked at her just like it did in the cage. It made no attempt to run away even though it was free to. She wasn't going to go chasing after it.

"Go," she encouraged. It stayed. "So you just a normal hare then?"

"Who would have guessed?" Vrai commented humorously.

She wasn't shocked that this was just a regular hare, but there was still faint disappointment. Either way she was going to set it free. No way could it be comfortable being caged like that. Besides, she had one more. She could just tell her dad Amron gave one away. He wouldn't doubt her. It was Amron, after all. She turned her back and started to walk away feeling disappointed in herself; disappointed in the hare for just being a hare; disappointed that she didn't just give them vine like she was supposed to. How does Tegan know who to talk to and who to leave alone? She wondered this, but abruptly her train of thought was jolted by the sound of rustling leaves behind her. When she spun around she caught the faint sight of a little girl disappearing in the taller bushes, naked. When she looked down the hare was gone.

Her heart pounding in her head she couldn't decide if it was the right time to smile or scream. The phenomenon that had just taken place, she had prepared herself for it, yet she felt caught off guard. Her whole life she was living oblivious to this side of the world. She felt pride that she had just freed some-one she was subconsciously keeping captive. Though, the thought of how many more were there wouldn't leave her head.

"Get the boy." Vrai said sending Giselle racing back to the house.

Her predicament now was that it wasn't time to go in. In fact it was the dead of night right now. Later on that night before she left for Majesty she caught a snip of GBN news. It was about the ten-year-old girl that had gone missing some time ago. The same one she heard about when she was watching TV in a depressed state a few weeks back. Only, she wasn't missing anymore. They found her naked not far from her house, too traumatized to say where she was. Giselle's body felt as cold as ice.

She walked in Majesty independently for once. No guides, no one saving her life, no manhandling from Vrai. On arrival Giselle went straight to the female room to get into the outfit that Marcel had given her. Leaving now to search for Tegan she found the place was deserted. There was no one in any of the rooms she peeked in. Ariel could have been in the kitchen, but Giselle wouldn't know unless Ariel wanted to be seen. She was probably down in her little hide out. When Giselle approached the door of the Rec. Room she heard a hushed discussion.

"The attacks start early this year," she recognized Ecoli's voice.

"Reckon they know something?" Marcel asked.

"Of course they know." Ariel spoke up. "Somebody run they mouth."

"We doh know that, okay." Ecoli stated.

"Somebody tell them 'bout we security. I feel we have a spy here in Majesty." She continued. She sounded like she was talking to herself.

"Doh make assumptions." Ecoli said strictly.

"I'm hypothesizing." Ariel corrected. "I want to investigate this."

"That's fine." Ecoli allowed it. "In the meantime, we need to hold a press conference."

There was uproar of disagreement in the room. Ecoli's voice could be heard trying to quiet them down so he could explain himself.

"Why?" This sounded like Marko now. "Don't tell people things you're not sure about. Just beef up security at the terminals."

"If we increase terminal security and say nothin' the denizens goin' to notice. Is better we tell them." Ecoli sighed.

"I agree," an unfamiliar, whispering, male took the mic. "May I recommend that my unit take care of this."

"I'll prep my medics." Marcel accepted.

"I can hold off on recruits until January if you want. Reckon there's no need to bring new comers into this right mess." Tegan said.

"I'll help Ariel find the culprit or culprits." Ming volunteered.

"Good." Ecoli sounded satisfied. "Good. Hozen I want to know what you plan on saying before releasing anything to the public."

"Wait." Tegan cleared his throat. "What about Giselle?"

She gasped instinctively at the sound of her name. What did she have to do with any of what they were discussing?

"Wha'ya mean what 'bout Giselle?" Marcel asked and an awkward silence towered. "Ecoli?" Her tone was demanding.

"Talk 'bout it later," he said.

Giselle stepped back from the door at the sound of the meeting adjourning. She pretended to be walking up to it when they started exiting. The air escaping the room was heavy and tense, but when they saw her they all contorted a smile into their features.

"Hey! Ready for ya first trainin' day?" Marcel greeted.

"Yup," she showed thumbs up.

Her eyes strayed to Ariel for a few seconds then she looked away again. She wasn't sure how she felt about being in the presence of a real-life werewolf.

"Still en comb your hair." Marcel stated.

Giselle grew a sheepish grin on her face.

"Next week. I promise. I go bring the comb and every-thin'." Giselle said pulling on her hair instinctively.

"So you and Tegan." Ariel's voice was less threatening now than it was the day before. "My girl, I gon pray for your sanity."

"He not that bad man." Giselle backed up.

"Almighty, I hope not." Marcel went on.

Ming walked by them as they spoke not saying anything. Marko followed not too far behind making some stupid comments that forced Ming to flip him off. Then Ecoli came out. They all greeted her as they passed by, but didn't stop like Marcel and Ariel did. They had things to do. Giselle could see on their faces how preoccupied their minds were.

"Anyway, we have work to do so catch you later." Ariel stated taking Marcel with her. As they walked away she struck up a conversation. "Ming not supposed to be working with me? Where she going?"

"Marko bothering her again." Marcel sighed as she waved Giselle good bye.

Giselle entered the rec. room. Tegan didn't come out, so he had to be in there or in the training room she saw before. She was unsure of any other entrance to the training room and she hadn't a clue how to get to the bunker from outside. She hadn't had the chance to explore yet. When Giselle went in, there was another one of the Guardians present; one that she hadn't the chance to officially meet yet. Name- unknown. He was the headphone guy. She remembered that much. He was standing by the bar with the headphone around his neck and a clip board in his hand. Giselle wasn't sure whether she should go up and talk to him or carry on like he wasn't there. What would she say? She made her way over to the counter with the intention to just go straight by, but her conscience wouldn't allow it.

"Hi," she said to him.

He raised his head slowly from the clip board and acknowledged her. Hair messy, eyes bloodshot, face frozen and unbelievably skinny. Was he sick? Was he on something? He didn't smell of anything, but he looked like he'd have a hard time walking straight.

"Hey…" He had a heavy voice.

He squinted, attention still fixated on her, his breathing low and heavy. Giselle felt uneasy and compelled to step back, but she didn't. He looked back at his clip board.

"Only foreign name 'ere's Giselle so that belongs to…" he pointed her with his pen. She wasn't sure if he was asking or telling.

"Yeah. That is mine," she nodded. "And yours?"

He turned his attention to a phone he'd fished from his pocket. Not knowing what to do, Giselle asked his name again.

"Scout." He had a careful way of talking.

She felt so put off by him.

"Ok." This meet and greet wasn't going anywhere. "I goin' in the trainin' room."

"Wait." He called after her. "Ya need to sign this." He slid the clip board across the counter.

Giselle looked down at it and observed that everyone on there had about one or two titles to their names, but her name was bare. All it said was Giselle, time in and time out. Maybe Ecoli was respecting the fact that she wasn't sure she wanted to work there yet. Maybe that was what Tegan meant by 'what about Giselle'.

"Making sure we're all still alive." Scout smiled.

Giselle looked him up and down taking in the fact that he wore the same clothes as the others. They let this guy carry weapons? She pursed her lips. This was the Scout from dispatch; the one that worked alongside Marko. He didn't come off as a hard worker, but he also didn't come off as a slacker. She didn't know what to feel. Did he have skills enough to land him that position? Maybe. Maybe not. She signed in and descended the steps not even saying good bye.

~*~

"Uh, Tegan…" Giselle mumbled.

First and only thing on her list of things to do was tell Tegan what happened earlier.

"How ya going?"

"I find a hare, well a girl that was in the form of a hare today."

He stopped walking. "How?"

"I had it as a pet and I figure I go just check to see, but when I take it out it turn into a girl and run away," she explained.

"Any idea where she went… or who she is?"

"Yeah kind of," she gave an apologetic look for not taking more information from the news.

"S'ok. Good work locatin' a shape shifter." He tapped her shoulder then kept walking. "And thanks for lettin' her out. I can find her."

"So, what we doin' today?" Feeling considerably better Giselle was skipping alongside Tegan. "Where we goin'?"

"RQ2," he stated. "Recruit Quarters."

"What the two stand for?"

"Just to differentiate between Recruit and Recon."

"Oh," she digested this information. "Wait, I thought you had patrol today?"

"Yes, but like I told you, I lead recruit. Sometimes I stay in RQ2 until ten o'clock MT then I go about my schedule."

"I still don' see the point of you doin' all this other stuff if you already leadin' a whole unit."

"They're not permanent jobs. S'kind of like I'm in trainin' too. We call it exchange programs. That way we don't spend forever and a half in trainin'." That still didn't explain anything. "Answer this. In a world with no exchange programs you're a recon member. Recon members rarely end up in situations requirin' excessive physical energy or resultin' in injury. But one day things didn't go as planned and one of your men gets hurt and nobody in the recon unit has any trainin' in first aid to do a first response. The reaction to that injury could be the difference between life and death, but because we don't have exchange programs nobody knows what to do. What happens then?"

Finally realizing the purpose of the exchange program she said, "Oh. So that is why recruit is the last on your schedule? When you finish with the others you go back to that?"

He nodded. "And after a few months of steady recruit I might do three different jobs on the exchange program again. You choose when you want to do it."

"Well you see now this make sense." She slapped his arm with the back of her hand. "You must learn to explain yourself man."

The RQ2 was yet another unique room. The common symbol was painted on the wall behind a big brown desk. This room seemed more modern than the Rec. Room as it had a mini fridge and smooth painted walls. Giselle assumed they were out of the mansion and in the building she saw on the map now. There were maps plastered on the walls with specific countries and about eight thumb tacked globes in there. Two long thin legged tables were in the center of the room and it was surrounded by men and women chattering over papers. Right down both sides of the room there were computers giving live feeds from surveillance cameras; each screen showing at least four different angles. They weren't even showing public places. One video looked like the back room of a privately owned shop and a good few of them looked like people's homes. There were a few people there studying the surveillance, zooming in and out at certain points, observing the surroundings and even people.

"Sir!" A recruiter called the moment she realized Tegan was in the room. He went over to her. "We've confirmed cam fourteen. She's in East India…" the woman trailed off giving a whole bunch of coordinates and codes Giselle didn't understand.

"You have a team?" He asked her.

"Yes sir."

It was funny how she referred to Tegan as "Sir" and she looked way older than him. Giselle couldn't see herself calling him sir. No way.

Sir. Giselle laughed at the thought.

"I want them out by ten am MT," he said.

The woman looked at her watch. "It's eight now."

"Then you should get ready," he said and moved down the room. He turned back, "Good work by the way."

Giselle watched as the woman gathered her maps and left the room with two buff men and a manly woman. Tegan made his way over to the desk with Giselle in tow where there was only one chair.

"You can go ahead," he offered the chair.

"As if you had a choice," she told him already seated. He snorted.

Tegan sorted through some papers first before taking a stack of them and going over to a big white board and flipping it over. He then did a little magic like back in the training room and the thumb tacks on the board immobilized the papers that were floating towards it. Giselle admired this sight.

"This is the mission board," he said while the papers were being pierced. "There is one in almost every unit; especially patrol and recon."

"Ok. So dependin' on what is here that is what you doin' for the day?" She asked feeling like she finally understood something on her own.

"Something like that." Close enough. "Most of the work here is done on schedule, as I'm sure you've noticed. So sometimes people call HQ directly if they want something specific done and depending on the nature of it Ecoli would hand it over to one of our units. Then the leads decide if they want to assign the mission to certain people in their unit or they post it on the mission board and whoever is interested would go do it independently, or Ecoli could just make us do it ourselves."

"I like that idea. You ever do missions from here?"

"Most of the time my work comes from this board," he smiled and fidgeted. "Otherwise I'd be stuck invading people's privacy on those cameras." He pointed the surveillance area. "We watch people we suspect first before we approach them."

She nodded to what he was saying and turned back to read some of the papers. One read:

Suspected Succubus
Albina Barak of Prague, Czech Republic.
Report to: Berta Faix

213

"That is all the information you get?" Giselle pointed the one she read.

"Recon and recruit could track a person anywhere so that's actually a lot to go on," he sounded proud.

Besides the mission board there wasn't much to see in the RQ2. Everyone was busy studying maps, doing research or on the phone doing what sounded like an interview. Occasionally, a person would come in from outside, take a paper from the mission board, sign out and leave again. But that was all it was. Giselle, although she was supposed to stick around Tegan and see what he was doing, idled in the room and watched the monitors. He didn't bother to call her though. He knew indoor work was boring. By the time it was ten o'clock she felt like the whole day had passed.

She was dozing off until she heard, "You ready?"

Then the energy seemed to just flow from out of nowhere.

"Ok, so what's your favorite food?" Tegan asked out of the blue.

"Oil down. Why?"

"Just gettin' to know my shadow," he shrugged.

She smiled. "Well doh ask me my personal business if you not tellin' me yours."

"Sorry," his nervous twitch returned.

"You supposed to answer 'ok and my favorite food is so and so'." She poked. "Let me go again. My favorite food is oil down."

"Ok and my favorite's barbequed prawns." He laughed as they entered PQ- patrol quarters.

PQ was brutal. First and foremost; man stench. It really stung your eyes if you didn't prepare for it. Nothing was in order. No one was fully clothed. It was like a bar and a gym in one. And again with the tattoos.

"It's a miracle they keep it together outside." Tegan hung his head in shame.

"Aye, rematch! Now!" A guy was shouting after he got beaten in arm wrestling.

Tegan brought her over to a desk where they both signed in to patrol. At least it made her feel good that her name was printed on the paper and not scribbled in. Or maybe they used the Gumshoe pens. She was tempted to hear who's voice would say her name. It would most likely be Ecoli, but who knows right?

It was Ecoli.

"He work fast," she said.

"Ecoli doesn't slack," he scanned a different paper before turning to leave.

They moved through the mass of manhood in the room and out through a different exit. So far, every exit had led to a balcony of sorts. This one was actually the front of a building and had a concrete road that lead straight into Floral Cove. Tegan rounded on a tube which Giselle outwardly disobliged, then ended up taking a patrol car to Allen Shorts Back Street. It was a shabby yet well put together cross road that had nothing but merchandise shops. It had everything from toys to awkward knick-knacks that you really had no reason to have in your house but bought them anyway. The people there were fairly normal with the one or two fangs, claws and dump of tattoos. With their outlandish appearances it wasn't hard to spot Marko and Ming in the crowd of busy civilians. If they had been any more normal, Giselle would think they didn't belong in Majesty. From the time they had taken to the streets Tegan was getting just as much attention as Ecoli did when she had gone walking with him. The only difference was there were absolutely no negative glares fired his way. People seemed to adore him. It was the same with Marko and Ming. Everyone that walked by wanted to say hi and tell them they were doing a 'bang up job'.

"Ello gov'ner!"

Marko couldn't be more wrong with both the accent and what he said. Still he bowed to Tegan and looked confident like it was the top answer on family feud.

"Please don't." Tegan said.

"Alright, whatever. Giselle," he raised his hand like he just wanted a simple hi five. When she raised hers he took her wrist and started moving her in all directions making a movie length handshake. "…and then you do that and that and Boom! Let it explode." She was laughing.

"Ninety-nine percent of that was unnecessary." Ming rolled her eyes.

"Your existence is unnecessary." Marko retorted.

"I hope you enjoy reality TV." Tegan gestured the two in front of them. "They bring all the drama all the time."

"That's not funny Tegan." Ming flipped the hair she praised so much. "It wasn't funny the first time you said it and it isn't funny now."

"I'm tired of hearing your voice. Would you pipe down?" Marko didn't even have the decency to look at her.

"Seriously, does Ecoli even know who he's working with? How dare he send me on a job with that?" Ming wallowed and chucked her thumb in Marko's direction.

She had a really stuck up way of pronouncing her words and sassy body signals to go with it. Added to that, her personality wasn't hard to decipher. Just the way she wore her uniform compared to the others spoke millions. It was like she would do anything to show off her auburn skin and cover girl figure. And her hair was always in perfect place to show up her pimple free, squinty eyed, pouted-lipped face that always seemed to have beef with everybody. After a long, hard, crossed-eyed stare out the corner of his eye Marko broke his gaze from Ming and addressed the two in front of him.

"So where we headed?" The lively young man invited himself. He sounded like he was trying to get away from his partner.

"We reach." Giselle stated.

"Yeah, we're doin' patrol in the Back Street today. So we're technically workin' right now." Tegan shrugged. "This is it!" He let out a fake enthusiastic tone and smiled nervously.

"Yeah Tegan, bring the girl to do boring work on her first day."

Marko shook his head. He draped his arm over Giselle's shoulder barely because she was so short. Then he started to walk off with her.

"You should've hit up the mission board. Minor setback. Back Street is where the good shops are."

"Marko, what do you think you're doing?" Tegan caught up.

"Exactly what I said before you asked me that rhetorical question. Hitting up the shops."

"You know what rhetorical means?"

"Word a day calendar." He brushed off Tegan.

"Uh!" Ming shook her head. "Let me talk slowly here." She started dragging her words using excessive gestures. "We have important information for Ecoli, remember?"

"Ming go away, nobody likes you." He said, then quickly addressed a woman who interrupted to shake his hand.

The banter between the two did not fail to amuse Giselle. She stayed utterly gratified by their insults and expressions when the other person answered back. Were they always like this? Tegan did just call them reality TV. This was the expected result of putting a laid back joker and an uptight potential perfectionist together. It would never work. In defiance of Ming's "oh so helpful reminder", Marko started guiding Giselle down the streets and telling her about the different shops he liked going to. The Back Street had a lot of corners and turns and

218

endless places to get lost. The shop keepers looked sketchy, but then again, the people in the town looked no different. Tegan and Marko were comfortable, so why not? The first shop she saw when they turned the corner was Confections; a one story grey building with, glass doors and its name in red just above it.

"Confections like sweety?" Giselle asked. "Let's go there!"

"Nope." Tegan dismissed the idea. "You can get sweets at the Rowdy Ruby for free."

She fretted and puffed her already fat cheeks.

"You can get sweets anywhere for free, Tegan." Marko spoke on her behalf. "Just let her go."

"What is she five? She can walk around on her own. Let's go Marko." Ming interrupted.

"Not today Satan." He showed her his palm.

Giselle laughed. At this Ming stalked away. Was that a good thing or a bad thing? Wasn't Marko supposed to be on a job at this very moment? Wouldn't Ecoli be mad that he abandoned Ming? Or was he used to this by now? Well, either way the she-devil was gone now so it really didn't matter to Giselle. It didn't seem to matter to neither of the boys either because they just continued on with their previous conversation.

"Marko, you need to know when to stop playing." Tegan gave him a warning finger.

"It's not like it's illegal," he folded his arms as if he was a little kid.

"Not here it's not, but in Grenada it is."

"What illegal?"

The talk was just ridiculous. All she wanted was some glucose in her system. Tegan gave her a stern look as if he was trying to suppress her interest in the place with his mind.

"This is a drug store. And I don't mean prescription drugs," he huffed.

"For real?" She piped.

"No. For fake," she glared at Marko for his sarcastic response. "Yes. for real. It's not illegal here."

"Not the point." Tegan, again, was trying to sway her mind from the store.

"So I could just walk in and buy something and they wouldn' say nothing?" She asked ignoring him.

"Guys…"

"Yup. You could buy ten brownies and they won't care."

Tegan finally gave up. "You should know," he mumbled.

Marko grinned guiltily. "I was curious and Scout gave it to me."

Tegan shook his head and snorted in a high way as to say he would never stoop so low.

"Don't say you've never been curious. We all have. I'm just brave enough to explore." Marko defended himself.

"You." Tegan pointed Giselle. "Confections is off limits. You're only fourteen."

"I wasn' goin' to buy. I just want to know." She was annoyed. Why did he have to bring her age into this? "So people don' overdo it?" She turned back to Marko.

He shook his head. "I guess because it's so easy to get there's no thrill in buying now. Mind you, it's still a very popular store."

"Cause they're practically giving it away." Tegan grumbled.

Whether or not he approved they were still going to discuss it so why not give his insight, right?

After long, staring at the blond boy standing next to him Marko suddenly said, "Don't let Tegan trick you into believing he's innocent."

Giselle looked at Tegan whose face was getting considerably red.

After a very long time of distracting them from their job Marko left. He had to "handle some business" according to him. From there the day wasn't so much energetic, but it was still mind warping. They patrolled the area and Giselle stood back while Tegan reprimanded a few people. Plus, she got to explore Floral Cove a little more. When her five hours were done they signed out and Tegan saw her off. He explained that she shouldn't stay longer than three o'clock pm MT. That way she could get home and get some sleep before she started her day in the normal world. Before she left, Tegan gave her a Handbook. It was really just the guidelines given to denizens when they first entered Majesty. They had to sign a contract and everything. However, it was mandatory that patrollers read those guidelines in order to enforce the law. The version meant for patrollers had a few more pages than the original.

Giselle lay on her bed, head where her foot should be, with the book opened in front her face. The moment she set foot back into her house she became studious. She was too eager to see what was inside, but after some time she lost interest. Fifty percent of that book was obviously directed to Nocturn Niche, forty percent to Floral Cove and ten to Heavenly Heights (if they even needed rules at all).

She groaned, "everythin' is Supernatural society blah, blah, blah, do not over kill, blah blah, blah, jail, blah, blah, wait what?" She shot to an upright position on her bed to read over what she just brushed through. It read:

Seeing as Majesty is supernatural society it is absurd to ask the denizens to change their diets completely. However, restraint is required. **_DO NOT OVER KILL_**. *Denizens are allowed to hunt, but are restricted to two kills a month in designated areas. Substitutes have been provided for the various groups to make use of. Any denizen found guilty of more than the allowed killings per month will face disciplinary action. Disciplinary action may take the form of suspension, jail time and banishment and any other punishment deemed suitable to the crime by the chief of Majesty. Sentence time may vary.*

"Wait, hunt what?" She muttered not sure how to feel about this.

Did that outline really say hunt? After a long meditating pause, she found it best not to think about it too much. Don't hunt. That was good enough for her. She looked down at the book again to see what else she had been jumping over. The laws of Majesty were strict and specific. After going through it cover to cover she found herself at the end where it read:

These laws may be adjusted or changed without prior notice. Denizens **will** *be held accountable if new laws are not adhered to.*

She heard her dad cough in the other room. That was record breaking time for her to put a book away and throw her covers over her. By the time she was lying down he wasn't even done yet. Frightened wouldn't properly describe what she just experienced. The goose bumps on her skin were doing it well though. She took that as a warning to take off her lights and go to bed. In the twilight of her room her mind grew restless. Why did that always happen? When she was surrounded by people or busy at work she would completely blank out from her personal life. It was like all her problems in the world would melt away and she was fine again. Then the moment it got too quiet or too comfortable she would stress out again. All her bottled up thoughts would take top priority in her mind. She was not over her grandmother's death. She wanted her back. She wanted her to be here to explain all the things she was seeing now and explain why she had kept it a secret. She wanted to make sure that her family would be ok. However, that one she worked way too hard not to think about. If only there was a way to convert all her points from Majesty into cash. According to the handbook she could exchange, but the exchange rate wasn't worth it. She sighed and rolled over.

Don't think about this now. She was telling herself.

She needed to surround herself with more people. The ones she had found weren't enough. It wasn't enough if it couldn't help her forget all this. Drum Corp, the guardians, Majesty; it wasn't enough. She needed to do more. She needed to work harder; anything to clear her mind. With all the efforts to push those thoughts out of her head she found herself roaming back on the little girl from earlier now. Was that really the girl that was missing this whole time? Did her dad really mindlessly lock a ten-year-old girl in a pen and keep her from her family for weeks? Why didn't she just change back and run away? Giselle slid out of bed unable to find peace of mind and slowly made her way to the window that looked over her rabbits. Except she didn't see just rabbits. There were four people there. One was directly in front of the cage talking with the rabbits it seemed. Another was looking into a light from a device on his wrist and tapping around on it. Then across where she had released the hare two people stood. One feminine figure was stooped low. She picked up some of the dirt and sniffed it then looked up at her comrade readily like she had caught a scent. Then the other guy was someone she felt too good to see. A tall, fidgety, tattooed, blond haired guy making hand signals to his comrades. If she hadn't looked out the window she wouldn't have known they were there. And without much thought she escaped into the night air to be with them.

CHAPTER NINE

MORE THAN A MAGICAL WORLD

AS FAST AS her feet would carry her thick figure she looped around the house to where she saw Tegan. She couldn't explain, nor did she care to, why the sudden surge of excitement raised within her. Never mind the fact that she only went back to Majesty in hopes Vrai would never speak again. Nor did she try to remember that she was still in two minds about the Magical world itself since it had a huge role in making her family what it was; broken. All she knew was that he was there and she wanted to be there too. Technically speaking, it wasn't as though she was running off to Majesty again. She was only in her back yard. This time they had come to her.

"Tegan!" She yelled in a whisper, but her voice was loud enough to carry through the air.

At the exact same time all four of the recruiters raised their heads and readied their weapons. Giselle halted in her tracks skidding to a stop.

"S'ok," Tegan assured them once he saw who it was.

Obediently they lowered their weapons.

"Giselle," he spoke her name with some agitation. "Why'd you come out?"

"You lookin' for the girl, right?" She asked and there was a flicker of something in his eyes. What was it?

"Who be this?" The mysterious woman beside him stood up. "And how does she know the mission?"

Giselle narrowed her eyes in confusion. "Am..." she began to speak, but was taken aback by Tegan.

"Giselle," he rubbed his hands together nervously as he approached her. "I met her in the Back Streets today while I was patrolling. We talked a bit too much about life as a guardian. She alerted me about Alana." There was a confusing mix of lies and truth.

"Huh," the woman turned up her nose. "Small world."

Once she joined up with the other two men and indulged in discussion Tegan clasped a hand on Giselle's shoulder guiding her away from the group.

"Why you lie?" She asked him as he made no attempt to speak first.

"Why'd you come out?" He spoke softly.

"Because I see you, but... but why you say you meet me in Back Streets?"

"Technically, that's not a lie. We were in Back Streets." He glanced over his shoulder and rushed his words.

She couldn't believe his response. She couldn't even understand why he was acting the way he was. Why didn't he want to introduce her to his friends? Why was he keeping her a secret? Why was she even a secret to begin with?

"Tegan," she started.

"Look," he spoke over her. "I would feel a lot more comfortable if you went back inside. That way I'd know you were safe."

"From what?" She exclaimed and earned some glances from the recruiters.

Tegan's jaw hung open for a while; his expression revealing his debate on whether to tell whatever precious information he had or not.

"We can talk tomorrow," he finally said.

"But I want to help you find the girl." Giselle whined still clutter minded about his behavior.

"Alana," he breathed. "Her name is Alana and I can manage."

"But I s'posed to be followin' you around and learnin' how to be a-"

"-this could be dangerous."

She groaned in frustration. All the while Tegan's fidgety habit prolonged. He kept glancing back at his friends and talking over her. Not to mention how fast and secretive he was making the conversation. Everything he said only made her suspicious and want to stick around more. Why was he acting as though he suddenly didn't want her around? She should feel offended about it, but the way he was going about it did not give off the faintest bit of insult. It was more as if he had to say what he was saying. As if, if he was given the option he would introduce her to everyone and take her along with him. But he couldn't for some reason and that was why he was nervous.

"Ok fine," he said wary of Giselle's persistence. "You can come with, but you have to do exactly as I say."

Orders like that did not suit his voice or his appearance. He was feigning tough and authoritative, but his soft blue eyes gave away all his concern and worry.

"Ebba," he called to the woman. "Remember that man we were lookin' at this mornin'?"

"Yes sir?" She answered.

"He's in your hands now. Handle it. Take Roscoe with you," he told her.

"Yes sir," she saluted and she took her leave with the guy that was talking into the light on his wrist.

"Why the sudden change?" asked the last man remaining.

"Make things faster, you know. Alana's only ten. How hard could she be to deal with?" Tegan shrugged and smiled that smile Giselle got the first time she saw him.

"Think ya will soon find children very troublesome," the man said whilst eyeing Giselle.

"I can manage," said Tegan. "In the meantime, let's try the impossible and kill three birds with one stone. There are a few people who saw Alana after she ran off from Giselle. You know what to do, Adman."

Bowing humbly the graying Adman took off on his own journey.

"Why you send them away?" Giselle asked following Tegan into the bushes as he instructed.

"Cause the two of us are goin' to get Alana instead," he said.

"But you was goin' to get her with all three of them initially?" She kept poking at him.

"Plans change." Tegan shrugged.

He guided her through the bushes along the path Alana had taken in her hasty escape. Giselle, being on a roll, paraded one question after the next. She wanted to know how he knew so much about Alana and where to go. He said that this was actually the simplest mission he had ever gone on. Since the story of Alana's return was still fresh in Grenada all he had to do was listen to the news and hang around a few old shops and listen to gossip. From what he gathered he deduced that Alana was a Shaman that was capable of shape-shifting which wasn't uncommon. Most female shaman's had an animal they could take the form of if necessary; it was usually a hare. He went on to explain why that was the exact reason why the people of the normal world had so many superstitions about them. As easy as the words slid off his tongue Giselle still couldn't believe that in the short space of time they had split up, he had gathered a team and was on the move. She continued to question him about his recruiters and why he was so protective of her identity, but he did well to evade those questions. Surely impressing her with some magic would take her mind off it. They were bordering St. David's and had the task of finding their way deep into St. Johns. That was no short travel. In efforts to shorten the trip Tegan had jinxed a broad piece of wasted ply wood. It was now floating at light speed through the town of St. George; every now and then Tegan glanced at a digital map to check that he was heading the right way.

"Majesty is actually way more advanced than Tlos ever was," he struck up a new topic.

"What was Tlos like?" She asked.

Pieces of Ecoli's story danced its way through her mind. It must have been an extremely violent and backward place. The way it destroyed itself so easy was almost impressive. Giselle couldn't imagine what it must have been like back then when it was everyman for themselves.

"Brutal," was all Tegan said to describe it. "I've never been there personally, but my parents aren't exactly young even though they appear so." He chuckled.

"They born there?" Giselle was beyond interested at this point.

"Yeah," said Tegan. "They were only children when everythin' went down. They didn't know each other back then. They're both Shamans. Majesty's elders."

Giselle chuckled.

"I'm not complainin' though. If they didn't choose to live this long I might not have been born." He shrugged.

They crossed over some great expanse of bushes that had mist wound between it like hair in a used brush. Checking his map again Tegan announced that they were almost there. Knowing this, they started descending a great deal.

"So…" Giselle paused briefly.

Should she ask him what she was thinking? With the way he had been acting tonight he might not even tell her the truth. Plus, this was something she had originally wanted to find out herself. Still, Tegan was considerably easier to talk to than Ecoli. He didn't have an air that made her nervous nor rapid mood swings. And he wasn't intimidating seeing that he wasn't the chief of anything.

"Tlos," she hesitated. "Who… what it have there now? Is it deserted?"

He noticeably seized in front of her jerking his steering of the ply wood.

"Um-uh," he stuttered. "Yeah."

His words were too crisp and uncertain. She narrowed her eyes taking in view of the back of his head for a while in a suspicious sort of way. Why won't he answer her truthfully? Tegan was good at keeping secrets as he clearly displayed here. He was just terrible at lying. In spite of the awkward silence dawning on them Tegan pulled the ply wood to a rough landing on a river bank surrounded by trees. The water was rushing naturally down its path beating against the big rocks and making crashing noises. The bank, just like the river, was plagued with rocks as well. They were exceptionally large, protruding their round, smooth heads from the ground all over the place giving footing for them to climb. The path from the river had an upward slope. At first glance, one would think they were in the middle of the woods; no sign of life, the darkness, the rushing of the fresh water, and bustling of the trees. But there in the darkness, almost hidden in the mist of the night, was a little old wooden house. It was engulfed in the trees and standing lonely on top of the hill. The lights in the house were off causing the blackness of the window and giving the house a sense of abandonment.

With ease Tegan made his way up the rocks zig-zagging through them looking for the easiest way up. Giselle on the other hand was having a hard time keeping up. It was too much climbing, too much turns and twists and slipping for her liking. After only thirty seconds she was already panting leading Tegan to offer her a hand. Who could build their home in such a deserted uncivilized place? She was cursing to the ends of heaven and earth about the location of this house and how hard it was just to get there. Why would Tegan land so far off if he knew where he was going? This wasn't funny in the slightest. She was starting to regret asking to go with him.

"Tegan," she called breathlessly in the darkness.

She couldn't see him properly although it was debatable whether it was actually that dark or if she was just that tired.

"Stop for a minute," she said.

"I was stoppin'," he spoke casually. "We're here."

Giselle glanced up at him, clutter minded, knowing that they were only half way to the house. Before she could form the question, why they hadn't gone all the way up, he pointed to a concrete tomb structure that stood largely across from them. It lived ominously among the rocks like a dreaded king reining over all; tall and lit by the moon.

"She's in there," he sounded disappointed.

"You sure?" Giselle asked stealing another glance at the crooked house.

"I'm sure." Tegan confirmed.

He walked easily alongside the path, Giselle stumbling to her feet to go after him. It was a warm night. Or maybe it was because she was moving so much it felt warm. The mist certainly gave a different definition of the night. As they both made their way around the tomb Giselle could have sworn she heard sniffing. It was faint and almost went unnoticed. Stifled; as though the person it was emanating from was putting effort into staying silent. Where was that coming from? Surely, she hoped, it wasn't from the tomb. She prayed the tomb wasn't housing the source of this desperate cry. When they got to the front of it there were metal bars forming a blockade at the mouth. They were rusted and bent and had a huge padlock dangling from the brand new latch in the corner that didn't match its surroundings. Stooping low enough that his head was leveled with the tomb Tegan peered into the darkness. The moon light was in such a convenient position that it shined light directly down on it. Still, it wasn't enough. Light doesn't bend corners and so only the back wall of the tomb was alight. The corners and direct front of it was shaded hiding the whimpering soul within.

"Alana." Tegan called gently.

Watching from behind him Giselle was skeptical. What made him believe it was Alana in there? She was only a ten-year-old girl; added to that she had been missing for weeks and was discovered not too long ago. If anything, she would be with her family right now. As far as Giselle was concerned Alana had the best care during the time spent with her so there was no reason she shouldn't be home.

"It's ok if you don't want to talk." Tegan continued. "Most people don't."

The sniffing stopped.

"Most of them have already been through enough and think I'm just another person coming to belittle them." He eased closer to the tomb. "I know you're not afraid of hearin' voices this late at night. There's not much for you to be afraid of is there?"

He paused and waited as though he was giving her time to digest the few words he had spoken. Meanwhile the area around them had become considerably quiet. Suddenly the rushing of the river and rustling of the trees and random snapping of sticks and calling animals were all distant sounds. They didn't matter much anymore. Her own breathing had become distant to her, Giselle, as she was so enticed with what was happening. She was caught off guard when a young, scared, tortured voice reached out of the dark lifeless hole.

"No," it said.

So Alana was really in there? Why?

"There's not much for me either." said Tegan. "There are a lot of things people hope aren't real. Those things are my life. I bet you could say the same."

This time she said nothing.

"My name is Tegan. I can do magical things too. You're not a freak. I know you probably think you are, but you're not."

"Magic is not real," the girl's voice rose weakly.

"That's what you were told." Tegan fully sat down next to the tomb crossing his legs like a pretzel. "But you know better, don't you?"

"Mommy say magic not real!" She screeched.

Overhead Giselle heard a few birds scatter from the trees.

"But you've done it before, Alana. You're a shape-shifter." He told her.

"No," her voice was small again. "How you know my name?"

"Well," Tegan started up conversationally. "My friend told me that you needed help. You were her pet, I think. So naturally I did some research so that I could find you. It's my job to help people like you, you know."

It was the moment of truth. Once those words left his mouth they could hear echoed shifting noises. It was as if some interest was sparked and the little girl was aroused now.

"What frien'?" She asked.

"The one that took you out of the cage. She apologizes for keepin' you in there." Tegan stole a glance at Giselle giving her a weak smile.

More shifting noises. They were becoming regular now. Almost persistent until a small head popped up at the far side of the little set up, outside the reach of the moon light. They couldn't see her face or any type of detail, but they knew that the girl was watching them hard now. She was standing still in the corner.

"Tell me," Tegan began again, "why are you out here?"

"You," Alana's voice had some realization in it. "You take me out of the cage."

Giselle felt rigid. She didn't expect to be addressed at all; she would much rather watch Tegan work. He was so good at it. Knowing Alana was now looking directly at her, Giselle nodded.

"I didn' want to come out!" She snapped. "You think if I wanted to I would still be there?"

Giselle hadn't a clue how to respond. She could feel herself sinking deeply into her pit as the seconds ticked by. Why was this whole thing so tense? They were only talking.

"Why not?" Tegan asked.

"Cause if I was there I wouldn' be here." Her head sank again and Giselle assumed she was sitting.

"Want to tell me more about that?" Tegan rubbed the palm of his hands down his lap.

"No," she growled. "I don' know you. How I know you not just like everybody else?"

"Good question." Tegan seemed to be waiting on her to ask this. "For one, I don't talk like you so you know I'm not just some local messing with you. Secondly, do you really think anyone would come this close, this late at night, to someone they thought was a shape-shifter?"

"Not even my mother," Giselle could have sworn she heard her mumble.

"And last, but not least," Tegan stated then went to work.

He rubbed his hands together in preparation for whatever it is he was about to do. His eyes were closed and he focused for a second; still rubbing his hands a bit excessively now. Then after speaking the words "give me light" he pushed his hands forth and a small blimp of orange light illuminated the tomb.

"I'm just like you. You're safe," he said.

Alana must have been in just as much shock as Giselle. Giselle had seen Tegan do magic ample times since she had come to know him. Yet every time she saw it, it felt like the first time. Alana stood up again. This time they could see what she looked like. She was skinny and had a head that was slightly too big for her body. Her eyes were wide and hard and she had a rather defined lip complimentary to the wound making home on it. Her appearance gave the look of exhaustion like someone who had struggled their whole life. What type of trouble could a ten-year-old get into to land herself here?

"You do that?" She gaped at Tegan.

"I can do a lot more than that," he assured.

The little light blimp floated lazily to her and landed on her shoulder. Staring at it emotionally a sob left her lips involuntarily and her eyes became flushed with tears.

"So.." he went closer to the bars pulled a hand kerchief out of thin air and handed it to her. Instead of wiping the fresh tears welling up in her eyes she wiped her bloody lips.

"Why are you out here?" He asked again.

A few more sobs left her before she said, "I hate my mom."

"Don't say that," Tegan instructed.

"I hate her! I hate her!" She yelled defiantly. "She put me here."

Alana squeezed her eyes shut to hold in whatever she was feeling.

"My mom was cussin' me and my dad was beatin' me. They see me make somethin' float once and ever since they been doin' that and callin' me a witch. I tell them I didn' get involve in anything bad. I just know how to do that somehow, but they wouldn' believe me. They say am the devil," she confessed.

"I don't think you're the devil." Tegan spoke easily as Alana continued to swallow her sobs.

"I run away from home. But she," Alana pointed Giselle viciously, "she find out I was there. I didn' know if I could trust her so I run."

Giselle could feel the guilt build in her, but also a little rage from the accusations. How was she to know Alana was in hiding? How was she to know that anyone would rather a life as a pet?

"I assure you Giselle is good people." Tegan spoke on her behalf once again.

"When I get home they pretend they happy for people and then beat me for runnin' off. They think I went and get mix up in more witchcraft. That is why they put me in here to sleep." She broke down causing the little light on her shoulder to shake casting dancing shadows. "I don' want to be here. I want to run away again."

"Don't be rash." Tegan said. "I can talk to your parents. That is, if you want me to."

"No!" She snapped at him again. "I doh want them to take me back. I want them dead."

"Don't ever say that again." Tegan wagged a warning finger at her. "It might just be words now, but words can become actions faster than you realize; especially for someone like you who only has to think about killing a person to make it happen."

Alana noticeably withdrew from the opening at the sudden seriousness in Tegan's voice. Giselle couldn't take her eyes away from him either. Where did that come from?

"Well is the truth," she clung to the hand kerchief timidly.

"Still, don't let what everyone else think of you define who you are. You can't force people to accept you-"

"But is my mother! My mother..." she dropped to her knees. "I shouldn' have to ask her to. I shouldn' have to make her. She jus' should."

"Something as common as blood doesn't change a person's beliefs," Tegan stated.

This conversation had more effect on Giselle than she ever thought it would. Here was a little girl realizing that she had all these strange abilities. Here was Alana innocently thinking that she might be different, but she was going to have help getting through it. And then there were her parents and their reaction to the whole situation. The way they treated her was excessive and uncalled for. Giselle couldn't help but question how bad she must have been treated to choose to live as a pet for the rest of her life. On top of that, knowing her father, she wondered if she'd soon know the answer if she ever revealed to him anything whatsoever about Majesty. Sure, he was sweet now, but what if he did a complete 180 on her? What if she ended up just like Alana; running? Tegan didn't see, but in the same moment Alana fell to her knees Giselle plopped back on a rock dazed in unwanted thoughts.

"There's a place I can take you." Tegan spoke after silence that was too long. "It's filled with people just like you and Giselle and I. No one is going to ridicule you for being different. Actually, it's quite the opposite. People love hearing about what each other can do. They're all very accepting there. I can even find you new parents and get you enrolled into a school. You can make friends that might be far weirder than you are. You can levitate anything you want in front of them without them running off. They may even make a game out of it. There's no need to worry about anything because a lot of effort goes into the wellbeing of children. I have a friend named Hozen; he makes sure of that."

Giselle was listening keenly and oddly enough everything Tegan said sounded inviting. Even Alana was bought. She raised her head hopefully to look at Tegan eating up every piece of his words. She was almost in disbelief that a place so wonderful truly existed. It was then Giselle understood. Majesty wasn't just some spring chicken magical world. It was so much more than that. It was a stronghold that provided shelter for the lost, weak and fallen. It was a place for people who felt like they had nowhere else to turn. It was for people who felt like they didn't belong in the normal world anymore. It was a place that allowed those people to just be free and be themselves without fear of being torched by an angry, ignorant mob. And as a guardian, it would be her job to ensure that those people continued to feel safe and welcomed and like they had someone looking out for them. Guardians were responsible for making sure cases like Alana's never flourished. If they did, it was their job to make sure they weren't prolonged. They were the sense of security that people like Alana needed. Majesty was a place where they could go to feel alive and accepted. Instead of living like a hobbit in the normal world. That was something Giselle didn't mind being a part of; especially since she was risking her own home life to do so. If indeed she did fall on the other end of her father's wrath she knew that there would be a place she could turn to. With that, finally, she had a reason to overlook her grandmother's secret-keeping and her grudge and accept the offered post as a guardian. Sure, she still wanted to understand what went down between Ruby and her mother, Grace, but it wasn't influencing her decision anymore.

~*~

"I don' like none of you." Giselle said from her position on the couch Monday afternoon.

Amron and Andre had been gone since morning and just now returning. It was Carnival Monday. She was especially mad because she wanted to go with them and her dad told her she couldn't. She was "too young" for that crowd. Typical. Emma got to go and she was only fifteen. She knew children younger than her that took part in Jouvert. When she presented this argument to her dad he simply said, "Well that is other children business." Stupid Amron and Andre always had to milk every opportunity to tease her and boast. All weekend they were giving her hell. This added fuel boosted Amron to wake her up every morning even more annoying than he used to before. Every damn morning!

He would shake her awake and say, "Come listen to dad sayin' why you can' play jouvert small girl."

Then Andre would be by her door to chorus behind him. "Maybe when you start wakin' up by yourself in the mornin' you could lime with big people."

"Well I wouldn' know if I could wake up for myself if you doh leave me alone in the mornin'." Then she'd walk away from them.

During the time leading up to Carnival Monday, her conversations with Vrai had become more frequent. Giselle didn't want to talk to Vrai. She had nothing to say to her actually, but Vrai blatantly didn't give a dime about what Giselle felt. She kept going on with her "Now that you are a guardian in training" speech in the most random places. A few times Giselle had to pretend she was the one talking and lie about reciting lines from an old show called "Wizards of Waverly Place". Vrai kept telling Giselle that she had to keep on her toes and pay keen attention to her surroundings and be considerate of others. To this point Giselle hadn't a clue what there was to be paying 'keen attention' to. She also told her to look deep within herself and find what she was really exceptional at. That way it would be easier for Ecoli to place her in a group. Apparently most guardians entered Majesty already highly classed in whatever skill they needed to do service to the place. The training period was to develop their skills in other things they weren't so fortunate to be good at and to get them acquainted with Majesty. Giselle on the other hand, alongside the others, came off as talentless. Or at least that was what Vrai said. She gave Giselle a hard time about the fact that she learned not too long ago that she could fly and she wasn't making any effort to learn how to do it well. Not only that, she made it quite clear that she found it absolutely hilarious that Marko felt the best way to teach her was to throw her off of high places in hopes that she had just as much luck as the first time. It was like deja-vous all over again with him. That was how she learned Marko could manipulate timelines; he could fast forward it, rewind it or even freeze it. He'd become so skilled that he could control the timelines of several people at once without affecting anyone else around them. At the end of the day Giselle was more stressed than she had ever been. Vrai's voice had become like a woodpecker working at her skull.

She had just made her appearance in Majesty for yet another day. She was already mad at her brothers for leaving her be-hind; mad at Vrai for continuously making her existence known and mad that she, after all this time, still couldn't master flying. Wasn't she supposed to be good at this stuff? Why was it prov-ing so difficult? Not to mention Tegan was behaving just as awkward as he had the night they found Alana. Boys! They were so annoying. This was enough to keep anyone angry for days. Now seeing Marko leaving the girls room looking all sus-picious made her madder. Why she felt ill about this? She couldn't answer that.

"Um, what you doin'?" Giselle asked.

He spun around like he didn't expect to be seen.

"Oh, Gizzy!" He held his heart.

"That sign say female, Marko." She folded her arms.

"Oh it does?"

He turned around and scanned it for a minute. He strategically rested his hand on the door blocking out the first two letters in the word.

"I see male."

Giselle shook her head as she approached him. She moved his hand.

"Well would you look at that!" He feigned surprise.

"Move." She pushed him out of the way.

"So hostile," he exaggerated the push by throwing himself back. "What's wrong?"

"Nothin'," she shrugged opening the door.

"Nope. Something's wrong," he said pulling her back and hugging her around the neck. "Hugs make it all better." Giselle tried to push his arms away. "No, no. Just let it happen."

She exhaled loudly and rolled her eyes. He finally let go.

"Feel better? Yes? I knew you would." He grinned, snapped his fingers and walked away.

All she could do was fight back the smile and change into her jumpsuit uniform. He was so strange.

Giselle was currently working in the medical unit with Tegan. They completed patrol last week. It wasn't that bad. She was studying her manual during the day and seeing the laws put in place when she went on duty. It was just like Tegan said, Floral Cove was a very self-controlled place. There weren't many scenes for them to take control of. She hadn't yet been introduced to Nocturn Niche or Heavenly Heights. According to Tegan they had their own patrollers who originated from the respective cities. They all still operated under Ecoli's orders, but there were division leaders that relayed messages between the cities.

While working with him she was known as "Giselle, the girl I met in the back streets". It bothered her that he wouldn't introduce her properly to people. No one paid mind to her presence anyway. They were all briefly interested in why he paraded her through the Sub HQ, but none cared beyond that. They didn't even know she went to the Official HQ or else they might have brought that up in their hushed discussion with Tegan as though she couldn't hear. Added to that, these people didn't seem to have a clue who she was. What happed to people wanting to know the granddaughter of Ruby? Then again, if Tegan would just introduce her properly maybe they would.

She entered the Rec. Room on her way to meet Tegan when she ran into Marko again. He had the silver thermos that belonged to Ecoli and he was pouring a strange glittery liquid from a small tube into it. He looked up frightened for a second time, but calmed down once he saw it was her. Second time this morning he was acting strange. What was he up to?

"Oh," he wiped his fore head. "It's just you."

"What you doin'?" She made her way over to him.

"Helping Eco-loco," he said nonchalantly and covered the thermos.

"By doin'?"

"Exactly what I just did."

He smirked and headed out the door. She followed him. Something about this didn't seem right.

"So, I was thinking we could go to the falls and I'd help you with your flying."

"Ok," she said torn between discussing flight lessons and figuring out what was in that thermos.

Marko made his way to the kitchen door then turned around and stopped her.

"Don't come in. Mission 'evade Ariel' in progress."

He spoke like he was in some sort of James Bond movie. Then he disappeared behind the door. Seriously, what was he doing? She walked back to the Rec. Room door to continue along her original path when Tegan entered HQ. He looked exhausted, sweaty, flushed and in dire need for some sleep.

"Oh, g'day," he greeted. Attest to Giselle's examination of him he said, "Shaman and a Loveland Frog got into it. You don't even want to know."

Marko came back out talking into his shirt. "Mission completed. Damage - negative."

"You know is not really stealth mode when you talk so loud before you go in and when you come out," she scolded. "Then again there is logic and then there is Marko logic."

"More like common sense and Marko sense." Tegan chimed in.

"Who christened today 'gang up on Marko day'?" He asked while looking up in the air like a diva. Neither of them responded. "Good," he headed out the way Tegan came.

Tegan smiled and ran his fingers through his hair.

"What he does do again?" Giselle inquired.

"Honestly, if I got that question on an exam I would fail," he chuckled. "Marko's brain is like… like the wheel in price is right except with pictures. And whatever the red arrow lands on that's what he does."

Giselle laughed at Tegan trying to make sense of Marko on a whole. While they were talking Ecoli came strolling from the Universal Passage.

"Hey," he greeted them. "S'up?"

"Nothing, I'm just here dying because I'm thirsty. No biggy." Tegan joked casually.

"Thanks for the advance notice. Gon have to take care o're-cruit while I look for a new lead." Ecoli said.

"No prob," Tegan showed thumbs up.

"Giselle?" He looked at her.

"Waitin' for trainin', but I have a feelin' it might be canceled," she felt good to join their banter.

"I'll find a replacement for ya." Ecoli joked and went into the kitchen.

A few seconds later Marko showed up again.

"Oh yeah, Gizzy when I said I'd help you I meant right now."

He gestured her outside in an authoritative manner. She looked at Tegan for confirmation. He showed her thumbs up then disappeared into the male's room. Right after Ecoli came out again holding the thermos Marko had a while ago.

"Eco-late!" Marko greeted.

"One day…" Ecoli defended. "A little more and ya might kill me."

"I just might." Marko smiled.

Ecoli chuckled and disappeared down the steps. Giselle did not like Marko's choice of words.

~*~

"Pious falls." Marko answered Giselle's questions as he made his way up the slippery rocks.

They were at the falls; Giselle, Marko and Scout. It was a small secluded place. The water was clear, sparkling even, and appeared as if it was floating. If she didn't see the massive slab of red rock beneath she would have thought it was. It was flowing airily into a wide and deep pond that seemed to never overflow. There were a lot of trees around the place keeping it hidden. If someone ever went there on their own and got in-jured, crying out wouldn't attract any attention. The place was too secluded and something about it suggested that it blocked out everything outside its premises and caged whatever was in it. It was breathtaking. To get there they had to walk the same path Ecoli took her on to get to the grave yard except they took a detour on one of the many twisting bridges.

"They say its s'pos to be sacred or holy or whatever, but Scout's here so it can't be," he continued with his playful tone.

Scout's lips crawled up in a slick, easy smile. "Ha.Ha."

In all her life, Giselle had never met such an unenthusiastic, person. He didn't put effort into his words or anything at all.

If he was any calmer he would be dead. Something besides her having to inhale his second-hand smoke just didn't sit well with her. He was just too mellow.

"It's probably semi-religious."

Marko finally made it to the top. Giselle was lost. There goes that Marko sense again.

"Scout, I'll give you fifty points if you get in the water."

"Ya don' like me, d'ya?" Scout groaned coarsely.

Marko laughed.

"Can' swim or somethin'?"

Sure, she was asking about Scout who was right there, but she directed her question to Marko. He was too difficult to talk to. Yes, Marko was random, but his random was funny. Scout's random had you questioning yourself. Without answering her, Marko heaved forward and did the most ungraceful dive mankind had ever seen. In the process, he must have splashed all the water from the pond onto Giselle and Scout. Giselle jumped to her feet shielding herself as if she wasn't going to get wet anyway. It was weird, but the water felt sensational. It was smooth and perfectly cool against her skin as if it was hugging her with a mother's love. Or like she was rolling in on a cloud. Scout didn't seem to think this at all. The sudden sound of his voice surging through the air shocked her. One thing she didn't know and had no idea was even a possibility; Scout can shout.

"MARKO!"

Her head snapped in Scouts direction where he was rubbing his arms and legs furiously. He was acting as though he had an itch that he couldn't bear. Every place the water had touched was smoking and singed. He looked like a piece of wood whose fire had died out.

"Blasted son of a bitch!"

The look of horror on Giselle's face matched Marko's. Scout didn't even acknowledge Marko shouting, "It was an accident!" He just left still rubbing the smoking patches on his skin. Both of them watched him leave before Marko spoke again.

"I guess it is religious."

"Wha…"

"Don't worry about him. Come on, climb the rocks. Time to fly."

"Right now? Wait, what happen to Scout?"

"He needs prayers." Marko choked out a laugh, but it wasn't his confident, boisterous laugh. It was nervous and shaky.

"Come on slow poke."

The humor wasn't even trying to stay in his tone anymore. Maybe it was an inside thing. After all, both Marko and Scout were in dispatch which made them partners. Maybe Marko crossed line a that they had set. It was obvious Scout wasn't much of a joker and probably Marko's playfulness rubbed off as annoying to him. That didn't explain why he had such a dramatic reaction to the water, but it still said something.

Giselle reluctantly started climbing up the slimy red rocks. Patches of moss and grime washed over it and it was nothing but a delight to touch; not in the slightest. Luckily Giselle wasn't as scornful as Ming or she'd have never made it up. Those rocks were disgusting up close. Scenery- A plus, feel- F. The whole way up she was thinking back to the first time she figured out she could fly. When Marko pushed her over a cliff and instead of feeling terrified she felt winded and confused and drenched in déjà-vous. She was also thinking about all the rock climbing she had been doing and dreading the whole physical aspect of this guardian gig.

"How you go help me? I just have to keep fallin' until I learn not to?" Her tone was full of resentment to that plan.

"Unfortunately, no." Did this fool just say unfortunately?

"Thank God." Giselle sighed relief.

"You little coward. You'll be swimming." Marko teased. He was climbing up behind her. "You're lucky Tegan's your trainer. He was all like *'Marko you can't push her of a cliff. There's so many ways that could go wrong. Just cause you can control time doesn't give you permission'.*" He mocked Tegan's accent and failed. Giselle laughed. "Like, dude, grow a pair. Yeah, so I was like Gizzy's tough she doesn't look like a cry baby and he's all like…"

At that precise moment she reached the top and the view wasn't even the source of the satisfied feeling inside of her. Sure, the view was like bait to the eyes. The river on the top swerved all the way back to the horizon and the abundant number of flowers that swarmed the banks put the botanical gardens to shame. Surprisingly, all that fell into the okay region because Marko saying she was tough took the top spot.

"…and now I have to use my head because apparently I never do that. I guess they think I've been thinking with my ass my whole life," was what she caught in the end of his long-drawn rant. She didn't even notice that he made it up and was standing next to her.

"You really think that?"

"Well obviously I don't think with my ass, geesh! You too?"

"No dummy," she shook her head. "If you think I tough?"

"Oh." he was rubbing his hand over his bare water painted chest. "Yeah. You look it."

"Well you, my brother and my uncle is the only people to think that," she mumbled to herself, but Marko had sharp ears.

"Hey, how others see you is not important. How you see yourself is all that matters."

He stared deep into her eyes. She nodded. Marko started to grin.

"I so copied that from a facebook picture, but it makes a hell a lot of sense doesn't it?"

He moved behind her. She turned around intending to follow his lead, but he held her shoulder and kept her facing straight forward.

"Ok clear your... wait, you should probably take your stuff off unless you're ok with your clothes getting wet." He rambled.

"I don' mind," she confirmed after kicking off her shoes.

"Okay. Just relax for a bit and when you feel ready jump off, but not like your diving. Do it like you're a bird about to show people you're the shit because you don't have to walk to get places." He tapped her shoulder for reassurance then stepped back.

Giselle tried to do as he told her, but her mind was congested. She was in Floral Cove in some other world. Apparently, her grandmother was chief there and she wanted to share this world with Giselle, but for some reason only after she was dead. She was an Ersatz and she could fly, but she didn't know how to do it on her own. She had to go through training to be a guardian and it was way more underwhelming than she thought it would be. No one wanted to accept the fact that even though she was fourteen, she could handle herself. Plus, she had finally seen with her own eyes what Majesty was worth, but she still couldn't see the importance of the documentor, dispatch, and recon units. She still couldn't figure out what Majesty had to be protected from and whenever she raised the topic no specific answer was given. The way they went on about it, she could tell it was more than just the normal world they were hiding from. A world filled with supernatural creatures couldn't protect itself? All this was running through her mind. Every day she seemed to have a new sentence to add to this list of uncertainties. It was bothering her; weighing her down. She took another deep breath before telling herself "be quiet and jump already". Then, after opening her arms like they were wings, she jumped off the edge.

Why was it so hard to climb up, but so easy to fall back down? She was slipping and sliding on those rocks on the way up and had to use everything she had to get up there. Yet in less than a second she was splashing into the water beneath her. Jump number one: failed.

"That's all you got?" Marko shouted from the top.

"Look so," she shouted back from the water.

Her clothes were soaked all the way through and her hair was wet and dripping. She swam over to the side and climbed onto the bank making her way back to him. She needed to get this. She needed to do it right. What was the point of having the ability to fly when she couldn't take off? What did Marko see anyway? She was just like a big log tumbling off a cliff over and over again. Jump number two: failed. Jump number three: failed. Number four, five, ten, thirty-five, all failed. Each time she was getting more frustrated, winded, annoyed and heavy. Even the day was growing tired of her as the sun slowly began to set and shy away from her failure. Turns out water made you tired; who knew right? Note the sarcasm.

The last time she climbed back up she wasn't even in the mood to try anymore. To make it worst some song birds came around to terrorize her. Fashioned in different colours, they swarmed around her head with their unblinking bug eyes each singing a different ballad. The one she heard the loudest was:

What goes up must come down

Unless it's you, you'll never leave the ground

She flopped down on the river bank and covered her head screaming. Marko had to save her from them just like the first time they met. She was just as helpless now as she was that time. No change. Marko prodded her with his toe.

"Come on, you can't fly if you're lying down."

"I can' fly at all," she covered her face with her wet hands.

She was too busy beating herself up in her head to think about anything now. The next time those birds attacked if she couldn't fend them off then she was officially useless. That was her rule. That was the standard she was setting for herself. She at least had to fend off a songbird.

"Yes, you can. Don't even say that."

He grabbed her wrist and pulled her up. About five birds were lying unconscious around her.

"When you fall, I don't know if you notice this, but you glide. You don't just drop like a normal person would. You need to know how to take control of that."

She glides? She doesn't glide. She hit the water like a brick.

"Close your eyes," he spoke in a soothing tone while bringing her to the edge of the fall again. "Clear your mind. Forget all those failed attempts. Forget the outside world. Forget everything. Just focus on you and where you want to go." He smoothed out her hand so that her fingers were straight and together as if she was about to swim. "When you're ready."

For a long time, all Giselle could hear was her breathing and the rushing sound of the river emptying below. Slowly she was becoming relaxed. She submitted to the darkness brought on by her eyelids. The wind was blowing gently and made the atmosphere cool and in the distance she could swear she heard a howl and a few birds chirping. There were so many strange sounds around to be honest. None of which she could identify, but she didn't notice them before because her mind was so loaded. Sometimes we get so entangled in the world and what we must do that we forget to slow down and take in the view. After the long silence, she felt herself step forward. Almost involuntarily, her arms lifted a little beside her and before she knew it she was dropping off the cliff. She wasn't thinking about hitting the water or plummeting helplessly or even how to steer up. She was just falling and for the first time in her life falling felt so sensational. The wind was blowing through her hair and against her cheeks and beating against her ears. Maybe she did glide when she fell. She liked the weightless floaty feeling she was having for once.

"Gizzy! Look down!" She faintly heard her name.

Was Marko calling her? Why did he sound so distant? Why look down; why not look up? She opened her eyes to see what his yelling was about, but she didn't just see him. She saw landscape. The trees formed a perfectly thick barrier around Pious falls and it separated it from everything else just like she had assumed. Beyond it a wide mouthed river flowed down to Floral Cove. On the other side, where the river seemed to dance off into the nothingness of the horizon there was another waterfall that appeared to be flowing up instead of down. Then, way below her was the tiny outline of the person she called Marko waving excitedly at her. How did she get this high? And how was she maintaining it? Last time she opened her eyes she ended up on the ground. But this time she stayed afloat and in motion. She felt right at home up there; like the sky was where she needed to be. Her arms were opened out beside her as she curved around and prepared to go in for the landing.

"Holy crap! Marko! You seein' me right?" She yelled at him as she got closer.

"Where are you?" He yelled back looking everywhere, but in her direction.

She laughed. Giselle was overjoyed. Never in her wildest dreams did she think she would be flying one day, but here she was. Flying. Not landing.

"Ok slow down." Marko put up his hand. "Slow down or stop or something, Gizzy!" He yelled as she got closer, but she had no clue how to do that and ended up ramming into him head first. Marko stumbled back to the edge and both of them went tumbling over the edge and into the water.

Marko shot up kicking his legs and treading the water to stay afloat.

"That was awesome!" He spit some water before talking in a choked voice. "You killed it!" He hi-fived her.

Giselle grinned. "I know cause I'm a boss!" She picked up a superior tone too thrilled to keep herself from giggling when she finished talking.

"Now that we got you in the air we need to figure out how to get you back on land." He wiped his face again.

"Yeah, but in the meantime swimmin' race!" She pushed him under water before taking off to the bank.

"You dirty cheat!" He yelled when he resurfaced.

They practiced some more and she was getting good on the takeoff, but not the landing. Marko joked about having a concussion by the time they were done.

"I like your chain," Giselle randomly complimented while they were resting up. "Especially that stone."

They were sitting on the banks drying off before putting on their shoes and heading back.

"Oh this," Marko lifted it. "Thanks. It's an Opal. This is my most favorite thing I own."

"You don' have much stuff I guess?" She smart mouthed and raised her brow.

"Say what you want," he chuckled. "I'm never taking this thing off. The opal glows with body heat. The day it stops glowing is the day I die."

They let the talk fall before conversing again.

"How was patrol?" He asked.

"Borin'. That all it have in Patrol? Jus' walkin' the road and tellin' people don' litter."

Marko chuckled. "No."

"That some kind of pre-trainin' or somethin'?"

"No," he denied again not furthering his reasons.

"Then what is the problem? Me?" She asked suddenly feeling insecure. "Or everybody jus' busy?"

She remembered the conversation she had overheard. Something big was happening faster than they had expected it to and they seemed very secretive about it. Since that meeting, Ming and Ariel were a bit scarce and Marcel was doing overtime in the hospital. She had also heard Tegan say he intended to stop bringing people into Majesty. One morning before they went out on training he told his unit that they wouldn't be bringing in new denizens. Instead they would keep watching over the ones they had intended to bring in and only act if that person was in desperate need. There was no more specification. Everyone seemed to just understand what he was talking about and when she asked him he diverted her attention to basic medical practices.

"The other day Ecoli wanted to tell the country something," she brought up.

Marko didn't appear surprised in the slightest that she knew of this discussion.

"That's what chiefs do. They talk to the people," he shrugged.

"What it was about?" She asked.

"A lot of important things the country needs to know," he stated vaguely.

"Like what?" Giselle grew impatient.

To her growing irritancy, Marko responded unrelatedly. "I think Tegan just doesn't know what to do with you."

She narrowed her eyes and screwed her features at the abrupt change in topic, "meanin'?"

"Well from my knowledge Tegan never does a job unless it's from the mission board. And all new guardians are trained in weapon control, combat and first aid right off the bat. And while all that's going on you do one mission after the next to gain experience, learn the country and meet people. Then after two months you're introduced to the public as an official guardian." He explained carefully.

"Then what the hell?" Why wasn't she doing that?

"Ecoli asked Tegan to look after you and I think Tegan thinks the best way to protect you is to not say anything. Ignorance is bliss." Marko started picking at his fingernail carelessly. "What? You thought you didn't have weapons because it wasn't time yet? Hell, I had mine the second day."

"That not fair. He didn' even give me a chance." She stood up.

"How responsible would Eco-leader be if he handed a fourteen-year-old girl a gun?"

"Since when you thinkin' about bein' responsible?"

"I'm not. That's why he's the chief because if I was, you'd have had the whole stash by now."

"I goin' and talk to Tegan."

She spoke through gritted teeth, grabbing her shoes and storming off. Marko took off running after her.

She couldn't believe it. She thought this was the place she could come and not have barriers because people thought she was "too young". Turned out the whole thing was a conspiracy. Ecoli took one look at her and shut down all her training and tried to fool her into thinking she was doing it. What was their problem? She could handle it! He didn't even have the courtesy to ask if she had ever been in a fight. She had been in plenty; enough to write a whole book series. That had to stand for something. Right? As a matter of fact, this whole thing didn't make any sense whatsoever. He was the one asking her to be a guardian in the first place. She was the one apprehensive about the whole idea. Yet he was the one withholding training and she was the one angry about it. How did that turn around happen? She couldn't help but question, what if Ecoli never wanted her to be a guardian in the first place. She stormed into RQ2 in search of Tegan with no success. Her next move was the training room, the rec. room, and kitchen. No Tegan, until finally she burst into the Male's room with no restraint from Marko. He was just strolling behind her.

"Tegan, you're about to get roasted!" He spoke overhead the fuming Giselle.

"Pardon me?"

Tegan rolled over in his bed. The room was set up just like the female's room only it was a bit messy.

"Why you didn' train me properly?" She rolled out the question.

Tegan, eyes barely open, put up his hand as to say stop.

"Whoa, whoa, whoa…" He paused and looked around confused. "What time is it?" He said hoarsely.

"That is not the topic of discussion!" She yelled.

Tegan pulled his pillow over his head. "I have a head ache," she heard his muffle voice.

"Tegan…"

"Look, I don't know why you're mad, but I'm sorry. I promise I'll make it up to you, whatever it is, tomorrow…"

"You're gonna regret saying that." Marko sang as he threw his stuff in a corner and started changing his clothes.

"Can one of you call Marcel please? I don't feel too good," he rolled over again this time facing the wall.

Giselle took a deep breath and tried to calm her nerves. He was sick. She couldn't blow up on him now. He even took front and apologized even though he had no clue why she was yelling at him. How could she stay mad at that? Sure, she was still irritated, but it wasn't specifically with him or anyone really. It was just the circumstances.

She sighed. "I goin' home. I go tell Marcel you lookin' for her."

CHAPTER TEN

FIRE-DEVIL OR FIRE ERSATZ

GISELLE MADE SURE she was in Majesty early the next day. Since finding out the whole training thing was a trick it was all she could think about. It put her to sleep that night she went home and haunted her all day. As if she didn't have enough to think about. Life wasn't exactly like bathing in a pot of gold at home. She had to catch Ecoli right when he came in. She knew he was always there early, but she never saw where he went after. Giselle already felt helpless at home; there was no need for him to make her feel helpless here too. When she stepped out of the mirror she caught a glimpse of him going into the kitchen so she followed.

"Ecoli," she called him when she entered.

He was making tea for his thermos. "S'up?"

Was that a new one or was that the one Marko had put the mysterious substance in? The memory of him acting all suspicious had just flown back into her head. Ecoli didn't appear sick so maybe what Marko put in there wasn't deadly. Or what if it was some sort of slow poison? Marko didn't seem at all like that type of guy so maybe she was just jumping to conclusions here. Him an Ecoli were close. They were friends. He would never do something like that, would he? Or was he one of those people that didn't like him and just wasn't open about it. Marko was too playful for such a change in character. Then again she had seen too many TV shows where the good guy turned out to be the mastermind behind the entire plot. Should she tell Ecoli or was he aware of what had happened? Maybe she should tell him, but not before she dealt with her problems first.

"Why I not doin' combat, weapon control and first aid trainin'?"

His attention snapped up to her. "Huh?"

"You know what I talkin' about," she folded her arms.

He sighed. "Is not time yet."

"When is time? Marko say you train guardians in that from day one," she responded.

Ecoli pursed his lips like he had been caught in a lie. He looked away from her and with an expression that said "damn you Marko". He took the plate with breakfast food that sat on the counter.

"I go tell ya when, yeah." He left.

Giselle pursued him straight into the Rec. Room. "You don' think I could do it?"

"I never say that." He sat down.

She noticed how he looked less friendly now. His movement was stiffer. He picked up his fork and started to eat like nobody's business.

"Then tell me what you sayin'," she insisted.

"Ya so persistent. I sayin' that I decided that ya not doin' that now. Just accept it," he responded impatiently.

"Why?" Giselle demanded.

"Because."

Was steam rising off his skin right now because Giselle could swear she was seeing steam? She wanted to think she was seeing things, but she was standing in Majesty. She was fully engrossed in a world where she could fly, and shop keepers turned into hares and her teacher could make things disappear with the snap of a finger and a few simple words. If she was seeing things, then this whole world had to be an illusion.

"Because is not an answer," she said. He kept eating. "Just give me a valid reason that don' have to do with assumptions and I go leave you alone."

"I make decisions for the safety o'the guardians and Majesty. If I say no trainin' then ya best understand that there is a damn good reason and I don' gotta explain myself!" He snapped.

"Ecoli! Stop behavin' so, nah!"

Suddenly his hair lit up in flames and he didn't even flinch. Giselle stepped back stunned. She wasn't expecting that. He stabbed his fork in the table and it stayed standing. This wouldn't be a big deal if the table was wooden, but it wasn't wood. The loud clang sound she heard could only be made from two pieces of metal hitting each other. The same time that happened Marko walked in.

"OH!" He gasped and grabbed Giselle's shoulder and walked her out. "Just borrowing her for a minute chief."

"Marko I not playin'. You can' see me havin' a conversation?" She was not intimidated by Ecoli one bit- not when getting what she wanted was on the line.

"Take as long as you want."

It annoyed her to hear Ecoli say that. He just retrieved his fork and went on eating once his hair fire went limp. When the door closed, Marko dragged her back to the Males room to talk privately.

"What you doin'?" She was mad.

"Saving your life." Not the answer she was expecting.

"What that s'pos to mean?"

"I guess we should start telling people this when they just step out of the mirror now? Don't shout at Ecoli."

Giselle was more taken aback that Marko actually said Ecoli's name right than she was about what he just said.

"Excuse me?"

"He's a fire Ersatz with anger issues. That's not a good combination. Yelling at him is like literally adding fuel to the fire; he will hurt you. Not intentionally, but he will. He's been trying to keep it under control, but that's really difficult when his magic is always pushing him to burn everything in his path."

Giselle, not caring about any of this, geared up to talk again. He was the chief. He had to listen to them.

"Well…"

"No. Listen to me," Marko stopped her. "I bet you saw how some people looked at him when he took you out the first day. That's because he probably had a run in with them for one reason or the other. They fear him. They act angry, but if he was to approach them they would run. Some of them think he's just pretending to be nice. That's not what he wants. That's why he hates his job."

She was seriously shaken up by Marko talking to her like her father. She had never seen Marko serious before. He usually failed at trying to look serious, but this was real. Giselle stared at him wordlessly trying to take in what he was saying, her own anger receding. Was that why the waiter told her watch her back?

"Then why he doh jus' step down?" She asked rudely.

"Ruby passed the torch to him. Ultimately Majesty choses, but she mentored *him*. Marcel, Ariel, Trevor or Hozen could easily take his place. Hozen and Trevor refuse and Ariel wants him to stop backing sown from challenges. Marcel told him not to let his insecurities run his life which means he's stuck with the job." Marko's tone was calmer now. He sat down on the bed in the corner of the room.

"Ok." She mumbled.

"There's more," he mumbled.

"K…" Giselle sat on the bed opposing him not knowing what to expect.

"There are spirits that live in Majesty commonly called fire-devils. All they do is scheme, trick, possess people and cause chaos. Everyone hates them."

"I thought only good people could come here."

"Who's to say they're not good people. They are what they are and that's what they do," he corrected. "The devils commonly travel in fire balls wherever they go. I don't know if you know this, but Marcel is from Heavenly Heights; she's an angel. With Ecoli being her brother people think he's a devil. They refuse to believe he's just an Ersatz with fire magic. Not many trust him as chief. He's under a lot of speculation."

"What you think?" She asked.

Hearing this cleared up a lot of things Giselle noticed about the sibling pair. Giselle always felt such a light, welcoming air around Marcel. She seemed to radiate beauty no matter what she did. Then there was Ecoli who walked with a noticeably, probably unintentional, hostility. There was a possibility he was a devil. He did have fire power and he blew up a little too easy. And, if devils were supposed to be these infamous schemers and tricksters then wasn't there a possibility he was pulling a fast one on all of them?

"I think he's my friend and I don't care what he is." Marko firmly stated. "What I care about is keeping him tamed. The less explosions he has the more they trust him. If you want something just talk to him. You'll get the answer."

"I go try. But…" she sighed. "He not exactly the "give-you-what-you-want" kinda person."

"If he gave you everything you wanted he wouldn't be a good chief, now would he?" Marko gazed at her sternly. Giselle couldn't respond- a familiar shame was growing strong within her. "Sometimes what we want is not what we need. The Ecoli that took you on a tour, the pleasant one, that's the real Ecoli. Remember that always. Don't shout at him. He has your best interest at heart."

With the way Marko spoke maybe he did just do her a huge favor. She probably would have been barbeque by now.

"Alright. Sorry," she sounded defensive.

"No need to apologize. Don't get all Tegan on me," he smiled. "Remember that time you saw me put stuff in his thermos?"

"Yeah?"

"I won't tell you what it was, but it helps calm him down. I don't do it every day just once in a while. He thinks he's being calm on his own and then on other days he tries to mock how he felt on those calm days. It works. Don't say anything though, because he doesn't know about it."

"You can' do that!"

"Yes I can," he said. "Don't worry. He's healthy."

Giselle shook her head. That was the end of that conversation.

For over a week Giselle focused on home. She went to Majesty, but only a handful of times for about an hour or two exploring headquarters and other places. She stumbled upon a hotel, where ideally the guardians were supposed to live. Ming made use of it as far as she found out, but the others either already had a home in Majesty or were comfortable outside of it. It was difficult for her to get into certain parts of headquarters since next to no one knew who she was so she kept getting put out when she was discovered. They wouldn't even let her explain. From there, Giselle wandered in Floral Cove for a bit. She travelled down new, to her at least, cobbled roads that lead to parks, malls and residential areas and made full use of the Rowdy Ruby. She discovered the National Magical Enlistment Centre, Ragunds Training Arena, Ghost Life Insurance and Claw Salon and Fang Repair. A distance from Floral Cove Square she ended up in a place called Silver Meadows where a very busy auto mechanic garage was operating. She found that the more she walked and the further she went signs- 98 miles north-east to Heavenly Heights, 280 miles west to Nocturn Niche- became frequent decreasing and increasing in values respectively. In a lot of ways Majesty was just like any country in the normal world. It had businesses, recreational and residential areas, government and denizen's that were just trying to make a living. It wasn't any different, she was learning, between being in there and being back home.

Tegan was sick so he couldn't train her. And she refused to do flight practice with Marko. Imagine all the things she could have known by now. She could have been trained in proper combat. She could have known how to wield a sword or have a katana of her own to call baby. She could have been out in Floral Cove patching up sick people until the Medic Squad showed up. She could have been out on missions. But no, Ecoli didn't think she could handle it. And now she was skeptical on whether to confront him again because of what Marko said. She wasn't afraid of him; not at all. She just wasn't confident in her ability to not shout. She tended to raise her voice when she got worked up about something. So now, in an effort to resist Majesty's pull, most of her days and nights were spent wastefully on social media, talking to Emma on the phone, dealing with her annoying brothers and praying that staying away was the best way to keep her family oblivious about the whole thing. Shutting Vrai up had become a true concern. She would be going back to school soon. Form 3S at The Anglican High School; new class, new teachers, new subjects. She should just worry about that for now. No second world problems. She needed all new books for that class. She managed to wrangle up a few from her older friends, but not everything. There were new books on the book list this year. On the topic of school, she needed new shoes, socks and a white belt. Amron needed new shoes and socks too. God alone knows how that foot of destruction worked. Andre was starting college, so he needed new everything. Brent wouldn't admit it, but he just couldn't afford all that. Andre was willing to use the school library for books instead of his dad getting them, but knowing

Brent that wasn't even an option. Giselle crossed him sorting out his budget and bills a few times over the summer vacation. Every time she asked him about it all he said was, "Don't worry". How could she not worry? He was having a hard time and it made her guilty every time she had to go to him for something new. That's why she always saved. That way she could afford her own stuff and not burden him.

There was a Facebook group for the band and the chat box was busy twenty-four-seven so she just joined in talking to them. She got satisfaction and a few good laughs from Amron because he kept typing "Stop talking to me!" All the while she was on the phone with Emma plotting how to mess with Cheddi and Rayanna in the group. Amron was on the couch outside listening to her in her room and selling out all her business in the group. After a while the conversation turned into the whole group planning a get together because they missed seeing each other every day. Amron was yelling "I doh miss you!" to Giselle from the living room.

Soon her room door opened without a knock and without checking she said, "Come out of my room." She thought it was Amron.

"Hang up the phone," her dad's voice made her freeze.

"Emma I have to go," she hung up.

"I bought four rabbits and a hare. It only have three animals in there now," he stated.

Three? She thought. *Oh God, we didn' lock the cage!*

"Where the rest?" At least he didn't sound mad at her. He was curious.

"Ummm," she hummed. How was she supposed to tell him Tegan, an Australian boy from Majesty, checked the cage for shape shifters and didn't lock it back. "Amron give them away."

Like that maybe?

Her dad had a sudden flash of anger across his face when he stormed out of her room. There was no doubt he was going to the living room where Amron was innocently talking in a group chat. Her stomach churned with guilt. Nope. She had to tell the truth. Could she?

"Tsk, tsk, tsk," she heard Vrai's fake disappointment.

"Shut up," she snarled at the chain and she dashed out after her father.

"What wrong with you, boy?" Brent took Amron's phone right out of his hand.

Amron was relaxed. "Right now or in general?"

"How you could give away our rabbits? You buy that?"

Amron was still relaxed, "Dad, I never…" he began, but noticed Giselle pleading in the back ground. She was terrified of telling the truth. "… thought you would realize." He finished smoothly.

"Well I did. Who you give?"

"Raheem."

"So if I ask him he go say he have it?"

"Yes," he said confidently.

Giselle knew Raheem had no knowledge of the rabbits, but she also knew he was Vice President Liar to President Liar (Amron) in Liars and Co. He would back up Amron first and ask questions later. That was exactly what Amron was doing for Giselle now.

"And you give him two? What happen to givin' him one?"

"Cheddi wanted one too."

"You either get it back or pay me for it," their dad ordered.

"No prob." Amron put the TV on.

Brent, mad at how calm Amron was said, "Take of that damn TV!" Then he left the room.

Giselle ran back to her room without a word. She was panicking. Her dad was mad at Amron, which wasn't anything new, but this time it was her fault. She had enough money saved up. She would just give Amron the money and let him use it as his own. Then they'd be even, right? When she snapped out of the daze she was in she went back on her bed and looked at the group chat. There were new messages:

Raheem- What the hell going on in your house?! Your dad talking to me on the phone right now @Amron @Gizzy

Emma- Lol. That's why you hang up?

Oh Brent. He didn't believe one word of what Amron said. It was a proud and terrifying moment for her. If he took Amron's words without investigation, then he didn't know his own son. He was smart to call Raheem. Giselle might have done it too if she was him. Giselle responded:

Gizzy- Tell him Amron give you two rabbits and you give Cheddi one.

Raheem- Way ahead of you.

Cheddi- Guess I should wait on my call then.

Rayanna- LMAO!

Now Chief Executive Liar was in on it too.

Her room door opened again. Instead of talking first, this time she looked to see who it was. Oh great. It was really Amron this time. She was not thrilled to see him. Now she had to explain why she had him lie for her and listen to him probably tell her she was crazy. She didn't even have enough time to come up with a proper lie for her father. She sighed. She already knew what he was going to say, but she just wasn't ready to confess.

"What you do with it?" He asked easily and not at all upset. This made her feel guiltier.

"I can' tell you," she responded. In a way that was the truth.

He narrowed his eyes. "Since when?"

"Today."

Amron made his way over and sat on her bed. "I jus' lie for you."

"Thanks." She clicked her tongue and went back to using Andre's laptop.

"Giselle." He stared at her. It felt awkward to hear her full name come from his mouth. "Just tell me what you do with it. You know I won' sell you out."

"I know, I jus'… maybe later." She stammered.

He took one last look at her before saying, "I hope so."

"Poor boy. Then again he has his secrets too." Vrai spoke once Amron left the room and was completely ignored by Giselle.

"Damn it!" She shouted in a whisper after he left. "I should have say they died." Why did the good ideas always come after the action?

~*~

She went into Majesty that night later than usual. It wasn't her intention to go, but Amron wouldn't give her a break. He really wanted to know about those rabbits. She went to bed around eight o'clock. An hour later her dad came to check on her and boy could she win an award for best leading actress in a one man play. She faked sleep like it was her job and she nailed it.

Tegan was back today. He was feeling better thanks to Marcel. His cheeks weren't red, his eyes weren't heavy and his fore head wasn't like a hot skillet. Seriously, you could have fried some bacon on there. Probably wrap him around a cake pan and you'd have an oven. She didn't exactly go for her fake training though. She went so Marcel could comb her hair. She'd been saying she'd do it next week every week. They were in the female room. She was sitting on the chair from Ming's dresser and Marcel standing behind. They had just finished washing and drying and now it was time to style.

"Think I got too accustomed to ya afro 'cause as I'm doing this I'm tempted to just leave it puffy," she joked while putting grease in Giselle's scalp.

"You could leave it if you want." Giselle joked.

"Rest in peace afro." Marcel responded. They laughed.

Once Marcel had finished pleasing herself with Giselle's hair, she left for the hospital again. She said that things were increasingly busy over the past few weeks. Emergency patients were flying in left, right and centre. Marcel at least gave her some insight on the problem. Between December to January every year Majesty had some tragic misfortunes, but for some reason it started earlier this year. She couldn't stay long enough to explain her theory or even what caused the said misfortune as she had to run off to work. Making her way down the hall Giselle could hear the volume of the TV in the Rec. Room booming. The TV was only ever on whenever Trevor was in there. Other than that it stayed off.

"…as the annual crisis draws nearer extra measures are being taken to ensure the safety of all Denizens. The cities are still raving about the curfew Mr. Ecoli, Chief of Majesty, inflicted upon the country." The news reporter was saying.

Then Ecoli's voice boomed from the TV speakers.

"Majesty is now Officially under curfew. At seven o'clock pm to six o'clock am MT six of our major terminals will be shut off. Those are the inter-world terminal and the inter-city terminal of Floral Cove, Nocturn Niche and Heavenly Heights. We asked that everyone be in their rightful homes before that time as no one will be allowed to enter or leave Majesty or anyone of the cities once the curfew takes effect. Business will continue as usual in the inner-city terminals throughout the cities, however, there will be an increase in patrollers on duty."

It was back to the news reporter now,

"Questions have been aroused as to why the guardians are taking such drastic early actions as the annual Christmas Hunt is still another three months away. Some say Ecoli has information about Weyden Empire that he is withholding from the public. Elleb has more on this…"

The TV shut off and some heavy, incomprehensible, grumbling followed. She didn't stay to sort out what it was about, but she was beginning to realize she'd soon see what Majesty had to be protected from. If Ecoli, being the person he was, felt it necessary to call a curfew on Majesty in order to withstand this, then just how much danger were they in?

After they finished, she took to town for no particular reason. Down the long steps, up the side walk to the purple shuttle stop. She wasn't exactly waiting for a shuttle; she was just enjoying the surroundings before heading home. It was late afternoon there so the sky was orange and the air was uncharacteristically warm. There weren't many people outside. A lot of the houses had their lights on and their doors tightly locked. Birds were flying to their nests for the night and businesses were closed. There was a little mini mart on the other side of the road. That was the only place she saw so far that was open. Funny how here was dead, but Floral Cove Square was probably still bursting with life.

She turned her gaze to the enigmatic street lamp. Somehow this pooled her interest more than a lot of other things she had seen or heard. Her mind was entrapped in the wonder of how they kept the flames alight. Who tended to it? They seemed to just dance carelessly in midair. The flames reminded her of Ecoli and all Marko had said about him. Since then she couldn't stop analyzing his rapid mood swings every time she questioned him too much or gave him an attitude. She also couldn't stop eyeing him every time he took a drink from his thermos. What was Marko feeding him? Did it really keep him calm? It looked more to her as though he was still a ticking time bomb. Especially with the whole "He might be a fire-devil" thing, she faltered to see how anything Marko could possibly give him would make a difference.

As her mind wandered she heard a faint humming noise creeping nearer. Dropping her eyes to the street, the flare of the fire followed. She had to blink a few hundred times to rid herself of the orange glare before she could make out anything in the consuming darkness. Finally, she recognized the shuttle before her. Gently, still humming, it slowed to a stop.

"Wha's a youngster like ya doing ou'ere this late?" the driver called. "S'my last trip to the terminal. Need a lift?"

"No." Giselle sighed looking up at headquarters. "Headed in that direction."

The man chuckled.

"Big dreamer, yeah. We all want to get up there and if we don' we want our kids to get there."

He clearly didn't understand what Giselle meant when she said she was headed there. More so, she didn't further her explanation.

"S'not the same," he gazed up at headquarters when she looked at him.

"Headquarters?" She asked curiously.

"No, the guardians," he corrected. "S'almost a complete different group o'guardians than eight years ago. Only veterans up there now are Mr. Hozen, Mr. Trevor, and darling Ms. Marcel. Whole load o'youngsters up there we got, yeah. Almighty watch over us!"

"They not that bad." Giselle defended in an un-offended voice.

"Ya wouldn't know that." He seemed to forget he was in the middle of doing his last trip to the terminal. "Things 'ere are different now. Barely a year without precious Ruby and we're already on lockdown. Bet it's that damn worthless Weyden Empire stirring up again." He spoke that unfamiliar name with utter hatred. This was only the second time she had heard about the mysterious Weyden Empire, but it felt like the third. What if the "they" the guardians were talking about a while back was Weyden Empire? If that were so, then what was this Weyden Empire and what was its significance to Majesty?

"Ecoli doesn' know what he's doing, yeah. He'll run us into the ground, that one."

"How you know that?" Now she was defensive.

"The flames m'dear," he pointed the street lamp.

She looked up at it lacking understanding of his statement.
"New 'ere are ya?"

She nodded.

"These flames change whenever we have a change in leadership. S'how we knew Ms. Ruby was gone. This here flame used to be the brightest red. Shaped like a ruby it was. The ruby jewel is a powerful talisman against evil. S'why we never knew misfortune when she was in charge. Then one night it changed into this careless flame." He sighed. "Imagine being with ya family thinking ya safe an all o'a sudden the lamp, it goes from red to orange."

That was how they found out Ruby was dead? In a way, Giselle felt that was probably more traumatic than being told; the fact that this red light from the street lamps always gave them comfort and one day it wasn't red anymore. What was worst, they would never get that type of glow again.

"What wrong with Ecoli fire?" She asked.

"His? Just a wild flame, yeah. Shapeless. Meaningless."

Giselle watched the lamp again understanding that it was more than just an outdoor light to these people.

"The fire changes shape and colour depending on the leader o'Majesty. S'controlled by the magic used to create this place. The leader before Ruby, Malcolm, his flame was a blue hope diamond. In the history books they say the founder, Hubable, his flame was emerald green."

Probably Ecoli's wild flame contributed to the whole fire-devil controversy. She couldn't see how it wouldn't. He could trick people, but could he trick magic?

Giselle went back to headquarters deeper in thought than she was when she left. If someone asked her how she felt about Ecoli she wouldn't be able to answer. She didn't know how she felt about him. New information kept inserting itself in her mind every day. He was only twenty yet he was running a country. That was already a hard job and seeing as half the country didn't trust him and the other half was divided between doubters and supporters he was probably stressed out twenty-four seven. Maybe that was why it was so easy for him to blow a gasket. Probably, it wasn't that easy to make his head catch fire in earlier days. She couldn't help but feel he was getting worst even though she hadn't known him long enough to diagnose that. Marko's help, although generous, wasn't help enough. Why didn't his fire have a shape? Why wasn't it a unique colour like all the chiefs before him? Was it because he was really a fire-devil and the magic governing Majesty knew better than anyone that he couldn't do anything for them? It couldn't be. She couldn't accept that as the answer because if it were so then why was he even a guardian to begin with? Why was he put in charge of the patrollers preceding his chief days? They were the ones that instilled order and carried out justice. From the sound of it, fire-devils weren't about that. But his flame…

"Oie, Gizzy you- nice hair- but you should have gone home a long time ago mate." Tegan said when he saw her enter head-quarters.

"I was just walkin', but I goin' now. And thank you." She flipped her hair in a really sassy way.

He smiled. "You seem happy."

"Barely." she responded with a half-smile on her face because she couldn't contort a facial expression to show exactly how she felt. "I was talkin' to one of the shuttle drivers."

"Oh." he made creases on his forehead. "Someone figure out you're Ruby's granddaughter? Fandom starting? I can't imagine."

"Says the one who have fifty woman walkin' behind him every time he step outside." She raised an eyebrow.

Tegan rubbed his shoulder nervously. "I-I suddenly don't feel comfortable having this conversation."

They talked some more until she was standing in front the mirror bidding fare well. Her foot was only a third way in when she pulled back and turned to face him.

"You talk to Ecoli?" She asked.

"Um," his nervous twitch started up. "Yeah I did."

"So you know what I want to ask next."

"You're mad at me." His innocent face puffed up as he rubbed the back of his head.

She shook her head. "No. Just tell me why you not doin' real trainin' with me?"

"Because chief orders," he said. "Obviously."

"Yeah, I know, but why?"

"Um-I-um… you see… Giselle you're putting me in a tough position here," he admitted childishly.

"If am a guardian then I should know about whatever it is that happenin'-," she stated.

"-yeah, but-" Tegan started but Giselle wasn't done talking.

"-like why you keepin' secrets from me and why you keepin' me a secret? Or why Ecoli flame don' have shape or like what is Weyden Empire?" She rambled.

"Wow," Tegan gasped after her rant. "For someone who shouldn't know much you know a lot."

"I pay attention." She folded her arms. "At least give me the proper trainin'. That thing that you does do, like that night with Alana, I want to do that too. And I want to help bring people here."

"You understand that I can't right?" He put his hand on his chest when he said this. "It's Ecoli's call."

"Why you have to listen to him anyway!" She spoke out of annoyance.

"He's the chief." Tegan sounded scared.

She sighed. "Yeah, I know." Giselle attempted to go through the mirror a second time, but stopped again. "Wait."

"What now?"

"You say you would make it up to me."

"No I didn't." He defended.

"Yeah, you say…" and she started to mock how he spoke. "*…look, I don't know why you're mad, but I'm sorry. I promise I'll make it up to you, whatever it is, tomorrow.*"

"I don't sound like that." Tegan got defensive.

"That is not the topic of discussion." She pointed out.

"This is not tomorrow." He stated.

"Yes, today is yesterday's tomorrow. And you was sick. So, tomorrow in that sentence mean 'when I get better'." She smartly twisted his words.

Tegan huffed and folded his arms staring at her through un-bidden eyes as if to say, "Really?"

"Please, please, please, please…" Giselle hung onto his arms and weighed down his tolerance.

"Huh! Fine. I'll work somethin' out." He hung his head.

Tegan was too easy. She launched forward and hugged him. He just smiled and patted her back.

CHAPTER ELEVEN

SURPRIZE ATTACK

"YA GO ON one mission, one mission, and if ya prove that ya responsible enough then maybe… maybe I might…"

"I hearin' a lot of might's and maybe's in this sentence." Giselle interrupted Ecoli's compromise.

They were in the chief's office having the discussion she was longing for. It was a narrow, but lengthy office embedded in the earth beneath headquarters. The rectangular room was mostly underground with a wall of window on either end. From one window, Floral Cove could be seen in all its glory; the colours like a portrait of a million flowers, the yellow sandy shore like a crescent moon laid to rest, the tall glass buildings like a bar graph of Majesty's growth in wealth over the years. From the other window Nocturn Niche appeared as a muted illustration from a book of fairy tales. It was like watching split personalities. The walls were as busy as the wide desk that sat closer to the Nocturn Niche side of the room. Along the right side of the room stood an armoire; in it were photographs and relics of the past chiefs.

Tegan had spoken to Ecoli and two days later he agreed to sit them down and have a talk.

"Just hear him out." Tegan insisted.

"I will authorize trainin' if the mission is successful and I get a good report." He concluded more crisp.

Giselle stared at Tegan. So Ecoli needed a good report, huh? That should be easy. Tegan, noticing the devious look in her eyes, averted his.

"A good, honest report," she realized how hard Ecoli was looking at her.

"What is the mission then?" She asked determined to prove herself.

"That's up to Tegan, yeah. Should know ya enough by now to choose wisely." Ecoli sat in his chair.

"Right," Tegan said. "Any specific unit?"

Ecoli's eyes wondered over Giselle for a while then he sighed and looked out the window. "Ya doh want anything easy, d'ya?"

Giselle snapped her finger. "Right."

"Well then," Ecoli went back to Tegan. "Patrol. Four-man team."

"Alright," Tegan obeyed.

"Ecoli," Giselle called him.

She had gotten what she wanted; more involvement. After debating whether or not to be a part of Majesty and deciding she should, then being held back, she could genuinely say she was satisfied. Now it was onto the harder questions. Why, after he was trying to get her to join, was Ecoli trying to keep her from the real tasks of a guardian? Was it something Ruby said? Was her grandmother still pulling strings from beyond the grave? This thought made Gisele all levels of agitated. Why didn't Ruby just talk to her about all this before she died? Why did she have to make it so complicated?

"S'up?" Ecoli addressed her unprofessionally compared to how couth he was before.

"Tell me about my Gran'mom," she requested.

Tegan observed how tame she had become and stood up.

"I'll excuse myself," he said as he left.

A look of confusion crossed Ecoli at first, but after a few seconds his expression smoothed out with understanding. Still, it took him a while before he spoke. In fact, he didn't speak. At first Giselle thought he was probably thinking, but after a while in the silence she realized something. That was a pretty raw question. He appeared as though he had so much to say, but it was all painful memories he was trying to suppress.

"I ask cause you say she mentor you." Her voice was low.

"Yeah," his tone was equal. "Um, she was nice."

She waited for more, but it never came.

"That's all?"

He nodded, "Ya don' meet people that genuinely nice any-more. She liked to help people and she believe in second chances. Actually the chances ya get from her was infinite, yeah. Somehow she could see the good in everybody. When everybody else see waste, she see potential. Even in me."

That last part seemed to have slipped out without permis-sion. He consciously sat back and cleared his throat.

"She was nice," Ecoli concluded.

"Ok. I was jus' want to know cause," she paused. "Cause you know her. I mean, she wasn' hidin' nothin' from you."

The green monster was alive and feeding inside of her, but she was trying hard to starve it. Ecoli bowed his head slightly. He must have picked up on her vibe.

"She could talk about her family for mass time, yeah," he said. "S'why everybody kinda know ya would show up one day."

Giselle remembered the first time she fell in Marko called her by her name. He even knew her nickname. Most of the guardians acted casual with her actually. Listening to Ruby for so long, they must have felt like they knew her.

"Ya play too much and ya want people to treat ya equally, but is so hard to. Ya the youngest one in the family and a joy to be 'round and she want it to stay like that. Amron is her favorite trouble maker. He think he smart playin' tricks on his dad, but she already know all the lies he tell whenever his dad tell her things about him. Andre is a bit stiff, but that's because he always had to fight for his mom attention. She started to show signs when he was two and he always thought it was his fault. That's why he always tryin' to be perfect. And BJ is just like her. He genuinely nice. I meet him. I couldn' believe it, but he really is."

It felt strange having her family summed up by an outsider. The things Ecoli said, she never knew. The reason why everyone treats her like a baby, it was ok with her. It actually stitched a smile on her face. The part about Ruby not buying any of the shady things Amron did made her laugh too. And she was right, BJ was just like her. He was lovable just like Ruby. He got it the best out of everyone. He had their mom, Grace, before things went in a loop. What he said about Andre though, that was something Giselle would have never guessed. She never knew that about her brother. It was actually sad that he felt like he had to be perfect for Grace to stay sane. She didn't though. She got worst and died. He must think it had something to do with him. She always thought Andre was easy to read, transparent, but now she wondered just how much she didn't know about him.

"I didn'," her train of thought started straight then took a sharp turn. "Wait, when you meet BJ?"

Ecoli looked her dead in the eye when he responded. "Grenada. In Andall's. Ruby talk 'bout him enough. I just know was him."

Giselle didn't respond, but analyzed him.

"Tegan should be upstairs, go to him first then go meet Marko." Ecoli suddenly stretched and dismissed her. "I hear ya flyin' need improvement. And later the guardians go be at Pious Falls. Not often we all free at the same time so we takin' advantage o'it. Stick 'round." He smiled.

They were in the weaponry. Giselle was glad to be in there again. It meant she was about to get her first weapon. Was he going to teach her how to use the bizarre stuff in there? That was what she thought until Tegan walked straight through the room. He approached a strip of bare wall and for a few seconds Giselle was confused. Tegan rubbed the wall and just like in the female room, a door appeared. They entered. It was really roomy and dark in there. Dead ahead there were some lengthy cages lit by small red bulbs and surrounded by barriers that lead straight to either a target or dummies. Across the room there were more dummies and punching bags. A few mats were set down and she was sure they weren't for sitting. Then on the other side there were endless draws.

"Physical trainin' room." Tegan said. "In light of our up-coming mission here are some safe weapons you don't need excessive training to use."

He made his way over to the draws.

"Keep in mind our deadliest weapons are hidden in plain sight. That stuff you saw out there, nothin'." He said as he pulled a draw opened and took out a dark coloured apparatus. Then he got a ball.

"What could be more deadly than a scythe?" She asked.

"This," he handed her the thing he took out.

She inspected it and the first thing that flew out her mouth was, "a door knob?"

It was a matte black door knob or at least that's what it appeared to be. The handle was round and the end part was circular and open like a door knob was. The only difference, the neck was more extended and was hollow like a tuba.

"It's a peg missile," he played with the ball in his hand. "It's new. It never used to look like this. We have it in a different design. It's just that since workin' here Marko made a lot of suggestions about our weapons and the group of geniuses who makes them actually listened to him. He thinks we should have some weapons hidden in ordinary objects just in case."

"In case what?"

"I don't know, honestly."

Tegan went back into the weaponry and moments later came back with a sniper rifle. "This and that is the same thing. With the peg missile you don't need target practice. You just need to aim. It reads what you want through your palm. That's the difference between the two. With the gun version you have to have perfect aim and once it's locked on the target it does what it has to do." He tapped something near the neck on the tool in Giselle's hand and the back of the round handle lit up. It looked like some kind of computer chip. "Mixing magic and technology, remember?"

He led the way over to the cages and told her to stand back. Tegan skillfully pulled the rifle shoulder length, leaned in to the cheek piece and closed one eye to look into the day scope. With little to no noise he fired. Easily, a purple bullet shot out and rammed itself into a dummy at the end of the cage. The bullet itself was the size of a pebble, but the crater it created was ten times its size. It wasn't even a bullet anymore. Giselle could see thin, spider-like, mechanical arms embedded in the rim of the crater constricting. Tegan lowered the rifle coolly.

"Damn," Giselle gasped.

"Admittedly my favorite to use," he smirked. "Alrighty, your turn. But you'll be usin' this ball and the peg missile."

Tegan slung the rifle over his shoulder and onto his back. He narrated her to the yellow line he stood behind when he made his shot. Then, carefully, he adjusted her hands to suit the proper use of the weapon.

"So hold it like this and then, there you go, take a shot." He offered.

Tegan threw the ball and used magic to keep it aloft and zooming around. Giselle, unsure of what to expect, raised the peg missile and aimed.

"Keep it focused in the general area of the ball and when you're ready, turn the knob to the right." Tegan instructed.

She did as she was told and instantly there was pressure surging through her arm. From the open end a black bullet shot out and there was an electric looking purple string attaching it to the peg missile. Then, after a few seconds, it sprouted some airy purple wings and started chasing after the ball that Tegan was controlling. The longer it flew the faster it got until all Giselle could see was a purple blur floating around. Alas, it impaled the ball and once the bullet was planted inside the wings grew up on the ball and it stayed in the corner of the room where it accomplished its mission.

"There's no escapin' a peg missile bullet. Doesn't matter where the person runs; once its set it's only a matter of time."

"Damn." Giselle repeated with even more interest.

"You think that's it, huh? Turn the knob left." He urged.

Again she did as she was told and this time instead of a flying winged bullet, the ball started to fly toward her as the purple string wound up and the equipment vibrated. It only took a few seconds for the ball to be snugly sitting in the nozzle of the peg missile in her hands. Tegan took it, plucked off the wings and pulled on the now black string that was still connected to the bullet inside; except, a bullet didn't come out. It was this little black spiked sphere that tore the original ball apart when he wrecked it out. Once it was out it turned into a bullet again. Giselle's jaw hung, wordlessly astonished.

"Try being on the receivin' end of this." Tegan laughed nervously and rubbed his shoulder. "Not fun."

Giselle looked at the torn up ball again. Imagine having that in your arm and having to pull it out. That had to be painful. It didn't look like it could be deactivated without being pulled out.

"There are three types; black, red and orange. You won't be usin' the black." He took this time to retrieve his precious peg missile from her.

"How come?" She sounded disappointed.

"Do you want this mission to happen or not?" He asked her as he headed over to the draws. He pulled out the exact same thing from a different draw, but this one was orange. Handing it to her he said, "the orange is an electric net. Basically, it does the same thing. But, it wraps up its target in a net. That is what you'll be usin'."

"Ok," she groaned. At least it was electric; that made it interesting.

"It's all yours now. Smile. I just got you your first weapon," Tegan grinned.

She mirrored his facial expression faking reluctance. In truth, she was happy.

He proceeded to another draw which contained about forty little clear cases that looked like medicine boxes. Inside there were two puzzle pieces for each slot. They only had one space to connect. The rest of it was spread out like corner pieces. Some of the puzzles had pictures on them and others were blank.

"These are summoning snaps." He took one out. "You stick the pieces together and whatever is on the picture is summoned to your side. Like this."

He connected the two pieces in his hand. There was a picture of a bastard sword on it. Suddenly she was witnessing the broad blade sword materializing out of nowhere; ready for use. Flipping the sword on the flat side, he pointed out some almost invisible markings. He explained that to summon something you had to first put spells on it. Then put the name or picture of what you wanted on the puzzle pieces. People could be summoned too. It was done the same way as would be done with an object. Also, the summoning spell took one month to wear off. To send back a summons all she'd have to do was bend the pieces forward as if she were closing a book, or tell the summons 'your services are no longer needed'. Tegan showed her a few other things she would be able to use, like; a transponder which was what they used to communicate with each other, sensor plates which were flat lifeless objects. They could be set to make noise that would wake up the world if stepped on or in proximity in order to chase predators. The alarm could also be set for silent. And finally, night vision glasses.

Once their session was done, they headed to Pious Falls for her flying lessons. She had slacked out too much and Tegan insisted that she do something today; although, Ecoli had already instructed her that she had to. No matter how much she begged to go to the mission board Tegan had already convinced himself that they'd go there another day. At least she was prepared this time. She wasn't going to be jumping off the falls in her training jump suit like last time. Tegan made her go home for swimming clothes. He also made sure he was there for the lessons so that Marko couldn't say things he wasn't supposed to anymore. He didn't directly tell Giselle this; she guessed that was why he tagged along.

When they got there she practiced her takeoff and landing as usual. Instead of jumping off the cliff now she was able to stand on flat ground and rise. Easy. Then came Marko's least favorite part where she came down out of control and she was too far to fall in the water so she knocked him down. Seriously, he might get injured. He started running away from her now and she found it funny to chase after him. Evening started to crawl in and soon they were all relaxing around the water. She was still in her swimming clothes, swimsuit with shorts over it, and cold. Meanwhile Marko and Tegan were just in swim trunks; Scout wore a dry vest and long pants. They were unaffected by the temperature. Were they even human? Maybe not. Scout seemed to be avoiding past experiences by steering clear of anywhere wet. During this time, she got a good look at Tegan's tattoos. She knew he had a lot, but it was only when he took his shirt off she saw the whole thing. His entire left arm, neck, chest and back and checkered parts of his right arm were covered in patterns, shapes and other impressive creations; just like Henna. Scout had a tattoo as well; it was a pattern that centered on the ball of his shoulder and stretched to his neck. Other than that it was nothing really.

"Why all the tattoo's?" She asked Tegan finally.

"Um, because." He shrugged.

"You jus' wake up one mornin' and decide to become a human canvas?" She responded.

He laughed. "I don't even remember getting these mate. I just always had it."

"What you mean?"

"It's a cultural thing from The Land of Spirits. They mark their children when they're about three or four years old. Women do their left arm only and men do all this mess here to show that they're stronger than women. Then Shaman's took it further to tattoo their faces, but Ersatz don't." He explained.

"That kind of sexist." Giselle commented.

"Hey, I didn't start the trend." He said. "Only the old families from Tlos do it like this now. These days, people get tattoos in here just 'cause its common. One thing everybody still does though is the sun and the moon."

He pointed to the simple sun representation at the top of his arm then the crescent moon on his wrist.

"Just reminds us that everything has a beginning and an end, even life. Doesn't matter what magic you have. So use your time wisely." She looked at Scout again and on careful observation she saw the sun and the moon centered in his tattoo.

"Marko has his on his wrist."

She was intrigued. "I want one."

"Right, like your parents would allow that."

"My dad won' see it."

"How do you know that?"

"Cause I could get it somewhere he can' look."

"I didn't hear that. I'm not responsible." Tegan got up and walked away from her. She laughed.

It was tiring treading around in that water and keeping vocally active. After a while she stayed seated and watched as the guys fooled around and enjoyed the freezing cold water. Except Scout; he stayed far smoking his joint. They were discussing past events, making bets, pranking each other and doing other stupid stuff she couldn't make sense of. Boys will be boys. Amron would fit in perfectly here in her opinion.

"No, you big ass, cause it's like if you're wet and everything around you is wet then you're not really wet. That's what he said…" Marko was trying to explain something to them and they were deep into it like it was a project for school.

"Ya know what's trippy?" Scout started. "Like, if ya clean when ya come out o'the bathroom then why does ya towel get dirty?"

"Cause…" Marko started then stopped. "…I don't know."

Tegan laughed. "But are you ever really clean though? Cause dirt on you is mostly just dead skin cells. No guarantee that all washes off in a five-minute shower."

The boys stopped to think hard again. This even had Giselle thinking.

"I don't know anything about the world anymore." Marko joked loudly.

"Questions you ask when you're high, mate." Tegan pretended to point the words in the air.

"Hey, no wonder Scout brought it up." Marko laughed.

"Bruh," Scout glared at him, but smiled eventually.

Giselle started observing Scout. As her eyes rolled over him she went into her spells of disapproval. She just couldn't get what was so good about being high all the time.

I bet you he can' remember half of what he do last week. She thought. *That's if he even know what goin' on now.*

Scout was half way through a drawl speech to Marko, who was going on like it was the funniest thing he had ever heard, when he broke out in a yawn. Really though, if half the stuff Scout said was on a Facebook status, she would die laughing. But she was determined to remain annoyed with him. Then again, she was just treating him like Ming treated everyone; cold. She hadn't even gotten to know him. One of his hands were stretched out, mouth like an O and eyes closed as he yawned. How could he be so tired and he hadn't done anything all day? Then out of nowhere his eyes opened and he became stiff with focus. His body went rigid with alert and the usual slackness he had about him was no more. The hand that was stretched during his long yawn was now in front of him clamping tightly onto the shaft of an arrow that was pointing between his eyes. Giselle let out a loud gasp. She didn't know if it made sense, but her respect for him was far greater than it was a mere five seconds ago. Did Scout, her Scout, just catch an arrow that was shot at his head? Unbelievable. It wasn't like she hadn't seen something like that before, but that was on TV of course. It was on Teen wolf when Stiles accidentally shot an arrow at Scott and he caught it. But that only worked because Scott was a werewolf and because the scene was edited to look like he actually caught it. This was real.

"Bruh, if I die, I'm blaming you." Marko broke the chilling silence.

Scout's eyes roamed from the arrow head that was no more than a centimeter from his face to the direction the arrow had come from. Giselle followed it and noticed a dark figure disappear into the nearby bushes.

"Like hell if ya think ya can run now!"

Scout took off into the bushes. That was new. She had never seen him run before. Let alone walk straight. His speed was unnatural. Marko shot out of the water taking off after him. Tegan got up too and she was about to follow.

"Wait," he stopped her. "You should probably stay here."

"Why?"

"Because you're just..."

"Fourteen?" She asked him.

Then she pushed her way past him and ran after the guys. She was a guardian for Christ sakes! She was just getting ready for her first mission this morning. When were they going to let her just do things without telling her she was too young and it was dangerous? *Life is dangerous!* said the hysterical voice in her head. If she was meant to stay young and cute then she'd have never been chosen to be a guardian. When she finally caught up to them in the bushes the scene unfolded in front of her. Scout was standing on the back of a man who was face down on the ground groaning. He was holding a bow and arrow which Giselle assumed was the attack weapon that started all this. The arrow was drawn and pointed at the man's head. It was official; she respected Scout now. That was pretty bad-ass.

He didn't even break a sweat. Now she saw why he was in Dispatch.

Marko grinned. "Slay!"

"Don't be rash." Tegan followed up.

"I know," Scout said stepping down. "Not 'til I see his face." He kicked the guy in his side causing him to squirm and turn over. "Roscoe."

"Roscoe!" Tegan amplified the shock of the situation.

"Oh, this makes a lot of sense now." Marko relaxed, not that he wasn't before. "You know, if you're going to upset someone you need to expect an arrow or two threatening to potentially take your life. Just saying." He leaned back on a tree and folded his arms.

"Get up." Scout said, arrow still drawn and aimed.

"I hate ya." The guy growled.

"Tell that to the patrollers." Scout nudged him with the arrow head urging him to walk.

"Looks like someone's spending the night in the slammers," Marko sang.

Giselle didn't understand one thing that went on. Wasn't this the same Roscoe that was working with Tegan some nights ago? Why was he here attacking a guardian? There were laws against that. She knew. She read the hand book. He was going to be charged with treason for sure. Not as if he could kill Scout anyway; not like that, and definitely not with the reflexes Scout had just displayed. She looked at Tegan for a breakdown of the situation.

"Roscoe's sister did some things against Majesty with a group of her friends and Dispatch was sent after them two days ago," he said. "Only two of the eight of them are in patrol custody now and Roscoe's sister is not among them."

"Oh."

"'Cause he's a murderer!" Roscoe spun around pointing at Scout who didn't even bother to tighten his grip on the weapon. Instead he dropped it and assumed a still stance staring Roscoe dead in the eye- his iris went completely silver.

"We only need one to confess. That other guy was lucky." Marko's mumbles almost went unnoticed.

"Ya sister led a group that burned a village flat. Out o' 158 people, eighteen are in critical condition and six still aren' stabilized. The rest o'em are dead. She openly swore her allegiance to Weyden Empire. She's part o'the reason Majesty's under curfew. I don't pride myself on taking lives, but she was a threat to Majesty. Too bad they couldn't deceive Ariel and Ming. I should lock ya up too cause I think ya knew about all o'that." Scout spoke to him carefully and freely like he did with everyone. He was unafraid. Still, somewhere in there like an undertone, she heard growling.

"I know nothing," Roscoe snapped.

"You told her to run," Marko's face wasn't joking anymore. "You're probably with Weyden Empire too."

"Where's the proof?" Roscoe grinned.

"I didn' have any, which was why I couldn' detain ya." Scout shook his head and smiled a deeply pleased smile. "But now I can."

Roscoe's face flattened knowing he made a big mistake trying to go after Scout.

All of them marched back to Pious Falls with the strange man leading the way. The only reason he moved silently was because Scout was intimidating him with some animalistic teeth. His canines were elongated, more than usual, and the rest of his teeth became pointe and sharp. Tegan did say he was something. What was it again? The word wasn't free flowing in her mind. When they made it back Hozen and Trevor and everyone else was there. They looked at them led by a strange man who was followed by a dog like Scout out of the bushes and acted like it was nothing.

This is normal then, Giselle thought.

Marko and Tegan spread out between everyone else and Giselle took her seat by the big rock. Scout's fangs were normal now. Roscoe made no attempt to run while standing in the centre of all the guardians. He wasn't going to get far.

"Too lazy to go down town," Scout muttered.

That sounded more like him now. He walked over to where he had hung his jacket and took out a clear ball from the pocket; it had green waterlogged confetti in it. He pushed the man against one of the big protruding rocks roughly. He then shook the ball and when it lit up he threw it at the guy's feet. A green gas swarmed him and by the time it was clear, Giselle could see green vines tying him to the rock and tightening when he struggled.

"If it makes ya hate me less, ya sister killed herself when she realized she was cornered." Scout turned his back ready to walk away, "although, I don't care how ya feel about me."

As if that weren't enough, he retrieved a syringe from the jacket pocket and injected something into Roscoe's neck that made him pass out right away. Giselle looked at him aghast.

"He's just sleeping, yeah." Scout told her as he passed by.

What kind of sleeping? She wondered this.

"Scout," she called him.

He stopped in response. She had always been annoyed with him for no particular reason. Scout never knew of this. Giselle didn't know how Scout felt about her. He never directly let her know whether they were friends or something. It wasn't as though Marko and Tegan did that, but with them things just kind of flowed.

"What are you?"

He glanced back and they locked eyes for a moment- his morphing silver to her brown. She looked at him so closely and intently that she could see her reflection sketched in his eyes. To her surprise it didn't look the way it was supposed to. She was flipped upside down.

"An Aswang," he spoke slowly with a slight amused look on his face.

Something told her he looked at her like that on purpose. He wanted her to see it. Then, without any explanation, he walked away to contact Patrol on his transponder.

That name had come up again; Weyden Empire. And no one was trying to explain to her what it was. Ecoli told them not to. That she knew for sure, after talking Tegan into getting her a mission. Why didn't he want her to know? She had to ask, but when was the right time? She barely saw him lately. This morning was the first in a while and the conversation she had with him she wouldn't wish for it to change. It was one of the more pleasant times spent with Ecoli. It was her intention to lead up to the Weyden Empire question, but the conversation took its own direction; it didn't follow the script she had laid out in her mind. She had to bring up the Weyden Empire talk some other time. When he couldn't take back the mission or wasn't talking about Ruby. As conflicted as she was, she wouldn't stop anyone from telling her about Ruby's magical chief days.

Things seemed to be getting busier and busier as time went by. Ecoli was always on the move. Apparently everyone else was busy too. She didn't even know dispatch was deployed to deal with a case Ariel and Ming had investigated. She had only learned of this now. People died. An entire village was burned. And why were people pledging allegiance to Weyden Empire? Was it a cult or something? Or was it possible that there was another magical world out there? Ecoli was trying to keep her in the dark and he was doing a damn good job at it too.

The guy's had a laptop and projector that they were setting up on a table they carried with them. Meanwhile Ecoli and Ariel were gathering fire wood. The rest of them were just hanging around. She couldn't tell if Hozen was happy to be there or not because, for one, she had never seen his face before. His brown cloak always covered every bit of him. And he had just come back from a mission he went on not long after their secret meeting (which she wasn't aware of until he showed up). It was the same with Trevor; she couldn't see his face either, but that was because he had half of it wrapped in gauze. She remembered he had his arm and leg covered before. That wasn't just a style then, he was probably injured.

"What happen to your face?" Ming pointed him with her cup. Giselle was listening in on their conversation.

"Ya know, a lil fight, but me deh ya."

"He got beat by a girl."

The voice of the mysterious Hozen caught her off guard. It was a rusty whisper spoken carefully and had a frost bite air to go with it. As if that weren't creepy enough, he chuckled and it suddenly felt like she was in a horror movie, and that one stupid character was about to say, "hello, is anyone there?" She was more interested in him now than ever. Tegan said he was a Slaugh, right? She had forgotten to google it. She should really get on that.

"Shut your mouth!" Trevor glared at Hozen. "Me just have nuff respect for 'ooman not to hit she back."

Ming let out a very uptight laugh followed by Hozen's crisp laugh that Giselle didn't find appropriate to laugh along with.

"We're going to project the movie on the waterfall." Hozen was saying.

"That gonna work?" Ming asked.

"Don't question the master."

Hozen put a brown, malnourished, hand on the top of her head, turned her around and pushed her away. Trevor laughed hard at this even though it seemed to bring him pain.

"I got a blanket. Thought ya might be cold."

Marcel distracted Giselle from the fit of laughter she wanted to let out. The fact that even Hozen couldn't stand Ming was funny to her. Marcel proceeded to wrap the thick blanket around Giselle's all too grateful shoulders. She was too tired to hold conversation at this point, but she was happy to be there and listen.

"What movie?" Marcel asked no one in particular.

Marko jumped onto a big rock and called everyone's attention.

"Guys! Ok, so we're watching, wait for it, We're the Millers!"

"Really?" Ariel spoke kind of skeptically.

"Yes!" He sounded like a big child.

"Wha's that?" asked Marcel to which Marko began explaining.

Marko and Marcel began to stray from the movie description onto other topics and so did Giselle's mind. How did Marcel feel about people calling Ecoli a fire-devil? They didn't appear to be distant. They probably got along really well. Why else would Ecoli make a point to say she was his sister when he introduced her? And why else would she make him face his fears and remain chief of Majesty. So how was she dealing with all of this controversy? Did she address the public at all about it? Surely people would believe the words of an angel. Or maybe she already knew what Ecoli was and felt it best to stay silent. His flame was wild and careless after all. Giselle glanced up at Marcel speaking animatedly with Marko. Then she looked over to Ariel and Ecoli who were over by the fire wood in their own little world.

"Look at this," Ecoli said.

He touched the tip of the stick with a flaming finger and it caught fire. Then he put it in his mouth and it was gone. Again the heat didn't even bother him.

"Impressive right?" He spoke with puffy cheeks, smoke leaving his lips.

"It was impressive the first ten times. Light the fire." Ariel didn't even spare him a glance.

"Alright, alright," he chuckled.

He blew over the pile of wood they had set up. Flames flew from his mouth engulfing the wood. Now there was an orange dancing light filling Pious Falls.

That was impressive, Giselle thought.

"That's new." Ariel seemed impressed too. Giselle stared at them for a while dozing a little.

"We need more girls here. This is like a man…" there was a pause where Marko took the time to glance at Hozen and Scout, "…and beast fest."

"There are girls here," Ecoli said.

"Well yeah, but Giselle is Giselle and Marcel is Marcel. Ariel… I like myself. I'm not trying to die and…" he looked over at Ming and made a face like he smelled something foul.

"Maybe you should take a bath if your own body odor affects you that badly." She smirked. A few of them laughed.

"You want to cuddle someone?" Hozen called across to him. "Come here." He was moving over to him with open arms.

"Naw, dude. No! Stay away from me! Hey! Hozen! Guys! Help, I'm under attack!"

He started to run as Hozen chased him with open arms. His whole body seemed to hover above ground never making one foot-print. She would run if Hozen tried to hug her too. Though, it would be for less comedic reasons. Scout was sitting around the water. He glanced up at the wild pair.

"If ya jumping in the water then warn a brother."

On the side, not caring at all about the display, Ming pulled out a piece of red paper from her jeans pocket. This was the first time Giselle saw Ming in something other than the common pants. It was her first time seeing all of them in casual clothes actually.

"I'm curious," Marcel suddenly said.

"About what?" Giselle looked up at her.

"The note," Marcel said as though it were obvious. "Ming got a note from a secret admirer. She found it at headquarters. No one but guardians can go up there so I'm curious as to who it is."

Seeing them all together Giselle couldn't help, but wonder which one of them gave Ming the cute note. They were just so corky and never serious. They didn't seem to have any interest in relationship's or the personalities for writing love notes at all. In her opinion, it would be a miracle if they actually put two correct words together to tell a girl they even liked her, especially Marko with the way he talks to Ming. Maybe it was Tegan. He was the only sensitive one here. From the looks of it, Ming was probably still thinking about it. She was sitting a little distance from Scout observing all of them with a thoughtful expression, red paper in hand. Finally, Trevor finished his tinkering with the projector. The movie appeared on the falls. There were no plugs here or any electricity so she had no clue how he did it. The point was he did.

"Okay! Popcorn!" Ariel was digging into her bag. "Trevor, Marcel, Ecoli, Tegan…" she called their names as she tossed the sealed bags. She was just throwing it over the water and Trevor waved his hand in the direction of the owner. The popcorn followed. When it was Marko's turn he was standing with his hands opened, but the bag went straight through and hit him in the face.

"Nice shot Trevor." He said sarcastically.

"Was Ariel," Trevor defended himself.

"Aided by Trevor." Ming stated.

"Basket hand." Ariel remarked. "Scout and Hozen no salt for you and Ming, butter for you. Um, Giselle, I don't know what you like."

"Butter," she found some energy to say.

Her popcorn was delivered. Giselle looked around at all of them; their smiling faces and comfortable composure. The way they interacted with each other, they were like a little family. She looked down at her blanket. Then she felt Marcel's arm around her comforting her. She must have noticed how tired Giselle looked. She snuggled comfortably under Marcel's arm. Now she was part of the family too. And again she was the baby.

~*~

Wake up.

She was still at Pious Falls. We're The Millers was a good movie; almost impossible not to laugh at. She didn't see all of it, but the parts she did see were awesome at least. She almost wanted to watch it a second time, but they put something else on after. Everyone was commenting at random scenes in the movie and making it funny even when it wasn't supposed to be. Then after a while they all faced her and started speaking in unison.

"Wake up."

What was happening? She kept hearing it.

315

"Wake up!"

She opened her eyes and the first thing she saw was her brother's face, Andre, right in front of her. She jumped out of bed holding her chest only to turn around and see Amron standing on the other side of the bed.

"You can' jus' throw all this ugly on people in the mornin'!" She growled in a whiney manner.

"Ha, ha." Andre faked a laugh at her insult.

"Time to wake up. School today." They left.

"Just one mornin'." She whispered to herself.

"Stop complaining." Vrai made her presence known.

"Good mornin' to you too," Giselle moaned grumpily.

She got out of bed and did her morning routine for school-cussing Andre to hurry and get out of the bathroom. Then she went in the kitchen for breakfast where her dad was expressing how happy he was that he didn't have to see them home all day. Amron made a few stupid jokes and got embarrassed by Brent. Andre combined some weird food then washed it down with some cocoa tea. His school opened a week ahead of Amron and Giselle's so it was just another day for him. Meanwhile Amron and Giselle were making sure they had their uniforms together for the first day back. Amron in his grey pants, maroon tie with yellow, green and blue stripes and a white shirt. Giselle in her navy blue pleated skirt, a red and navy blue tie with yellow and green stripes, a white shirt and long white socks. Both wore black shoes. It was time to deal with Tanteen again. There were five schools in that one area; three secondary, one primary and a college. Then the ministry was right on the hill next to it. There were two bakeries, a fast food shop called The Greens and the tennis court which also doubled as a fast food place; all very popular. The roads were going to be busy this morning.

She did the usual meet up with her friends. They hugged and talked excessively. She went to assembly where the principal gave her big speech and talked about how happy she was to have them back safely and "alone" which was code for not pregnant. New teachers and prefects were introduced. Form teachers were listed. Then they gave instructions for the different classes to leave one by one with their teacher. Now she was in her new class listening to the register being called and the new teacher trying to learn her students' names. She made a few announcements from the office all of which no one was happy with.

"All students are banned from going into the following areas while in uniform: Tennis Court, Net Ball Court, Basket Ball Court, The Greens and the Playground." She called out the long list of her students' favorite places.

"Why?" Was the general summary of what all of them were shouting.

"Because you go down there and make confusion with the other schools and too many of you doh know how to leave the GBSS boys alone." She stated.

That last line certainly hit home. Half the class had a boy-friend in GBSS. Ironic that they call The Grenada Boys Secondary School and The Anglican High School brother and sister schools and their students were always in more than friends relationships. Giselle had no interest in any of them. For one, all her brothers went there and she only knew their friends. Second, some of the boys there acted like animals that were let out from a cage. However, Giselle and Emma did have a problem with this news.

"Miss, that is where I does buy my breakfast!" A girl cut them before they could voice their concerns.

"You should eat at home. Is not healthy to have that greasy stuff in the mornin' anyway." She shot down.

"Miss?" Emma called her.

"Yes..." She was thinking hard.

"Emma. Yeah, so me and Giselle in the National Drum Corp and…"

"Oh, you played at the carnival launch?"

"Yes, we did." Giselle answered.

"Yeah, so the band have a meetin' on the tennis court this afternoon and usually we have practice on the netball court on Friday's." That last part was news to Giselle, but then again she wasn't in the band as long as Emma was.

"I see," she hummed. "I'll talk to Ms. Howard and tell you."

Great. Now they had to depend on their hard-headed principal's response. Luckily for them their principal was in a good mood today. She gave them permission to go and told them to ask that the band's meeting place be relocated. They weren't going to do that though. The rules said they couldn't be there in school uniform. They just had to change clothes. Plus, there was no way you could keep the AHS girls from the courts or The Greens. It drew them in like mango did flies. This was going to be a long term with a lot of suspensions and detentions.

The school day seemed to go by fast. They weren't exactly doing anything seeing as it was the first day. It usually took about three to four days before they got their official time tables and started to work. So basically the day was wasted. It was just them burning out all the holiday energy. It felt weird to be back at school where things were normal. She had spent the entire summer in Majesty. Night-time was becoming a strange term to her since she left home at night- fall to go to Majesty where day was just beginning. So it was more than shaking off the holiday energy for her. She was going to have to balance school, training and her upcoming mission.

After school they headed down to the tennis court that was already crowded with the other schools; not excluding AHS girls. You just can't stop them. They bought ham and cheese sandwiches and stood in the tiny car park waiting for some of the band members to show up before going in. Children littered the little space as though they had no home to go to. A few of them had on their sport shorts and vests, tennis rackets in hand, bouncing the balls off the tall cracked green and white wall. They were careful not to let the balls escape them and land on one of the four cars parked directly behind them. Just behind the cars another broken wall stood erect. Its dust like ash on the ground in front of it. Beside it, where the vine woven, rusty fence stood blocking the large drain and the main road, some boys and one girl sat on a rotting bench eating chicken. It was loud. They could hear people ordering food inside the shop, the constant bop of the bumping balls, heavy foot falls, laughter, fights. Looking out through the great brown gate that never closed, just across the road, they could see college students walking along the side walk to and from classes. It was from this bunch that some of the band members came, doing exactly as Emma and Giselle had done-sought out food first. Not too long after, Amron, Cheddi and Raheem showed up playing as usual. The only time you would catch them groomed and looking presentable was on the first day of school. This was running though Giselle's mind as she took in her friend's haircuts.

"Gizzy! Sistren!" Raheem raised his hand for a hi-five. "Up high! Down low! In space! In your face!" Both of them swung to smack each other in the face and both of them ducked and missed.

"Yes!" Raheem shouted in triumph having finally succeeded in getting Giselle to do the handshake again. He had been trying every band practice. It was really just a game that little children played to get a cheap shot at slapping their friends, but had developed into their greeting for each other.

"Alright people!" Rayanna and Serene exited with food in hand. "Let we get this started. I have a Maths class in ASPS buildin' in half an hour. That is a long walk."

Mr. Williams was already on the benches in the court waiting for them when they went in with the rest of the band. He must have passed through the playground to get in undetected. He sat them down and discussed a few important stuff like; the ministry getting new Yamaha drums and they won't be able to use it as they'd like, when they would have practice again, playoffs available and talk of a new official uniform. When that was done they moved on to less important things like the outing they didn't have because of all their different schedules. The band was made up of a bunch of different secondary school students, college students and a few working adults. Though Giselle didn't really consider them adults; they certainly didn't act like it.

"Alright, so we agree with the fifteenth because that's when we could get everybody. That sound good?" Mr. Williams was saying.

"Yeah!"

"I is a broke man. So either everybody bring money and put up to buy food or we bring food." He rubbed his stomach.

All the boys started to chant, "buy KFC! Buy KFC!" This definitely drew some attention from the crowded court.

"No man!" Serene shut them up. "Every damn time is KFC. That costin' a lot of money. I could bring water, Rayanna could bring juice, another person snacks and somebody

321

cook. Not Raheem because we doh want shittin's." She said this rather seriously.

"A-a!" Raheem placed his hand on his chest, drew back his head and looked at her like he was offended. They all knew he wasn't.

Mr. Williams laughed. "I go cook."

"No, not you either." Serene said and cut his laughter short. "You could provide the ingredients and let Tracey mom cook. She does make some nice food."

Everyone seemed to support the idea. "Everybody agree?" Mr. Williams needed confirmation.

"Yes!"

"Alright, BBC Beach for twelve o'clock. When I say twelve I mean twelve. I doh want to see nobody walkin' in after two. All-yuh Grenadians always late."

"That's we nature, dog." Cheddi put his foot up on the bench in front of him and crossed it.

"As a matter ah fact, come for ten so by twelve half of us should be there." That was how the meeting ended.

Before entering Majesty that night she felt way guiltier than ever. Giselle was home alone with her brothers and they went full NCIS on her ass. Amron brought up the rabbits again. He wanted to know where they were and why Giselle was keeping it such a big secret. Andre even brought up the fact that she had been going to sleep really early of late. He knew she wasn't sick and he just found it strange. After she made all her excuses and they let it slide, Amron took his investigation a step further.

He wanted to know who was responsible for the new hairstyle she was sporting out of nowhere. When she told him it was Emma's mother's doing he skeptically let it slide. Then he said he found it harder to wake her up in the morning. Giselle retaliated that he should just stop waking her up all together, but Andre cut her off. He stated that for someone who goes to bed so early she shouldn't be so tired. In the end she concluded, in her mind of course, that she should stay home tonight. Just to be safe. She made a good call too. They kept bothering her all night; just randomly calling her for no reason whatsoever.

Around twelve they finally fell asleep. She didn't want to go to Majesty now anyway, but she was so used to being up after twelve that she couldn't fall asleep. What now? She was tossing and turning in her bed and she could hear Amron snoring loud in the other room. That was something she hadn't heard in a while. Actually, seeing her room so dark and lifeless wasn't something she had seen in a while either. It felt strange. Imagine that. She got up. She had brought home her training jumpsuit with her from last time. When she changed out of her swim suit to go home she had gotten so used to wearing it that she put it back on instead of her home clothes. So now she had it buried in her closet until time to go back. She dragged it out from the depths of the black hole that was her closet. She didn't want to turn the bed room light on. She sat on her bed in darkness appearing to admire the style of her jumpsuit. It was the same colour as the pants everyone else wore and it had six pockets too; two small ones on her chest, two near the waist area and two at the back. Sewn on the top right pocket was the Majesty symbol. Her mind was going through loops. Her dad said BJ would be back in Grenada tomorrow so she was looking forward to that. And she couldn't stop thinking about all the things she had researched before bed seeing as she couldn't enter Majesty. According to google another name for Slaugh was secret keeper. She found it ironic since Hozen was doing a good job at keeping his face a secret. She spent half an hour after reading in detail about it scrolling through the abundant images on google. They all claimed to be Slaughs, but every one of them was so different from each other it was hard to tell. Which one would Hozen most likely look like? She wondered this. When she googled Aswang, she found out it was '...*a vampire-like witch or ghoul...*' which explained Scout's teeth. It also explained why he couldn't stand the water of Pious Falls. It was holy and he wasn't. What concerned her was the fact that some Aswang's had several forms they could assume and they made a habit of eating people.

So the no huntin' rule apply to Scout, she remembered the handbook.

Shaking this thought out of her mind she changed subjects. Weyden Empire could not be found on google. No matter how she phrased it she found nothing that put the two words together. Google kept suggesting she change Weyden to Hayden; still nothing of worth. Majesty wasn't even on there, not that she expected it to be. That ended her search for the night.

"Why the sudden interest in the supernatural?" Vrai asked.

"That's a question?"

Giselle sat on her pillows now, her jumpsuit strewn across the bed, head against the head board.

"It is almost obsessive," Vrai answered.

"I just wanted to know stuff," Giselle breathed.

"Did you find what you were looking for?" Vrai continued casually.

"Most of it," she confirmed. "I still can' find out anythin' about... Vrai?"

Suddenly flanked with an idea she sat upright and pulled the mirror into view.

"Yes."

"What is Weyden Empire?" She waited on the edge in anticipation.

"Everything must begin somewhere. For a human it is in the womb of their mother. They then come forth into the world under man made lights in a four wall, concrete building. For the magical-supernatural world we begin in whatever unique ways our species require then come forth under the natural light of on an island far, far from here." Vrai spoke cleverly.

"Yeah, The Land of Spirits, but it didn' have war there or somethin'?"

"Giselle," Vrai addressed her. "Countless countries have been in war, but they still remain inhibited, do they not?"

Realization suddenly setting in, she raised her gaze to think, but was greeted by an unpleasant surprise. Even though briefly, Giselle could have sworn someone was in her room. There was a dark figure looming around her bed closing in on her. With the panicked gasp that left her lips she must have scared the person away. They disappeared. From then, she wasn't comfortable in her room anymore. She didn't feel safe. Would it be ok if she went outside and flew around for a bit? She would feel much better out there than she did in her own room. Grabbing her jump suit, she fled the house.

She circled around her house and flew low in the bushes in the area to hide. Taking practice of flying left and right and eating a few branches with her face when she failed. Everything takes time. Though she felt she might have dodged a few more branches had she not been so distracted. Who was that person and why were they in her room? Was it someone from Majesty? The person did disappear. Still, that didn't make any sense. Why would anyone from Majesty sneak up on her like that? They didn't know she was a guardian; actually they barely knew she existed. There was no reason for anyone to come looking for her. None of the guardians would show up like that.

As she got further and further from her house Giselle flew low in some thick branches getting a little handle on dodging them. She found it amazing that she felt so refreshed and relaxed like the sky was where she needed to be. The cool air in her hair and the comforting tireless composure of her body; she was made to fly. She was looking down scanning the ground as she hovered along when something caught her eyes. A body. A motionless body. Pale. Dry. Lifeless. Seeing this gave her flashbacks to her mother and grandmother's funeral and so she faltered and struggled to keep herself aloof. Should she do something? Call the police maybe. No. Maybe not because then she'd have to explain how she found the body all the way out there at this hour. She couldn't call Tegan or Marko either. This was a situation in the non-magical world, if there was even such a thing anymore. This had nothing to do with them. No. She should just go home. Giselle, still trying to keep her mind clear of the fact that she just saw a dead person, probably another missing person, decided home bound was the best direction. This would never leave her mind though. Even if she went home she would still remember it was there and she'd feel guilty for not helping. And what about the stranger in her room? What now? Where to turn?

Apparently her mind decided it was a good decision to turn back. She couldn't leave it there. Not like that. She had to find a way to make sure that body was found no matter how freaked out she was. Somewhere out there a family was moaning and on edge hoping that whoever was down there would come home. She couldn't leave the body there. Her conscience wouldn't let her. Connecting her knee's to the dirt she didn't land in any manner Marko would be satisfied with. But at least this time, just this once, she could be excused. With the dead man lying no more than ten feet away from her, she had reason to be nervous and out of focus. Trembling and trying her best to stay calm she crept up to him not finding the strength to walk. She couldn't help wondering how he died. Why was he out here? Did someone murder him? She got closer to his body. There was a still aura about him that she could not bear. The aura of death. There was no smell- maybe he hadn't been there long enough. The closer she got the more noticeable the bite mark on his arm and on his neck became. Those two puncture wounds that she knew too well. Everyone knew them actually. They were the signature of a creature whose existence some thought was debatable. She knew the truth. If Majesty was real and if Nocturn Niche was real then vampires had to be real.

The rustle of the bushes in the night air raised her hairs on end. Her goose bumps were so bountiful and so high you could use it as a scrubbing board. She shouldn't be here. She should have run away initially. That was how she felt now. The good girl inside of her wanted to do something, but everything else was saying she should pretend she never saw this. At least she had proof that this was supernatural. Now she could call Marko and Tegan in and it wouldn't be pointless. A vampire had clearly murdered someone. Weren't they not allowed to do that? She remembered reading something along that line in the patrol book, but she couldn't think straight enough to recite it now. There were a lot of different ways to express fear. Some people were loud, some people ran, some people even turned into professional boxers within two seconds. Giselle froze in fear; where people would run, or scream she stayed still and silently lost her mind.

The sound of chuckling locked her joints, making it difficult for her to get to her feet. Once she did, once she was able to turn around, she saw she wasn't alone. Her chest tightened. The man was tall and pale with long sleek hair running down his back and a pointed nose. He pulled a girl he had in his arms up in a death grip and held her head back. Then she saw it. The man had fangs. She guessed right; it was a vampire. She started breathing heavily, but her composure now didn't match what she felt. Straightening up she tried to talk sense to herself.

Ok. Brave up. You a guardian. Relax!

When the vampire made his move to bite the girls neck Giselle shouted, "Stop!"

He froze taking in every detail of the tough outer appearance of the panicking Giselle.

Help the girl. Help the girl. This is what you wanted to do. She said in her head.

Watching the girl tremble madly was unnerving. Then, as if the vampire didn't care that she was reprimanding him, he bit into the girl's exposed neck. Giselle ordered him to stop again unable to think of anything else. What should she do?

If I could only summon… she began a thought, then remembered something vital.

Dipping into her pockets that held the same magic as Ecoli's she retrieved her orange peg missile. That should help a little bit.

"Drop her!" She demanded pointing him with her new found confidence.

Taking his last sip the vampire let the girl's body fall lifelessly to the floor although she didn't seem completely gone yet. He hadn't finished her off. In fact, he looked as though something else, much better than blood, had sparked his interest.

"Majesty," he snarled.

Ignoring him she continued. "Walk away now and we go pretend this never happen."

She knew she wouldn't be taken seriously if she told him he was in trouble. She couldn't go quoting the handbook at this moment. So she settled with asking him to leave. His eyes carefully roamed her stopping suddenly when it reached her neck. Giselle was nervous. Was he thinking about eating her instead?

"Sui Generis," he muttered lowly.

"Move I say!"

She stepped forward, but when she got closer he disappeared. She froze. Where did he go? The thud noise behind her answered her question. Slowly she turned around trying to force her joints to comply. Her eyes roamed up to the sleek man standing wiping his lips with the sleeve of his shirt.

"Another meal."

His accent was thick and not one she could put a country to. That wasn't how people from Majesty spoke. Yet, in a weird way he reminded her of Vrai.

"You-you get permission to go huntin'?" She asked gripping her peg missile tighter realizing he wasn't going to leave.

The vampire chuckled ominously. He rubbed his hands through his hair as if he was worshiping it.

"You are one of those armatures from the New World. Permission?" he laughed at the idea like it was the most absurd thing he ever heard.

"What you call me?"

He flipped his hair. "I called you an amateur. What is the problem little girl? Need a dictionary?" This angered her. "Inept." He was suddenly directly in front of her then disappeared again. "Incompetent." He spoke from behind her. She spun around backing up in the process. "Coward."

"Am not a coward!" She snapped. "If I was I would be runnin'. I doesn' run."

"Because you cannot." He found his own bullying amusing. "You are a coward. You are a part of that generation that fled when hell became more than just a nickname for The Land of Spirits. You disgrace."

"Shut up!" His one word insults stung more than they should have.

"You do not deserve to live, more than she deserves to die." He pointed the girl.

She raised her weapon to his head to defend herself when she saw him step forward, but he grabbed it and tugged her closer to him with it.

"Ah, Ah, Ah, not so fast. I have been presented with a gem; a guardian. While you lot fled we stayed behind and suffered. We are still suffering. But now, I have a guardian." He inspected the chain in her neck.

Giselle tugged on the peg missile in attempt to set it free. She couldn't. She wasn't even able to set it off because he had some of her fingers in his grip as well. He was cold. With envy and greed etched across his face he reached for her chain, but she smacked his hand away with her one she managed to work free. Enraged, he bent her fingers backward causing her to cry out in pain. He clasped his icy, pale fingers on the gold chain, but wasn't even allowed the opportunity to tug on it when a bright white light flashed from his hand followed by a popping sound and him letting her go. He grabbed onto his wrist and looked at his smoking, charred fingers in shock. Bewildered, Giselle glanced at her chain of which the mirror was stirring.

"Vrai?" She called breathlessly.

"Focus," was the instruction she received.

Looking up at him again and shifting the peg missile into her other hand she aimed struggling hard to ignore the pain in her fingers.

"Insolent…!" He was saying when she turned the dial right and shot a very purple net at him.

He sped away from her the net following in a wild chase. A sudden pain across her chest made her drop to her knees and when she looked she only caught glimpse of his hair disappearing in the trees and not far behind a blurred net. What did he do? Why was she suddenly feeling so warm and sticky?

"Leave the weapon. Go to Majesty." Vrai ordered her.

Giselle tried to move, but evidently she was in a lot of pain. It was a bad decision to look at her hand because she was greeted with too much of her own blood. She couldn't breathe.

"I will take you in," Vrai said.

"No," Giselle spoke between breaths. "Take… her… too" She nodded her head in the girl's direction.

"I cannot." Vrai was stern.

"Why!"

Giselle shouted and she could see purple string endlessly rolling out of her peg missile. The thread was wound around the trees, but slowly somehow it seeped through and was now stretched in the direction she had last seen the vampire.

"I jus'… I stay to… help her!… Take… her… too!" She clutched her chest.

"The magic used to make the Sui Generis will not allow me to carry her to the universal passage," Vrai sounded annoyed and sorry at the same time.

"Fine," Giselle choked out tasting blood in the process.

In her second attempt to rise to her feet she was successful, but not without screaming pain.

"What are you doing?" Vrai asked.

Giselle had stumbled across to the dead man's body where she tucked the peg missile whose thread had stopped moving.

Then she went to the girl's body and was attempting to stand her up. The girl's groan was barely audible, but it was hope.

"Hospital," was all she could get out while trying to stabilize the extra weight.

"You cannot make it all the way there and live," Vrai raised her voice.

"Watch me," Giselle growled.

In all the searing pain Giselle took off in flight. She was going to make it to the hospital no matter what. She didn't care who saw. That was all Vrai seemed to care about; her secret being exposed. She kept shouting orders at Giselle who blatantly ignored. She had to make it. This was the reason she became a guardian. She wanted to help people. Her job was to offer protection. Though her protection was technically meant for the magical- supernatural world it didn't mean she should exclude this girl. She couldn't. She wouldn't forgive herself if she did. But the pain became too much and so did the weight and the blood loss and suddenly she found herself descending and unable to go any higher. The hospital wasn't close. What now? She went down, down, down until darkness surrounded her. She was sure it wasn't from the trees but from an onset black out.

She needed Marcel. Badly. She felt a familiar tug. It was like the one she felt when Vrai had sucked her in the first time. The thirsty desire she had to yell profanities at Vrai for not letting her do her own thing was too intense. All she wanted to do was drop this girl to the front of the hospital. When that

334

was taken care of Vrai could do whatever she felt like. Why was she interfering? The pull became stronger; that ride was not at all like hers. The pain made it something different. She wasn't even sure she was awake. She didn't see herself appearing in Majesty. Instead she was caught up in a whirlwind of colours. The heat was intense and she felt like she would be torn apart if she didn't melt first. Straight ahead she could see a familiar frame. The entrance to Majesty, but how could she get there. There was no ground beneath her feet. She was suspended in space. She couldn't swim.

You could fly, her exhausted mind encouraged.

That was the last thing she could remember thinking before the world went dark again.

CHAPTER TWELVE

TIME TO RETURN

"HEY, YA UP?" A voice whispered.

Why people keep wakin' me up? Why I can' sleep peacefully for one mornin'? Every day is the same thing. She thought to herself.

She refused to open her eyes. She stirred in her bed trying to block out the voice beside her.

"False alarm," the voice said again.

"We must wait then," another voice said.

It was masculine, though, it didn't sound like Amron or Andre; not even her dad. Who was in her room?! Giselle shot up to a seated position in fright, not oblivious to the pain spiraling in her body. Whoever was there had another thing coming. She wasn't about to lie down and cower. If it was the vampire, if somehow he escaped her net, she was going to stand up and fight. She was already very agitated and high on adrenaline; best to finish what she started. To her disadvantage, the speed she rushed forward with made her dizzy and suddenly she felt so nauseated. The room was in a blur.

"No, she's up." the male voice said again cheerfully.

She could faintly see an outline of a person in a white coat in front of her. He had a clip board, she assumed, in his hand and was walking toward her. But who was he? She didn't feel comfortable with the fact that she couldn't see his face clearly. She started backing up wildly blinking excessively to try and clear her vision. It helped little. For some reason as she thrashed her arms there was a pull to go with it and what was on her face? Reaching up she grabbed at the plastic material. Was this an oxygen mask? She needed a weapon; that was all she kept thinking.

"Stop. Leave the room. I will deal with it."

A familiar female voice ordered. The coated outline stopped. She could see now that it was a lab coat. She looked to her side where the female voice had come from, panic still in her system. This outline was settling though; the long, thin, curly locks; the broad hips and the glasses. She froze blinking a few times again and bringing her hands to her eyes. Why did they feel so heavy? After a good rub she could see now. Not perfect, but clear enough.

"Marcel." Her voice was barely there.

Marcel approached as she said, "Thought we lost ya."

"Where am I?" Giselle blurted out coarsely. The nerves were still concentrated in her system.

"Hospital."

"Which hospital?" She was lost.

Marcel sighed. "Majesty's City Health Centre."

Majesty? How did she end up there? Last time she checked she was at home because her brothers wouldn't give her peace of mind. They were all over her about the rabbits among other things. Urg! They were so annoying and always up in her business. Honestly, they should just tame already. It wasn't like they hadn't reason for their suspicions or anything, but still. After she dealt with the both of them that was when all the chaos took place. Remembering the girl and remembering the vampire clearer, now she was also reminded of her wounds and the pain it brought. This memory only made her more aware of her chest still trembling with pain. Her breathing was rough and ragged. Marcel rushed to console her. She could not be consoled.

"Calm down, darling. Deep breaths."

Marcel tried to get these words through to her. After fighting for five minutes the words finally sunk in. She was on her knees now. When Giselle looked down at herself she noticed an excessive amount of drips hooked up to her. Worst yet, her arms had a whole lot of red patches like rashes all over it. They seemed to be moving; fading into nonexistence leaving a caramel mark as fresh and smooth as a baby. She could see the movement even though it was slow.

"Ya can't move like that." Marcel put both hands on Giselle's shoulders. "Might open ya stitches."

"Stitches?!"

"You don't know what happened?" Marcel asked, her voice full of hurt.

"Where the girl?" Giselle sniffed, her whole body moving in accordance.

Marcel lowered her head, "I'm sorry."

"What?"

"I'm sorry," she whispered again. "What happen to her was beyond my expertise."

Taking a few moments to comprehend this, pressure built up in Giselle's chest.

"Ya passed out and ya Sui Generis delivered ya 'ere. But ya didn' wanna let go o'the girl and because o'the magic that created and protects the mirror she was burned. Ya got burned too," Marcel pointed the pink patches. "I can make the scars go away once ya heal completely."

"That's not good enough," Giselle growled.

"Huh?"

"That's bull! You can' jus' do the same for her that you doin' for me?" Giselle snapped.

Giselle seemed to have caught Marcel off guard. Heck, it would have caught anybody off guard. The amount of rage and emotion that was embodied in Giselle's tone was nothing Marcel expected.

"S'more complicated than that. To this world she does not belong. She suffered the worst o'the mirror because o'that." Marcel observed how worked up Giselle was becoming. "If ya don' calm down I'll have to sedate ya."

When she opened her eyes again she was feeling extremely serene. The room was dark. Giselle was lying flat on her back and the only thing in sight was the flat white ceiling. She could hear the pronounced beeping from the machine near her bed. It was very slow paced. And there were faint respiratory sounds in the corner of the room. She felt like she should be mad, but her mind was too lazy to pursue that emotion. So she laid there in silence.

All she could think about was the fact that she caused that girl to die. She held on till the very end and caused her to be burned by the mirror. Wasn't there anything Vrai could do about it though? She was the spirit that completed the Sui Generis. Surely she should have a say in the activation of this protective magic. As much as she tried to convince herself of this, she knew this had nothing to do with Vrai. If she could control the protective magic in the chain, then Giselle wouldn't have been burnt too. Vrai tried to help her; she knew that much. Lazily, she turned her head to the right. There was a muscular figure sitting in the corner in a very uncomfortable looking chair. That couldn't be her father, could it?

"Dad?" She squinted.

She knew the individual heard her because he jumped out of sleep looking startled. Then he got up and made his way over to her. He wasn't her dad. The youngster sat on the side of the bed groggily. It was Marko.

"There's my warrior," he yawned.

He stretched before he started to talk again.

"Ming found you in front of your mirror and called for help. Everybody was losing their minds thinking you were done. Not me though. I was calm."

The mention of his composure was an obvious lie.

"And then Marcel came and dealt with everything…" Marko went on in his rant like they weren't in a hospital room. "… so Tegan started to freak out." She caught the end. Wait what? Why was Tegan freaking out? Giselle was finding it hard to focus.

"…but at least the scars are gone. Well, most of them."

She slowly raised her hand remembering faintly that there was something on there earlier. She expected to see healed bruises or something, but her skin looked untouched. She could have advertised for cocoa butter lotion. Great, she thought. Bring on the guilt for shouting at Marcel.

"Just your stitches now. Two more days and your good; then Marcel can take away the scars. It would be like it was never there,"he stated casually. "It was a really big slash so the medicine took longer than usual to work."

"Where?"

"There."

He pointed her chest and traced the air down to her stomach. She copied his motion touching her chest. She could feel a bumpy irritated area through her hospital gown, but it wasn't paining like before. She found herself stretching. How could she be so comfortable? She just got stitches.

"How long I been sleepin'?"

"Second time or altogether?" She just stared at him. "Altogether then? Just over two weeks." Her eyes widened in alarm. "Don't worry. Duplicate Giselle's been in your place for a while; I don't like her. She's actually a bit ruder than you are which shouldn't be. Or are you just holding back your rude comments because you haven't known us that long?" He gave her a knowing look. "Anyway, when you feel better I can give you her memories. Painless. It would be like you never left."

Giselle sat up preparing for an argument again; probably even shout. She just ended up moaning. Not in pain, but like she was tired. Then she yawned.

"Feeling really relaxed, aren't you?" He smirked.

"Yeah," she nodded.

"That's how Eco-losing-it feels on those days. He wants to shout, but he just can't get it out. Hey! That rhymed."

He repeated it a few times in a sing-song voice. Giselle's lips twitched into a small smile at the nonchalant guy on her bed.

"It's the water from Pious Falls. If you have a mind like Marcel's, you can do great things with it." He explained then oddly started to chuckle. Giselle stared at him with knitted brows. "If you have a body like Scout's then you need to do great running from it."

She giggled weakly.

"The water, they mix it and use it for a lot of different things. In your case a sedative and a pain killer." He poked her arm when he said his next few words. "I could cut your arm off right now and you wouldn't feel a thing." She rubbed her arm.

Marko took the time to explain in detail everything that happened. He said she did a good job protecting the peg missile. They were able to find the vampire that hurt her. It was at this time he handed back her peg missile and assured her that Ecoli was really impressed. He also told her that Marcel worked tirelessly to ensure she was alright. He said she knew the girl was gone the second she saw her and she still tried to do the impossible. It didn't work and Marcel was troubled.

"I mean, what's the point of doing magic if you can't even keep the people around you from dying, right?" His voice was shaky. It sounded like a weak laugh used as a blanket to hide sadness. "It's worth a shot."

Giselle nodded.

"I know you're mad for some reason. Like, is that a Grenadian thing 'cause Eco-lunatic, you know what, never mind. Off topic. Just, don't let this weigh you down, ok?"

"People doesn' jus' get over this stuff, Marko," her voice was slightly annoyed.

"I never said get over it," he rushed these words together. Then his voice was light again. "I said don't let it weigh you down. I watched my... you never get over it."

She couldn't help longing to know what he was going to say. He made no effort to follow up on it. Instead he wrapped his fingers around his opal pendant.

"Next time you're throwing a tantrum call me. I'd like to get that on camera." He smiled. "Don't rip anymore stitches," he said before exiting the room.

Marko really had her mind busy once he left. She had so many questions running through her mind and so much to think about. Number one on the list, apologize to Marcel. Number two- was her training still on? He did say Ecoli was impressed with how she handled herself. How did they even know about that? How did Ecoli know how well she handled herself? You know what, it didn't matter. They used magic; end of story. So what, she was out cold for two weeks. She hoped that didn't change anything. If anything, she wanted training more now. She was never going to end up in a situation like that again. She wanted to be prepared. There was nothing to be impressed about; the girl was dead. She couldn't save her.

~*~

"Are you serious right now?" Tegan asked her.

They were standing outside RQ2. Once she left the hospital, two days later, she was taken to sub HQ by a guide. Marcel didn't want her walking alone just in case and left word with her workers to make the necessary provisions. Her initial goal was to find Marcel, but she couldn't open the door to the medic room. She found herself fumbling just like Tegan did to go in. Marcel might not even be in there; she fully considered that, but still…

From there she found Tegan in RQ2 scanning the mission board. He was preparing to take on his third mission since she had been hospitalized. She was fully prepared to hop onboard this train.

"Yes," she responded simply.

"But, you just got out," he stared at her skeptically.

"Yes and I make up my mind so don' try to change it. I want to do the mission. I have to. So let's go pick one," she rushed him.

He sighed and rubbed his head. "You know you could be really annoyin'."

"Thanks," she smirked.

He smiled and shook his head. "Alright, here's the deal. I'll pick a mission with you first thing tomorrow."

"Why?"

"What do you mean why? You just got out the hospital. I'm pretty sure Marcel's waitin' for you at headquarters." Tegan observed her face full of disappointment. "Why do you want to do this so badly?"

She couldn't bring herself to look at him, but she did answer her trainer's question.

"Cause I mess up," she was soft.

"No you didn't," he stooped in attempt to get her full attention.

"Yes I did. The girl didn' survive."

"Giselle, to be a guardian one thing you're going to have to learn is you can't save everybody. As long as you know you did everything in your power to carry out your mission successfully its ok. And you were alone. For the most part, as a guardian, you'll never be alone."

She sighed.

"Hey, your peg missile caught a vampire. Do you know how hard it is to catch a vampire? Especially one from Wey…" he stopped himself.

"Weyden Empire? You could say it. I doh get what the big secret is. Is just Tlos new name after the war, right?" She dryly enlightened him with her new-found knowledge.

"Seriously, where do you get your information?"

"I ask a lot of questions," she shrugged.

"Really? I didn't know that." Tegan was very sarcastic.

Following this discussion Tegan guided Giselle back to the medic room in headquarters where, surely, Marcel had been waiting on her along with Marko. It was hard and only to herself would she admit a little embarrassing, but she had to apologize to Marcel. In the heat of realizing her own failure in the hospital she was a bit rude to Marcel. That shouldn't have happened no matter how down in the dumps she was. To her surprise, Marcel waved the apology saying she forgot all about that and that she had heard worst things.

"Ok, you'll need this."

Marko handed her a small stoppered tube. The liquid was brown and thick. What was this? She took the tube from him staring at it unsure. Marko called it Anamnesis Solution. He explained that this substance was going to combine her and the duplicates memories. He said her brothers and father were out of the house so she could take it at home. Once swallowed, she would be totally out of it for five minutes while her memories combined. He also made a point to mention that she should have water at hand; the taste was revolting. Simple enough.

Giselle was on her way home for the first time in what felt like forever. She had to do her routine walk from Ruby's house. The entire walk home she was so nervous. Why? Because she had to leave Grenada when she was fatally injured and her dad didn't even know she was gone. She was going to be awkward and nervous knowing the truth. She hadn't seen her family in over two weeks. How would they react when they saw her? They might not even react; technically she'd been there the entire time. The duplicate. Was combining her and the duplicate's memories going to help deal with that? Since it was there the whole time, would joining eliminate the awkwardness? Had they really fallen for that replacement? Were her brothers and father so oblivious to her behavior to be fooled by such a cheap trick? She hoped they weren't, but at the same time they had to be. They had to be gullible or else she couldn't stay in Majesty for as long as she did. She couldn't run the risk of them finding out. And for some reason the thought that if they ever got suspicious and she had to give up Majesty for more than a day burned. If it was her choice to stay away it wouldn't matter, but if she had to because of the circumstances she'd miss it badly. The thought of possibly never seeing Marko, Scout,

Ecoli and Tegan again and never having Marcel to treat her like a daughter brought on new levels of hurt. Choosing Majesty over her family wasn't an option she wanted to be aware of. That wasn't something she wanted. She wanted to go and come in Majesty as she pleased secretly.

"So you are alive," Vrai suddenly spoke on Giselle's chest.

Giselle didn't respond.

"I had to take you," Vrai continued. "You would have died."

"And you would of get a new owner," Giselle retaliated as she bent the corner by the community's church.

Vrai took a while before she spoke again. "I made a promise to protect you."

"When?" Giselle sounded annoyed.

"The contract."

Giselle sucked her teeth in a very pronounced way.

"You were doing your job so I did mine."

"No I was just helpin' a random person," she clarified.

"That vampire was from Weyden Empire. If he managed to kidnap you or take me, Majesty would be in deep trouble. You stood up to him and in turn I protected you."

Understanding Vrai's motive Giselle softened. It didn't make her any less confused though.

"So Weyden Empire is what Majesty need protection from?"

"Yes," Vrai confirmed.

"And Weyden Empire is The Land of Spirits?"

"Used to be."

"So why? Who is Weyden then?"

If The Land Of Spirits was stable enough to form an Empire why wasn't Majesty aligned with them? Why weren't people travelling back and forth from the two as they wished? And why was Ecoli so careful about any information concerning Weyden Empire?

"Weyden Empire refuses to associate with Majesty." Vrai spoke gravely.

"How come?" Giselle asked.

"They consider Majesty the worst generation," she said.

"But people there not bad behave from what I see. I barely had to do anything as a patroller." Giselle couldn't see the point to Weyden Empire's recoil.

"It is not that type of worst generation," she said, quickly following up with, "talk to your chief. He keeps this hidden for a reason."

Stubbornness prevailed, she stopped talking to Vrai altogether. She was giving Giselle the answers then just stopped so suddenly. Why? For a while her only company was her footsteps. They were dragged and not in any hurry.

"I am proud of you," she heard Vrai again.

Again, Giselle said nothing. Not to be rude. She was just acknowledging the fact that for once something snooty didn't come from Vrai. She was surprised and appreciative that Vrai didn't use an uppity tone with her. She didn't have to ask why she said what she said. She already had that conversation with

Tegan and Marko and she knew Ecoli was impressed. So Vrai was proud, huh?

"I chose you for a reason," she continued.

Giselle, knowing she had to say it eventually said, "thanks for helpin'."

They both left it at that.

"I can teleport," Vrai revealed one of her many secrets. "Hide."

Trusting her, Giselle looked around ensuring she was alone then stood on the far side of the road beneath an overhanging branch. There was a muffled thud sound like a pillow hitting against the surface of a mattress and she felt wind brush against her. Before she knew it she was standing at her front door.

"Lock your room when you drink the solution."

The mirror ceased rippling. It looked like a regular mirror pendant on a unique chain. For the first time since knowing of her existence Giselle genuinely appreciated Vrai. Imagine what could have happened if Vrai chose to leave her stranded that night…

Placing a light hand on the door knob she turned and peeked through the crack. No one was supposed to be home, but she couldn't fight the feeling that she had to sneak in. It was weird. It was a fact that everyone's house had a different smell, but no one ever knew what their own house smelled like. Yet, somehow the smell she was never aware of was the greatest welcome back she could ever get. From the time the door was opened, she was greeted with a whiff of axe body spray that reminded her of Andre; a musty kind of air that sent images of her dad rushing through her head; then a fruit smell which reminded her of Amron because he like the outdoors just as much as she did. There was so much more mixed into it that she couldn't define, but it was unmistakable that something was missing. She assumed it had something to do with her not being there for over two weeks.

Giselle entered.

The center table was cluttered as usual with the newspaper and mail for Brent; bills. Next to the couch there was a basket of her and Amron's school uniforms. Above it was the ironing board. She could tell that was Andre's designated job when he returned from college. The floor didn't have much scattered across it which meant that Brent along with her duplicate had probably recently cleaned up. Something she never thought she'd miss was helping her dad care for the house. Off to the corner, just behind the door was the shoe rack with Brent, Andre's, Giselle's and one side of Amron's shoe. The other side had toppled over onto the floor. Feeling delighted to be back she put his shoe on the rack for him; something she would have never done without incentive. Then, in anticipation to see her room, she started a half run half walk to the hall. Customly the door opened.

"You home?" She heard Amron behind her.

She spun around to see her tough, oval faced, coffee brown, reckless, partner in crime almost smiling at him.

"Yeah," she had to hide the joy in her voice.

"How come? What Ms. Howard tell you?"

She froze. Was Ms. Howard supposed to say something?

"Um, why you want to know?"

"I was jus' askin', gosh!" He was irrationally annoyed. Kicking off his shoes he didn't look back to see if it landed properly on the shoe rack; it didn't.

"Excuse," he motioned her to move out of his way and then disappeared down the hall to his room closing the door tightly behind him.

What was that about? She couldn't deny that she was hurt by that reaction. Were they in a fight? A real fight? That didn't happen very often. It was usually them against BJ or them against Andre or them in a two second quarrel. So what happened? It felt raw to be on Amron's other side. What did the duplicate do? Rushing to her room now and ignoring sentimentalism she fished the anamnesis solution out of her pocket.

"Leaving a duplicate on its own long enough can make it develop into its own person," Vrai informed wisely.

Breathing heavily with unsettling thoughts about what that duplicate could have possibly done to make him treat her that way she locked her room door, sat on her bed and drank the nasty brown liquid as if she'd die if she didn't. Instantly, as it touched her tongue, she remembered Marko's advice to have water at hand. It was horrid; metallic, sour and regurgitation worthy. By some miracle she managed to swallow. After that she fell back on the pillow waiting to see what would happen next and tearing up from the after taste. Like a speeding truck sleep struck and so the movie of her past two weeks began.

CHAPTER THIRTEEN

ANAMNESIS SOLUTION

"YOUR BROTHER SHOULD be in the country."

Brent absentmindedly mentioned this as he crossed the living room. Or so he wanted it to appear. He was just as worried as any parent would be whenever their child traveled. He wanted to know if BJ had a safe flight home or not. That explained why he was flipping through every news channel he could find; looking for plane crashes maybe? Brent was a bit dramatic, which explained his children. Amron constantly drumming on his bed room wall wasn't helping. In fact, it was grating his last nerve so much so that he confiscated Amron's drumsticks. It wasn't long after that, the front door opened. In walked BJ and the weight that melted off of Brent was almost a visible puddle on the floor.

BJ came in tall, skinny, broad smile across his chestnut face. He strutted in. The only thing leaving his mouth was, "family!"

He said it in the most enthusiastic way possible. After that their dad swallowed him in a hug tapping his back and everything. In the midst of all the love Brent let him go and smacked him upside the head.

"Why you didn' call?" His tone wasn't rough though.

"I was already comin' here," BJ shrugged and embraced Giselle who was already under his arm.

She was overjoyed or at least the duplicate was. She couldn't help but agree that that was how she would react though. So far things were normal. She was looking on, but not in a physical form. Even Giselle didn't know where she was. She felt no attachment to the duplicate. It was almost as though she was a ghost overlooking the gathering.

"That's not the point BJ," Brent was trying to correct him, but the happiness wasn't allowing the stern in his voice to break through.

"Next time," BJ sat down. "Where Amron and Andre?"

"BJ!" Amron broke into the living room startling everyone.

Excitement raining through he rushed over to BJ and dropped all his weight in his big brothers lap with no other intention than to hurt him. In anticipation for it BJ attempted to move out of the way, but was still pinned by Amron.

"All these years and you still slow." Brent chuckled at the two boys' now rough housing.

Letting Amron go on for a few seconds longer before throwing him aside effortlessly, like he always could but pretended he couldn't, BJ got up to address everybody.

"So I have somethin' to tell all of you, mostly dad, but still all of you. Where Andre?" He rubbed his hands together.

"He have extra afternoon classes," Giselle told him. "I think it finish a while ago so he probably on he way home."

"Oh. Ok, ok." BJ couldn't defuse the look of excitement on his face.

"What this about?" Brent asked him.

"Um," BJ ran his hand over his low-cut jerry curled Mohawk.

"You do somethin', ent?" Brent accused.

"No," BJ's voice was humorous.

"Oh yes," Amron joined in on the finger pointing.

"Chill, chill, chill!" That was BJ's way of shutting people up. "Ok, so is about a girl."

"Jah!" Giselle sighed exasperatedly.

BJ had a reputation when coming to girls. Not one girl he ever dated, checked out or had a crush on was approved by their father. Not one. Brent disliked all of them. Every single one of them was a mess and a half. BJ seemed to be drawn to the kind of girls that liked drama, were boisterous, had too much attitude and confidence, and were territorial. Basically his phone couldn't have a password. One time Giselle called him and she could hear one of his female friends in the background asking him who it was. Quite frankly, Giselle was thoroughly annoyed with them all as were her other siblings. Amron low-key used to bully them, although Giselle felt like BJ knew about it. Andre would talk. BJ just didn't care. He wasn't going to try to change his little brother. The day he found a girl that could tolerate Amron he'd know he found the one.

"And what is this one name?" Brent wasn't taking him seriously.

"Why you usin' that tone?" BJ was unsuccessfully swallowing a laugh. "She different."

"Yeah right," Amron chastised.

"You go away for a while and all of a sudden you have a girl and she different," Giselle summarized smugly.

"For your information, big mouth, is not all of a sudden." He faced her then turned to include the others. "Been eight months now."

"Eight?" Brent and Amron spoke completely out of sync.

Brent seemed to be taking him seriously now. "Eight months?"

"Yes. Now hold on." BJ sounded proud of himself as he made his way to the door.

"What the hell? She here?" Giselle exclaimed.

"Watch your mouth." Brent corrected then faced BJ again. "You bring her here?"

BJ said nothing. He just had this really smug look of amusement and excitement as he stepped outside. The three of them waited quietly to see who he'd walk through the door. On an occasion like this, when he announced that he finally had a girl he was sure of, they'd never give him the time of day. After the third time, when he was only seventeen, they couldn't be bothered. Clearly BJ didn't have his life together in terms of relationships. It was best to ignore him instead of falling into the trap. They all went the same. He met someone, all of a sudden they were dating and then one dramatic tear filled story later they were broken up and he was over it. This time however was different. What made it different; he said he was with this girl for eight months. That was longer than any relationship he'd ever been in. Accusing him of lying would never cross their minds because if there was one thing BJ was always open about was his love life. They all knew every detail of everything.

It didn't take long before he stepped back in the house holding onto someone's hand. They couldn't see her tiny frame behind him though. Then once he got in he stepped aside to reveal the mystery girl. The dead silence that had awakened in the room pressed on. Nobody said anything. They all stared at the young lady with critical eyes not intending to make her feel uncomfortable, but it was their nature. BJ wasn't oblivious to how they were staring; it all came back to- he just didn't care.

"Everybody, this is Aibell Airlie. Aibell this is my dad Brent and my sister Giselle and my younger brother Amron. The other one not home yet," he introduced.

"Hi everybody," her face lit up without the faintest hint of discomfort.

"Hi, nice to meet you," Brent spoke first coming out of his shock.

List of things missing from this girl: she wasn't wearing leggings, jeggings or a really short skirt or pants; her clothes weren't tight at all; she wasn't wearing a million earrings on one ear which Brent had a big problem with; she wasn't chewing gum; she didn't have any visible tattoo's; and she greeted everybody pleasantly like she was happy to be there rather than forced. That was a game changer. Giselle blinked a few times to ensure Aibell actually looked the way she did. She was short. Anybody would look short next to BJ; he was unnaturally tall. But Aibell was short. BJ had nothing to do with that. She had on a pale blue jeans and a purple, long sleeved, plaid shirt. She rolled the sleeves up to her elbows and kept the shirt half way buttoned exposing a white vest beneath. Her hair was pulled back in a bun. The roots were black, but everything else right out to the bun was green. That was the only dramatic thing about her. She was decent. That was what caught them off guard. That and the fact that she was Caucasian.

"How are you? I'm so sorry about what happened to Ms. Ruby. Am I allowed to say that?" She glanced at, BJ but she sounded like she was talking to herself. "I don't care, I'm saying it. BJ won't stop talking about her. I wish I met her. She sounds great."

"She was," Brent responded still a bit odd.

"You know what," she scrunched up her face in thought. "I actually shouldn't bring that up so long after, is that ok? I just felt like I had to say it, you know?"

BJ stood at her side gazing down in total admiration as she rambled.

"No, no. Is ok." Brent shook his head. "Sorry, what was your name?"

"Aibell Airlie," she happily reminded him. "So you're Mr. Thomas, Giselle and Amron. Am I right? Don't be afraid to yell at me if I'm not."

Giselle nodded. "That's my name."

Amron folded his arms and squinted as though trying to seek out Aibell's darkest secret.

"Yeah, you're Amron. Just by that look I can tell. Sorry, BJ talks a lot. I wish he would shut-up sometimes."

"Well I know that for the future then," he scoffed playfully.

"You're welcome," she smiled and took a step forward as though she was about to walk deeper into the house before halting. "Is it ok if I come in? I'm very aware that this loaf of bread over there had a reputation for girls in this house. Sooo…"

"*Has* a reputation," Amron corrected her.

"No, no sweetie, *had*," she said pleasantly. "I'm here now."

The confidence was still there that was for sure, which wasn't a bad thing. Giselle wasn't sure if she would label her as territorial yet though. She had to let the evening play out. After a few minutes of small talk Brent took BJ into the kitchen to talk to him. He was very vague on what he wanted to talk about although everyone already knew. During this time, Andre came home, Giselle and Amron found out that Aibell was twenty-two and that she was from Brooklyn. She openly admitted she enjoyed singing, but her true dream was to be a police officer.

"You still in school?" Andre asked her. He was just as shocked as the others when he saw her.

"No, I don't like the idea of being judged by some third party who decides if I'm smart enough to have a good future. I decide that. Thank you very much," she was very front-ish and straight forward with her response.

"And you want to be a police officer?" Andre evidently didn't like her attitude. Giselle and Amron on the other hand were very intrigued to like this girl. Still, Amron being who he was, he had to say something smart.

"Is that the real reason or you just too dumb to keep up with your subjects so you skip university?" He looked her dead in the eye.

"Amron! Say sorry," Andre reprimanded him.

Aibell chuckled and for a minute Giselle thought she might be crazy. "I don't imagine your grades leaving you in a position to criticize anyone."

Giselle stifled a laugh and Andre had a look of disapproval on his face. As for Amron he seemed to respect and hate her at the same time.

"You're funny though," she pointed Amron. "And you're the nerd of the family. I can tell." Her eyes flicked to Andre. Without a word, he got up and went into the kitchen.

Giselle could like this girl.

A few uneventful days went by where the duplicate behaved just as Giselle would. She was shaken awake by her brother and experienced some annoyance. She went to school less than enthusiastic to learn. She hung out with her friends and after that she took a bus and made her way home. Life was simple. It was basically in repeat other than the few times BJ and his lady friend came over. Their dad was having a hard time accepting that BJ went away then all of a sudden he came back with a girlfriend and they'd supposedly been together for months. He refused to believe it. And Aibell didn't seem to pick up on the fact that Brent was uneasy when she was around. She was just talkative and rude to Amron in the sweetest way that even Andre didn't know how to phrase it when he wanted to run and complain.

The morning was young, but with the growing habit of getting to school late, Brent sent both Giselle and Amron on their way. They were upset about this mainly because they had to wake up earlier than usual. The time they woke up in the morning had nothing to do with their lateness to school. It was the time they wasted messing around with each other. Brent even went to the extent of waking Amron. He was not thrilled about it, but Giselle felt no sympathy for him. She simply said, "Now you know how it feel?" Slowly, still a bit grumpy about their new schedules, they made their way out of the house and down the road hoping a bus would pass by soon.

"I have Spanish with Mr. Gravesandy today," he stated and stopped as though in mid-sentence.

Giselle waited a while before speaking again. "Sooo?"

"Nothin'," Amron shrugged. "I just can' stand him."

"Stop doin' that!" She smacked his shoulder.

"Doin' what?" He rubbed the spot she assaulted.

"Talkin' like you have a story to give and then cuttin' off," she specified.

"I doesn' do that," he defended himself.

"Oh yes. Doh argue," she shut him up. "Why you pick Spanish if you don' like it? You in form four now. You could choose anything you want."

"I like Spanish, I jus' doh like the teacher," Amron slowed his speech and exaggerated his tone. "We have two Spanish teachers. I thought I was goin' to get Mrs. Carol. I like her."

"Because she's a lady," Giselle pointed out matter-of-fact-edly.

"Nooooo!" He dragged, though she could tell that he honestly meant he didn't like her that way. "She's a good teacher. She used to teach me in form two and three. I thought she would teach me in form four too."

"You behave like you don' know they change teachers," Giselle rolled her eyes.

"I know they do, but I doh like when they do that. I spen' two years learnin' with how a certain teacher like to teach a certain subject and now I have to deal with this big-head man. He not even makin' it lively."

Giselle sniggered. "That's like my History teacher. Miss. Riggs used to make it fun and now boring Miss. Harris teachin' me. She make me want to sleep all the time. If I havin' trouble to sleep in the night I jus' have to see her face and I would knock out, one time."

Amron laughed so hard he actually had to stop walking and put his hands on his knees. He laughed enough to have his sister break out in a fit as well and it wasn't even at what she said. It was just him amusing her.

"What you laughin' at? I give you a joke?" She asked hilarity in her tone.

She grabbed onto his bag strap in attempt to get him upright and walking again. She refused to believe Amron was even laughing at her joke anymore. He was just being his stupid self at this point. It was probably one of those times where the laugh was funnier and sweeter than the joke and it was too good to stop. When Amron decided it was time to sober up he lifted himself up not without unrequired assistance from Giselle. He wanted to talk, but the laughter was still dying away in his throat. And as he was about to make eye contact with her, as his eyes strolled up her school uniform to her face all the humor washed off of him. He sprang up eyes fixated on something behind Giselle and moved her briskly away from whatever. Startled she stumbled in her attempt to turn around only to be greeted by nothing. Nothing was there. But when she looked back at her brother his face was set as if something unwanted and repulsive was nearing. Then, in the moment of him looking away from what he was transfixed on and her gearing to ask him questions, a bus pulled up beside them. Without a word Amron took his sister by the wrist, entered the bus and remained silent until he said good bye when they parted ways twenty minutes later.

This was the first time she had seen him act that way, but to her dismay, it wasn't the last. When he got home that evening he did his best to avoid all talk about his behavior. He was even thrilled when BJ passed by, without his girlfriend, to hang out with them. He spent his time rough housing with him and arguing with Brent who was complaining about him. Brent felt that Amron should realize that summer was over. He was in form four now and CSEC examinations were just around the corner. He wanted him to hit the books more. As always Andre agreed which added more anger in Amron's argument.

Since the duplicate was set to copy Giselle's actions, even though it didn't have to, it made an excuse to run away to Majesty every night. That was how she became aware of Amron's weird behavior. He was out of the house more than usual after school now and when he did stay home he went to bed as early as Giselle did. One night after she got home from Majesty she was making her way back home and saw Amron doing the same. He was alone, but he seemed to be saying good bye to someone before going in the house. How odd. At first she didn't really care about his strangeness. She was just glad he didn't catch her sneaking home, but then things got bad. She was seeing things. No matter where she went, no matter what she did she felt like people were watching her. It was easy to tell when you weren't alone, especially when the people stalking you were making themselves visible. She kept seeing different strange people appearing in her everyday life and frankly it scared the living crap out of her. It was odd. There was a new

IT teacher at school. It was a stumpy broad shouldered man with beady eyes that kept staring at her whenever they were in proximity of each other. She didn't study IT so they never had any reason to exchange words. Emma said he had a strange way of talking though; so proper. Then there was this albino boy, at the supermarket, that kept showing up everywhere she was. When she was choosing drinks in the fridge isle with her friends he was there examining a yogurt cup and casting shady glances at them. When they went to the snack isle to get cookies he was there getting a bag of chips. What was off about it was he had no yogurt or drink. Why was he over there then? Even at the cash register as she was about to pay for her things he was behind her in line. She dropped her coins and both of them bent down to retrieve it at the same time. When he handed the money to her he didn't look her in the eye. His eyes went straight to her chest where her grandmother's gift was weakly hidden. She said thank you after accepting her money, but he said nothing in response. He just left his can of tomato sauce he picked up with the cashier and left. They could just as easily be normal people, but something about their vibe didn't seem right; especially when the strange phenomenon's continued on at her home life with her brother acting crazy looking at air, people not from the neighborhood watching her walk home and seeing strange figures looming outside her bedroom window. She even heard talking.

"Are we sure that this is the one that caught Orygen?" The first shadow whispered.

"Yes," the second one said. "She is the one. She had New World weapons and a Sui Generis."

Giselle laid still in her bed as they talked with incredible details about things they definitely shouldn't know.

"She is young, this one. The new world seems to have gotten desperate for candidates." The other shadow chuckled.

"She should be an easy kill. The fact that she caught Orygen was mere luck. He was never smart anyway."

They both let out a gargled, unpleasant chuckle.

"Let us report to the Empire. We have found the girl."

Then they left.

Things were kind of strange after that. It was then Giselle, the real Giselle, was reminded that these were her duplicate's memories. They weren't hers. Hers were of the hospital when she was irrationally rude to Marcel the first time she woke up. That night, after the people had left her window, the duplicate folded itself in her bed tightly and squeezed its eyes shut in fear. The second it did it was like it blacked out and that created an opening for the real Giselle. When she had first woken up after the accident in Majesty the duplicate had just gone to bed. Her memories were fusing. As soon as she had finished freaking out on the hospital bed and was sedated she was taken right back to Grenada being woken up by Amron.

She woke up from the sound of Amron's voice. He was shouting her name. Though, this morning was unlike any other. The duplicate was different. Un-Giselle-like. It woke up with a new type of annoyance. Not an- I can't stand my brother, but I secretly don't mind him waking me up annoyance. It was more of a- do that again and I will literally murder you- type of annoyance. The glare that Giselle gave to Amron had him thanking the lord that looks couldn't kill. That was the first morning. She spent all the time they were in each other's presence that day questioning her brother. She, for some reason, was more serious now about why he was acting so strange. She wasn't even going about it the way Giselle would. After asking a few times she'd usually tell Amron to feel free to talk to her when he was ready which was what he did to her. This Giselle was almost holding him up with a stake for the answers that she did not get.

There was a meeting that night in the Rec. Room that was held in her presence for the first time. It was Ecoli talking to Tegan, Marcel and Marko.

"I can't leave it any longer," Marko was saying. "Duplicates can become their own person."

"We doh have anythin' better we could do?" Ecoli was asking.

"No," Marko shook his head. "The only person that ever successfully made and controlled a duplicate is Madge."

There was an uncomfortable silence in the room.

"Unless Weyden wants to lend us his people, which is highly unlikely, all we can do is rely on Tegan's magic and that voodoo crap," he pointed Giselle's duplicate. "And that voodoo crap is becoming unreliable."

"As if you are of any use to this establishment," The duplicate said.

"Oh my god, it's alive!" Marko reacted.

All of them looked shocked at Giselle's duplicate.

"Was it not sleeping?" Marcel asked.

"It is." Tegan said nervously.

"See, this is exactly why we have to remove it from that home. It's going to become a problem really fast. These kinds of duplicates are only good for a week. After that they become their own person if you don't extract the memories and destroy the shell." Marko seemed to be demanding action from Ecoli, but still holding his tone. He didn't want to make him upset.

"How Giselle doin'?" Ecoli faced his sister.

"Pretty damn fine," the duplicate carefully picked each word.

"Tegan! Put that thing to sleep. It's freaking me out." Marko yelled at Tegan.

Tegan nervously ruffled his hair. "I did!"

"Well damn, do it again!"

"Giselle not awake yet. Even if she was, I'm not willing to send her home with wounds so severe. I at least want it to a point where it's manageable for her. She can't go home acting like she needs rehab when her family didn't know she was hurt to begin with."

Ecoli rubbed his temples in a frustrated manner.

"Fine, fine. Fine," he said. "I jus'... maybe we should..."

"Ecoli," Marcel pulled his hands. "Ya not stupid. Stop tell-ing ya self ya don' know what to do and do what ya feel is right."

"Ok," he gazed at her. "I doh want to rush ya, but see if ya can speed up her recovery. Tegan, Marko keep the duplicate goin' for four more days. If Giselle not well enough to go home by then, well, I jus' have to talk to her dad and tell him what goin' on."

"Are you sure, mate?" Tegan asked. "The plan was to hold out until January. We'd have more time then. It'd be safer."

"Yeah, but how safe are they with that demon in their house?" He jutted his thumb in Giselle's direction.

"You're one to talk." the duplicate, that was more and more sounding nothing like Giselle, criticized. They tried their best to ignore it.

"True," Marko sighed. "Ok. I can monitor it for four more days. Tegan you up for it?"

"Sure," he nodded.

Marcel gazed around at them and then said, "I'll do every-thing I can to help her."

After that memory, Giselle's confusion was cleared. What-ever it is they were doing to control the duplicate was no longer working. It was now acting on its own impulses rather than what Giselle would do. When Amron woke her up again the next day she didn't greet him with a glare. First of all it didn't even feel like the duplicate had just woken up. The speed and strength it got up with was unnatural for anyone getting out of bed; even if their crazy big brother was making an unnecessary ruckus. The duplicate spun around and chucked Amron so hard when he tried to wake her up. The strength, to him, felt supernatural because frankly it was. No fourteen-year-old girl was going to push a sixteen-year-old boy and have him fly across the room the way he did. After that mishap Amron never woke her up again. The duplicate was nasty to everyone it came across that day. The beach event that the band had planned had finally arrived and she was nothing, but a nuisance the whole time. It got to the point where the band members were asking Amron what her problem was. Raheem was the only one trying to look past her attitude. He even attempted to do their handshake, but she refused.

Giselle woke up again in Majesty that night. This time she was seeing Marko and she understood why he was there now. He wanted the duplicate gone, but the only way that would happen was if she woke up or the four-day time limit ran out. She was beginning to realize he preferred her waking up. Although she couldn't' tell if it was because he wanted the real her back or if he wanted to keep whatever secret they had a secret. She was awake now. And she'd be well in two days. Ecoli had no reason to open his mouth to her dad now. Unnecessary confession. The memories were kind of bunched up after this; in and out of Majesty. Whenever she would rest in the hospital, which was often, it was a gateway for the duplicates memories. That was where she saw it. She was hounding Amron again for something she had seen him do. The duplicate was full on spying on him. Everywhere he went, everything he did, everyone he spoke to she kept tabs. Giselle could hear her thoughts. The duplicate couldn't shake the thought that Amron was magical. It almost became an obsession between causing trouble at school and making unnecessary mischief at home. The real Giselle however found that absurd. There was definitely nothing magical about her brother. Yes, he was strange, but he wasn't magical. She would have taken time to figure out why the duplicate felt that way about Amron, but fleeting thoughts of Weyden Empire running through its mind stopped her. The duplicate was trying to figure out how to get Weyden to trust it and prove that it could be an asset. It kept thinking that it was in the house of *'The Ruby's'* family. This was strange to Giselle. Why would the duplicate know anything about Weyden Empire and why did it sound like it wanted to betray Majesty. Because of the duplicates hostility toward Amron he also became suspicious trying to see where she ran off to at night (because somehow he had become aware of that).

"Who are you?" Amron growled one day after school. It was just him and Giselle, but Andre was sure to be there soon.

"What you mean by that?" Giselle responded coldly.

"I mean you not actin' like my sister so what goin' on?" he asked. "Where you went last night?"

"Not your business," she said.

"Yes it is," he retorted.

The duplicate gazed at Amron for a while and Giselle could hear the thoughts again. It was wondering if it took Amron alive to Weyden if it would be accepted. Amron's gaze shifted from Giselle to something overhead and so did the duplicate's. She started to smile.

"I see nothing, but you see something, do you not?"

"Where the hell you put Giselle?"

He was sure now. This wasn't his sister. Bravery being a part of his genetics he approached the duplicate and gripped her bicep tightly refusing to let go.

"Where Giselle?"

"Hopefully dying. That would work out perfectly for me," it responded.

"You little shit!" He snarled tightening his grip.

The duplicate punched him square in the jaw and started roughing him up in an attempt to free herself. Amron tried to hold on, pin her to the floor even, but he couldn't bring himself to fight how he usually would. This impersonator had his sister's face. He couldn't just punch it like it was some unrelated boy from school. In his efforts to restrain her without hurting her he was kicked and scratched until she had him pinned on his back instead. Her knee was on his throat and he couldn't breathe. His eyes were turning bloodshot and watery and she wouldn't get off. Then, as if by magic, Amron saw a concentrated lightning shaped light fly over his head and strike down the duplicate. She flew backward hitting against the wall near the door way. Choking and holding his throat desperately gargling air and feeling the pain as he did he flipped his body over. Whatever did that to Giselle might do it to him too. But it didn't. In the split of a second he could have sworn he saw a blond boy standing in his hallway, but just as fast as he appeared he disappeared. Then Andre came home.

From there her memories cut to her talking to Tegan about doing her mission. He lied to her. Maybe it wasn't all a lie. He said he'd been doing missions since she was hospitalized. Maybe he was free to for the first week, but for that entire second week he'd been babysitting the duplicate. He never told her anything about saving Amron's ass. Was that the mission? She had no clue what happened to the duplicate after that. All she knew from then on was that she was given the Anamnesis Solution and sent home.

The duplicate was no more.

CHAPTER FOURTEEN

A HINDRANCE

GISELLE HAD TO do the mission. That was the only way she would feel right. That was the only way she could prove that she was useful. If she proved to Ecoli that she could actually protect someone then maybe he might trust her with Guardian secrets. Maybe he might tell her about Weyden Empire and whatever it was that had to wait until January. And, she couldn't make the connection yet, but maybe it might help her with her brother. If someone were to walk in between them they would freeze to the bone. There was no communication going on there; as far as he was concerned his sister tried to choke him, she was up to no good and his dad was on his ass more than usual. Yet, like he always loyally did, he never told their dad what really happened. If Andre didn't walk in their dad wouldn't know anything at all. As far as Brent was concerned right now, Giselle and Amron had a disagreement that lead to a fight. Amron had every right to be mad at her or her duplicate really.

It was about three in the morning when she woke up hungry enough to eat the world. Continuing the tradition of every teen ever, she snuck out of her room to seek a midnight snack. And following the tradition of every house ever, everything chose to creak and make noise all the way to the kitchen. The whole point of creeping was to not be heard. She probably might have made less noise just walking normally. The soreness she had was making creeping even harder. Every time she thought of that night she was cut, the night she was burnt, it was as though she could feel the pain all over again. A familiar faded gold light was falling through the door frame. Someone was up; most likely Andre. Seriously was there a time when this boy wasn't hungry? She eased up to the entrance and peeped around the corner to see her partner in crime before going in. The whole point of going stealth mode was to not be seen. She couldn't just waltz in there.

Uhh, she groaned in her mind.

She would have preferred it to be Andre. Amron was standing in front of the fridge just staring in it. It was unclear whether he wanted something or not. That was the exact reason why his dad had to ask him questions like "You pay bills inside here?". She had only been spying for like two seconds when he turned around. He just glared at her like he expected her to be there. One thing about Amron you could not scare him. There was no sneaking up on him, there were no pranks, no scary stories and no horror movies that would make him flinch. He was rock solid. She had a better chance scaring Andre with a lizard; he had a phobia. Giselle walked into the kitchen bravely. She had already been spotted so why stand there hungry. Her stomach was crying for attention.

She walked in and went to the cupboard. The fridge was her target, but he was there so she had to avert. Nothing in the cupboard peaked her interest now. Sighing, she attempted to leave, but the sound of Amron clearing his throat made her turn around. She didn't even fully see him before she caught sight of an apple flying her way. She caught it. Giselle stared at it for a while; apple was her favorite fruit.

"Thanks," her words were barely audible.

One word. That was a record amount in days. She crept back to her room to enjoy her snack in peace, but now she couldn't. She was more upset than she was when she went out. What would her grandmother say to her? She could be the pompous, front-ish, I-don't-care Giselle and tell him stop being so cold. But the truth of the matter was as tough and hard boiled as Giselle thought she was, Amron, was ten times tougher. Knowing this she couldn't stop the tears welling up in her eyes. Why did she have to know about Majesty? If she didn't then she wouldn't be crying right now. She'd be focused on school; probably over the depression stage of losing the women in her life. The thought of this made more tears flow. If it weren't for Majesty she might still have them. Letting the apple fall to her sheets she laid on her side. The hot tears ran over the bridge of her nose and soaked the pillow. Amron didn't even say anything to her. Why won't he say anything? Why didn't her grandmother give the chain to someone else? What if it went to one of her brothers instead of her? She could bet things might be a bit different. What was her purpose as a guardian anyway; all she did was fly and she wasn't even good. The house was quiet for a long time. She wondered if he was still out there burning current. Then finally she was absorbed in miserable hazy sleep.

School was not like school. She had to clean up the mess that damned duplicate made. Detentions. Apologies to friends. Scowls from teachers. Uncertainty from the band members. It was a horrible atmosphere to be in. She just wanted to go home. That way she'd be alone. That way she could run off to Majesty. And she did. When she made her appearance that night everyone was happy she was ok; everyone there at least. Hozen and Trevor were off on another mission. They weren't a team or anything, but Hozen and Trevor always went on missions together if their work load allowed it. They became good friends when they met there some years ago and now they were always in each other's company. Ariel was off on another mission as well and Giselle couldn't help, but wonder if it was one like last time. Would Ariel need dispatch to come and clean up a mess she uncovered? Ming was locked away in another room just beyond the air bunker. She was handling excess paper work; copying information from her little black book. Tegan said as documenter she had to do background checks and keep logs of every denizen, guardian and event in Majesty. The fact that she was an invisibility Ersatz helped with that. She also had her own team, though they weren't as bountiful as the others. Right now Ming was recording things she found in the past two weeks. Giselle's accident included. Marcel was busy at the hospital as more and more injured people were flooding in with the International Emergency Medical Service; the IEMS. Giselle found out they weren't even injured in Majesty. They were injured in whatever country they were from and called for the IEMS. And Ecoli had serious Majesty affairs to deal with; probably answering the denizens and news people hounding him about what was really going on. On top of that he had patrol to command.

Giselle, quite contrary to what you'd expect, was quiet. She was quiet about her accident, about her home life, about what was revealed in the memories, about everything. The dying urge to know more and ask questions was being repressed. Anything that might jeopardize her chances of doing the mission was to be kept secret until after. She didn't want to provide Ecoli with reason to change his mind. Silent was the game.

"Is your flying right mate? Did you try doing it at all since recovering?" Tegan asked.

"No," she said. "I still can' land. I know that for sure."

"Why do you sound so down?" Marko asked noticing her lack of spirit.

"Is nothin'," she shook her head.

"Talk up, mate," Tegan encouraged. "We know something's wrong. It hasn't been that long since waking up."

"Is not that," she denied.

"Then what? Is it about the duplicate?" He bent to her eye level.

Without waiting her response Marko said, "Sorry about that. We should have intervened sooner."

"Is ok," she shook it off. "How you make a duplicate anyway?"

She felt this was a harmless question.

"Well," Tegan straightened up and went around the bar to get himself a drink. "You use a dead body as a shell and you charm it to look and act like the person you want. It can't be any dead body though. They need special maintenance."

"Wait what?" The response was more out of surprise. Her family was making home for a dead carcass?

Marko took over the explaining from here. "There's a place you can get them, but you need two valid pieces of ID and a reference to get it. People usually donate their bodies and the high security is a way to respect the dead and avoid having wasteful or unnecessary duplicates."

Giselle nodded. Never in her life did she think something like that was possible. Not even after finding out about Majesty.

"The disadvantage is you can't reanimate a person for more than a week. That's dangerous. They tend to stray to the dark side."

Soon Scout entered the room looking more ready than anyone. He had on his common pants and a fresh black T-shirt with a jacket to match his pants. His pants didn't look sluggish and like protocol uniform though. For some reason, it looked crisp as though he had just washed and ironed it after a long time. He and Marko matched. On his left shoulder, a large camouflage bag hung by one strap, in his hand another. Then on the other shoulder a sniper rifle and a silver tonfa blade in his hand. Swinging the bag by the straps he threw it at Marko who attempted to catch it. The weight made him stumble backward and unintentionally take a seat in an empty chair. Giselle and Tegan laughed. The dangerous smile brewing on Scouts face showed he did it on purpose.

"Guess ya don't want me to throw this?" Scout held up the tonfa blade.

Marko narrowed his eyes and pursed his lips.

"Giselle, Tegan," the nonchalant Scout greeted. "We're leaving for a week."

"Where you goin'?" She investigated this new information.

"Ecoli needs Dispatch to head out for a while. Try to do something about Marcel's increasing workload." Marko said this as he stood up and swung his bag on his back.

"Oh." She experienced mixed feelings about this. "How?"

"If we reduce the attackers we could reduce the injured." She noticed he looked over her head in Tegan's direction. Then with a guilty expression he said, "But don't worry about it."

Did Tegan just shut him up? Turning around to get her answer she caught Tegan turning away briskly and pulling a cup to his lips. What was the damn secret now?! She wanted so bad to scream this, but held her tongue. Facing Scout this time she spoke again. Scout didn't look like he'd stop talking for anyone. If he let something slip Tegan couldn't correct him nonverbally over Giselle's head.

"So is just two of you?"

"No," he spoke tiredly. "Two elites from patrol and one medic is coming with. Can't take this one lightly, yeah. We could die."

Scout looked over Giselle's head in half annoyance half incomprehension.

"Bruh," he raised a hand. "So wha'? I could die."

Scout said this and this time Giselle refused to look behind her.

"And Marko too," Scout said with less care. Then his attention was back on Giselle, "So yeah, see ya soon I hope."

Scout made his way over and gave a horrified looking Giselle a fist bump.

"Don't worry too much. We're too bad ass to go out easy," Marko pointed himself and Scout.

Marko read his watch then collected his sniper and tonfa blade from Scout. This seemed to be routine for them now, getting ready for missions. They were so natural about it. As Marko retrieved his sniper Scout took it upon himself to pull Marko's jacket and ensure that the hand gun he was carrying was still there. Then Scout reached over his shoulder and pulled a two sided, wooden handled, battle axe giving it to Marko after collecting a small package of summoning snaps that Marko pulled from inside his jacket. Seeing Marko carry most of the weapons Giselle assumed he needed them more. His magic was controlling timelines; not much could be done with that in a fight. Scout on the other hand was a shape shifter. He could hold his own without weapons.

"We have to go. But I'll see you sometime next week."

Marko gave her rushed hug and patted her head. Giselle watched as the two, distinguishable only by their faces at this point, left the rec room to the simulation training room. They were about to start a dangerous mission. She could only hope that she indeed saw them again.

~*~

The two mission boards at Patrol Quarters were endless. The missions kept rolling in and as fast as they came they went. When Tegan and Giselle arrived, there were a few people hovering looking for work. By now Giselle had been in there quite a few times and was used to the environment. It was like a "tough-guy" station; a lot of indecent men hanging around trying to prove their strength and talking a load of nonsense. She had never hung around long enough to talk to any of them though. Tegan didn't like to stick around there; he wasn't that type of guy. He was like a little princess between them; although, that was an unfair comparison. Giselle had never seen

Tegan officially in action before. He had free magic; he was bound to be just as good as any of the air heads in there.

"Ok, so a mission," Tegan let out some air when they came to a stop.

An overly muscular guy was standing nearby with his pea sized head reading a paper. The guy looked at Giselle from the corner of his eye then turned back to his paper. Then he turned again, this time making his staring obvious.

"Tegan, sir," he addressed respectfully. "Don't mind my asking, but who be this?

"It's u-um," Tegan's natural nervous stutter came to life. "Giselle."

The big guy observed her some more, "She been in here mass times, yeah?"

Normally at this point Tegan would wrap up the conversation and usher Giselle away, but he didn't. He couldn't. They had to be there.

"I 'member Miss Ming wearing something like that when she just got 'ere last November- or was it December?" The man continued.

"I have a shadow," Tegan smiled. "Watching over her for Ecoli. I'd prefer if you didn't ask questions."

The guy nodded.

"Alright," Tegan went back to Giselle refusing to explain to Giselle what just happened. She wasn't going to ask about it. She'd wait until the mission was complete.

"So I could pick anything or you pickin'?"

"You pick what you like and I'll tell if we can or not." He pushed his hands in his pockets.

Itching with anticipation she scanned the board. She strayed to the board to the left side of her, but Tegan steered her away from it. Every one of those papers had the word "Urgent" in all caps and highlighted red. Those were top priority and flew off the board as the clock ticked. They were high classed missions that required immediate action from beyond exceptionally skilled patrollers. On the other board, there were more papers than there were on the "Urgent" board. The missions there had big black numbers pasted at the top. According to Tegan the numbers here represented the skill level needed to even consider these missions. Number one represented the easiest missions, number ten the hardest. There was a practical exam that people took to find out their skill level at the National Magical Enlistment Centre. Basically, he would allow her to take anything between one to three; three only because he was generous. The few missions she did fancy he seemed uncertain about them and denied her the chance.

"Tegan just doesn't know what to do with you." Marko's words came back to her.

Was Tegan just afraid to choose a mission period? Was he afraid of Giselle getting hurt?

"Tegan," she addressed him understandingly. "You choose."

"You sure?" He asked her.

She nodded.

"What kind o'mission ya looking for?"

The big man faced them. He had walked away a few seconds ago, but came back.

"Something inside Majesty, Floral Cove preferably." Tegan responded.

The guy looked over the board again then tore down a paper handing it to Tegan.

"How 'bout this? Some oldy's being a peeping Tom over at Hogback. Can't imagine what kinda lady he's into if he peeping over there." He remarked.

"But I said Floral Cove." Tegan refused.

Giselle made herself comfortable near his arm to peep at the paper. "That not in Floral Cove?"

"It's in Nocturn Niche," he said bored.

"Then let's do this," she hadn't been to Heavenly Heights or Nocturn Niche. Good time to see what it was like right.

"I like this youngster," the guy repeated, putting his hand on his hip. That was when Giselle noticed he was missing a hand.

"Nope." Tegan popped the 'P'. Giselle stared at him annoyed. Noticing, Tegan observed the paper a second time. "It's number one, but a bad place for us."

"By us you mean me," she folded her arms.

"No I don't…"

"Stop being a panty man and do the thing. Who wearing the boxers 'ere? The kid? Almighty will guide you." Giselle couldn't help, but laugh at the big guy's wording. Who says "panty man"?

"Giselle want to go," she spoke playfully in third person.

"If that's what you want then fine, but if we're going to Nocturn Niche I'm getting an NN patroller to go with us." He made his condition. "And you Twiggs, since you encouraged it."

"Twiggs?"

"That be me," he shook her hand. "Ya know where to find me Tegan sir. M'at ya disposal."

"Thank you." Tegan said while folding the paper. They started to leave PQ.

"Who name this big hard-back man Twiggs?" Giselle spoke in disbelief of his name. "That is a joke?"

"You haven't heard anything yet, mate," he responded.

~*~

Vrai, again, was expressing her unwanted opinions on things going on in Giselle's life. She was giving insulting criticisms on Giselle's abilities and questioning her chances of completing the mission. Although Giselle let her talk rather than shutting her up, her comments still fell on deaf ears. Vrai was annoying. That was all Giselle had to know. When she got to the house it was the second time since exiting Majesty that day she spoke to her. The first time she spoke it was to say, "who cares?"

"Ok shut up now. I home." She looked down at her chest. "You should know that. You teleport me."

"Rude." Vrai snarled, but the mirror obediently stopped rippling.

Strolling into her room she was brought to an immediate halt. There was something there that shouldn't be; or rather, someone.

"What the hell!" She tried to keep her voice down.

It was barely manageable though; she got scared. More so she almost pulled her peg missile on him.

"Where you come from?" He asked.

"I-I…" she thought and snapped back with a quick response. "From a walk."

"This late?"

"I had to go outside for a bit."

They had to whisper to avoid waking up Andre and Brent.

"You not actin' like yourself lately." Amron looked away from her.

The turning of his head showed he did. It was too dark to see and determine what was going on, on his face. To do that she'd have to go closer, but she was holding her ground by the door for now.

"You too," she threw back.

"That's different," he stated firmly.

"Is the same thing," she said.

After a long pause between them she made her way over to the bed. When she got a few feet closer to him, the memory of the stranger in her room flashed through her mind. Then followed the memory of her cut and burns and she winced with the enormous effort it took her to forget it. It wasn't anything serious. She just wished she didn't do that though; Amron took note.

"And since when you doin' that?"

"Amron, nothin' wrong. Ok?"

"Doh try that bullshit lie with me," he fixed his butt more comfortably into her mattress.

He wasn't talking to her for how many days now? And here he was in her room playing parent. What was his deal?

Giselle huffed, "Ok so two people I know dead same year. Excuse me for bein' sad," she spoke annoyed.

"Sorry…" and then the world fell silent as if in awe of what he said, "…but I doh believe you." Her eyes immediately shifted to his. "You give away the rabbits, behavin' suspicious and now you actin' all damaged?"

Giselle squirmed uncomfortably in the seat she newly acquired.

"What happen? What you been doin'?"

"Nothin'."

She knew if she told him he might laugh or probably he would over react. What would she do then? But Amron was also an expert at weaseling answers out of people. She had to tell him something. Once he understood, he would be accepting- maybe. Should she tell him?

"Gizzy you want me to get dad? Cause I could go and tell him all the lies I tell for you."

There it was; the blackmail. He never had to pull that trick on her before. It was easier for them to come to a common understanding. They usually pulled out the big guns when they were dealing with Andre. She stayed hushed for a while longer and he did too. How did they get to this point? Why was he parenting her? Couldn't they just get along and know all the gritty details about each other like before and not have secrets? Majesty was driving a wedge in their relationship.

"I didn' try to choke you." She whispered barely, but Amron caught every word of it. "It was somebody else." He waited patiently. She couldn't read his expression. "A vampire... it... I get hurt and I had to get a duplicate to take my place in Grenada."

"I thought you wanted us to get along again," he mumbled. "But you still playin'."

"I wasn' here..." she ignored him. "...I was in the hospital."

"Gizzy..." Amron was far from believing or was he. She still couldn't read him.

"It sound crazy. I know. But it have more to the story."

She divulged every detail of her August vacation to him. She told him everything except the fact that the Sui Generis had a spirit called Vrai and anything about Weyden Empire. Until she understood the deal with Weyden Empire she couldn't tell him anything. Her not knowing much wouldn't help her case here. She couldn't read his face when she was done, but she desperately wished she could. He just sat there soaking up everything like a sponge; a very uninterested and un-intrigued sponge.

"I know," he spoke finally and abruptly.

"You know?" She eased back on her bed.

"I didn' know what you was doin', but I know somethin' was wrong with the chain after you call me from dad phone to ask me about it," he cleared up. "I only find out a few days ago that you been goin' inside of it."

"How you find out that?"

"That is not the point," he shut down and she knew well not to seek more information. "You need to stop goin'."

"No," she refused.

He stood up. "Gizzy if gran'mom know you get hurt she wouldn' want you to go back."

"You doh know what gran'mom want!" She yelled in a whisper.

"And you know?" His eyes were wide and demanding humbling respect. "She had a whole other life and we didn' even know about it. Who the frick know what she want?" The scared expression on Giselle's face made him smooth out the tension in his composure and voice. "Ok, so say I doh know what she want. I know what I want and I know what Andre want and I know what dad and BJ want. Gran'mom dead and mom dead, we doh need you dead too."

Giselle folded her arms and shifted in her seat. Amron held out his hand.

"What you want?" She asked.

"The chain," he said.

"I not givin' you…"

"Giselle Samantha Thomas, the chain."

He kept his hand steady and open in front of her and so began the great waiting game. Giselle knew her brother. He wasn't about to walk away from this fight. She took off the chain and handed it to him. Vrai would come back to her anyway. In no time Andre's person was peeking into her room.

"What goin' on in here?"

Amron slipped by Andre and walked out. Andre exchanged a questioning look with his sister and she shook her head. That was how the night ended. That was how she was once again one step further from both her brother and her mission. That was how she began regretting ever finding out about Majesty.

CHAPTER FIFTEEN

THE EMPIRE

VRAI WOULD COME back to her. She wouldn't stay with Amron for long. She was going to wait until she was ready and then reappear in Giselle's possession as always. The fact that half an hour later she hadn't returned meant Amron still had eyes on her. There was no way he knew about Vrai or the fact that she was attached to Giselle. He couldn't know she'd go back to Giselle at the first opportunity she got. And, he definitely couldn't have figured out how to stop her. Then again, Giselle didn't know what Amron knew. He managed, somehow, to discover the portal. Her biggest fear at this point was of him sticking his hand in or something. He'd get burned to death like that girl did and Marcel wouldn't be able to save him. Hopefully he remained opposed to portal travel. They were in a fight, yes, but wanting him hurt or dead were the last things she desired. In the meantime, Giselle pondered Amron's sources. How did he find out about the portal anyway? She couldn't remember him being anywhere other than the living room, kitchen and his bed room every time she used the Sui Generis. It wasn't as though they had peep holes in their walls or anything so how did he know. He was acting so offbeat about it too. That wasn't one of the kickbacks she had thought up for him. He was either supposed to want a part of it or sell her out to her father. Instead he kept it a secret and wanted nothing to do with anything. She never thought about how he'd react on finding out about Ruby; his anger and dismissal of Ruby's wishes caught her off guard. Could his icy treatment be a representation of how her family would react? If so, she wasn't about to reveal anything to them; not now not ever. More and more she wanted Vrai to come back to her and in some weird twisted way she wanted her to stay away. Maybe it was good Amron took the chain away… or maybe not. She couldn't decide.

The next morning, she was awakened by a vibrating sensation on her chest. As expected Vrai was resting comfortably there. She rose out of the sleep groggily. Something was missing. What was it?

"Your sibling did not wake you today." Vrai stated.

That was what was missing. He didn't come wake her. She always wanted him to stop, but now she wished he was in there laughing at her irritation. It had just become a morning norm.

"He is a smart one." Vrai commented. "He knows things."

"Like what," she yawned.

It wasn't out of boredom for the conversation. It was just that Vrai woke her up early and started talking the second her eyes opened. It was a miracle she even caught any of what Vrai said.

"He knows that I am here. He tried to talk to me for a good half hour. I said nothing." Vrai informed her.

"He what?" Most of the sleep was shaken out of Giselle now. "How he know to do that?"

"No idea. I have a hunch, but I refuse to divulge any more without certainty." Vrai spoke as though she was discussing with herself.

"Well how you go find out then? What you want me to do?" Giselle was willing to help. She was curious as to how Amron came about his information.

"Let me think." Vrai said in that rude voice she always used.

"Doh talk to me if you doh know what you want." Giselle snapped back.

After lying down for about ten more minutes she went to the bathroom where she relieved herself and brushed her teeth. On her way back was where the main event for the next few weeks started. Giselle and Amron weren't on smooth speaking terms yet. She was beginning to think that was never his intention coming to speak to her last night. His curiosity was probably too overwhelming. She came across Andre in the hall who was telling her a story about a fight he saw at school.

"I doh know where it start, but the guy come runnin' down by The Greens and get jump by some other GBSS boys." He held onto the handle of the bathroom door.

"Yuh muh! What time was that?" She asked him.

He wasn't granted the opportunity of responding. Amron exited his room and things got tense. Andre must have felt it because he said nothing. He kept his eyes trained on his brother as if waiting for him to pour out his problems.

"You take it back." It was too obvious how hard he was trying not to shout.

"Take back what?"

"The fu…" his gaze temporarily strayed to Andre before he continued, "…flippin' chain."

She looked down on her chest where the chain was resting beautifully. Damn it! Why didn't she leave it in the room?

"I didn'…"

"What the chain have to do with you?" Andre chimed in.

"Mind your business!" Amron yelled at him.

He grabbed Giselle's shoulder and pulled her into his room to have a conversation. Andre, finding this suspicious, tried to follow, but Amron locked the door.

"Amron open. Why you lock me out?" He jiggled the door knob. "Amron! I tellin' dad!"

"Dre." Amron called him with shredded patience. "Leave us alone please."

They heard a loud screeched sucking sound and footsteps leaving the hall. Andre was gone.

"What the hell!" Giselle yelled.

"That's my line," he growled.

"I didn' take it back," she said full of attitude.

"So how it get back in your neck then?"

She thought for a moment. He already knew so much. What harm could it do to speak freely in front of him now?

"Tegan say if the mirror meant for me it go always come back to me."

He let out strong exhaust in his nose and looked at the floor almost laughing. He did not believe her. Andre came pounding again.

"For real, what this about?"

"Dre! If we wanted to tell you we would tell you! F off!"

With that Andre retreated to his room and that was the last they saw of him for that day. Giselle felt terrible knowing things about Andre now that she didn't before. He just wanted to be liked and not feel like he was the problem- she disagreed with the manner in which Amron shouted at him. When she brought it up they argued even more ending in him taking her chain and leaving. Now the three of them weren't on speaking terms and Amron had the chain again. A scene like that one went on for a few days; Amron taking the chain and it magically reappearing on her. He even went to the extent of dumping it in the water behind the terminal. Next day Giselle woke up with it in her neck- dry. Because of him she wasn't able to go to Majesty for a while and this pissed her off. She couldn't stop thinking about what was going on in there and if they thought she bailed on them. What angered her more was that she finally had her mission. It was finally time! What if they thought she chickened out and they were just giving her space? Tegan would sure as hell be happy to not take her anywhere. She felt like she should stay out and try to make things right at home, but if Amron's only concern was to get rid of the chain then it wasn't worth it. He wasn't listening to her. The mirror would always come back. Maybe now he would understand why Giselle buried it. Maybe now he'd feel like a fool for digging it up. To settle things, the last time Vrai came back to her she asked her to stay with Amron when he took her again. Vrai protested, but Giselle being her owner she had to respect the request.

Something strange lately was the fact that she kept having near misses. When she had Vrai one afternoon before Amron came home she tried putting bread in the oven. Her dad usually made a lot and put them in the freezer, so she was thawing one out. The second she drew the match, there was this great ecliptic explosion that was shielded and swallowed by Vrai. She didn't smell gas. How did that happen? She also kept running into strange people asking her about her chain. This one guy straight up whispered in her ear 'long live Weyden Empire'. She felt like she was being followed on several occasions; luckily for her an adult always seemed to appear at the right time. And one night she could have sworn some supernatural force had pinned her to her bed and tried to cut her breathing. She didn't know how Vrai found out because she wasn't there, but thanks to her showing up unannounced Giselle managed to survive. There was more too; how was a girl supposed to be comfortable living if this kept happening? Maybe she was imagining it. The explosion and the incident in her room were probably real. She had Vrai keeping an account on it. The rest though, maybe her mind was just paranoid.

She stayed up late trying to practice her math. She had a test coming up and she knew nothing. They were doing consumer arithmetic in math class. It was the first topic studied when school opened. Like the good duplicate she was, the other Giselle learned nothing. Absolutely nothing in her memory was related to education. She remembered being in the classes and she could hear the teachers talking, but the mischief the duplicate got into was the main focus of the memory. She had her notes though; notes that she peeked off of Emma's notebook. Hopefully that would save her. She couldn't fail form three before she even started. She also had a Principles of Accounts test. That was no walk in the park in her opinion. After what felt like a lifetime, she closed her books and shut her light off. Pulling her sheets over her she gave into sweet sleep. Her mind was obsessed with the fantasies of what she'd be doing if she had Vrai. Why wouldn't Amron just let her go and trust that she would be ok? He never doubted her before so why couldn't he be the "loosey" Amron she grew up with now?

Giselle didn't hear the creek of the floor boards in the hall, but she did hear her bedroom door ease open. For a second she couldn't see anyone. On first instinct, she froze in her bed. If someone was here she was going to pretend to be asleep; maybe it was Amron again. Unless he was coming with a peace treaty she was not interested. Then again what if it was that mysterious disappearing person? Her body was stiff in bed, but she couldn't force her eyes closed. She kept staring at the door until she saw Ecoli step in, his index finger on his lip. You would think relief would wash over her, but terror beat relief to the chase. Why was Ecoli here? How did he get in the house? How did he know where she lived? Did he spy on her? She could hardly relax running these questions through her head. Then Marcel came in. Marcel walked around Giselle's bed, leaving Ecoli standing by the door peering out. Looking for Giselle's dad maybe?

"Sweetie, ya ok?" Marcel whispered and rested her hand on Giselle's fore head.

Giselle, at a loss for words, just nodded. She couldn't sit up yet.

"Ya had a mission and ya didn't sign in for a mass time, love." She had so much concern laced into her voice one would think she was Giselle's mother. "Why?"

Giselle responded, but with all the air caught in her throat no sound came out. She sat up and tried to clear her throat without making too much noise.

"Um, Amron take the mirror."

Marcel had a protective look now. "He knows?"

"Yeah," the words seemed to be flowing now. "He mad that I get hurt."

"Thank the Almighty."

Marcel suddenly sunk into Giselle's soft mattress all the tenseness oozing out of her. Giselle knitted her eyebrows together. What was that supposed to mean?

"We thought somebody from Weyden Empire took ya or somethin'." Ecoli cleared up. "But we couldn' just show up in the middle o'the day cause ya dad look difficult."

Did this potential burglar say Weyden Empire? Why would he just mention that now? And why would someone from Weyden Empire take her?

"Weyden Empire?" She repeated.

Air caught in his wind pipe. "Sorry wha'?"

"You said it," she sat up straighter.

He played it cool. "Hm, never heard o'it."

Marcel glared at him less inconspicuous than she probably thought she did. Taking the opportunity, and regarding her silence as a waste, she took to telling them about the strange things that had been happening to her. She spoke about the strange albino boy and the conversation she overheard and even Amron acting strange that morning before school. She knew he had nothing to do with anything she was telling them about, but once she started venting she couldn't stop. She had to let it all out. Obediently, both Ecoli and Marcel internalized her story and waited for the end.

"The mirror s'posed to come back to ya, yeah?" Ecoli said not commenting on her horror stories at all.

"I tell Vrai to stay with him to avoid trouble," she mindlessly responded. She wanted him to tell her something about the other things, not that.

"Ya can' do that! Ya want me do somethin' 'bout it." Ecoli's hand lit on fire illuminating the room. A soft rushing sound filled the air.

"Course not!" Marcel yelled in a whisper.

Ecoli rolled his eyes. "Jus' scare him a lil."

"No." Marcel snapped.

"Amron doh 'fraid nothin' and nobody." Giselle discouraged. "But what you think about everything else?"

Ecoli doused his flame.

"Well…" Ecoli began, but the footsteps in the house hushed him up.

"You bring somebody else?" Giselle's eyes bounced between the sibling pair.

Marcel shook her head. The creaking got closer to Giselle's room. Marcel pushed Giselle gently back in her bed and pulled the covers up to her neck. Then she joined Ecoli who moved behind the door. Her room door eased open for a second time. Amron's head protruded. His attention was on Giselle initially and completely missed Marcel and Ecoli standing right behind him.

"I know you up," he whispered.

Then as if some sort of super human instincts kicked in he turned around. His movements were too slow this time though. Maybe there was something that could get by him after all. The time he took to speak to her Marcel had waved a weak good bye, held Ecoli's hand and vanished in thin air. Giselle rolled over in her bed and stared at him annoyed.

"Who you talkin' to?" He demanded.

"Harassin' me in the day is not enough? You have to do it in the night now?" She groaned from her position.

He glared at her. "You have people in your room."

"Yeah," she wasn't about to lie. "They wanted to make sure I was ok because they didn' see me for a while."

"And."

"And what? That's all."

He sighed and looked away for a long time. Slowly he made his way to her and sat on the bed. Giselle looked at him in speculation. What was his problem now? He already got what he wanted. He could sleep peacefully now.

"If I say you need to stop goin', would you?" He asked patiently.

"No."

The grave disappointment vining on his features grew a whirling emotion in her. She didn't want them to be at odds anymore. She should just tell him she wouldn't go back, but she couldn't. Not now. Maybe if he had come in there before Marcel and Ecoli showed up. Seeing them taught her just how attached she had become to that world. She didn't want to leave Majesty. Yet, everything since knowing of its existence had been a struggle. The simplest things were a problem. Why was she even staying in there? She could argue it was to help people or fulfil Ruby's wishes or find out what really happened to her mother. But it could easily be none of those things. One minute she felt strongly about it and the next she was just there to be there. Amron rotated in his seat so that he was facing her.

"One condition then- change your safe spot to my room."

"Huh…"

"I doh feel comfortable with you walkin' from gran'mom house three in the mornin'. That is a long walk."

If only he knew Vrai could teleport.

"Your room?" Her tone was critical.

"Dad doesn' go in my room and I could handle Andre. And I want to see you come home safe every night."

She couldn't argue with that reasoning. He cared! He was freezing her out, but it was because he cared! After the silent agreement of his conditions he hugged her, but she weaseled away from him. Smiling, faintly, he pulled the chain from his pocket and handed it to her. She tried to take it, but it was like he had it on a death grip.

"Amron..."

"Doh die," he whispered.

His appearance was soft and his aura was vulnerable and uneasy. She had never seen him like that before. A songbird would be living lavish next to him right now. Giselle leaned in and hugged him again wishing she didn't push him away the first time. He was just concerned. Their mother and grandmother were gone. She was the only girl he had left in his life that he was closely related to and cared about. After that he left the room and she could sleep peacefully knowing she was free again. Most importantly, her brother had her back. Finally! She could finally tackle this mission and win her real training session. Amen.

Entering Majesty had a giddy sensation to it this time around. She was back. It felt as though she had been released from prison. She missed seeing the universal passage and all twelve halves of the Sui Generis' standing loyally along the walls. She missed walking down the less than perfect hall to the rec. room. She missed standing out on the ledge holding onto the metal banister and looking over the beauty that was Floral Cove. The only things absent from the equation were Marko and Scout. They weren't back yet and from the sound of things they weren't coming back anytime soon. After soaking in the scenery and indulging in nostalgia she flicked on the TV in the Rec. Room. She was waiting for Tegan who hadn't ventured into Majesty as yet. To pass time she fed into the curiosity of what Majesty's media was like. It was just like TV was; sit coms and talk shows and game shows and reality TV following some train wreck of a person that society found entertaining for some reason. They even had news, though she already knew that part from overhearing some of it some time ago. The only thing different about Majesty's TV programs were the people and the fact that the strange appearances and magical acts weren't just make up, costumes and good editing. It was all very real. Locking onto the news channel, however, was how she learned of Marko and Scout's less than desirable extended absence from Majesty. There was a little after-news talk show going on. It wasn't your average report. It was more just a young man summarizing what was said in the official news and giving his and the public opinions on what was happening.

"As the Christmas Hunt draws near the new chief o'Majesty, Ecoli Sinclair, continues to carry out secret projects. According to our sources, Dispatch was deployed sometime around the eighteenth or nineteenth o'October. Their mission remains amiss. Seventeen days later and the dynamic duo has yet to be seen. Ecoli hasn't made comment on this. Shady."

The blue-eyed reporter made his distaste for this information very clear. He was like a hyperactive chipmunk sitting in his brown padded rocking chair with a greyish black pipe between his fingers. As unprofessional as he appeared he still honed a very prestigious mannerism. His bow tie was almost like a choker in the dark blue collar of his white shirt. Sleeves rolled up to his elbows neatly to expose a sleeve of tattoo's like Tegan's, but with different designs. On his devious, less than attractive, face he wore a tattoo like thorns slanted from his chin to his hairline.

"With the way things be now it begs the question 'Can we trust Ecoli Sinclair?'. In the past month there has been an increased amount of injured. Not to mention the mortality rate has risen by five percent since the great Ruby Thomas' reign ended. What does it all mean?"

The young man, whose name could be none other than Aubrey since the show was called Aubrey's Opinions, was over dramatically enunciating his own questions. Did he think this was all some joke? Why was he calling out Ecoli like that?

"All m'saying is if there is a rising nationwide issue he owes it to us to speak out. The young leader, whose flame has no shape need I remind ya, remains silent. If ya ask me I think s'the fire-devil he been trying to hide so much that's causing this chaos. For all we know he could be the one orchestrating this whole thing. My sources have also informed me about an incident he covered up. The fire in Nocturn Niche not too long ago that claimed the life of so many was anything, but natural. Seems Weyden Empire managed to sink its fangs in Majesty somehow, yeah. This begs the question, should Ecoli Sinclair be allowed to control the patrollers? If he can order them to lie to the public so easily why should we trust him to pull the strings of our most trusted unit- after Dispatch o'course? If I disappear after this episode airs, he did it."

"Not very nice is he?" Tegan's voice rose solemnly behind Giselle.

Emotionally and mentally aggravated she faced him. Why was this guy saying all these things about Ecoli? If he knew that there was a chance that Ecoli was a fire-devil, why would he provoke him like that? Giselle knew from firsthand experience how easy it was to get Ecoli to burst into flames. According to Marko, it wasn't intentional; he just didn't have that type of stable control over his fire. Was Aubrey trying to grate Ecoli into confronting him? Was it all a stunt to tear down the Chief of Majesty? And the scarier question was- if this wasn't just some stupid stunt were all those things true? Was Ecoli covering things up and where was dispatch? Then there was the case of Weyden Empire. There it was again. She couldn't fully comprehend the complexity and intensity of the issue because nobody would tell her the deal about Weyden Empire. That was the missing piece of the puzzle now wasn't it?

"Guess since you heard all that I don't have to explain what I'm about to say next."

Tegan nervously introduced his hands to his pockets.

"What happen?" asked Giselle.

"Well, um," he bent his head to the side and scratched his temple. "You're not, um, we're not going to Nocturn Niche anymore."

She smiled weakly as though it would calm her. "Because you choose a better mission, right?"

He followed her kind gesture and blessed her with a weak laugh. "No. No, that's not quite it."

"What the news have to do with anything?" Her voice was an octave higher. "If he mad why he have to take it out on me?"

"That's not exactly it either." Tegan defended.

"Then explain. As a matter of fact, where Ecoli?"

"You're not gonna do anything stupid, are you?" He gazed at her with those innocent eyes.

She exhaled loudly. "No. I jus' want to talk to him."

Tegan gazed her for some time before pulling the door to the Rec. Room open again.

"I don't believe you, but whatever. I'll take you to him."

In silence, they made their way down the steps to Ecoli's office. She personally, wanted to yell at him for throwing her around the tracks like that. Why won't he just let her go on her mission or train? It had nothing to do with that stupid Aubrey. Plus, if it was something to do with Weyden Empire, for some odd reason, then it still had nothing to do with her mission. She wasn't leaving Majesty and she'd be with Tegan and that big-guy Twiggs the entire time. She was safe. Why did he want to 'protect' her so much? Well, she was about to find out now, wasn't she? When they got to the heavy brown door that sealed away the chief's office, Tegan requested entrance with a respectful knock after which (and without response) Giselle opened the door. Inside Marcel was fuming with folded arms at Ecoli who sat humbly on his desk avoiding eye contact with her. Seeing Giselle burst in heatedly like that, momentarily shut down whatever it was the two were arguing about. This gave Tegan enough time to sputter a million apologies.

"Ok good! See, Giselle is here. Talk to her!" Marcel ordered her little brother.

"Marcel…"

"Ecoli it was ok before when she didn' know anything, but too much happen since then." Marcel flung her arm in Giselle's direction.

"Ya tell her to come here?" The increasing irritation in Ecoli's tone was sending Tegan's nerves off the edge.

"I'm sorry." Tegan grabbed onto Giselle's shoulders. "We can come back later."

Giselle shook him off. "You talkin' about me?"

"Yes."

Marcel turned her back to Ecoli and addressed Giselle as though she hadn't just barged in. Whatever it was they were arguing about, Giselle's showing up seemed to work to her advantage. She fully embraced it and didn't question it once.

"Well what this about? Ecoli why I can' do the mission?"

"Yeah Ecoli, why?" Marcel faced her less than thrilled brother again.

"Maybe I'll leave." Tegan excused himself.

"No ya won't." Marcel ordered him. "Cause ya been keeping secret too, yeah. Ecoli didn' work alone."

"You make it sound like I was an accessory in a robbery," he whined.

"Marcel, leave this alone." Ecoli lowered his voice dangerously.

Tegan took a not so subtle step back.

"I refuse!" she cried.

"Somebody tell me somethin'!" Giselle demanded.

The three of them obviously knew something, the same something. They were all on the same page except Giselle. What was it that they were keeping quiet?

"I say-"

"-I hear what you say, but what ya keepin' secret is irrelevant now." Marcel barked over him.

"Marcel!"

Ecoli stood up, his hair ablaze; his cheeks, neck and arms seemed to be setting off sparks. Giselle had never seen him that bad before. She had only seen him mad enough to set off steam and light his hair. Other than that she had only seen his fire in a casual occasion (if you'd consider his being in her room in the dark of night threatening to scare her brother a casual occasion). It was unreal. The sparks played about his body like a scratched match that wasn't heated enough to catch fire, but if brushed in the slightest a second time would erupt in flames. Somehow fire looked like a part of him. It wasn't outlandish to see it slowly threatening to engulf him like that. The fire seemed to add something to his body. If anything, the flames finally completed that uninviting aura around him. In response Marcel started to act up too. Her behavior wasn't quite like his. Her dark skin and solid appearance faded into this yellowish glowing ghostly figure with beautifully sculpted wings. If someone turned the light off in the office they'd still be able to see because of her- because of both of them actually. They were like the embodiment of the contrasting windows- Marcel being Floral Cove and Ecoli being Nocturn Niche. Marcel looked the same, but there was somehow a more glorious buzz in her translucent features. Watching them together they looked like a feuding demon and angel. It was hard not to lean toward the theory of Ecoli being a fire-devil standing in front of Marcel right now.

"Oh shit." Giselle heard Tegan gasp lowly behind her.

"Don' change on me!" Marcel stared him in the eye.

"Then don' go changing on me like ya wasn' arguing and ya could do no wrong!" he countered.

Giselle backed up to Tegan's side not knowing what was happening. Were they about to fight or something? Surely not. They couldn't right? From her side, as she sought refuge, Tegan took control of the situation.

"Stop this. You turn back and you out your flames." The two refused to do as he said. "All right, fine. I'll do it for you!" He flicked his arm in Ecoli's direction and water washed all over him engulfing his whole person in steam to the point where they could barely see him anymore. Then he did the same arm motion in Marcel's direction muttering words Giselle couldn't decipher. Terrible screams emanated in the room as blackness circled Marcel's body. The heat from it was so extreme it sent out waves. Then lowering his arms he said "release," and all was well with them again. Marcel looked terrified and Ecoli traumatized, but they both were physically normal again.

"This is stupid. You two are even fighting about it now." Tegan strolled forward. "Marcel I agree that keeping this hushed at this point is irrelevant- it truly is by the way- but Ruby left the well-being of her family to Ecoli. If Ecoli's not ready to sell out yet then just let it be. And Ecoli you have to sell out now. It's not helping any of them. If anything, Giselle's in more danger now because she knows about Majesty and Weyden Empire knows about her, but she doesn't know about them."

The two said nothing for a long time, though Tegan didn't seem like he expected them to.

"I'm taking Giselle to the training room for a bit and when I get back you'd better have yourselves together and be ready to spill."

As he said, so they did. Tegan took her to the physical training room where he coached her in self-defense moves despite being opposed to it when she first came here. They were at it for a while. Whatever secret they were keeping he was over it. He first taught her the basics and then once she was getting the hang of it he challenged her a bit by fighting her and using cheats- his magic. When she called him out on it he told her she was in a magical-supernatural world and she had to be ready for anything in a fight. Expect the worst because no one was going to play by the rules; there were no rules. The excessive amount of time she spent being dropped on her ass by Tegan didn't annoy her one bit. She was already in a rage and a bit shaky from the whole showdown in Ecoli's office so she was releasing the tension in their fight. Once that was over he allowed her a break, but she didn't want it. She wanted to keep going. If she stopped the anger and shock in her would just get pent up again. So, he took her into the shooting range and helped her with her aim. The first two times she shot she didn't quite have the grasp on the pressure involved in pulling the trigger; it took a little getting used to. During all this, Tegan kept telling her that she was going to be fighting a lot for the rest of her life. She was in for some rough days because of who her grandmother was. He didn't get into detail because he wanted Ecoli to tell her. Though mentioning it was just his way of informing her that she could always call for help no matter the time. She was a guardian; she could borrow emissaries and patrollers and recon members and anyone else for that matter whenever she felt something wasn't right and she needed to take action. They were at her disposal.

By the time this was over it was night-time which meant morning was well set in Grenada. She hoped Amron would cover for her seeing as she changed her safe spot to his room. Vrai was opposed to this; she said Amron stared at her too much. Giselle neglected to hear her cries.

Meeting up with Ecoli again wasn't as dramatic as the first time. He was calmer now. He still had that repulsive air about him, but that was just part of him. She understood that. He took her on a walk just like he did when she first discovered the place. This time instead of going over the bridge and to the grave yard he took her on one of the multiple bridges that strayed from that path; this one lead to a flourishing park that was sparsely littered with playing children. Making their way over to a wooden bench a distance from the sandy playing area neither of them said anything. They hadn't spoken a word the entire walk there. When she went to his office the second time, mindful of knocking, he told her they were taking a walk and that was pretty much it. They sat down and took in the surrounding for a while. There was this one kid who found it funny to turn into a reptilian creature and chase his friends around. They were laughing and screaming and having the time of their lives. Giselle couldn't help but think that if this was Grenada the reaction to this would be the complete opposite. That made her mind run on Alana and she wondered how well she was adapting to the change in environment. She must love it.

"You calm now?" she spoke first.

Ecoli nodded humor on his face. "Sorry 'bout that. Siblings fight. S'what it look like in Majesty."

"You never actually…" she trailed hoping he'd understand what she was getting to. He gazed her for a while before making a face of realization.

"Oh, no. Never. Is more an intimidation thing, yeah. She usually backs down."

"Ok." She breathed relief.

Could you imagine Ecoli and Marcel getting into a physical fight? She didn't want to.

"So," he rubbed his hands together leaning forward. "I got some things to tell ya. Things my sister and Tegan apparently would murder me to spit out."

"Before you say it, tell me why you been keepin' it a secret?"

"Ya go understand when I done," he said looking over at her. "So ya know Ruby was chief o'Majesty and Tegan tell me ya know a lil 'bout Weyden Empire. So yes, Weyden Empire is what is left o'Tlos. After the war ended The Land o'Spirits had become a waste land. Was left open and venerable to intruders, yeah. The Shamans was able to somehow gain stamina again and rise up durin' this period of weakness. From then they been quietly livin' as Gods in Tlos, which is what they wanted to begin with. Soon they caught wind o'another Magical-supernatural society said to be growing more powerful than Tlos ever was or could be; that society was Majesty. With they need to be in absolute control all the time Weyden Empire was formed. Weyden did not form it himself; he was too young. Instead it was created and named after him by one of his elders. Weyden is in charge now though. Weyden Empire and Majesty are arch enemies, which has plenty to do with why anybody in Majesty dies. Weyden Empire calls Majesty the New World. They have a grudge against Majesty. They say we the worst generation because we ancestors abandoned them durin' the war and create a haven and leave them to suffer, but the truth is they just want to take over."

"But is true." Giselle commented and this evidently upset Ecoli.

"They had just as much freedom to leave as we ancestors did. There was nothin' holdin' them back," he defended Majesty. "They choose to stay. And now, because o'that stupid grudge, they make a habit of tryin' to kill the chief and guardians o'Majesty; tryin' to destabilize us."

Ecoli saying this clarified so many things for Giselle. This was why Tegan said she'd be fighting for the rest of her life. Weyden Empire would be hunting her down, not exactly from a personal grudge, but because of the bad blood between the two magical-supernatural societies. This was also good reason why the guardian grave yard was so big. And it said a lot about why that vampire attacked her that night. She also remembered the whole thing about the burning city and Roscoe's sister pledging allegiance to Weyden Empire. Of course Ecoli would cover it up. He didn't want the Majestic's to know that people were converting.

"They have this thing called the Christmas Hunt where they kill denizens instead of just the guardians. And for some reason this year they start huntin' us earlier. Earlier as in since Ruby died. I think they celebratin'. When she was in charge it was hard for them to get away with anything, yeah. They did kill people, but not many. All this is why I was keepin' ya a secret. At first I was goin' to have ya trained so by the time Christmas Hunt roll 'round ya could defend ya'self, but since it start earlier I felt it better to jus' wait it out and keep ya involvement in the magical world to a minimum. That way they would never find out who ya were. They hate Ruby and now that she gone they go hate on ya. I underestimate how much o'a trouble maker ya were. Because ya run into a Weyden Empire vampire they be very aware o'ya existence now. According to Recon for now they just think ya the guardian who got Ruby chain. They doh know ya her granddaughter, but that won't last long. As much as I hate to admit, Marcel was right. If I told ya this from the beginnin' ya might o'been more careful. I didn' want to 'cause imagine on top of tryin' to accept that Majesty was real ya found out there was a rival Empire out to get ya. Ya wouldn' want to stay here would ya?"

She shook her head.

"So that was one o'my reasons. As for the other reason, early last year Weyden reach out to Ruby sayin' he wanted to call a cease fire. He was goin' to stop attackin' us and in return he wanted he people to be welcome in Majesty; said he found it safer. Majesty does have a void city. S'the black hand on the flag. Each hand represents a city. When Hubable made this place he knew the war was still alive in Tlos. He made space for them to come live if they agree to stop the fightin'. It was goin' to be a neutral ground where all the different types could mingle. That way they could stay together if they refuse to mix with us, yeah. They refuse it. Out o'respect the city was left empty for whenever they were ready. Weyden said he was ready; admit defeat to Ruby. He wanted a face to face meetin' with Ruby to discuss instead o'talkin' through Majesty's emissaries. For a long time nothin' came out o'the request. Weyden kept tryin' to reach out to Ruby, but she wasn' convinced. Then he pulled a stunt on her. Ya mother, Grace, she was very close to Ruby. She was a seer; had visions. She used to tell Ruby dangerous things she envisioned happenin' to Majesty and that help her to fix it before it was a problem. That was why Ruby was considered the greatest chief. Grace had an unclear vision 'bout a peace treaty. S'why Ruby met Weyden, but I'll tell ya more on that in a bit. Ya mom used to be fine workin' with Ruby until she had her first son."

Thirsty for more information Giselle rotated in her seat and leaned in to hear more. So, her mother was more involved than she realized. And what did having BJ do to her?

"Her first born died."

It was like having glass shattered in her head. She never knew that there was a child before BJ. She wasn't even sure BJ knew about that. If he did, he surely kept that under wraps. Why wouldn't her father mention this? Was it too painful or had he forgotten him.

"Ya mom predict his death before he was even conceived. She wanted to have lots o'children though. It was a dream of hers so she went ahead and start her family thinkin' she could do somethin' about the future like she always did. She thought havin' and losin' the first child would be a gateway to her big family. But bein' a mother, she still tried to protect him. She thought if he get involve in Majesty he'd die. So naturally, she kept everythin' about magic a secret. Ruby wasn' even allowed to see him. He didn' die because he was involve in magic; he was jus' in the right place at the wrong time. He was lured away from his church camp by Lajabless- his body was never found. From then ya mom was kind of weary of Majesty. With her first born gone, she try to have her big family and that was when

BJ came. Then Andre. And the visions got more intense and that's when she started losin' her mind. For some reason she couldn' find ways to cheat her destiny like she used to. Ruby reckons s'cause she wasn' thinkin' rationally. Then she had the last two and when she saw the immense danger they would find themselves in she couldn' deal with it. She left Majesty makin' sure none of her children ever got involve and because she was so paranoid she was committed to the mental home. Ruby visit her mass times and Weyden saw how much she cared about her. Ruby did an amazin' job at keepin' her family separate from the magical-supernatural world so Grace was the first lead Weyden had to her outside life. Knowin' that, he used Grace as a bargainin' chip to gain entry into Majesty and when Ruby refused he kill Grace before we could rescue her. Rumor has it Grace had a life-changin' vision about Majesty and that was the real reason Weyden took her. He didn' want anyone to hear it."

Never had Giselle felt so low in her life. All this was going on around her. All these complicated battles were being fought and she was oblivious. How was she supposed to feel? What was she supposed to think? This was too much.

"Finally, givin' in to his persistence, in June this year Ruby gave him the time of day. As usual, it was her seein' the good in people sayin' maybe Weyden changed. She wanted to forgive him for what he did to Grace; Ruby was all about forgiveness as you already know. So they pick a neutral town to meet in; Dysen."

"Dysen? Where is that?" Giselle interrupted with a soft sorrowful voice. Her eyes were inflamed and fluid.

"Ya go soon learn that it have hundreds o'small magical-supernatural societies around. Majesty and Weyden Empire are just at the top of the food chain. Everyone wants to form an alliance with either us or them to survive. Dysen is the only exception. It small, but independent. They refuse to align with either of us. Ya mom peace treaty vision was the reason why we chose Dysen as the meeting place and not one of the aligned magical-supernatural societies."

She leaned back soaking all this in. The longer Ecoli spoke the more she realized how big being a guardian of Majesty was. Majesty was one of the top two magical-supernatural societies. She was starting to realize it was more than just a place for leisure now. She was starting to see that the world wasn't what she thought it was. There was so much more going on.

"Ruby, two other guardians and a few patrollers went to Dysen that day. When she came back she call a meetin' with us sayin' she deny Weyden access into Majesty. If he was a changed man he would have never done what he did to Grace. She shut down what could have been the biggest merge in the history o'magical-supernatural existence. It was all over the news that the rulers o'the big name magical-supernatural societies had a meetin'. She couldn' trust him though; she felt he was just tryin' to gain easy access to take control. The next day Ruby and everyone who accompany her to that meetin' died; poison. I think she knew she was goin' to die. Somethin' wasn' right with any of them when they came back. I know all o'this because like I said, she was my mentor. She tell me everythin'. I doh know why she thought I was most suitable to do this. She asked me to look over all o'ya and only introduce ya to Majesty when I thought it was safe. She knew there would be uproar if she died. I had one job; to keep a secret. I failed her. All this is the reason why we are where we are now."

Gisele looked away from him so he wouldn't see her cry. Why was she crying anyway? Her mother was the seer who made Ruby the great leader she was. She was murdered as a bargaining chip. Her grandmother died in the line of duty and still made provisions for their safety once she was gone. She was supposed to have four brothers instead of three. Her first brother was born as a sacrifice for the family she had now. There was a magical empire out there that would stop at nothing until every memory of Ruby and Grace and Majesty ceased to exist. She was kept out of all this for her safety and she understood why now. What was the right emotion for all of this? Was there an emotion? Why was she crying?! She couldn't even speak to Ecoli. It was hard to find the words. She had no questions. Everything he said was pretty clear. She had no comments because she'd only be repeating his words and hurting herself more. She just couldn't react. So this was it. This was the big secret that had to wait until January when things cooled down. This was the reason why she couldn't train or go on missions or be introduced to the public as a guardian.

Not yet. This was why she had to be 'Giselle, a girl I met in the back streets'.

Shakily Giselle brought the back of her wrist up to her blared eyes spreading the tears instead of erasing them.

"Sorry," Ecoli sighed. "But ya have to learn how to fight now."

Hearing him say this made her sob loudly. She covered her face trying to contain it unsuccessfully. From the side, she felt an unnaturally warm hand pull on hers and insert a kerchief. He made no attempt to comfort her because he wasn't that type of person. Still the concern on his face and giving of the kerchief was genuine. He did care for how she felt. It took a few minutes before she was able to swallow her cries and resort to sniffs.

"Ya have full permission to train with Tegan."

Ecoli was giving her everything she was asking for before she knew why she needed it. She didn't need training before because like Tegan said in the start she wouldn't be getting into dangerous situations anytime soon. He was right. That was because to the magical-supernatural society she didn't exist. But now that Weyden Empire was aware of her she would have to learn to fight. Either that or die a shameful death. This was all getting too real now.

"The strange things ya been sayin' ya were seein', that's Weyden Empire. They been watchin' ya because they think ya too young to be a guardian. They been tryin' to figure out if your chain doesn' just coincidentally look like Ruby's. They know now that is the real deal. The chain spirit will protect ya. Keep it close. Don' give it to Amron." He informed. "For now, go home, but please return soon."

CHAPTER SIXTEEN

ICED OUT

GOING HOME DIDN'T require excessive walking or tele-portation. She was safely transported to Amron's room where he waited with faded breath for her return. He sat on his bed with the chain on a chair in front of him. Giselle appeared sitting in the chair with the chain snugly around her neck. He exhaled loudly, showing how worried he had been. He knew full well he couldn't go into the mirror looking for Giselle if she were ever late and he wasn't aware of any other entrances. All he could do was wait and trust she was ok. It was only a moment before his relief turned to concern again. She didn't look ok at all. She was teary and low in personality.

"Gizzy," he called her.

She said nothing, but sought comfort in his arms still doing her best to hold in whatever it was that she was feeling. He said nothing either, taken aback by her behavior. He just hugged her in silence and waited until she was ready to pull away and talk to him. She sniffed on his shoulder swallowing hard trying to find her voice.

"What happen?" he asked once she sat up straight.

She lowered her head in thought then responded. "I was talkin' to Ecoli."

"The chief? What he say?"

Amron knew a lot about Majesty now that Giselle could confide in him. He just hadn't been there or met anyone. He couldn't. Normal people weren't allowed so she never tried to bring him and he never asked to go.

"He tell me I can' do the mission." She told him carefully.

"Again?"

"Yeah. And he tell me why," she said.

"What was the reason?"

That question was the key to her voicing what had happened. It was the gateway of her repeating Ecoli's upsetting story to Amron. She couldn't explain to him exactly why she was so bothered by this. There was no specific reason. Every detail of this story just got to her; especially the part where her eldest brother died. When she told Amron this his reaction wasn't what she expected. For the entire time he remained dead in the face refusing to reveal whether this information affected him or not.

"You know about mom first born dyin'?"

"No," he shook his head still showing no surprise to hear this. "News to me."

"I want to ask BJ if he know," she voiced her thoughts.

"And how you go tell him you find out if he know?" Amron spoke with raised eyebrows.

"I-I doh know."

"Then doh ask him," he advised.

"But-"

"-leave it alone Gizzy. We still doh know what any of them go say if they find out about this." He spoke with a voice of reason. "If Ecoli serious about Weyden Empire tryin' to kill you then I think you should start learnin' to fight as soon as possible."

"You do?"

"Yeah," he encouraged. "I tell you not to die. So you have to learn how to fight and I have to act like I doh know about magic- maybe that might help me somehow."

"Ok." She sat up straighter on his bunk bed.

Amron's room was pretty big, but because it was messy it felt clustered and small. He used to share a room with Andre, but now Andre was using BJ's old room. This was why he still had a bunk bed. He slept on the bottom and kept his clothes on the top. It was a pretty cozy set up since he had about five pillows. It was like a fort in there.

"So mom was a seer," Amron said more to himself. "And she used to help Gran'mom protect Majesty."

"And she had visions about us gettin' in trouble and she get crazy." Giselle spoke to herself as well.

She couldn't help, but wonder if the predicament she was in now was what her mother saw. She also wondered how different her life would have been if she and her brothers had been introduced to Majesty from birth. What if them being introduced to Majesty changed everything? Maybe if they had Majesty then those things her mother envisioned, whatever they were, wouldn't have happened. Maybe the first born would still be here because he would have been able to see the danger when he was approached by Lajabless.

"Dad know anythin' about this?" Amron asked.

Giselle didn't catch being absorbed in her own thoughts.

"Gizzy, dad know about this?" he called her.

"I doh know. Ecoli didn' say anythin' about him."

"I mean, if mom was so involved then dad had to know. Gran'mom is his mother anyway."

He did have a point, but how would they get around to asking him. It was not like their dad was known for inviting that type of talk. Plus, if he did know about it and said nothing it was because he wanted them to remain oblivious. Maybe he blamed Majesty for the loss of his wife and mother. Giselle knew she blamed the magical-supernatural world for their loss. However, she was seeing more clearly and knew that Weyden Empire was the one to be mad at; more specifically, Weyden Herwend. He was the one that called a fake cease-fire and used her mom only to kill her in the end. Then when he got what he wanted, Ruby to meet him, he killed her too. It was a good thing she never gave him access to Majesty or else they'd all be screwed. Majesty might not even exist anymore or at the very least it might not be what it is now.

"Well now we have to make sure he doh know we know," she shrugged.

~*~

Reluctantly, she awoke and got ready for school like she was supposed to. She kept yawning the whole time. At school, she dozed off in her first three periods. Then, as planned, she slept through religious education. Half an hour wasn't enough though. She was still tired, and would have to suffer through math before lunch break. She wasn't doing well in that class or in geography. The term was half way through and she was thinking about dropping classes. She couldn't let Brent know of this either. With laziness kicking in and heavy minded about school and everything else, she had Emma get her lunch and bring it to her. Emma was on the lunch program. Then they stayed in class with a friend chatting about upcoming Christmas plans. Speaking about casual things had its appeal.

The weeks that followed surely delivered. Between school, training and telling all the details of everything to her brother, she was being stalked and attacked. There were times where she narrowly escaped the situations she found herself in. The training with Tegan was helping, but it wasn't enough. Her favorite thing to focus on was weapon control. She was good at firing a gun now. Should they need a sniper to cover them on any given day, Giselle was the girl for the job. Every weapon Tegan suited her with she managed to master it, but when it came to bare, hands on, head butting combat, no defense other than body parts, she failed dramatically. She was no good at all. What were the odds that she was going to have a weapon at her disposal should she be attacked at school? Conclusion- she needed to be better at physical combat. She had weapon control down to a science. It was the physical combat training and first aid that held her back. For some reason she wasn't getting that right either. Her reaction time was slow and she panicked. Every animated dummy Tegan told her to fix died or got worst before she could do anything. At least she could fly; she flew away every time she felt nervous about something. Her landing was no more stable than an egg on a tilted counter, but it was better than before. That could help, but for how long?

She finally got her gumshoe pen; red with thin, fiery orange designs. She probably used the emergency button on there more times than she could count. What scared her was the fact that Ecoli said her attackers were weaklings. Weyden Empire wasn't taking her seriously because of her age and that was why it was so *easy* for her so far. "Easy," he said. One day she went to the washroom at school and there was a tarantula woman hanging from the ceiling trying to take her chain. *Easy*. He found it *easy* that Vrai constantly had to teleport her from places or randomly suck her into Majesty. He found it *easy* that she had to keep lying to her father about knowing of the big secret that her mother, Ruby and probably he himself had. It wasn't easy. If anything, it was a nightmare brought to life. She felt like she was in prison again because although Ecoli authorized her training and allowed her small, discrete missions in Majesty she was not allowed to fight outside if Weyden Empire had attacked. He wanted them to continue underestimating her. If she pulled out a tomahawk and proved how good she was becoming, things would get worst. He should know; actually all the guardians should know because fighting off enemies had become a daily hobby for them at this point. Ecoli told her to call for help- always. No matter how small the problem was and whether or not she thought she could handle it, she had to call for help. It was one of the conditions he gave her in turn for training and Amron insisted it was a good deal.

Late November rolled around. In some countries it was really cold. Majesty sure enough was cold, but in Grenada it was as though they were in an outdoor curry pot. Since Ruby left them they had never found a new pass time for the weekend. The only thing entertaining about the weekend was that for two days school was closed and they used that time to procrastinate on doing homework. To fill the void BJ opened his doors to them. He said they could come by his house whenever they felt like it so they took him up on the offer. Andre went too, but he had to leave early since he did Saturday classes. To Amron's dismay Aibell was there.

"Gizzy, you know how to cook?" BJ asked. They were outside cooking on a coal pot in an attempt to be recreational and get fresh air.

"Not really. I know how to bake bread and stew chicken, but that's all."

"Alright, well pull a seat cause class about to start. Let me show you how to make dumplin'." BJ flexed his arms as though he was about to do some great task.

"Oh, be quiet. You're no chef." Aibell chastised.

"I hope you remember sayin' that when you starve," he didn't even spare her a glance as he poured some flour into a bowl.

"I will," she chirped as she took some used utensils into the kitchen.

When BJ finished tending his pot, he verbally directed Giselle on how to make the dumpling and when to add it to the pot. They were making oil down. According to him, "one doesn't just throw dumpling into a pot of oil down. It is an art."

"So Amron, you doh have a girlfrien'?" BJ asked out of the blue after listening to Giselle talk about Emma.

"No," Amron responded dryly.

"How come?"

"Cause he ugly and nobody like him." Giselle rolled her eyes and half laughed as she peeked into the pot.

"Hush your mouth!" Amron frowned. "And am not you BJ."

"You sayin' no could mean you gettin' some action somewhere, but you jus' doh have a girlfrien'."

"Let dad hear you sayin' that," Amron smiled. "I doh have a different woman every week."

BJ held his chest in offence, "A-a, I doh have a different woman every week. Even if I did, am a grown man."

"And you still have to ask dad approval of your girlfrien'?" Amron raised a brow and sat back on the stone ground.

"Out of respect," BJ confirmed.

"Yeah, right! How long it go take before we see the bad bitch side of Aibell?" Amron spoke so casually as though this was a topic long overdue.

"Let dad hear you sayin' that," BJ warned jokingly.

Giselle chuckled, "For real though, Aibell can' be that nice. Be honest."

"You been here all day. Why I go make her dress up for two of you?" BJ placed his hands on his hips.

"I doh know." Amron shrugged nonchalantly stripping a leaf. "Because you doh want us to be right about her not bein' different."

BJ pulled the cover off the pot and randomly gazed into the steam. They were all hungry. If only somebody had started cooking when Aibell told him to they wouldn't be there watching the pot take its sweet time.

"She is. Why would I lie?" He couldn't scratch the hideous grin off his face.

"Because," Giselle poked his rocky bicep and repeated her brother's words, "you doh want us to be right about her not bein' different."

"All-yuh annoyin'."

"Then why you tell us to come here?" Amron threw his strips of leaves at BJ who instinctively covered the pot again.

"Aye, watch the food."

"But be honest BJ. That's how Aibell is for real?" Giselle asked tired of the talk.

Right as BJ was about to respond Aibell popped up again shutting down the conversation.

"You two want juice?" She asked.

Amron and Giselle nodded, their lips glued. As was BJ's.

"Am I interrupting your little sibling gossip session?" The amusement on her face was too evident; though, she probably wasn't trying to hide it. "I'll make myself scarce."

"I want juice too!" BJ called after her green, loose hair bouncing back into the house.

"Get your own juice!" she yelled not stopping.

"Feel the love." he hugged himself. "Yeah, but I doh know. Aibell feel different to me. Like, we have we problems here and there, but we work through it instead of breakin' up. And whenever I see her I just feel… happy. I feel like everythin' right even when she mad at me; she look cute when she mad. If we ever break up I doh think I go be able to get over this one."

This was new to them. Unless this was rehearsed, he had never spoken about a girl like that before. It didn't sound re-hearsed; it all flowed so naturally off his lips. Whenever they asked him what he saw in his girlfriend at the time, he usually went right to the physical features. So far they hadn't heard about how 'sexy' Aibell was once.

"So you like her?" Amron summarized as though he was just now hearing this for the first time.

"Yeah." BJ answered in a lost sort of way then repeated himself more surely. "Yeah, I do."

"How long you say it been?" Amron scooted closer to BJ.

"Eight months," BJ leaned against the house. "A little secret, we never even do it yet and I want to, but at the same time I could wait. That even normal?"

"You shittin' me? How long you say it been again?" Amron shouted.

"Lie!" Giselle called him out.

BJ laughed at them judging him. "Ask her. She doh care, she go answer."

While Amron and Giselle were telling BJ that they didn't believe Aibell would answer them, she came back out with a tray carrying three glasses of juice and a beer. She gave one glass to each of them keeping the beer to herself. BJ looked at his juice then at her.

"You said you wanted juice," she grinned deviously.

"So Aibell,.." Amron had his mischievous business voice on. "BJ just tell me somethin' and I doh believe him."

"Did he tell you he sometimes wears my Bras? It's true. It builds his self-esteem." She sipped her beer as though what she just said was no big deal.

"Learnin' stuff about you bro." Giselle grinned.

"Chill." He rolled his eyes.

Amron let this joke fly over his head as he had more important questions to ask.

"So I hear, not sayin' who tell me, that two of you never do it before." He said all this while keeping a turgid finger pointed at BJ's chest.

Aibell shrugged, "We haven't."

Giselle almost choked on her juice. She was expecting Aibell to blow up on BJ for telling two children about their personal life. She was hoping to finally see the "bad bitch" side of Aibell as Amron so nicely put it.

"Wait what? You just answer me like that?" Amron shared Giselle's shock.

Aibell scoffed and spoke with a duh tone. "You asked a question. I answered."

"Well damn." Giselle sat down.

BJ on the other hand was highly amused by their inability to make Aibell angry or act differently. She was showing how truly different she was and they were conflicted. Amron wasn't able to embarrass her for Giselle's entertainment. Amron cast a look over to Giselle as though asking her if she just heard everything he heard. She pursed her lips and raised her brows. The dulling silence that took over forced Aibell to speak again.

"What was I supposed to say?"

"I doh know. Mind your business little boy," he suggested.

"But you're sixteen. And I already know BJ tells you two everything." She explained herself.

"Ok, so what have you done?" Amron got more confident in his questioning.

"Chill, chill, chill!" BJ butt in now though he was probably going to tell Amron later when the girls weren't around.

"Anyway, if you two are done minding our business, want to play some cards?" She offered.

"Why not?" Amron went inside the house still upset that he couldn't embarrass Aibell.

They ran off the wait time for the food by playing cards. They all had a few wins except BJ who only won once. Aibell wouldn't even let him enjoy it. She kept telling him he only won because the cards weren't shuffled properly. She was so loud and sarcastic and rudely smart about everything she said. Giselle kept whispering to BJ that he was secretly dating a female version of Amron which actually annoyed him beyond entertainment. Every time she said it to him he'd get mad and walk away from her and she found it to be the funniest thing in the world. She followed him everywhere he went. She didn't tell Amron this though; him being angry was a whole hundred levels higher than BJ. Knowing this she poked a conversation with BJ about how Aibell got when she was angry and then when he was done spilling, compared it to Amron. As planned, BJ was annoyed again. Amron was on his own personal mission trying to the best of his abilities to find out some deep dark secret about Aibell to which he was failing. She was answering his questions way too easy and carefree and he didn't like that. He was the stubborn one of the bunch. Amron's ignorance wasn't a mystery though. Given the chance to hang around him, it would become apparent that Brent behaved the exact same way.

They sat inside; Giselle watching TV and Amron and BJ at the dining table oogling over something on the laptop. It was the original plan to return home by night fall, but due to BJ's laziness they decided to spend the night. Bottom line- he didn't want to drive them back. This didn't bother them one bit. They weren't ready to go home anyway. They liked spending time with BJ; he was fun. For Giselle, she increasingly liked Aibell. Speaking of, Aibell sat on the couch coating her nails in a light purple colour. As she painted, mid conversation too, Aibell began a rumbling low tune. Giselle and Amron stopped what they were doing to admire her. They could barely make out the words, but they didn't need words to immediately determine how beautiful her voice was. The song was low and Giselle could be sure if she caught some lyrics it would be tragic. Deeply engrossed in her nail polish, Aibell sat there in and out of humming. She was timely losing herself in the music as though she was the only one there. She didn't glance around once to see if anyone could hear her. She simply minded her own business. Only for a quick second Giselle glanced over to BJ hoping to make eye contact with him. She hoped that the chased stare would tell him she was starting to see why he liked Aibell. Looks did speak volumes after all. That was exactly why she ended up doing a double take. Quite opposite to Giselle and Amron's seduction by her voice, BJ stared at his girlfriend as if singing were the absolute worst thing she could do right now. His face showed that he wanted nothing more than for her to stop. It wasn't as much a look of disgust as it was of discomfort and budding edgy jitters. Tearing away from her, BJ rolled his fingers aimlessly across his laptop.

"I think I leave the coal pot outside," he said.

"Nah," Amron broke his gaze from Aibell who remained singing. "We bring it in."

"We did?" BJ asked. "I feel like I didn' bring it. I have to check or it go bother me all night."

Without waiting for a response, he exited and raced to the back door in an odd fashion. Giselle watched him leave, suspicious as to why he would suddenly want to get away from the room so badly. It was quite obvious that's what he was trying to do, but why in the middle of Aibell's song. And why didn't Aibell seem to realize what was going on around her; like BJ dodging from the room or Amron following closely after him talking rather loudly. It wasn't like Giselle expected her to care about every little thing that went on in the room, but it was human nature to respond to stimulants i.e. people suddenly moving around you; especially when it had been dead for so long. But Aibell stayed humming.

"Aibell?" She ignored the idiocy of her brothers and checked up on the unmoving young lady before her.

And Aibell raised her head with the innocence of a five-year-old that lost sight of her mother. Her eyes were both lonesome and worried and her attitude didn't have that impassive vibrancy about it. She, just slightly, reminded Giselle of herself when she had just heard of her grandmothers passing. That first second of cognizance and shock overdosed with disbelief.

"Where is BJ?" Audible wasn't the best word to describe how she spoke in the slightest.

"Outside." Giselle answered almost in question.

Before any more conversation could be made Aibell was half way through the kitchen to the back of the house. Curiosity taking control of her body and guiding her feet she sprinted along to see what was about to happen. It was all so uncouth. As she made it outside a scene so ghastly came to life. BJ was instinctively guarding Amron as he spoke with utmost displeasure to a wrinkled face man only ten feet away.

"Oh, see!" The way the man's eyes landed on her the second she appeared in the door made her want to turn tail and run.

"Why you come outside?" BJ asked. She had recollection of this same question very many nights ago.

"Yesss," the pure pleasure with which the word was whispered, almost had this man gargling. "I would be rewarded if I brought him a guardian."

At the sound of this Giselle was desperately willing to retreat. They were here. Weyden Empire's sadistic people had located BJ's house and they were going to try to kill her like they always did. They were going to stop at nothing to take her which meant going through her older brother who had no idea what he was facing. BJ was going to stand in front of Giselle, Amron and Aibell and try to protect them and this man was about to pick him off like a leaf. What should she do? Summon help? She had her gumshoe pen, but it wasn't in reaching distance and she was too afraid that if she turned her back something would happen to BJ. She could fight. She knew how to fight, but she didn't excel in physical training as she did in weapon control. If only there was something here that she could use. Either way, he was going to find out tonight about all her adventures. Looking at Amron as if asking him for advice he looked just as in between as she was. Yes, BJ was standing in front of him for his own good, but it was obvious if BJ told Amron to run he wasn't going to leave his side. He would stay there and die with him if he had to. How was she going to protect her brothers? Gathering her thoughts on what the best move was, she was shaken so abruptly by an ear piercing, ferocious scream that she leaned onto the door frame and grabbed her ears almost begging for mercy. She felt as though her ear drums would burst and her skull would split. Her hair was standing up all over and the atmosphere became an icy sting. Her eyes squeezed shut initially; she now squinted to catch sight of what was happening. She wasn't the only one clipping her ears like her life depended on it. BJ and Amron were in distress. Even the grouchy, un-ironed man was groping himself desperate for this noise to seize. The only person unaffected was Aibell because she was the one screaming. She dropped with a thud onto her knees once she was done. And in the twenty seconds it took everyone to recover Giselle un-matted her hands from her ears.

"A banshee? She knows who is going to die tonight."

The raggedy man smirked. Without another word or so much as a warning, skeletal bat like wings sprang from his back and he pounced forward in attempt to bypass everyone and go straight to Giselle. She clenched her fist hoping beyond hopes that this was one of those moments that she miraculously excelled in the one thing she was miserably horrid at; physical fighting. The oncoming incubi didn't seem like anything she could fight off with sheer will. He had short black claws etched from his scrawny fingers and horns to match raising from his skull. Viciously he lunged forth. Then, out of nowhere, a sharp transparent blue, icy blade pierced right through him from his back to his stomach and pinned him to the floor. Her eyes slowly climbed from the twitching body up the blade to unexpectedly land on BJ. It was only then her mind welcomed the full scene of what was taking place in front of her. BJ's entire arm had somehow transformed into the subzero blade that held the incubi losing life beneath them to the earth.

Motionless.

Giselle and Amron, slayed for words, gazed in horror at their brother. Pulling his blade from the dying creature and having it take the form of his hand again he dashed to Aibell's side. Gently and with much love for her, he lifted her off the ground. Then, facing Giselle and Amron with the guiltiest expression on his face, he spoke.

"I have somethin' to tell you."

CHAPTER SEVENTEEN

NECROMANCER

IT WAS INTENSELY quiet for a while as BJ pondered his next words and Giselle and Amron questioned the authenticity of what they'd just seen. They had moved into the house after which BJ pulled out a very familiar piece of equipment; summoning snap. When he joined them a very handsome young man with budding, but properly groomed facial hair appeared. He had on a uniform like the patrollers except it was green which meant he was an emissary. All the units had the same uniform, just different colours as well as different symbols on their chest. When he showed up he didn't act as though he was called without knowledge or as though he was seeing BJ for the first time. He openly greeted him as an old friend; BJ entrusted him with the task of taking the body to Majesty. He also entrusted him with a message that he did not let anyone in the room, but the young man hear. Once the snap was broken and the man was gone (the body as well) it was awkward again. The stiffness of the silence had become too much. She had to know. She had to find out what this all meant.

"Shaman or Ersatz?" This was all she said. She gave no further detail of what those words meant or where they were from. She didn't try to tell BJ how those words applied to her or possibly him nor did she tell him where she learned it. She just expected him to know.

"Ersatz," he said back to her and Aibell gaped at him.

So their family had a higher percentage of inferior knock offs than she thought, huh? So far it seemed Ruby was the only Shaman. Their mom was a Seer; Giselle wasn't sure what category that fell under. She was probably part of the few in Majesty that could live anywhere they wanted.

"Blades?" She said again, the word carrying weight.

"Ice."

"So," Amron's voice added something frighteningly new to the atmosphere. "We wasn' s'pos to know?"

BJ's eyes glided over the two before he said, "I wanted to tell you, but I couldn' at first. And then when I could I didn' know how. That's why I didn' bring you home tonight."

At this point it was clear Amron didn't care anymore. He dropped everything and retreated to the counter where he began picking his nails. He didn't try to carry on conversation or even investigate. That seemed the least important thing on his mind. He just hung back with a dry, emotionless face and opted out of all human interaction.

"So you know everything that going on?" As if it wasn't obvious already, Giselle asked. BJ nodded.

"And you a Ersatz. And Aibell?"

Aibell, looking disappointed about being dragged into the conversation spoke on her own behalf. "Banshee. That means I…"

"I know what it mean. I watch TV," Giselle cut her off rudely still trying to grasp the realness of the situation. So this was why BJ said Aibell was different, huh. She was barely human. She was a so called mythical creature that screamed when someone near her was about to die; an omen.

"For how long?" She was back on BJ's case now.

"Seven years, but-"

"-what happen to Gran'mom keepin' the family out of Majesty? What make you the exception? You go tell us you not we biological brother now?" So began Amron's interrogation. He was finally ready.

"I am your biological brother and I wasn' the exception. I find Majesty by myself only to realize Gran'mom was runnin' the show. Since I already find out she couldn't tell me not to come back so she let me stay and figure out how to control my ice magic. Then when I get good at it and I get the job as an emissary she say I had to move out because people from Weyden Empire would know me now and I couldn' lead them to you. That's why I didn' make a fuss when dad talk about me movin' out."

"And I been in there since end of July and you couldn' say anything?"

"I didn' know you was there. Am an emissary. I was gone for weeks on a job. That's what the whole me 'visitin' uncle Rohan' was about. I wasn' by uncle Rohan."

"But dad call you there," she said unbelieving.

"And Uncle Rohan cover for me," BJ responded. "He is a Shaman."

Amron said nothing in response to this.

"So the family Gran'mom tryin' to keep out is just me, Amron, Andre and dad." Giselle summarized what Amron must have been thinking.

"That's what mom wanted. Gran'mom was just respectin' that." He had all the answers didn't he? "Ecoli call me up a while after I come back, which was strange because the last time I went in that office was when Gran'mom was in charge, and he tell me what was going on with you and I been lookin' out for you ever since I just didn' know where to start tellin' you."

Giselle wanted to speak again. She had so much to say, but Amron beat her to the chase.

"I find it upsettin' that you know how Gran'mom died and you didn' even try to confess then."

Once this was out in the open Aibell excused herself and disappeared down the stairs that led to their room. Tearing his eyes away from watching her leave, BJ rubbed his head and took a few wasted steps. He had been rooted in one position for so long and in the spotlight. This was probably just to get life in his legs again. Giselle took a seat on the counter next to Amron who was holding up his own weight now.

"Doh even bring that up," BJ shut down the talk Amron was digging.

"Because God forbid I find out the rest of your secrets!" Amron shouted at him and pointed him with his whole hand.

"Aye, you doh know nothin' about that so doh try to shoot me for it." BJ's voice raised as well, but it wasn't equaled to Amron's.

"Well duh I doh know! You know dad spend a lot of money on school and the least you could do is remember what the word secret mean. If not, oxford dictionary."

Amron was not Amron right now. Actually scratch that. He was too Amron right now. He usually let things slide off him giving sarcastic responses and acting uninterested or too cool to care. Whenever he let something bother him to the point where he took the time to carry out an argument, it worried Giselle. She had no compassion for that side of him and wished he'd keep it sealed up all the time. Why was he so angry anyway? She was upset too and she was probably going to be hard on BJ for it, but she wasn't going to yell at him. She wanted to hear all he had to say even though she acted like she didn't.

"Chill."

"Why? Because the prince ask me to?"

"Prince?"

"Yeah, the one that had all access to Gran'mom country."

449

"Amron."

"If you didn' realize," Amron paused. "Am mad."

"Well fine! You have all rights. Go ahead, verbally abuse me, but Gran'mom died and that wasn' somethin' I could just come out and talk about. She never tell me she was meetin' Weyden. She send me on some special mission to one of the farthest allied societies we have because they have the best military forces accordin' to her. It took me a week to get there. Then I had to round up troops and send them to the outskirts of Dysen to catch any Weyden Empire denizen comin' out without fail. She didn' even tell me why. I just assume Weyden Empire was tryin' to take Dysen and she wanted to get it first. From what I hear they get everyone except Weyden. Then it took me a week to travel back. I come back the day after she died expectin' her to tell me whether or not the troops meet her expectations. Imagine my shock. The last words I got from her was on a piece of paper sayin' she know I would want to go with her so she created a diversion to protect me. She was right to do it because I might have died too, but maybe if I was there things might of happen differently."

"I understand," Amron showed signs of having a heart. "But it still had a lot of years when gran'mom was still alive where you could of say somethin'. Forget that mom wanted us to stay out. Since when any one of us ever know a secret about dad that we didn' share with one another. Since when gran'mom plan a surprise birthday party for one of us we and didn' spoil it. Since when dad put medicine in we food to trick

450

us into takin' it we didn' tell each other. You see my point? You my brother, not just any old friend. We doh share selective information. We share everything. So mom and Gran'mom tellin' you to keep quiet should of make you want to tell us more."

BJ folded his lips undeniably thinking deeply about what Amron said. It was a fact; whenever they came across some information that was meant to keep under wraps they spoke millions about it amongst themselves no matter how mad the person it was about got. They sold out everything to each other- from Andre's first failed test, to Giselle breaking her dad's phone and acting like she didn't know about it when he asked, to BJ kissing a girl on the playground, to Amron getting in a fight in the bus terminal and BJ picking him up from the police station and not telling dad about it. Sure BJ was quite older than them all being twenty-five, but he still carried out his sibling duty of gossiping and upsetting them. Yet, up until this point they never had anything serious to argue with him about.

"What you want me to say?" BJ asked.

"You know what?" Amron's face loosened. "I shouldn' be mad. I have a secret too and I only, as Giselle tell me about Majesty, realize how it connected. So I go jus' say it now and make things even. I see things."

Giselle was lost even more so when BJ responded, "I know."

Amron left the room.

~*~

451

"He say he could see things," Giselle spoke aloud although she was alone in the room. It wasn't unusual anymore. Amron wasn't going to come knocking on her door asking who was there. He knew about Vrai now. Although he had never heard Vrai speak he knew she was there and that she frequently spoke to Giselle.

"Does not surprise me," Vrai responded.

"That was what you find was suspicious about him a while back?" She asked Vrai.

"Yes," she responded. "Many things he has done since my belonging to you has lead me to believe he is a Necromancer. It means he is able to communicate with the dead."

"Why you didn' tell me that before?" Giselle watched the stirring mirror, her reflection not gazing back. "When you find out?"

"I was not yet sure. That first time you broke down because of me and he entered the room he did not search carelessly like your other sibling. He was looking at something behind you, something I had not noticed at the time. When he took me away from you, being a spirit myself, I was able to see things about him you would not. I did not relate this to you because I felt he would tell you when he was ready." Vrai elaborated clearly remorseless about keeping Giselle's brothers powers from her. So BJ was an ice Ersatz and Amron was a Necromancer; was Andre hiding something then? What about their father? If Uncle Rohan was a Shaman there was a chance Brent was something.

"Ok," she hummed not satisfied with what Vrai had said. "Tell me more. What you see him do?"

"Well, he speaks regularly in his room and in the house when he is alone. There is a young boy. Amron calls him Isaac. He is always in the house and always telling Amron when he is in danger. This is why you cannot come up behind him without his knowledge. The boy seems much attached to this house and to Amron. If your brother had put me down once since taking me away I could have spoken to Isaac and found out what his connection to this place was. Unfortunately, I do not know."

Giselle stood with her sheets in her hand. She was cleaning her room, but with all that had happened the night before she couldn't concentrate. It was like finding things you didn't know you had and spending half an hour playing around with it. Except her toy was her family's secrets.

"He asked Isaac if he wanted him to tell," Vrai's voice sounded distant amongst the swirling thoughts in Giselle's mind.

"He what?" She threw the sheet over her bed and began fitting it to the mattress.

"He wanted to tell you about Isaac. Isaac was there every single time you told Amron about Majesty."

"So why he didn' tell me," she stopped again. This bed was not getting made anytime soon.

"Again, I do not know. Speak to him."

Saying this was so much easier said than done as everything else was. Amron point blank refused to talk. He didn't want to hear of anything magical. He refused to discuss how BJ was able to transform any part of his body into ice and use it as a weapon. BJ had sat down and spoke to Giselle and answered every question she had for him. She wasn't upset about it anymore. There was nothing to be upset about. He kept a secret, but that was because he had no other choice. It was what their mother wanted and it was safer if he stayed away. If she wasn't being hunted by Weyden Empire she might not have understood this as well as she did. But she was and so she did. Amron was blowing this way out of proportion. It wasn't as though it was any different with Giselle. When he found out about her going to Majesty it wasn't as though she had just came out and told him. He found out about it and they had a whole big thing. So why was he excessively mad at BJ and not at her? When she made this point he kept saying it was different.

"Amron you realize if BJ did stick around Weyden Empire would of kill all of us a long time ago," she pressed. "And we might not even know why people was lookin' for us."

"I realize," he pulled on his bag straps and hoisted his bag higher.

"And you remember the story about mom. She had visions about bad things happenin' to all of us if we go in Majesty," she dragged Ecoli's confession into the mix.

"You ever think mom was wrong?" His voice had some arrogance in it, though it was controlled.

"Wrong how?"

"She had visions of bad things happenin' to us so she keep us out of Majesty. Her first born died. Gran'mom died. She died. BJ had to stay away from us when he find out and we barely see him. You struggling' in trainin' and tryin' to learn about yourself and bein' a Guardian of Majesty at the same time while people from Weyden Empire tryin' to kill you. People go start tryin' to kill me too if they find out what I could do. They go try to get dad and Andre because we related to them." He paused and gave her a deep meaningful glance as though waiting for her to get some obvious point.

"So maybe this was the bad things she was seeing, but maybe this was the only part she see. She thought it was happenin' because we was in Majesty. She was wrong. It happenin' because we didn' get to go in Majesty and prepare for the day we do find trouble. And now we catchin' we ass to stay alive."

Giselle did think about this before; when she had just learned of her mother and grandmother's past. She did wonder what her life would have been if she had been introduced to Majesty earlier. Everything would have been so different. She might have been a complete different person too. Nothing like who she was now. Evidently Amron was considering this as well, though he was more detailed about it; more real.

"If we knew earlier and we went earlier am sure gran'mom would have make sure you was ready for the day you become a

Guardian. am sure she would have tell me what was goin' on with me…" he didn't speak rocky then.

"Am sure," she mumbled gazing at him concernedly. "But you can' blame BJ for mom mistake. And you can' get mad at him for obeyin' Gran'mom- the woman who take care of us."

"I could do what I want," he smacked the dust around the base of a tree wildly. That poor tree.

The afternoon was bright as they made their way across the careenage talking about their troubles stopping only when a stranger passed by. The smell of salt water was so rich in their noses that they were becoming senseless to it. The sound of the water beating against the concrete bank was frequent; the endless amount of boats lined along the walls weren't making it any better. Giselle adapted the custom of training her eyes in the shallow waters whenever she took this rout. There were always some unique fishes there. That was how she found out there was such a thing as a cowfish. It wasn't often she found them, but when she did they were usually wondering around aimlessly with their ugly, brown faces and horn like structures at the top of their head. Once she even found a manta ray in there. Beside the fact that it was dead it still looked majestic being the first one she ever saw. This often led her to wonder what it was doing in the middle of the careenage waters. She felt like if she could ever dive down there one day she'd see an abnormally large octopus among other strange creatures.

"What make BJ different from me? I didn' tell you about Majesty."

"You didn' know about me," he responded not looking at her.

She couldn't possibly see how different it was. He said it was because she didn't know he could see dead people. This still meant nothing to her and being the stubborn animal he was he didn't go into much detail. He never once brought up Isaac either. Giselle refrained from asking him because he was already so upset. Why push him to renew his anger toward her. She wasn't that determined. Like everything else he had been through, he'd eventually get over it.

~*~

It wasn't betrayal. It was not betrayal if the people you trust kept secrets from you with good intentions. It wasn't betrayal. This was how Giselle tried to convince Amron to forgive BJ. Ruby didn't introduce him to Majesty, he found it himself. Added to that, there were dangers involved in being a part of a magical world. It wasn't just Majesty; there was Weyden Empire and Dysen and all these other allied societies she kept hearing about. It was a justified silence. He had to forgive BJ for that fact. Forgiveness wasn't for the other person. He had to forgive BJ so he'd stop being miserable.

The blunt force and irrational rush that coerced through her body as she swung her weapon failed to push away the ill feelings she had about this squabble. She had just delivered the final blow in an intense battle. Some people were trying to jump her, but her increasing skills with the tools from the weaponry had worked to her advantage. She took care of them all herself. Taking refuge behind a semi-demolished wall she tried to regain energy for the completion of her mission. It wasn't one from the mission board; Tegan was testing her. She had to get to a check point on the outskirts of Floral Cove within a certain time limit and in her opinion she was doing borderline well (and that was her speaking highly of herself). She had an hour to get from the air bunker in headquarters to Neport which was the borderline village of Floral Cove and Heavenly Heights. She'd been at it for forty minutes now and the check point was in view. That was good time. After Giselle outwardly expressed how easy this would be, Tegan chuckled and said she should be fine then. She couldn't wait to meet up with him and drop kick his lying face now. The mission was horrid. She started off her mission leading a four-man squad and now it was just her. Just her! How could he do this to her? It was all so real. She had to watch her comrades get picked off one by one.

There was no one up ahead that she could see. It was a clear path to the house and considering the past events leading her there she found that suspicious. It was too easy. She felt as though she was about to walk into a trap. No matter how many times she scanned the area she couldn't see anyone. She searched the ground for disturbed earth to see if there were hidden traps there. Tegan taught her this. Things that she wouldn't usually check were the things she had to pay the most attention to. She observed the trees around the house for any sell out that someone might be hiding there. There were few animals in the area, but she still tested them by chucking rocks and watching their reaction. So, no one was here? No, someone had to be. She only had two weapons with her now; the rest were dropped clumsily along the way. She carefully put her mace away and took out her extendable swallow; it was anything but blunt. This should be useful right now. It would keep distance between her and her enemies.

Giselle cautiously stood up, hopped the wall and slowly made her way to the house. This was it. She was almost at the check point. Unfortunately, she wasn't going to make it there. Her time was up. And not the mission time, she still had fifteen minutes left; however, her life time wasn't lenient. The spear that had buried itself in her back saw to that. Stumbling forward from the traveling force of the spear, eyes wide and heart rate increasing, she reached around. She could feel it. The shaft was standing in her back as though that was where it was originally supposed to be and the head of the spear buried within her spine. It felt… scary. That wasn't supposed to be there. She didn't like the added heaviness. More strange, it didn't hurt one bit. There was a sting, but it was like the after math of being pinched on the cheek. A tickle.

"That's not how you do that," Tegan criticized as green digital lines peeled over everything around her exposing the white of the simulation training room. She said nothing as she reached for the shaft of the spear again only to feel it wither from her grasp. The tickle was gone, but her back was bruised.

"What did you do wrong?" He asked her.

"I-I, um…" she was still in shock. Where did that attack even come from?

"Never leave a man behind," he retaught. "Four man teams are used for a reason, if you're not highly skilled anythin' less could be deadly, which you've just seen. If one of you is injured to the point where you can't go on, and the mission isn't dire then retreat and recalculate. You should have done that now; I would have passed you if you did. Not to mention you entered unknown territory with no back up or even an escape plan."

She stayed silent as he called out everything she did wrong over the mic.

"Now, all that bein' said, good fightin'. I'm impressed with how far you've come so fast. I liked the way you scanned for enemies as well," was the better part of what he had to say.

"I didn' do it good. Somebody was there." She sulked.

"It was good. You remembered to test the animals." He stated pointedly. "Don't be so hard on yourself mate. Learn to appreciate the small things and in time everything else will fall into place."

The large rectangular window that provided the only visual aid to outside had finally reappeared on the wall. She could see Tegan and Marko again. Tegan was leaning over the control to the mic that he used to talk to her and Marko was the one creating the simulations with his million little controls. Marko had been back only a few days now. He was so generously gifted with wounds to take back. None too serious. All of them could be healed and earn him a pat on the back from Marcel, but he didn't want it. He didn't accept Marcel's treatment. Tegan said it was because to him, every scar had an interesting story to tell. He always healed at his own rate and kept the scars. Ecoli offered him the chance to go home and relax before getting back to work, but he refused. He said life in Majesty wouldn't wait for him to get energy again. It was obvious he was tired though. Scout wasn't spared of damage either. According to the half story Marko told Scout really took care of him like a brother when he couldn't help himself; he had been paralyzed for a whole day. She never found out how Marko got paralyzed or even why and when he got better because Scout would not let him finish the story. As much as he denied it, Giselle figured he was just embarrassed. He warded off all affection that was thrown at him relating to the topic. He even went as far as bearing his fangs and silvering his eyes when Marcel tried to treat his wounds. He said he'd heal without her hell treatment. That part was mostly because most Marcel's medications were made from the water collected at pious falls and it was like a poison to him as it was to the majority of shape shifters. She had alternatives, but he didn't trust medication period. He had a natural ability to heal himself and he was more than willing to rely on that.

Since Marko and Scout had been gone and even after they came back, the mortality rate had certainly decreased. There were less and less injured being rushed to Majesty's hospital.

Marcel was rejoiceful about this. Ecoli made a public announcement letting Majesty know that their two favorite people were back and less people were going to get injured for the time being. Of course, Aubrey had a lot to say about that. His obnoxious response was that Ecoli had only acted on the current events because of the harsh feedback he (Aubrey) had given on his show and he was going to continue to bash him until things in the country were right again.

"It's done. You can come out," Tegan instructed.

He made his way over to the door to meet her when she came out.

"I doh like this room," she swore as they met up. "The missions in there is so much worst than the real-life ones I do. People always dyin' on me."

"Good," Tegan smiled.

"Good? What make that good?" She didn't understand. "If I can' take care of some fake people in a fake room then how I go take care of real people in a real-life situation? I trainin' to be a Guardian. That mean everybody in Majesty go be my responsibility once I officially complete trainin'. The missions I do so far in real-life was easy and you know that. I doh think I could do this."

She was breaking down. All she wanted was to pass one simulated mission. She had done twelve. Every single time she had come so close to passing, but didn't.

"Giselle, you are so much better in real-life than you are in here. In real-life there are no second chances, but in here there are. The reason you fail is because, I've noticed, when you make a mistake in here, you don't put in as much effort anymore. On real missions you do." Tegan expressed his thoughts as her trainer.

She lowered her head.

"Honestly," Marko's voice was low and rusty. He needed sleep. "I can't guarantee you're going to be a perfect guardian. And I can't guarantee that anything you learn in here is going to prepare you for the real world. So, there's no point in stressing. Just learn as much as you can of the basics to stay alive and do what your heart tells you to do when you go out on a high-class mission because your enemies aren't going to attack you according to the program in your simulation training. They're not going to stop after five minutes like Tegan does."

She nodded more for his benefit than hers.

"Anyway, Ecoli needs to talk to you." Tegan packed away his trainer belt and went back to just being her friend.

She accepted his words and headed to the door. She just wanted to sulk. Was that too much to ask without people always saying some positive spiel to her? She just wanted to be upset and hard on herself for a while. Maybe have some quiet time to herself where she could sit screw faced and point out everything wrong with her life even though it was unrelated to the initial problem. Was that too much to ask for? Were guardians not allowed to sulk? Maybe that was how Amron felt with regards to BJ. This mind frame took her all the way to Ecoli's office and into the blue cushioned chair in front of his desk. This was where a whole new problem began.

"So, the whole point of tomorrow is to hide?" Giselle spoke with a touch of disapproval.

"More or less," he answered.

"Who say I doh have plans for Christmas Eve?" She meant to sound rude, but he twisted the question to his favor.

"I did, jus' now."

"You even Grenadian?" She cursed.

Ecoli gazed at her as if trying to determine if she just said what she did.

"Ya doh prefer stay alive long enough to reschedule ya plans?"

Giselle rolled her eyes, "I been trainin' hard. Let me go out for Christmas Eve. I could take care of myself."

"Jus' 'cause ya know how to fire a gun now doh mean ya invincible." He sternly disciplined. "Ya still have plenty to learn."

"How old are you?" She continued with the snide comments.

"Twenty," Ecoli responded with confidence simply because he knew she never intended him to. "And it doh matter my age. I say ya gotta come here tomorrow."

Giselle didn't respond. He won this round.

"If ya safety is the only thing I get to guarantee tomorrow then ya go be safe whether ya like it or not." He spun in his chair casually. Giselle questioned his understanding of the word 'safety'. He sounded as though he was daring her to do something which naturally made her want to act out.

"Fine. Tomorrow I come here for Christmas Eve. No excuses," she recited his first words to her.

"All I ask, yeah'," Ecoli was satisfied. "Ya could bring ya blood if ya want."

"How?"

"How ya think other people get in here?" She glared at him and his smart behavior as he smirked. What was with him this evening? "BJ could bring ya in. He go show ya the other way."

So Ecoli wanted her in Majesty. Christmas Eve was sure to dawn tomorrow and with it came the Christmas Hunt. The Christmas Hunt was this self-gratifying purge that Weyden Empire saw through annually. It was one thing that every guardian and denizen unwillingly anticipated and was always prepared for. This time around however it was going to be particularly rough being the first one in sixty-seven years without Ruby. With so many people already injured and the new Chief having all eyes on him to pull off locking down Majesty from Weyden Empire, it was like Ecoli was being tossed into the belly of the beast. This one day was going to determine his capability. Right now, all Ecoli wanted to know was that he had a handle on something. That something was Giselle.

She got up with the intention to leave his office not without showing how unpleased she was.

"Giselle," Ecoli called her again.

"What?"

"Come here tomorrow," his cool seemed to slip out from under him.

He looked at her with warning. Did he think she was going to bail? Did he really believe she was that reckless? There was an Empire out there that was willing to kill not only her, but all of Majesty if they got the chance. Did he think she'd disobey him now? Giselle gazed at him her expression conveying all this and more, but Ecoli could sense some amusement about her features.

"I comin'. I promise." She showed him her pinky finger as though this would solidify things.

Going through the mirror she found Amron waiting on the other side like he always did. Giselle didn't know what ran through his mind whenever she left, but he was always there waiting as though he was afraid she wouldn't come back. Was he?

"I have a headache," he said once he saw her.

He flopped down in his bed and pulled a pillow over his face. She observed the rehearsed way he carried on and decided against questioning. Whatever. Whether he was fishing for a reaction or blockading one he wasn't getting it anyway. She had her own things to be concerned with, like how on earth she was going to spend all of Christmas Eve in Majesty. As she neared the door she realized she needed to talk to him. Damn. She had to give him a reaction to his faked, bizarre behavior which she really didn't care for. He had a headache? Jokes.

"Amron," she called him exasperatedly.

"Headache," he said.

Ok. So he was refusing conversation, not begging it. Beautiful. Giselle sucked her teeth.

"Stop playin' before I give you a real headache." She threatened him. "I have to go in Majesty tomorrow."

"You doh know what I have a headache mean?" Amron thrust the pillow into his lap.

"Yeah it mean you doh have one," she rolled her eyes and shook her head at him.

He exhaled loudly. "You go in Majesty all the time. I know you goin'. Why you tellin' me?"

"So you comin' or you coverin' for me?" She asked him.

He sat up with narrowed eyes and question upon his face for a second. This conversation evidently didn't go the way he thought it would.

"Come with you?" He spoke the words as though they were foreign.

She sighed. "Ecoli want me there all day tomorrow. And not just like me leavin' here in the night time. Like from twelve o'clock in the mornin'. A full twenty-four hours. I can' stay in Grenada for Christmas Eve."

"Why he want you there so long?" Amron fully got up and put his two feet on the ground. "No." He forbid it right away.

"What you mean no? You didn' even hear the reason yet," she retaliated.

"I still say no," he held his ground.

"Ok daddy," she chastised. "Is Christmas Eve."

"And?" he urged arms folded across his chest.

She never explained anything about this Christmas Hunt to Amron before because frankly she didn't get it. Weyden Empire had all year, every year to attack and plunder and anything else they wanted to do to Majesty. Why did they have a special day for it? Why show up when Majesty was well abreast about their plans? How did that make sense? She got it, Majesty was basically the reformed version of The Land of Spirits, but couldn't they leave the past in the past? Just get on with life already! Why try to destroy a place that provided shelter and structure for the supernatural just like his own Empire did? As a matter of fact did Weyden Empire even have structure? Was anyone else working alongside Weyden? What type of place was it? Did it look as bright and inviting as Majesty did or was it muted and icy? Perhaps it was somewhere in between? She hadn't a clue. One impulsive question after the next she was seeing how little she knew about Weyden Empire.

"It have this thing called Christmas Hunt. People from Weyden Empire kill as much people as possible from Majesty as they could. Is not specifically me now, but I on the list."

Amron ran his hand violently down his face as though he was about to attack himself and let out a very frustrated groan. "Seriously!"

Her eyes roamed the room as if trying to find the answer to his reaction on the walls.

"You serious? Is a Christmas Hunt now!" He opened his arms. "Gizzy, you sure gran'mom wanted you there because honestly I doh see the benefits."

She carefully thought out her response. "I guess all this is why BJ had to keep it a secret."

He sucked his teeth. "And how I supposed to come with you?"

"BJ," she repeated the name.

"Oh," he sighed.

For some time he said nothing, but he continuously paced the room insanely bothered. There were times where he stopped walking and his eyes darted to the right of him. It was evident he wanted to say something. He wanted to voice his thoughts, but he didn't want to do it while Giselle was there. Even though she knew he was seeing things he still avoided contacting spirits in her presence. Why won't he just say something about it; elaborate more? She would openly welcome anything he had to say. She wanted to hear more about what he saw and how long it had been going on. She wanted to know how he felt about it; she was fascinated, but Amron would never talk about his feelings like that. He wouldn't just come to someone and admit to feeling an ill emotion. Did he even feel ill about it? Giselle didn't even know that. All she knew was that Vrai called him a Necromancer; did he know that was the name of his ability? She should tell him.

"You see anything right now?" She asked him.

"Like what?" He was disoriented. "What you talkin' about?"

"Like spirits," she answered calmly for his sake.

He congealed. "Why you… no." Amron answered as though that was the oddest question he had ever heard.

"Well," Giselle continued not believing him, but choosing not to pester him. "Vrai call you a Necromancer."

"I s'pos to be insulted?" He asked her, brows raised.

"No dotish," she gave him an insult he understood. "Like since you could see dead people and things like that it mean you a Necromancer. That's the proper word for it."

"A Necromancer," he repeated to himself.

His eyes floated inconspicuously to his left now. Whatever or whoever was there must have moved. His expression was almost unreadable, but something about it was like he was seeking approval of this new discovery. Or maybe he was feeling lighter about finally having light shed on this dark secret he had for so long.

CHAPTER EIGHTEEN

THE DOOR IS OPEN

SPENDING THE FULL day of Christmas Eve at BJ's house.

Christmas Eve at BJ's house.

BJ's house.

Was that going to be code now? Every time something magical or supernatural had to go down it was going to be at BJ's house. Did they just add a new thing to the list of sibling duties? They lied for each other, gossiped about each other, pissed each other off and now covered up magic. Interesting family. BJ told Brent that Giselle and Amron would spend Christmas Eve with him without Giselle even asking him to. He already knew of the plan. Either that or he had his own plans for protecting them. He told Brent they'd have Christmas Dinner at his house too. All Brent had to do was show up on Christmas day. BJ said he'd cook. After getting off the phone with his dad though he confessed he'd just buy food from the Rowdy Ruby and fake it. He didn't even have to find an excuse to exclude Andre because he took himself out. Apparently, he had plans like any normal Grenadian child would on Christmas Eve.

"If we have to come with you then what about Andre and Dad? What if somethin' happen to them?" Amron interrogated BJ with the roughest voice he could drag out of him.

"Recruit have that covered," BJ answered him.

"What that s'pos to mean?"

Giselle took the reins on this one, "Tegan say the recruit team go be watchin' anybody with magical attachment and they go help them if it became necessary. I guess dad and Andre on that list now."

"K," Amron humbled.

BJ had this flat fragile device that looked like a phone, except it wasn't. He called it the I.W.T. Key: Inter-world Terminal Key. He slid his point card in and the screen lit up asking him questions like a test. First he had to enter a pin. Then he had to tell the device where he wanted to go and how many people he intended to take with him. Once that was done the number 10 showed up on its screen. He said that meant they'd come out in one of the number 10 pods in the Inter-World Terminal.

"So we ready?" BJ asked looking over the small group. It was just him, Amron, Aibell and Giselle. "You seein' Majesty for the first time, excited?"

All eyes floated on Amron.

"Is no big deal," Amron shrugged and dunked his fist into his pockets.

Giselle felt like the response would have been different if she asked the question.

"Ok, let's go. It's ready." Aibell drew attention to the pods that were blinking to life in the center of the dining room where they were absent mere seconds ago. They were like the ones Giselle saw in the Inter-world Terminal in Majesty. Did they come here or were these the second half like the Sui Generis?

"This is the exact same one from the terminal?" Giselle didn't specify who she was speaking to.

"Would that make sense?" Aibell eyed her.

"You just have to say no," Giselle walked passed her and pulled one of the pod glasses open. She wanted to get this over with quick. If this felt anything like the Inter-city pods did, she already knew she wouldn't like it.

BJ chuckled and pulled the glass door to his own pod open, Aibell doing the same with the one in the middle. Amron approached the glass structure and inspected it for a while. He was about to see Majesty for the first time so no one questioned his uncertainty about everything. They were going to let him come at his own pace. Well, BJ intended to let him take his time knowing full well the pods wouldn't embark on its travels if all four of them weren't inside.

"Amron move your big head, nah. What you lookin' for," Giselle rushed him.

"Your face," he snarled. He raised a foot to enter, but was hesitant. "Um, I doh think I want to go?"

"Why not?" Giselle asked him.

"Cause," he thought deeply not excluding a glance at BJ. "I have to go in here alone?"

"Yeah," BJ answered him.

"You 'fraid?" Giselle teased.

"Didn' see that comin'," Aibell commented.

"I en 'fraid nothin'!" He sucked on his teeth again.

"So what then?" BJ tried to find the core of the problem, but Amron just glared at him and stepped into his pod. Once inside he gazed at the open space in the living room as if saying a silent good bye then looked over at the others. Neither of them, Giselle nor Amron, got to ask questions because once they were in there the pods shot into a frenzy. It felt just like the one Ecoli took her in, except, if it wasn't for the whooshing sound she'd have thought her own existence was imaginary. Visibility was naught and somehow she knew Ecoli wouldn't have a problem with lighting in there. Then, in a matter of seconds they arrived safely in Majesty. They were in the little plaza that housed the pods making up the terminal. All around them people were appearing out of nowhere within pods and coming out in large groups into the city. They were all trying to find shelter within Majesty before Weyden Empire decided they were ready to strike.

They left Grenada in pitch blackness, it being the middle of the night, only to show up midday in Majesty. Once they were all out and together BJ took them over to a little security booth that Giselle had never noticed before. He explained that it was set up there specifically for the Christmas Hunt and once it was over the booth would be totaled until next year or next time something threatening nationwide happened. There were about six booths cutting the terminal from flowing directly into the city. Beside each there were metal bars that corralled the crowd and forced the formation of a line. Choosing the shortest line they could find they followed the crowd.

"Why we have to go through the booth?"

Giselle had to speak a little louder than usual. It was noisy there. Everyone was talking. There was a constant cling every five minutes that was a result of people being let through the security booths. Behind them there was a zoop sound every time the pods were opened and closed and an airy swirling sound when people appeared within them. From where she was standing she could see beyond the security booths. There were vendors out there. That wasn't a norm either. Guess they knew how to make money… or points to be more specific.

"On normal days, people know their limits to go and come to Majesty, it shows up on the glass, but around this time sometimes things get out of hand." He responded casually as the line moved up little by little.

"Limits?" Amron raised a brow.

"Yeah. Limits between denizens and visitors," BJ spoke.

"Visitors could only stay for five months I think?" Giselle remembered reading about this in the handbook.

"It's six months now. Denizens can stay for as long as they want, but they can't leave here for more than a month." BJ explained more rules governing Majesty. "Well, more than a month depending on where they go."

"Think visitors can stay longer 'cause Majesty is more 'bout them comin' 'ere for protection." Aibell confirmed.

"Make sense," Amron mumbled, though the others might not have heard him. "How you become a denizen then?" Amron kept the conversation flowing.

"By fakin' ya own death in whatever country ya came from. That way ya don' exist anywhere, but Majesty." Aibell held BJ's hand as she walked forward. Her accent, ever since the big reveal was very distinct. "Never had to do that, yeah. Was born 'ere."

"That's why you talk different now," Giselle critiqued.

"That Majesty accent aye," Aibell shrugged.

Finally, they made it through the security booth where all, except Aibell, received a stamp on a detailed paper saying when they had to leave. Amron had to do a little more since it was his first time there- he had to get a handbook. He was allotted a longer time than they were to stay too. Getting onto the paved sidewalk they moved down until the crowd had sifted a bit.

"So anybody want to eat, cause I could eat," BJ announced.

"You could always eat," Giselle commented.

"You have to eat to live sister," he casted a comical glance her way.

"It have good food place here?" Amron raised a brow. "Like, I wouldn' end up in no shop where they servin' blood called survival juice or nothin' right."

"No," Giselle laughed, but BJ had spoken the exact same time as her and his answer made her cut short.

"Depends on where you go."

"Where I live, ya might find a shop o'two doin' that," Aibell carried.

"So what you eat?" Amron insensitively asked Aibell. As he spoke he kept turning to take in the scenery of the strange world. His reaction was far from Giselle's over dramatic behavior about everything. He remained mellow and walked along with his hands in his pocket as he saw people using magic to hold umbrella's over their heads and the shuttles floating by fully loaded.

"Food."

"Really?"

"Really. I sense when people are near death. M'not a monster." She rolled her eyes.

"Oh!" Giselle exclaimed. "You know where we should go?"

"Where?" Asked BJ.

"Start with R," she hinted and he immediately picked up.

"Yes!" He grinned looking down on Amron. "You have to see this place."

"Why?"

"Because I want you to. Stop bein' sour," BJ told him.

Amron granted BJ the pleasure of a glance. "Well I doh know who tell you I was a lime."

Although he said it in the most serious tone possible for mankind the three still cackled at his witty responses looking past his intended rudeness. They filled the travel to the Rowdy Ruby with a story of when Aibell saw the outside world for the first time. Apparently, BJ was the one that took her out of her comfort zone. Her mother was a Banshee and her father was a Selkie. Looking out her bedroom window seeing centaurs, foxes and trolls brought her comfort. That was all she had known the world to look like. Even coming to Floral Cove was strange to her. Everyone had smooth skin and could tolerate the day light. She called them shiny people. Still their magical factor made up for their appearance. But when BJ took her into the non-magical world she felt even stranger because there was so much manual labour. It looked like Floral Cove, but the people were talentless. The story came to an end when they arrived on the door step of the Rowdy Ruby and three of them were waiting for Amron's reaction. He looked at the large effigy of Ruby at the top and the classy layout of the deck and the wait staff busy at work.

He smiled.

Majesty wasn't huge on Christmas celebrations, but there were still decorations here and there and classic Christmas music pumping from different buildings. Inside the Rowdy Ruby there was a big Christmas tree in the corner that was decorated in glittering lights and colourful balls. The wait staff was wearing Santa hat's and had red snowflakes on their shirts. It was a nice vibe. Over the speakers, the famous 'All I Want For Christmas Is You" was playing. Before they could make their way deeper into the restaurant a hare hopped up to them. In the middle of the last hop it transformed and the friendly grey-haired woman grinned at them.

"Boss lady!" She exclaimed.

"Hi Ms. Lyn." Giselle smiled.

"How ya goin'?" She asked. She was dressed in the full Mrs. Clause outfit.

"I good. Chillin' with my brothers and Aibell," she responded.

"Brothers?" Ms. Lyn looked up at BJ and gave him a knowing smile. "I know ya." Then she turned to Amron. "But I don' know this one."

"Amron," he spoke.

"Alright good, good! Didn' know there were more o' ya. Almighty! Ya look just like what's his name," she snapped her fingers.

"Brent," BJ reminded.

"Yes! How he goin'? Ain't seen him in mass time." She put her hands on her hips.

"He good," BJ confirmed. Amron and Giselle exchanges looks. So she knew their dad.

As Ms. Lyn guided them to a table she carried on talk with BJ as an old friend. She was telling him ever since he found a lady friend he didn't come by to say hi or earn some extra points anymore. He outwardly denied it, but Aibell jokingly went along talking about things he didn't do for her too.

"So you work here?" Amron asked innocently.

"Before I get the job as an Emissary I used to work here." BJ confirmed.

"Oh," Amron sighed and his eyes dropped to the menu.

"Remember ya was so excited when ya got it as if ya won a million points o'somethin', yeah?" Aibell said to him.

"You like bein' an Emissary." Giselle didn't ask, she merely stated an observation.

As the three indulged in conversation Amron stayed quiet and listened. He inserted very little on the different topics. Sometimes he looked happy and other times he was unreadable.

"Yeah," BJ rubbed his stomach. They had ordered drinks and snacks. "That was the best worst day ever. I was havin' an off day in the kitchen so I asked to work the cash register instead. Then this girl come in and order a breakfast sandwich club without bacon and she refuse to understand that it wasn' club if it didn' have bacon in it. Ten minute argument later I had a best friend."

"Was a damn club. It had tomatoes," Aibell huffed.

"Doh start this." BJ shook his head.

"Awwww," Giselle put her elbows on the table and her face in her palms. "And they live happily ever after."

The drag of a chair being pushed interrupted them. They all turned to Amron who looked like he didn't expect that much noise to be made.

"I want to go see outside again," he said.

"Oh," said BJ. "Yeah, ok. Let's go."

"No," Amron stopped him. "You doh have to come."

That response sounded more like the anger about the secret again. He stood up and put the chair back in adjusting his pants before walking away. Giselle observed him.

"Can I come?" She asked.

He gestured her to come along with the nod of his head. Happy he said yes, she grabbed her bag and told BJ they'd be back soon. Then Giselle left side by side with Amron. She walked around the town and showed him the places she knew. Together they discovered places she didn't. They lingered in clothing stores, convenient stores the Majesty version of Subway and watched the population carry on with their life from some benches in a park they found.

"You like it?" Giselle asked him.

"Yeah," he smiled. "I think I would of prefer to grow up in here."

"I know right," she commented putting her sneakered foot up on the seat.

"That place have slugs as ah option for pizza though," he joked. "That's nasty."

"I'll pay you five dollars if you buy one and eat it. You can' spit it out." She dared him.

"You mad!" He remarked. "I like myself too much."

"You alone," she turned his comment against him.

"Well only my opinion matter." He flipped it again.

She sucked her teeth. "O'please!"

He faced her. "I want to go home though."

"Why?" Giselle let her foot fall.

"Cause," he hesitated. "I think… cause BJ so comfortable here when… cause Isaac."

He kept changing his answer. Giselle didn't try to interrupt him. He said Isaac. Was he about to tell her about this mysterious spirit he communicated with?

"Who is Isaac?" She asked as if Vrai hadn't told her stuff about him

"A boy," he answered vaguely.

"Ooookk."

"You know how mom had a child before BJ," he said.

"Yeah."

"He name is Isaac," he told her. "He always in the house."

"The one that died," she confirmed.

She was thoroughly creeped out at the thought of her house being haunted by her dead brother. Getting used to Amron being a Necromancer would take time for her. How awkward it must have been for him to see this ghost around them all the time only to find out who it was.

"Wait," she stopped him from answering. "You know about Isaac long before I tell you," she accused.

"Yeah," he said. She slapped his arm. "Ouch."

"Why you didn' tell me?" She barked at him.

"I would of have to tell you I could see dead people in order to explain," he rubbed his arm and met her softening glare.

"You lucky you had a good reason." She looked away now. "So you know what he look like and everything?"

Amron nodded.

"I wish I could see him," she mellowed. "What he like?"

"He behave like a drama queen just like you," Amron grinned. Giselle rolled her eyes. "He fun like BJ and he smart like Dre. When he get mad he behave like me, but I feel is because we hang out a lot." He rubbed his shoulder guiltily.

She tried to imagine it as he spoke; a boy with all their characteristics that they could have known, but time was against him.

"You barely home though," Giselle said.

"He could leave the house you know," Amron retorted. "Everywhere I go he go."

Giselle sat upright. "He here now?" She noticeably glanced around as if she'd see anything.

Amron seemed to lose his spirits again. "No. He stay back with dad and Dre."

"Oh."

"I want to go back and check on them," he announced. "I feelin' real uneasy about stayin' here."

"Tegan say they go be fine," Giselle reminded him of all the information she was given from the guardians before the day had rolled around. Their family was being monitored. They'd be fine.

"Trust me Gizzy," he looked deeply into her eyes. "I have a bad feelin'. Maybe we could go check on them and if everything good then we could come back and I might even eat the slug for you."

She wasn't sure how she felt about leaving Majesty, but the thought of his eating slugs for her entertainment was intriguing.

"Three?"

"Two," he confirmed.

"Three?" She asked again more insistent.

"Two and a half."

"Three?"

"Shit. Whatever, three." He folded his arms over his chest already disgusted at the thought.

She hopped to her feet. "Ok, let's get BJ." She was satisfied.

"No," Amron said. "We doh need him."

"Why you still mad at him?" She was tired of this fight.

"Because reasons." Amron stood up pulling something from his pocket. When it was finally out she saw it was the I.W.T. Key and BJ's card was still in it.

"You crook," she accused.

He smirked. "Let's just go real quick."

"I doh know. I not supposed to leave here. Let's just tell him." She was in two minds about it.

"I go say the magic word." He bribed some more then proceeded when she raised her eyebrow. "Pleeeeeease."

Was this a smart idea? Maybe she should just head up to headquarters and ask them to check things out. But they were like a billion years away from it. From where they were it could be seen in the distance; A castle with dots for windows and holes for doors. Staring at him and thinking for some time she responded, "Four slugs."

Amron made no argument. They walked around to some dense trees in the park. Giselle wasn't sure if they were allowed to use the I.W.T. key to leave Majesty during the Christmas Hunt so she didn't want to do it in broad daylight. It was too risky, especially since there were patrollers around every corner today. After Amron typed in the code that he managed to sneak as well, he punched in the address of their home and two pods came up. Both of them pulled the doors open. Stepping inside and closing her door Giselle heard Amron speak to her.

"Three and a half."

Then they were off.

In a matter of seconds the pods popped up in their front yard. Rushing to get out so that it would disappear they were laughing like foolish children. They never considered that the pod would appear randomly out in the open. What if someone saw? It was a big deal, but they couldn't help but make a joke out of it. They moved toward the house, Amron tucking the I.W.T Key into his pocket. Giselle was about to bring up the slugs again, but then Amron froze.

"Why the door open?" He analyzed.

Giselle looked at her house now realizing how uncharacter-istically dark and abandoned it was. It must have been around two am now. Andre and Brent should have gone to bed al-ready. What was even stranger, the door was wide open.

CHAPTER NINETEEN

BE A GUARDIAN

GISELLE ENTERED THE gloomy house not tinkering the door to let herself inside. It was busted wide open.

"Dad?"

"Shhh," Amron took her by the arm. "Doh talk so loud."

He didn't have to explain himself, she knew exactly why he preferred to move like a mouse. This wasn't a horror movie. They weren't trying to run into horrific avoidable situations. Still her heart was beating so loud she felt it would go against the atmosphere they were trying to create. She couldn't slow it down because she couldn't calm down. Not yet. They moved into the house easily looking for signs of a struggle; of anything. The living room sat untouched. Everything was in its place. In fact the busted open door was the only thing abnormal about the house. Her brother branched off from her looking deeper into the house, so focused as though he was seeing some obscure mess that Giselle wasn't seeing. He turned back, probably to steal an undetected glance at her, but she already had eyes on him. He hesitated for a moment then looked in the other direction and spoke.

"Where Dre and Dad?"

Giselle was sure this question wasn't for her. He knew she wouldn't have the answer to that. They had been together the entire time. It was more like he was speaking to the air yet his eyes were fixed upon a focal point that she couldn't find. She knew he wasn't crazy.

"He still here? How long ago this happen?" He carried on as if he'd gotten answers to his first question. Maybe he did. "Isaac, relax."

In the still of the moment the banged noise of a door being pushed so far back it hit wall begged Giselle's joints to give way. Amron didn't even flinch. He adjusted his head in the direction of the noise and searched for the source. There was a man there. He was bloody, limping and barely alive clutching his chest. They didn't know him, but they knew his clothes. His uniform was purple and just like that of a recruiter.

"Go..." he hoarsely slurred. "...still here. He's still here. Vamos!"

As he spoke and got closer he began to tear up.

"Tell Tegan... that-"

BANG!

A bloody hole materialized in his forehead like a tortured, but beautiful three D painting. And as life slipped through his fingers he fell forward on the dusty floor. Giselle screamed. This wasn't the first time someone had died before her. As the body hit the floor senseless to its final stop she could have sworn she saw that young lady with the two puncture wounds on her neck going down. And off to the side, as if she wasn't even in her house anymore a man with long sleek hair coming for her next. Her chest pained knowing what he was going to do and her head ached knowing the girl was going to die and it would all be her fault. She could feel arms making their way around her and she felt as though she was being trapped; as if this time she wouldn't make it out just like that lady.

"Gizzy," Amron called for her attention. "Doh watch, Gizzy. Watch me."

His voice drew her eyes to his. She stared at Amron as if this was the first time she had seen him in her whole life then back at the man lying on the floor. Her eyes wide and horrified. There was a clicking sound that Giselle had grown accustomed that followed. From the darkness emerged a man who was nearly identical to the man that had just passed before them.

"It is ok," he said coming forward, revolver in hand. "You do not need the one named Tegan."

He pointed his revolver in their direction ready to fire at any moment. Instinctively, Amron tucked his sister behind him and took charge of the situation. But what could a sixteen-year-old boy do to a grown, heavily trained elite pointing them with a gun? Amron was a fighter, but was he tough enough?

'You s'pos to be lookin' out for us," Giselle muttered. "You work for Majesty."

"Majesty is a waste," he spoke with the same accent that the vampire did which only sent her flashbacks whirling.

From her bag, she struggled to pull her gumshoe pen and push on the emergency button. Someone from headquarters or patrol had to show up. The second it was out and in view, however, it was shot from her grip sending it flying behind her. He didn't spend anytime between shots before pulling the trigger again. The only saving grace was Vrai. Amron stood brave as a soldier waiting, braced to be hit by bullets. Anything to protect Giselle. The bullets never came. Whatever Vrai did stopped them before it could get any closer. She deflected them causing the TV screen and the windows to shatter. Even though he didn't show fear, even though he was as cool as they came, Giselle could feel how tight Amron's grip on her arm was. She was certain that when he did decide to let her go there would be a print. Was he alright? In a matter of seconds bullets were flying again. Giselle closed her eyes tighter and Amron's hand stayed firmly where it was, his body cemented in front of her. Were the neighbors hearing this? Surely someone would call the police to their house right? Someone would be there to help soon right? Someone had to be. This was too loud not to draw attention; there was the bang of the gun and the loud crash resignating from the ricocheted bullets destroying all in its wake. It was as though the bullets had some sort of extra force behind them. There was no way this was a normal gun. It was made in Majesty after all; this should be no surprise.

"Ahhhh!"

A masculine voice rose above everything with a conquering power causing every conscious mind in the room to surrender. Giselle felt herself stumble as if she had suddenly lost all her energy or even the control to keep her knees straight. She couldn't stop herself. She could feel Amron falling too. His grip on her hand loosened and slid. Feeling her brother release her and fall was building a terrific horror in her that she'd never experienced before. Even the shooter was going down, but not without firing his last bullet. This time Vrai did not protect them. Whatever was going on affected her and the bullet went with full force to Amron's upper thigh. Giselle couldn't even cry out in horror. Her mind had gone lazy as if in a few seconds her consciousness would run away. This was a completely different to how she felt when Marcel had sedated her with that special medication.

Hitting the ground unable to stop she tried to at least prop her body up with her elbow. That was the most she could do as she wavered uncontrollably to the melody of Amron's stifled, pained groans. He obviously didn't want to sound hurt, but his injuries must have been too much. She forced her body to lean closer to him and check to see how badly he had been hurt. Lying on his back, he was clutching his left thigh, his face so screwed to bare the pain that it formed wrinkles. She fiddled with his fingers trying to get him to show her the wounded area, but he was holding too tight and she felt too weak. Footsteps emanated with urgency from the hall toward them. Was this it? Did that impersonator do this to them or something? He couldn't have; he went down too. Was someone else here then? How was she going to get them out of this situation?

"What goin' on," she could hear Andre's voice above her.

It was as if he was right in her ear one second then behind closed doors the next. Her sense of hearing was being affected by the mysterious force. With a shaky pull Andre helped Giselle to her feet. She still felt weak and as though she'd topple over, but she kept herself up long enough to inspect him. He had haziness about the way he spoke and there was something rolling down the side of his face. It was dark and Andre was dark skinned so it appeared to be thick black sweat. She knew it wasn't sweat. He rubbed his head, smearing the liquid pouring out of him, eyes less than bright. Stooping halfway he attempted to help Amron up too, but when he moved him he was rejected with a cry of pain and Amron jerking his arm away from him. Amron dropped to his back again grinding his teeth together rejoining his hand and his thigh.

"You get hit?" Andre kneeled down. Giselle stood over him watching hopeful that Andre would know what to do. "Let me see."

"No," Amron groaned through gritted teeth. "Leave it. Gimme a minute. It not hurtin'."

"Amron just move your hand," Andre grabbed his wrist and forced it away from the source of Amron's struggles.

There was a hole in his pants pocket perfectly torn as if it was part of the fashion. As Andre took care of him Giselle scoped the room making sure the guy wouldn't sneak up on them again. They were in no shape for that. When she looked for him though he remained in the same place she last saw him; near the entrance of the hall. He had collapsed and whatever it was that affected all of them seemed to have overpowered him. When she ran back to the living room to get the gumshoe pen she found that it had been snapped in half. It was useless now.

"You have to take off your pants," Giselle heard Andre say.

"No!" Amron protested.

"It bad," she asked.

"I can' see blood or anything, but I jus' want to make sure it not bad," Andre confirmed the reason behind his awkward request.

"No," Amron refused again sitting up with great difficulty. "No. Where dad?"

"Amron," Giselle wore a pleading aura. "Jus' take it off."

"I doh have to take it off. I feel ok!" He yelled at them. "We-urg-have bigg-er prob-lems. S-see? I good."

He spoke as he forced himself to his feet now and swallowed every cry of pain his body attempted to involuntarily utter. Amron wasn't nearly as discrete about putting all his weight on his right leg as he was trying to be. He glared at them before

Krystal Cyrus

trying to walk, but after taking one step he halted forming fists and exhaling loudly.

"Dre lead the way. Where dad?" He played it off.

"Amron it hurtin', don' lie. Come on. Jus' show me," Andre demanded in a 'I need to know everything about everything' manner.

"Ok so what if it hurtin'. You realize what happenin' right now? We doh have time to look after some little bruise." Amron folded his arms.

"Bruise? Amron, you got shot! What if walkin' make it worst?" Giselle voiced her thoughts. She just wanted to know he was ok. He got hurt shielding her.

He sucked his teeth loudly and began unbuttoning his pants. Once the zipper was down he tried to pull the waist of his pants down, but the left side didn't go down like he thought it would. He had pulled on it expecting his jeans to just drop to the floor and now he was grunting from that pain because it wouldn't. Andre pulled on the material trying to assist, but it was an ill move on Amron.

"Dotish!" Amron yelled at him. "It not goin' down! Jus' leave it!"

"Well I can' just leave it now," Andre fired back. "Why it not goin' down?"

He pulled with more gentleness on the material again trying to see what was hindering its path.

"What the hell?" Andre gasped.

494

Giselle was right on his heal looking too trying to figure out what the problem was. There were tips of spiderlike legs bursting from Amron's pants and holding onto his leg. At first she found it a strange phenomenon. He was shot so what was this? But then it clicked. She rushed over to the man lying on the floor, his gun lying next to him. She picked it up and inspected it. It was the Leacock .42 revolver. She had used one of these before. The bullets were nothing special. The plus about this gun was the fact that it fired twice as fast as a normal revolver. In training she used this one a lot because it was light and it had a bigger cartridge than the other guns. She had joked with Tegan about putting peg missile bullets in it; imagine it already being deadly because of how fast it fired and then having such a persistent bullet in it. Little did she know someone else had the same idea. And what was worst, she never thought the first time she'd see her brilliant idea played out it would be on Amron.

"Ah! Dre jus' leave it!" Amron's voice pulled her out of her investigative state.

"It movin'," Andre gasped.

"Because you movin' it," Amron quarreled.

"Dre not movin' it," Giselle told him. She got up and made her way to them leaving the gun where she found it. "It doin' that by itself."

"How it doin' that by itself," was all Andre could say to avoid calling her stupid. Amron understood though. He had heard all about the weapons in Majesty and the unusual things they did. When he heard Giselle confirm the identity of what was on him he looked in his pants again at the legs constricting in his skin.

"We have to pull it out," he said.

"I doh know any other way to take it out," she was sorry she didn't try to figure out if there was any other way to deactivate it. She was more than certain there wasn't. Tegan taught her a lot about the weapons in there so if there was some sort of deactivation for it she'd know. She never cared one bit about the deactivation though because she never thought she'd care about how it came out of the victim. She always imagined it buried in the chest of that vampire from Weyden Empire. She'd be happy to pull it out of him, not Amron.

"What you talkin' about?" Andre's gaze swept between the two.

Giselle considered spilling the beans to him, but she couldn't bring herself to. They had already left him out of everything. Instead she bypassed him and tried her best to help Amron. Maybe after he was ok and they found Brent they could tell the two together all the horrible things that were about to happen to them tonight. She peeled back the jeans material slightly trying to see where the bullet was to get it out. It was nowhere to be seen, but it wasn't hard to deduce where it was. The spider like legs holding onto Amron was coming through his jeans right where his pocket was so the bullet had to be in there. She pulled his pocket as far back as the mouth of it would let her and attempted to push her hand inside. She was greeted by a surprise; something flat and smooth and warm from Amron's body heat. She attempted to pull it out, but Amron bawled out again.

"What is that? What you do?" Andre joined them peeping in.

Giselle tried to get a better look, but it was too dark to identify what it was. Experiencing the same troubles Andre went to flick the light switch, but nothing happened as a result. Scanning the ceiling, they found the light bulb blown from the earlier hurricane of bullets. As a quick resolution Andre pulled his cell phone from his back pocket and shined it between them. Amron, curious too, bent his sweaty head forward to see.

"When you get a phone?" Andre asked him.

"The I.W.T. Key," Amron breathed.

"You lucky you had it," Giselle took in the dumb luck of the situation. The I.W.T. Key, that Amron wasn't even supposed to have in the first place, was the thing that saved him. The peg missile bullet had struck it and grown its legs through the screen of the key. It was just the protruding tips at the back that were clipping Amron.

"What the hell is that?" Andre shined his light closer pressing some buttons to keep it illuminated.

Giselle exchanged some looks with Amron over Andre's head. Should they tell him now? Should they spill everything they had been up to now and then repeat it again later for their dad? They would have to now, wouldn't they?

"Is a special bullet," Amron took the lead. "A peg some-thin'."

"Missile," Giselle added.

"Ook?" Andre awaited more information.

"The only way to take it out is to pull it out," she continued.

Andre looked back at the attached key and bullet as it con-stricted again. Amron sat on the coffee table that was beside him to cope.

"But it can' come out of his pocket like that," he thought out loud. "How you even know what this is?"

"That's a different story Dre," Amron closed his eyes and held the table beneath him. "Pull it."

"You sure you ready," Giselle skeptically stuck her fingers around the key.

"I would never be ready. Jus' pull the damn thing," he ar-gued and she excused his rudeness due to the situation.

"Ok," she took a deep breath.

"Let me do it," Andre spoke after she had taken a full twenty seconds preparing to pull it and building tension in the room. "Hold this."

Andre gave Giselle his phone and they switched positions. He held onto the sides of the key and after silently counting to three he pulled on it with everything he had. Amron near screamed as the spiny legs rooted in his own leg held on. He grabbed onto Andre's wrist impatiently.

"Wait, Dre wait! Shit, let it go!" He pushed his hand away and with the extra force it was done; the bullet and key were ripped out. It slipped from Andre's grasp and fell to the floor where the legs retracted. It was just a regular bullet making bed in a cracked screen now.

"You're welcome," Andre walked away from him to pick up the key.

Amron lay back on the table clearly relieved. Giselle shined the light on his leg where the bullet had been. There were eight streams of blood seeping from the holes, but it was nothing too serious. She took a deep breath feeling the same assuagement he was.

"How two of you know about this? That's some new thing that I doh know about yet?" Andre retrieved his phone to inspect the object in his hand.

"Dre," Amron breathed, already exasperated by Andre's need to know. Easing inch by inch, he stood up. It still hurt him, Giselle could see it, but the pain wasn't as intense. "We doh have time to explain all that. Hold on to it if you want- mostly because BJ might want it back- but we have to go and find dad."

Andre rolled his eyes and shook his head knowing any question he asked next would go unanswered.

"I doh know where dad is. He went in his room last time I see him. I was readin' in my room and somethin' hit me hard in my head. That's all I could remember," he recalled. He touched his head with the memory realizing finally that he was bleeding. "I go check his room."

He rushed down the hall after saying this.

"Maybe if they hear BJ know about it, it might not be a big deal," she spoke quietly to Amron.

He buttoned up his pants. "Dad already know. No way mom could of be involve and he didn' know. Let we jus' deal with tonight and we go figure it out tomorrow."

He took a cautious few steps to test his agility before walking normally. His leg was going to be fine.

"This supposed to stop once Christmas Eve in Majesty finish?" he asked confirmation.

"No, Christmas Eve in the normal world," she corrected.

Amron looked at the digital clock. "Two fifty-eight. That's too long."

"Maybe when the sun come up it might be better," Giselle looked at the bright side.

"We can' go back cause the key mash up and me, Dre and dad need it to go in there so we jus' have to wait and hope nobody find us. Isaac say nobody outside reactin' to the gun shots. They probably do somethin' to the house." He bent over like an old man and plucked the revolver off the ground. Then he tucked it in the waist of his pants.

"What you doin'? Giselle asked, but what she really meant was *'put it down'*.

"We might need it," he said and limped off to their dad's room as though carrying a gun was of little significance.

Giselle hurried after him not knowing what to expect. The recruiters were supposed to be looking after Brent and Andre. They were supposed to act only if there was a threat, but instead they became the threat. Was that it? Was that what happened? It was what she deduced from the scene that unfolded briefly. This brought up the question of what would have happened if they hadn't left Majesty without permission. She didn't want to think about that.

Brent's room reeked of anguish. Amron and Andre were trying to get him properly laid across the bed. He was out cold. There was no physical damage. Andre had a bruise on his head from being hit, but Brent was fine. This made Giselle wonder if the attackers got to go after him at all, or if things had only just begun when she arrived. Maybe Brent was knocked out by that mysterious force that had washed over the room. The recruiter still hadn't recovered either. He looked near dead the way he was sprawled on the floor. She hoped Brent wasn't experiencing the same thing the recruiter was.

"Daddy," she silently cried at his bedside.

Tegan promised her brother and father would be ok. He promised her they wouldn't get hurt. Well, they looked very hurt to her. Where was Tegan anyway? How were the recruiters here screwing things up without his knowledge? Were those recruiters Weyden's people in disguise or were they just terrible at their job? Once Brent's head was safely resting on his pillow as if he was in a coffin Andre pulled out his phone again. He was calling the ambulance. Realizing this Amron swiftly ended the call before Andre could even locate the green call button under his trembling fingers.

"What you doin'? I have to call an ambulance for dad," he reacted.

"Wait," was all that left Amron's mouth. He kept looking at his father's steadfast body as if he was hoping he would just open his eyes, sit up and make some broke man comment about him not paying bills in this house.

"We can' call the ambulance yet. What we go tell them," Giselle said what Amron neglected to relate. She had forgotten briefly, due to the nature of the situation, that Andre wasn't briefed yet.

"How about we tell them somethin' wrong with dad? You know, the man who take care of us? I didn' think I had to explain that." He raised his phone again.

"Dre, the ambulance might not be able to help him right now. I know somebody else we could call," she made a vague hint of a confession.

They needed Marcel. There wasn't anything visibly wrong with Brent so there was a chance he was under a spell. Giselle was no expert. She had no way of deducing the problem. Brent's state may have been beyond help from regular medical practices. Andre sucked his teeth, stood up poking the call button and pressed the phone to his ear.

"Dre put the phone down," Amron warned.

The phone was ringing.

"We know what we doin', Dre. You can' call people here. Just put the phone down." Amron faced him.

"Hello, yeah this is Andre. My dad…" Giselle watched as Andre tried to stay calm to explain to the people on the phone.

"Dre," there was a careful pause. "Put. The. Phone. Down."

Andre raised his eyes to Amron probably to make some silent curses using facial expressions. Growing up with two brothers and a rude sister if he didn't know how to flip them off discreetly by now then something had to be wrong with him. He didn't do that though. Seeing Amron pointing him with a gun didn't encourage pissing him off any more than he probably was. The phone slipped from his fingers and landed with a loud crash on the floor. Andre didn't spare it a glance or even show concern about its condition. He held his position.

"Where you get that?"

"Amron," Giselle screeched.

Amron lowered the gun and returned it to its hiding spot; the waist of his pants. Then he confiscated the phone.

"I wasn' goin' to shoot him," he spoke in a duh tone to Giselle. "I jus' wanted to scare him."

"Not like that," Giselle smacked him in the chest, though she considered hitting him in his wound just to make it count.

"What goin' on? You know somethin' I doh know?" Andre asked looking ten tons relieved he wasn't at gun point anymore, but still apprehensive.

"We always know somethin' you doh know," Amron snapped at him. "You need to listen for once and stop always runnin' off to tell."

"We can' call the ambulance, but you already did so they might show up now." Giselle got cozy by her father's side and gazed mournfully at him. She knew what she had to do.

"Why we can' call," his eyes bounce between the two.

"Is a long story," Giselle whispered focusing on Brent. "And we doh have that kind of time right now." Taking off her chain she handed it to Amron.

"What you doin'?" He asked her.

"You have to hold it. I go call Marcel and BJ," she explained.

"Ok," Amron agreed then he looked to his side as if retaining information.

"Isaac?" Giselle asked him trying to get used to his new behavior.

He nodded, "if you want I could tell Andre what goin' on while you gone."

She turned back looking at Andre who had been sponging up everything. She was feeling guilty for the first time that they did to him what BJ did to them. After learning that the whole family was involved one way or the other, spilling the beans to Andre hadn't crossed their minds once. It was even worst now because everyone was in on it except him. It wasn't necessary to keep him out anymore although it was a plus. If they had told him Brent would have found out that they knew much sooner. Maybe if he did they could have avoided this obstacle. She was beginning to see the appeal of waiting until after the Christmas Hunt to be introduced to Majesty. Ecoli knew what he was saying. She sort of wished she hadn't found out about it until things had calmed down and Ecoli settled into his position as chief. Looking away from Andre now, not knowing what she could possible tell him to minimize the freak out he would have once he saw what she was about to do, she stuck her arm into the mirror and was sucked in. Hopefully Amron could clean up the mess she just made. Secretly, she wished she had confiscated that gun.

Falling through the other half of the Sui Generis, rather unstable, she aimed full of intent at the hall. A voice stopped her. The voice that had brought her there to stay and constantly criticized and saved her life in the past was yet again on her heal. She called after Giselle willing her to stay and hear out whatever it was that she had to say. Whatever it was that was so important that Giselle had to put her father's ailing heath aside and hold a conversation.

"You will find that no Guardians are here." Vrai informed. "It is the Christmas Hunt. I have been around long enough to know that the Guardians have spread out within and without Majesty at check points to be sure infiltration is naught. The only people connected to the outside world are the Medics, Emissaries and Recruiters."

"Somebody have to be here," Giselle cried loudly.

"It would be wise to keep your voice down." Vrai told her. Her stirring glass had stopped for a mere second before she spoke again. "Touch my frame."

The urgency with which the words were said made Giselle bypass questioning and curiosity and grab on with obedience to the golden frame of the full-length mirror. The glass was its normal self again, but Giselle wasn't herself. She could see her body disappearing into nothingness until the brown of her skin was no more and the flowery pattern on her shoes had fallen into nothing. She couldn't see herself, but she was still standing there holding onto Vrai. It felt like the time she took the anamnesis solution. At the end of the hall a woman appeared; a patroller. Fully armed, her shirt with more personality than they usually had, gave away that she had on a bullet proof vest. Deep in speculation she entered the hall and searched behind each of the six doors ahead the Universal Passage. Then she did a quick scope in the Universal Passage and behind all the mirrors. She came so close to Giselle that she almost stepped on her shoe, but a strong force had yanked Giselle forward before it could happen. Vrai had saved her skin yet again. Then, still professionally, the patroller made her way out again.

"We must continue to speak like this for now." Vrai warned gravely.

Still holding onto the frame Giselle asked, "who was that? I though nobody but Guardians could come up here?"

"A high-level patroller protecting the second halves of the Sui Generis' from harm." Vrai said with utmost smarts.

"Why a guardian can' do that?" She inquired

"They already are," Vrai said. "The patroller is here for good measure. So long as they have the other halves nothing can happen to me or any of the others. So long as Amron stays alive, I am fine."

"An why I have to hide from her?" She went on.

"You were never openly introduced to Majesty. To say that you are a guardian now will only lead them to think you are an imposter. You cannot be seen nor present that ID you were given without an actual Guardian here to back you up. In other words, right now all you have is me."

Giselle fretted, wishing now that she had never strayed outside of Majesty without a plan should something bad happen. How was she to get in contact with anyone now? There had to be a way. There was a way. She just wasn't thinking clear enough. Panic was rising in her throat like water in a plugged sink and she was too flustered to know all she had to do was unplug it. She couldn't get the thoughts to flow with any order or sense. It was like that little voice that narrated her thoughts wasn't talking to her anymore. It wasn't telling her what to do or making suggestions or anything. It was dead silent, yet there were still flammable noises in her head that she couldn't tame.

"Why are you even here in Majesty? Why do you want to be a Guardian?" Vrai asked suddenly in response to Giselle's behavior.

"Because you won' let me go." She almost yelled, but tamed it knowing there was a patroller just outside.

"No seriously, besides that, you keep coming back. I have not had to force you nearly as much as I've had to convince people in the past. You went from not knowing the magical world existed one day to desperately wanting to be a part of it the next. Why?" Vrai asked simply.

"I doh know."

"There has to be a reason."

"I doh know. I jus'… can' walk away from it. I can' tell you why I want to be here. I feel like…"

"Like what?"

She took a sharp breath in attempt to keep her emotions in check. "I doh want to talk 'bout it."

"Well I need you to because whatever it is, it is hindering your performance."

"My performance?" She croaked. "Vrai, this is not jus' some mission. This is real life."

"Did you think you would stay in the simulation training room for the rest of your life? Or did you think you would just have to get to check points or talk people into coming to Majesty? What if you end up in Dispatch or Patrol or as a Medic or Emissary? It is going to feel just like this." Vrai preached with that cold truthful tone of hers. "I want you to treat it like a mission".

"How the hell I s'pos to concentrate on that when my whole family fallin' apart?"

"If your family is falling apart should you not want to put it back together?" Vrai questioned dubiously.

"How?" Giselle's tone softened. She wanted to sound angry, but it didn't come out that way. It was like being saturated with Marcel's medication again. "I remember when gran'mom was just gran'mom and mom was just the mental lady that couldn' take care of me. And when Andre was a perfectionist just because and Amron was just stubborn to be stubborn and BJ disappeared a lot because of work. And I remember when I just wanted to be treated like a grown person…"

Giselle heavy heartedly listed.

"Memories- intangible yet deliver the most pain." Vrai commented. "Same can be said about knowledge."

Giselle sighed running her hand down Vrai's frame, but not releasing.

"I wish I knew about Gran'mom in Majesty and I wish I got to spend time with her here and I wish Isaac was still alive and dad didn' cover the whole thing up from us."

For what seemed like forever neither of them said anything. Giselle rubbed her fore head not knowing where she was going with this speech.

"You cannot change the past. It is absolute." Vrai spoke wisely. "Nor can you plan the future. It is erratic."

"So what," Giselle analyzed. "I just have to accept that from now on things could go to shit at any point? Just deal with it? I figured that part."

Vrai's glass swirled as she gave an ear to Giselle's retort.

"I am saying, Majesty was a secret. That happened. Get over it. Think about now and think about the future and forget what could have been." She said.

Vrai- the truthful spirit. She remembered clearly that this was how Vrai chose to introduce herself. She'd been living up to the self-proclaimed title ever since. Right now was just like any other time they had spoken. She was telling Giselle as she saw it and right now, she saw Giselle's panicking as a nuisance. Nothing could be done about the events leading up to this moment. It was that way because that was what was meant to be. But what if she *could* do something about the past? Marko was a time Ersatz. What if he could travel back and convince Grace to let her children into Majesty. What would today be like then? If she did that then she'd have definite control over the future. The future depended on the past. It was the butterfly effect. Certain things in the past affected pointed things in the future. She believed it worked that way despite Vrai calling it erratic. But Marko's ability didn't work that way and she wasn't sure she wanted to change her family's past. If she changed it then she wouldn't only be wiping away the bad times, but the good times as well. And what if there were no good times in a world where she grew up in Majesty? What if one of her brothers had died many Christmas Hunts ago?

"Well what to do?" She asked advice, something she seldom did of Vrai.

"You have been training." Vrai pointed out what Giselle already knew.

"Yeah, but my dad need medical help." She was very aware that she was no medic.

"Exactly," Vrai used that stern stuck up tone Giselle detested. "So prove yourself. This is the ultimate mission. If you want a father tomorrow be a guardian today."

CHAPTER TWENTY

SURVIVE THE NIGHT

THE WEAPONRY WAS no longer an unfamiliar place. Her finger prints were all over the weapons, her sweat on the carpet and her scent in the shooting range. She was a regular. She could name everything in there and knew what it was used for and where it went. She had been knocked on her ass countless times on its concrete floors covered with red and orange matts and she'd been soaring through its air space on several occasions. It had been months of her going in and out of there. She knew the code to get in; she was the code. There was a hidden sensor on the wall that allowed access into it which only opened to the touch of a Guardian. After passing through the Sui Generis once, any person was well equipped to open hidden doors. The whole building was controlled by deep magic bestowed upon it by Hubable Gothany himself. And if those spells were to be lifted somehow one day, there had yet to be seen another magical genius skilled enough to redo it. To be more specific, there had not been another magical being allied with Majesty that was skilled enough to reproduce such complicated spells.

She pulled a brown leather carrier that went around her body like a graduation band. On it there were various sized pockets and openings where weapons could be stored.

"Dependin' on the mission we use these," Tegan's past voice spoke to her as she tried to figure out what she was going to do.

She threw it hastily around herself, then immediately took a deep breath trying to calm down. If she rushed she'd miss something. She couldn't afford to do that right now. Opening one of the many draws she revealed the peg missiles. Not even questioning her limitations on these weapons that were very well explained to her, she picked up the red one. It was like the black in that it shot bullets with strings attached, but this one didn't grow spikes. This one was designed to swiftly and undetectably shoot poison into the victim once implanted. It was very easily removed from the body, but that was only because the damage had already been done.

"You'll be right with the orange. Please don't hurt yourself with the others." She heard Tegan again.

Tucking that into the widest pocket she proceeded to pull some sensor plates as well. In the draw just above them were very high-tech radio like objects. They had antennas and green grid screens with very few buttons for use. To that the sensor plates could be synced so that she wouldn't have to remember where they were and guess which ones were tripped. Remembering the lights in her house were blown out and not willing to turn them on and attract attention anyway she pulled two-night vision goggles. She would need the help of her brothers to get through this. Amron could probably see more with his bare eyes than Giselle and Andre could. Pulling some more draws looking for things she might need she came across something so valuable she almost tore up in joy; summoning snaps. She could summon someone.

"To summon somethin' there must first be a spell on the object for the summonin' to happen." There went Tegan again.

Her shoulders sunk as the brief joy seeped out of her. Did BJ have a spell on him? He probably didn't. Even if he did, she couldn't just write his name on any old summoning snap. He'd be attached to a specific one. She took the marker from the draw just in case. She was willing to try. Scanning over the clear partitioned, plastic boxes they were kept in she noticed a stunning lack of guardian faces. They must have all taken them in case they needed each other. Groaning loudly in frustration she took a handful of the little puzzle pieces not looking at their nature and tucked them away as well. Something in there had to be useful. Tossing a cartridge of peg missile bullets onto her person she snuck over to the medic room.

"If the person is bleedin' have them lie down, apply pressure to and elevate the wounded area." Tegan echoed.

Brent was not bleeding, but Amron and Andre were. She grabbed a first aid kit from one of the cupboards making a mental note of the rest of the steps to treat wounds. Maybe she could tell it to her brothers and they could treat each other. What else did Tegan say?

"If it's a burn you'd want to remove any material from the burnt area." Tegan's voice carried on.

No, Brent wasn't burned either. What was wrong with him? Was it a concussion? What did Tegan say about concussions?

"Have the person stop movin' and rest. You should apply ice wrapped in a cloth to their head."

Well her dad was fully rested now, wasn't he? Taking another deep breath in effort to remain calm and keep Tegan's lessons flowing through her head she leaned against the counter. She didn't know exactly what was wrong with Brent. With that said there was no way she could treat him. At the same time she couldn't just leave him there and hope he'd make it through the night. If only there was something she could use to sustain him, something that would guarantee that as long as he had it he'd continue breathing. Rubbing the ball of her palm deeply into her forehead the skin became raw, but it was as if this action created an opening for her thoughts to fall free from her brain. There was something! She wasn't sure if it would work, but it was better than nothing. Opening the silver door of the very tall fridge in the wall of the medic room she searched the shelves. Near the top closest to the back were sterilized tubes of water from pious falls. Nothing had been added to it yet. It was pure; alkaline and void of harm. In layman terms, this thing was basically holy water and if that couldn't solve the problem or delay it then she didn't know what would. She grabbed the stool near the gurney and strategically placed it so she could get to her target. Capturing two viles as hers and placing them in the tightest part of her weapon holder she closed the fridge. Now she could leave. She should be capable enough with the tools she had chosen.

Hurriedly, but with plenty caution, she made her way back to Vrai. In the strained effort to remain stealthy echoed footsteps lost their way down the hall alerting the patroller. Giselle didn't turn around, but she could hear the urgency with which the patroller was acting. The patroller had abrasively welcomed her presence into the hall once again.

"Halt! Drop ya weapons!" Giselle heard the click of a gun being prepared to carry out its duties.

Wasting no time, from five feet away, she heaved forward toward Vrai. In that exact moment, she heard the fire arm go off, but she had just made it through falling wildly into the dark of her house on the wooden floors of her father's room. With an enraged vibrancy the entire mirror had caught flames for a quick three seconds. Vrai didn't have to outline it for Giselle to know she had just narrowly avoided being shot. The first thing in mind being to ensure she didn't break the viles she searched for them on her chest. They were still there safe and sound. That was good. There was no chance of her going back now that the patroller knew she was there.

"Gizzy," Andre pulled her up from the floor.

"I good, I good. I jus' had to… doh even worry about it. I good," she assured him, but once her eyes met his she saw a whole other question than the one she thought he'd ask.

"So it real?" His voice was airy, but stunningly heavy.

She gazed upon his perplexed features never breaking away unable to speak at first. So Andre knew now. He knew that a few months ago when Ruby passed away she gave Giselle her favorite chain. He knew that in the mirror, Giselle discovered a portal to an alternate world called Majesty where Ruby was chief. And he knew about their mom being a Seer and Giselle having to take post as a new Guardian and that Amron was a Necromancer and BJ was an Ice Ersatz. He knew that they all had an older brother named Isaac that was still with them in spirit and their dad never spoke about him as though he'd forgotten. He knew everything now. The question was, did he hate them for not telling him sooner?

"Ok," he breathed.

"So?" She watched him.

"Um, dad." Amron rudely spoke from the bedside.

Giselle hadn't noticed him there, but him speaking up reminded her of what she briefly forgot. She was in a race to save her father. Turning away from Andre she pulled a vile from her holder and opened the black cork skeptically.

"What's that?" Amron asked.

"Water from Pious Falls. Is like holy water. They use it in medicine." She answered him.

"Holy water?" Andre joined them. "So what medicine is this then?"

"Is jus' the pure water," she responded.

Andre raised his brow. "And that s'pos to do somethin'? I doubt it safe to give him like that."

"Dre, I doh know what wrong with him and I doh know what else to do," she tamed the sparking annoyance.

"I just sayin'. You say Pious Falls they get this from. Assumin' that is some waterfall that mean they have endless supply of this and they choose to use a little of it in they medication. Givin' dad a whole tube of it might not be safe," he analyzed.

"Well what we s'pos to do? How could holy water be dangerous." Amron, like Giselle, was biting his tongue.

"Because is not water they bless in an actual church or anything. Is water from some magical world that catch in the basin of a waterfall. You does see people usin' holy water in medication here? This water have to have something special about it." Andre presented his argument with more of an authoritative tone than a voice of reason.

Amron sucked his teeth and looked away from him.

"So what we s'pos to do?" Giselle corked the vile.

"I didn' say doh give him. Just doh give him all. You have a syringe? Give him like half that." He advised.

"I doh have one."

"How you was plannin' to give him then?" He asked, not very nicely.

"I doh know. I never did good in first aid so miss me!" She snapped.

"Watch," Amron spoke again, calmly. "Now is not the time to be annoyin' Dre. Let's just estimate and pour a little bit in his mouth or somethin'."

Refusing to put comment to Amron's words Andre nodded in agreement to the estimation. Once again, the vial was opened and Giselle looked into the rested face of her father. He looked dead. He looked like he had left them alone to fend for themselves. She moved the vile to his lips manually opening his mouth, but her own thoughts had her physically shaking. What if this didn't help him? What if Andre's speculation about the water was right? Would Brent be ok without this or was she making the right decision? Her hand shook so much that a few drops of liquid landed on Brent's top lip and the side of his face.

"Let me do it," Andre eased the vile from her grasp.

Moving out of his way all she could think about was this being the reason why she failed at first aid. She panicked too much too quick. She couldn't stay focused long enough to help someone in that way. Ask her to fight for you and she could. Ask her to cover you and ensure you never got caught and she could. But ask her to tend to a wound and it was a whole other story. Moving away from the bed she allowed Andre to do his do. When he was finished, she offered to treat their wounds. Andre took care of himself, but Amron refused. He said it didn't hurt however there was still a faint limp in his walk.

"Ok," she shook her hands to pull herself together. "We have to set up just in case more people come here."

"What you plannin'?" Amron asked ready to help.

"So wait? More people comin' here? Jus' how much people want to kill us?" Andre asked placing the first aid kit on the bedside table.

"A whole damn Empire Dre," Amron dragged. "You listen to anything I say to you?"

"Honestly, it make sense that Weyden Empire exists. I go give you that. It on an actual island. But Majesty? Where exactly that s'pos to be? Where exactly that mirror takin' you?" He asked something neither Giselle nor Amron had thought of before.

"I doh know," she mumbled.

"That really important right now? You want to stand up and discuss it or you want to ask the people if they know when they come to kill us?" Amron asked him casually.

"Well I think you should at least know where you goin'," Andre shrugged.

Realizing both her brother's personalities clashed too much to stand and wait for them to come to terms, she spoke up and changed the topic.

"I have some sensor plates so we have to put them around the house," she pulled them out of the pocket and held it up for one of them to take.

Andre was the first to reach out since he was curious and was probably formulating more annoying things to say. Giselle reached for the grid and pulled up the antenna then turned it on. The green screen lit up putting a sickly glow on all their faces.

"I have to scan the house," she announced.

"Lay it flat on the floor and press the scan button. It's the biggest one in the centre," Tegan said.

She placed the grind down between them, her brother's looking on carefully as a green light rose up from it. The light was divided just like the screen and it shot straight up to the ceiling. Then, slowly, it spread out at the top making an enlarging circle that scanned the room and took occupancy in every crack and crevice. It spread all the way out until it was just a flat layer on the ground then retreated into the grid. There was a soft constant beeping that followed this. Giselle picked it up pressing a few more buttons turning the beeping off. Looking at the screen now it wasn't green anymore. It was their house with grids going through it. There were some navigational buttons at the bottom which she used to display different parts of the house.

"We jus' have to put the plates down now." She said. "Oh, and Amron."

She pulled the new cartridge of bullets from her holder and handed it to him. She wasn't one hundred percent sure it was sensible to leave Amron with a weapon, but what choice did they have. Maybe him doing something reckless might just save their lives. She could see that Andre felt the same way.

"What?" Amron asked, though when Andre and Giselle looked at him he wasn't even paying attention to them. "I won' shoot myself," he dismissed.

So Isaac had concerns too, huh? He was more active in voicing them than they were.

"So jus' put them anywhere?" Andre asked.

"One in every room," she ordered.

Each of them taking two they spread out and placed them in their designated locations; the bathroom, kitchen, living room and the bedrooms. Once that was done Giselle was able to activate them. They showed up on the screen as green dots everywhere but her dad's room, which was where they all mentally decided to stay.

"Sensory plates have two settin's; incognito or loud. The loud one is to scare away unwanted attention. The incognito is to help you sneak up on the enemy before they get to you." Tegan explained.

"If it loud eventually the person might realize is just an alarm and come back. Then what?" Andre spoke.

"So you sayin' leave it on silent and attack people?" Amron swung the revolver as he spoke making both Giselle and Andre duck. "Relax. I not handicap."

"Miss me oui, I never say that," Giselle put noticeable space between them.

"Well I sayin' it. I prefer if you put that down," Andre ordered him.

Amron sucked his teeth again, but he did put the gun away.

"It have disadvantages either way so just do silent."

Andre went on and took post next to his father. In the time they were setting up their defenses and planning their strategies Brent had stirred a few times. He no longer carried the appearance of a dead man, but of someone who was merely taking well deserved sleep.

Once they had done everything, all they could do was sit and hope for the best. It would be absolutely perfect if there were no threats until morning, but there was no guarantee. For a long time it was dead silent. They could hear the noises of the rustling trees and the screechy croak of those small frogs that hung around their widows. They heard every time each other inhaled an exhaled deeply as if they weren't breathing the whole time or as if, if they didn't it would hinder them from staying calm. It was tense. The whole situation felt like being in a hurricane. Sitting there and hoping to make it through and putting up a brave front, but underneath you were really scared.

"How old is Isaac?" Andre suddenly disturbed the constant of the atmosphere.

"Would have been thirty-nine," Amron responded.

He was gazing out of the window. The moon light was glowing through the window giving his complexion a pale ghostly look. He had been there for a while.

"I mean when he died," Andre wasn't being irritating.

"Twelve." Amron's eyes flickered in his direction for a second.

"Ok," Andre accepted this response.

It was a while again before Amron spoke.

"He say he wish mom made us sooner instead of waitin'. Then maybe we could of get to know each other before he die."

Giselle sat with folded legs on the bed. She'd been picking at her nails for the longest time lost in thought. The most unnecessary things played on her mind now, like why there were different colour song birds. She also wondered how Scout had survived on his mission if his diet was people. She strayed on where exactly the water from Pious Falls came from and whether or not it would be inappropriate to eat now. Though, in between all of that she was obsessively checking the grid. No one was there. She eventually ended up thinking about that conversation she had with Vrai. If she wanted to fix everything she'd have to be a guardian. So far she wasn't feeling happy about how she was doing, but that was only because of the first aid thing. Hearing her brothers discuss Isaac made an unexpected smile play on her lips. She'd have liked to see what Isaac looked like herself.

"What Isaac look like?" The words naturally rolled off her tongue.

Amron stayed stationary by the window not saying anything and for some time Giselle thought he might not answer her. This wouldn't come unexpected. It was Amron.

"Amron?" Andre called his attention.

Amron's eyes strolled beside him and did a full scan.

"Like dad except he real short." At that he pulled his arm up semi-playfully as if he was defending himself from being hit.

"He might look ten times smaller than Aibell if he stand up next to BJ."

"Oh yeah! BJ!" Giselle gasped suddenly. "I was goin' to try somethin'."

She fished the summoning snaps from her holders and laid them out on the bed. Sifting through them she was seeing for the first time what she had in her arsenal. There was an axe, another first aid kit and a katanna. There was also one that had the name of a drink she couldn't pronounce and she assumed it was no one, but Marko to put that there. There was a laser which was one of the weapons Tegan told her she shouldn't use alone just to be safe. Then there were a few of those balls that Scout had used at Pious Falls that time to tie up Roscoe; it was called a Smoker. Then there were two blank ones. Pulling the marker and explaining to a critical Andre how it worked she wrote BJ's name, Brent Junior Thomas, on the pieces and connected them.

"What you waitin' for?" Andre asked after nothing happened. She sort of already knew nothing would.

"BJ," the disappointment in her voice was rich.

"Doh worry about it. We good," Amron consoled.

In all her sadness, she resumed the previous conversation. "Can you see mom or gran'mom?"

A crumpled look folded over Amron's features as he spoke. "No." The answer was simple, but it was clear it bothered him plenty.

"That a bad thing?" Andre asked him.

"I doh know," Amron answered honestly. "I wasn' worried when they died cause I thought I would see them still, but I can'. I think the spirits I see are restless. I not sure if I can see spirits that go to heaven or … I can' see them"

"Then that mean Isaac…" Andre began, but as he voiced his thoughts the grid began to beep in a low drawn out tune.

Breathless and frightened Giselle grabbed onto it to see what the problem was shutting the noise off immediately. Amron made his way across the room quietly to see as well. She shifted through the different sections in the house using the buttons. Everything seemed normal. All their rooms were fine. The bathroom was fine. The living room remained unaffected. The green dot in the kitchen had gone red. Someone was there. Either that or there was an animal big enough in there to trip it off. She hoped it was the second option. Connecting the summoning snap for the Smoker she was now holding her choice of weapon. She began shaking it waiting for that light to come on signaling it was ready for use. Each of them easing off the bed, they got ready for the worst. Andre instinctively pulled the sheets over his dad in a weak attempt to hide him. Amron didn't hesitate to pull out the newly reloaded gun from the waist of his pants and this made Giselle nervous. In all honesty, she didn't want to hurt anybody. But that wasn't realistic. She knew that at some point it may come down to kill or be killed. Having Amron here she was afraid he'd pull the trigger- and even worst- he'd feel no remorse.

Another beep had come up. It was in the living room now. There were no sensors in the hall so they'd have no idea where the intruder was once he or she moved in there. Amron's room gave off the next signal. Whoever it was, they were planning on searching the house it seemed. Giselle stood a good distance from the door since her weapon required distance. Amron was a bit closer than she was. With a regular gun she might have felt uneasy about that, but she didn't feel that way about this one. With gun's one needed distance, because on average, a person could move fast enough to avoid being shot. The Leacock .42 revolver, however, was made to fill that lapse in time so that it was harder to escape no matter where the shooter stood. Andre stayed back not showing visible wanting for any type of defense of his own. He was not up for fighting. Just like their silent decision to stay in their dad's room, they also came to a silent agreement that Andre would look after Brent.

The alarm for Giselle's room sounded next. The smoker began to flash. Easy clicking could be heard getting closer. It was the careful tap of something solid and thin hitting the wooden floor. It didn't sound like footsteps at all. It sounded closer to the way Amron's nails did when he drummed on the table lazily. No more alarms went off. In a matter of time the handle on the door knob turned and with ease the door cracked open. Giselle could feel her heart racing in her chest. Her grip was so tight on the smoker it could have possibly popped in her hand. Andre was anxious too. They didn't know what to expect once that door was fully opened. Amron remained calm though. He was ready. The door didn't swing all the way open. It stopped after a small crack. The flashing from the Smoker was throwing shadows on the walls of the room and maybe the intruder noticed this. The door was pushed fully open after the brief and stressful pause revealing a woman with wild brown hair. Her top half was of a woman who cared less of hygiene or grooming, but the bottom half was that of an animal. Long skinny, silky black legs that had nails like talons shooting out of it; it was like nothing any of them had seen before. Her eyes widened as she saw the three of them in the room as though she had hit some jackpot. Her first choice victim was Giselle. The speed with which she jutted forward almost swept a wind through the room. Giselle knew she had to act fast. She knew if she threw the Smoker it would miss and she'd be screwed. Thinking fast she constructed a plan. She let the Smoker fall a mere five feet in front of her exploding. The smoke erupted in the room and it was as though everyone was counting on it. She could hear footsteps beating across the floor now and a loud thud slamming the ground. She heard a feminine cry that didn't come from her so she knew she had done something right. The vines from the Smoker must have caught the woman. Making it to the bed she pulled on one of the night vision googles clearing her vision slightly. She could see that Andre had put his on too. Wasting not a second she connected the Summoning Snap for the katana. This was one weapon she needed more practice with. It was more than just swinging.

There was an art to using a katana. Tegan said this was something he couldn't properly teach her. For now she'd just swing and hope for the best.

The smoke was clearing as unnaturally as it had erupted. She saw that Amron had shut the door behind their unwanted guest. Speaking off, she was laying on the floor scrambling to get on her feet, but being pulled by the vines that were spreading out on the floor. Unexpectedly, she grew some claws and cut a few of them freeing one of her weird looking legs. When she had freed the second the leg she stood up with a push start toward Giselle. The gun went off and she fell again. She was clipping her ankle. Shocked, Giselle gazed up at Amron who was shaking slightly; he lowered the gun and stayed stationary by the door. Punctuated screams blasted through the house. Giselle wondered why the police hadn't shown up yet or even more, why the neighbors hadn't come by to see if something was wrong. It was Christmas Eve; it was definite that the majority of the population was already up.

The woman stayed rocking on the ground giving all her attention to the spidery legs that had invaded her flesh. This had to be more painful that what Amron went through. He had something to stop the bullet from hitting him directly, she didn't. Plus her legs were so skinny that around her ankle looked nothing more than skin and bone. There was nothing for that bullet to clip onto, but bone. Giselle backed up some distance to stay away from her bumping into Andre who was content on staying invisible behind the scenes. Not excluding loud cries, the woman dragged the bullet from its hold and flung it across the room. Handicapped she heaved to her feet as if fearing another attack while she was unprepared. Turning her eyes full of thirst and well placed hate toward Amron she attempted to attack again. He was the one that shot her. As she made for him, overlooking the pain of her visibly healing wound, she kept her claws out and ready. Amron fumbled lifting the gun again. He'd just shot it bravely a second ago so why was he grappling with it now. As he lifted his weapon it slipped from slack grip. He had to adjust and fast. Seeing him unprepared and a psycho gaining on him had an effect on Giselle. She had, if only for a second, gone blank. She wasn't even sure she was seeing. All she knew at that point was that if she didn't do something she might lose Amron forever. She felt herself lunge forward automatically. There was a slight pull on her arm, but it didn't last very long. Whatever it was that tried to hold her back was far from her now as she was right on the heal of the woman. Her Katana was raised over her head and with a protective rage she let it fall feeling physically that it could go down no more once something solid had been struck. And as she made contact she heard the gun go off three more times. The blackness peeling from her mind now she saw the blade neatly inserted into the arm of the intruder as if it belonged there. She wanted to think that she felt bad for doing that, that maybe she'd regret wounding someone in such a way. But she felt nothing, but relief that Amron remained untouched. She couldn't feel sorry for hurting someone who tried to hurt her brother. It was simply impossible. Unthinkable. Undoable.

With no other option, but to free herself and turn tale the beastly shape shifter pulled herself off the blade, visibly aching, and faced Giselle.

"I-I-I tho-ught you w-were help-less child-dren." Her tone was shocked as she clutched tightly to her stomach where the bullets must have implanted. It took longer for her shoulder to start healing than her ankle did.

…there are no rules…

…do what your heart tells you to do…

…they're not going to stop after five minutes like Tegan does…

"You should stop thought-ing," Giselle responded coldly not letting her guard down. She raised the Katana again ready to throw another attack, but the strange woman knew she was out of her league facing off alone.

Growling with a bellowing deepness at Amron she secured a clear passage to escape the room. Pulling himself together he took off down the hall probably to ensure that she really did leave. Neither of the two left behind attempted to go after him. Giselle looked at the Katana in her hand again breathing heavily.

…you want a father tomorrow, be a guardian today…

Andre stayed hooked to the bedside as if an earthquake had just ran through him. He couldn't move. He couldn't speak. He couldn't do anything. He had only just found out about this tonight and so much had happened since. He couldn't begin to formulate any sensible reaction. He made his eyes comfortable at the back of Giselle's head not seeing her, but trying to keep his own head right. Soon Amron came back…

"We need to block the doors," he spoke primarily to Giselle then carried his eyes over to Andre.

When Giselle was the only one that responded, by releasing her weapon, he accepted that Andre was not going to be a part of the moving team. Together and in silence they proceeded to the living room where they pushed the couch in front of the front door. Following, they pushed the homemade shelf that held the TV in front of the window. From there they went into the kitchen.

"Amron, you ok?" Giselle asked him. "You shoot her."

"You ok?" He raised his wide eyes to hers. "You cut her."

They both neglected to answer the question. They had an understanding of what they were feeling.

"The table might be too light. Let's put the fridge." He cut down the options for what should block the back door in the kitchen. After locking it again, with enormous effort, they plugged the doorway with the fridge.

"That should be good," Giselle stood and admired their work with less than a feathery feeling in her pit.

"Yeah that should be…" Amron began to walk as he spoke, but doubled over in pain griping his thigh.

"It still hurtin'?" Giselle ran to his side.

"I good. I jus' doin' too much," he straightened up much against his body's will. Then they proceeded to the other rooms blocking the windows as best as they could.

The ground was almost completely covered in vine. It was fine though. Unless disturbed, the vine was harmless. When they entered, Andre was standing in the centre of the room. He held the katana strangely by the hilt, the blade washed in blood. He was looking at it, but soon as he heard them enter he spoke.

"This is how it go be?" his voice was coarse.

No one said anything.

"I doh want you doin' this Gizzy," he near whispered.

"If I didn' do anything what would have happen to Amron?"

Short tagged breathing. Thoughts brewing. Emotions burning like trees in a wild forest fire.

"This not real," Andre squeezed his eyes shut.

"Dre you just see for yourself," Amron spoke.

"No," he denied. "I still doh understand why she was tryin' to kill us."

"Because," Giselle spoke with exhaustion. "Weyden Empire doh like Majesty. This time it was nothin' personal. Weyden Empire think Majesty abandon them."

"They kind of did," Andre gave his opinion.

"Oh no!"

Giselle was more passionate about the response than she knew herself to be. Hearing someone say this was so much different than being the one saying it. She remembered giving a response like that to Ecoli when he told her his story. She remembered his response too. The people from Weyden Empire had just as much liberty to leave as the people from Majesty did. They chose not to. They also chose to be an Empire of murderers attacking them for no reason and endangering their lives. They chose to stalk her for the past few months. They chose to take away her mother and her grandmother. It was all out of bitterness. She couldn't feel that way anymore. She couldn't defend the idea that Majesty abandoned them. Not anymore. To her, Weyden Empire was what was left after all the good people escaped.

"Majesty have four cities; Floral Cove, Nocturn Niche, Heavenly Heights and Neutral Ground which was made specifically for them, but they choose to stay out. I doh believe Weyden Empire stand for anything Majesty stand for. The devil is a liar if I let them do somethin' to Majesty or to any of us. You doh understand so doh try to talk like you understand anything!"

Andre looked at her as if she was insane.

"Since I go in Majesty I didn' meet one bad person. It was made to help people feel confident being whatever they were. Gran'mom and mom thought it was a good enough place to be in it for years," she went on.

"But mom keep us out for a reason," Andre reasoned.

"So," attitude was strong here. "Duh, she keep us out. You think if you had visions of your children gettin' in this kind of trouble you would of wanted them knowin' about all this? That doh mean the place bad. Is jus' the situation."

This argument was paused by the abrupt pounding on the roof. They all huddled near the bed looking up as if expecting to see something there. The pounding was in no way stealthy or carefully done. It was hammered. Whoever was up there was putting their all into trying to cave the roof in. Simultaneously they heard the front door rattling. The couch would not give way. Noises were coming from all over. It was like a race to see who'd get in first; the roofers or the impatient guest by the door. Startling the wind out of all three of them and finally waking Brent, the window on the other side of the room smashed. Two brutes had flawlessly jumped through landing on all fours. The first one was skinny, but sharp and had a dangerous edge about it. It landed on all fours, but stood up on its hind legs flouncing a towering height. It didn't take much for it to straighten out and their eyes to adjust on Scout. The second one was big and mean looking, very muscular. Something about the eyes were familiar though; those big glowing blue eyes. As the wolf contorted, a straight haired, light skinned cook looked over Giselle and her brothers.

"Ecoli go kill you," Ariel shook her head.

Then the roof caved in, but they hadn't much to worry about anymore.

CHAPTER TWENTY-ONE

THE REASON

PLENTY OF DAYS had passed since the Christmas Hunt, but that never stopped her from dreaming about it and thinking about it twenty-four seven. Turned out the pounding on the door that night was BJ. There was a nationwide alert that someone had gotten into headquarters. People in Majesty were on edge wondering if Weyden Empire actually managed to penetrate and in the Universal Passage of all places. When the Patroller reported what she had seen to Ecoli he knew immediately it was Giselle. He contacted BJ and told him that she'd been seen and that he'd take care of it, but BJ was too anxious to wait. Ecoli sent Scout and Ariel to make sure she was alright. They showed up just in time too with there being Ghouls trying to break in through the roof.

Ecoli didn't hold back on the yelling when they had finally met up. He was light-his-body-on-fire furious. He said he thought he had everything under control and then she popped through the Sui Generis. It took a lot of ass kissing for him to assure the public that they were safe and that he was competent enough to run Majesty. They still weren't sold. Ecoli had managed to keep Weyden Empire out and protected many people through his curfew, but it was always easier to remember the bad than the good. BJ didn't yell at them like Ecoli did. He was just happy to see them alive. Brent was fine medically. Marcel said that whatever happened to him left no scars or evidence of harm. She couldn't diagnose it. As a parent, he was far from fine.

"So you been runnin' back and forth in Majesty for years now?" He asked BJ, but it was very clear that any response to this question would be suicide. "I tell that woman. I tell her…"

He kept pausing not specifying who this woman was. They all knew who it was. He was never truly vague. The sunlight shone brightly through the opened windows of the cleaned-up living room that afternoon. The brightness was damn well joyous, but this wasn't the time for it. It was as if the sun was being entertained by Brent reprimanding his children. The four of them sat with zipped lips on the couch as their dad paced back and forth in front the TV trying to straighten himself out first. Even BJ being twenty-five years old was not ready to talk first. He made no eye contact at all. Giselle sat next to him with her hands clasped waiting to see where this would end up and at what point Brent would involve them. Andre was on the other end of the couch nervous enough to piss himself on the spot. Amron was the only one leaned back with folded arms nearly sleeping.

"Grace know what was comin'. That why she leave you out, but no! She had to put her hand where it doh belong." He argued some more not caring that they were hearing him. "And for what?!"

Giselle had an answer to this question, but she said nothing.

"I put away that life a long time ago for all of you and you jus' doin' what you want and lyin' for one another!" He faced them. "Nobody thought to tell dad nothin'?"

He waited. Giselle looked at him without the slightest urge to speak. He wasn't wishing for responses before so he probably wasn't now. BJ didn't even look at him. This wasn't his scene. He did not like being yelled at. It made him freeze up and he often thought of the right responses once he was able to leave and detox. Andre wanted to say something. When their dad had first corralled them and started ranting he tried to speak. He was cut of instantly. He never said anything after that. He was ashamed and afraid.

"Somebody say somethin'!" Brent yelled at them.

"Now we talk?" Amron lazily asked as no one else would.

"Doh try me today Amron," Brent warned him.

"Dad nobody en tryin' nothin' nah," Amron rubbed his stomach. "I wasn' runnin' left and right nowhere, but Grenada since I born and Dre only find out about this Christmas Eve morning."

"And when you find out?" Brent asked him.

"Giselle," he spoke, but he didn't leave it there. He wasn't the brother that would throw her under the bus. "She realize somethin' was up with the chain and she tell me about it."

BJ looked at Amron knowing that wasn't the story he heard, but he didn't make the stare last long. Amron was trying to take some of the heat off his siblings. It was up to them to back him up for it to work. Brent was well versed that Amron was the one most likely to lie here so if their stories and time-lines didn't match his they'd, be in trouble. This was why Amron had to talk first.

"So Giselle why you didn' come to me?" Brent asked her. "That whole mess on Christmas Eve would of never happen if you did."

"I doh know," she mumbled.

"Dad, so you been in Majesty before then?" Andre brought up.

"Yes," Brent stalled. "A long time ago. I choose what best for all of you and I choose to keep you out. What make you think it was best to sneak around behind my back."

"Because we didn' want to have this conversation," Amron told him.

"And BJ you should know better," Brent pulled up on his eldest again.

"Sorry," BJ apologized.

"Honestly, I doh see why you shoutin' at him because two of you in the same boat," Amron accused still, clearly, not ready to forgive.

"Really? Now?" BJ snapped at him.

"Cut it out. And watch your mouth boy," Brent refereed.

"No." Amron sat up straight now. "So dad, you knew we could do magic too?"

"I knew you could because the whole family could," Andre sank in his seat as Brent spoke. "But…"

"So you know BJ could turn to ice and Giselle could fly and I was seein' dead people?" Amron pompously threw his words at his father with more rage than he was ever known to.

"No," Brent confirmed not decreasing the parental superiority from his tone. "I know you would be able to do magic. Me and your mom jus' never try to find out what you could do. It was irrelevant."

Something about what Brent had said had awoken a raging beast within Amron. Giselle felt exceptionally uneasy sitting next to him as his aura was not welcoming. To her pleasure he got up, but not without putting his brown three quarter shorts in her face. That part she wasn't fond of.

"That doh make no sense. If you know we had magic then you had to know eventually we would start doin' things." He confronted Brent.

Brent did not like the idea of Amron standing up to challenge him. He was the youngest of the boys and the most troublesome. Where did he learn that from? BJ was good as a child and a fine example as a big brother, as was Andre. So why was Amron so brave and challenging? Brent believed Amron had too much influence on Giselle because she was testy too at times.

"You're magical not supernatural. As long as you doh believe things like that could happen, it wouldn'. You would suppress it. We never encourage nothin' about magic in here." Brent answered Amron's point with his own.

"Well it work on Dre alone then," Amron commented heartlessly. "Or you have somethin' you want to say?"

All eyes on Andre he hesitated with a fallen spirit-soundless. His lips fell apart a few times looking for the right words to say, but in the end he shook his head.

"What you gettin' at Amron?" Brent was annoyed.

"My point is," he dragged slowly and with that easily acquired calm tone. "You never say nothin' to any of us and you could be mad all you want, but we have right to be mad too."

"Excuse me?" Brent gaped.

"I not blockin' you," Amron responded cooly.

"Amron you need to sit down and have some respect," BJ warned him.

"Doh tell me nothin'!" Amron lost his cool for a second. The rage so real in him in that moment that his fingers contracted like claws at his side and the veins rose in his neck. His breathing was ghastly and his eyes had closed as if pressure had forced them shut. After that he began to march out of the room.

"Come back here! I not done talkin'," Brent shouted at him with authority.

"Oh yeah? Good," Amron turned back like he had just re-membered something. "Good, because I have another ques-tion. Isaac want to know why you actin' like you doh know him?"

Brent was ready to yell again as it was a natural thing for him, but the words clogged in his throat near choking him. The three left sitting on the couch were switching back and forth between Brent and Amron. They never intended for their dead brother to be brought up this way. It was never discussed, but they all had a much more tranquil setting in mind when think-ing about how they'd bring it up. Why did Amron have to be so blunt all the time?

"What you say?" Some of the intensity had lost its grasp on Brent's vocals.

"Isaac," Amron repeated the name. "Your son."

"How much you know?"

Brent wasn't necessarily asking in context of Isaac. He was just now realizing his children had discovered way more than he thought they did.

"Everything," BJ answered in Amron's place.

Brent tilted his head in BJ's direction awestruck.

"He always been here. He came home after camp. He didn' know he died," Amron continued. "He find out when mom kept cryin' all the time and she wasn' answerin' when he try to talk to her. Then two of you make more children and act like he never happen. He was mad for a long time and he used to haunt BJ and Dre until I born. I was the first person to see him in years."

Brent was enthralled in his story.

"Leavin' us out didn' make no sense," said Amron. "If you didn' do that everything would be different. I know that for sure. And you wouldn' of hurt Isaac…"

There was a long hesitant pause at the end as though he so desperately wanted to add something else on. Deciding against it he left the room despite his father telling him not to.

"Dad, why you never talk about Isaac?" Andre voiced this.

Brent's spirit was heavy; too heavy.

"We didn' forget him. I always remember him and love him. Your mom was real depressed about it for a while, but she wanted to have her family. She was still depressed when BJ born and her way of dealin' with everything was shuttin' it out. She love Isaac a lot, but thinkin' about him always used to make her cry," he answered. "And she jus' didn' want to cry anymore. Just so you know, she love all of you too. She was just in a constant mental battle and her obsessive efforts to pro-tect you turned her into the person you had to be protected from."

"What happen in her visions?" BJ asked his father. "What make her want to keep us out? Gran'mom never told me in detail."

"At this point son, I doh even know anymore. She saw so many things. Too many." He sighed. "Your gran'mom used to say for a long time, *Majesty have more disadvantages than advantages.* Just look at how they address themselves- the magical-supernatural world. Why not just magical, or magical-supernatural-mystical. The shamans still tryin' to remain separate. For some reason nobody sees it. I doh want you there, but all of you already reopen the door to that world."

"Dad," Giselle was taking her turn asking the question. "Shaman or Ersatz?"

He didn't seem to want to answer this question. He had to have known it was coming eventually though.

"Shaman."

CHAPTER TWENTY-TWO

OFFICIAL WELCOME

NEW YEAR'S RESOLUTION…

Everyone seemed to know what they wanted. Some wanted to be better people. Some people wanted to do more with their life. Some people wanted to do less; retire. Some people had it all figured out and here she was, she couldn't even decide what to wear to the celebration. She had been leafing through all her clothes unable to choose. What colour should she wear; she wasn't feeling like sunshine, but she also didn't want to go dressed like the grim. Should it be jeans, was that too casual? Or should it be a dress, was that too much? Nothing felt right. Maybe she should bail out. She sat on her bed and spaced out for a while. She wasn't thinking about anything. For some reason the dresser just seemed to be satisfying to stare at.

BJ showed up eventually. He told his dad he was going to take his siblings to a hang out. He did. It felt so different now though. They weren't just hanging out as BJ, Aibell, Andre, Amron and Giselle. They were; BJ the Ice Ersatz Emissary, Aibell the Banshee, Amron the Necromancer, Giselle the Flight Ersatz Guardian Trainee and Andre- plain old Andre. Conversations were much more open and tension was much thicker; especially between BJ and Amron.

"How come am the only one that can' do anything?" Andre brought up.

He had done a good job not bringing up the topic until then. Giselle had discussed it though- with Vrai. Vrai said she believed Andre did have magical abilities like the rest of them. They were the products of a very powerful family. He just had a more logical, scientific way of looking at life and thus his own technical mentality was suppressing his magical side. This was what their parents were trying to accomplish in all of them. He probably did have some experience when he was younger, being magical. In a family like this one, he had to. Like Marko said it was like learning how to swim. Andre probably broke it down and explained it to himself so much that it became nothing but a theory.

BJ shrugged guiltily as though he had something to do with Andre's sterile life.

"'s normal, I guess," Aibell responded.

Now that it was common knowledge she was born and raised in Majesty she brought her true self to the table. She was from Nocturn Niche and her father was one of the division leaders for patrol there. That was why it was easy for her to land a job as a patroller. She was exceptionally skilled and not one to anger as she had a sharp tongue. She was unique and had a morbid sense of humor and her hair colour changed like the weather; today pink, tomorrow silver. She had several piercings and tattoo's that she did well to cover up before. It wasn't surprising now why BJ was attracted to her. If they had seen this Aibell first they wouldn't have questioned it. Granted she was still a very nice person that openly spoke about anything, but her wacky side was a factor to consider now. She wasn't obligated to hold back anymore. BJ knew his dad knew about Majesty so bringing home a girl with the Majesty accent and sun and moon tattoo would have been a red flag.

"Most o'my blood's shape shifters, but my big sister, she can' do anything. She's athletic, plays any sport you can think up like one o'the boys, but that's as far as it goes," Aibell dished.

"Maybe she athletic because she have the gene to be supernatural," Andre commented. "Maybe there is somethin' there."

"Maybe," Aibell sighed and crossed her legs.

"Then I doh even have the same genes as all of you," Andre sulked.

"Dre, we not shape shifters. You won' be some athletic monster. If you have the gene it go be some psychological thing. Maybe that's why you so smart." BJ concluded.

This appeared to sit well with Andre. He liked that answer. It was obvious with the small smile tugging the corner of his lip.

"Anyway, we celebratin' the New Year as a new family," BJ raised his drink. "Let's not talk about this now."

Over all, it was a pleasant night.

When time drew near BJ took Andre home. Since he wasn't openly capable of magic he wouldn't be allowed in Majesty. The I.WT. key wouldn't let him pass; it would harm him. They never tried to bring him in Majesty simply because they were afraid of what might happen to him on the ride there. It may not have been as bad as the Sui Generis, but it was still better to be safe than sorry. Maybe in the future they'd test his abilities, but for now he had to be left behind. After bidding him farewell they headed off to Majesty. BJ got a new I.W.T. Key and made the bold move of joking with Amron about owing him points. Amron never responded. The three of them, BJ, Aibell and Amron, had to travel to Majesty that way. Giselle however had to use her own method. Ecoli asked her to.

~*~

There was a New Year celebration pending. Majesty took this celebration very serious. There was a time of nonexistence for them. They sprung up out of nothing and they'd been in existence for over two hundred years now. That was cause for celebration. They gathered in the South Side Playing Field every year and had a big party straight through the night. It was organized and held by the denizens, but the Guardians were honored there every year and the deceased remembered. Marko initially told her about it, but Ecoli asked her to attend and experience the good side of Majesty for once.

Being the responsible chief he was he didn't hold a grudge against her for running off on her own. He disapproved that she left, but he respected that she was strong enough to stay and protect her family. They all got out with minor injuries-their dad unharmed. He praised her for this; remembering what she was taught and applying it to a real-life situation. 'Not many people can do that. Most people only have book sense,' he said to her. After she pointed out that she never learned any of her training from a book and annoying him they were both on level ground again.

"Ecoli," she called him.

She was now entering the Rec. Room where he told her he'd be. He was already in there. Ecoli was never one to be late. In fact he was always on point and up to task with everything. She couldn't see why people would look past an important detail as that for something as irrelevant as his magical identity.

"Yeah," he answered.

"Tonight go be ok, right? Remember you tell me the first time I come to stay out of Floral Cove in the night time." She didn't know what to expect in this celebration. "Tell me now so I could brace myself for a heart attack."

He laughed. "Ya gon sight mass supernaturals, but doh worry. They harmless. I only tell ya that the first time because ya was new."

She nodded smiling brightly.

"They might maul me faster than they do ya," he joked.

Her smile faltered. "You go be ok?"

"Yeah, of course. Why it won' be alright?"

"'Cause, people doh exactly agree with you bein' chief," she said. "It won' be chaos, right?"

He took a deep breath. With everything that had taken place somewhere along the line Ecoli's problems had left her mind, but she remembered now. She recalled how aggressive the population was toward him. What if they didn't give him a chance to speak or they started protesting against him forgetting their own celebration. She hadn't been here long enough to see just how much Ecoli did for Majesty. He hadn't been in charge long enough to prove he could even do anything. Keeping Weyden Empire out completely could be counted as a victory, but few people spoke about that. Since day one he'd been dealing with the 'Ruby's dead' celebration Weyden Empire was having. Then there were the speculators. She hoped he kept his cool tonight and got through the celebration without any hiccups.

"Doh worry about it," he sighed.

"So why you wearin' that?" She asked taking note of the great difference in his attire.

The pants were the same colour as the one he usually wore, but this one was softer, crisper and less pocketed. It was like office attire. It fit him; made him look smaller and more professional than the other pants did. With it he wore a dressy button up shirt that was evidently well ironed and had Majesty's crest embroidered over the heart. Just beneath it he had three very important looking badges. One of them was light blue with, again, Majesty's symbol. The second one was the symbol of the patrollers; the horse. The third was purple with a sun wheel engraved in the centre. Over his shoulders, he had a green pallium regale that was equipped with a gold chain that ran from one side of the mantle to the next.

"This is the official Guardian wear," he smirked. "What ya usually see us in is the mission clothes. This we wear when goin' to other magical-supernatural societies, holdin' public meetin's and other important things, like tonight."

"I like it," she complimented. "What about the badge? What they mean?"

He looked upon his chest where they hung proudly. Pointing to the one with Majesty's symbol he spoke again.

"I got this the day I become a Guardian. We all have one." He said. "The hands holdin' onto each other represent unity. Each hand is a city in Majesty. The chief will give ya one and ya have to pledge to always give everything to protect Majesty. That makes it official."

"So I not gettin' one anytime soon," she bat her eyes as if trying to persuade him.

"Maybe next time," he laughed at her attempts.

She sucked her teeth, but she wasn't upset. She had come to terms that Ecoli thought she was too young and he was looking after her to honor Ruby. He was still going to let her train and allow her easy missions like finding a serial thief in Floral Cove. Judging from how it was when she had just decided she wanted to be a guardian, she was satisfied with that.

"This one," he pointed the horse. "I get this when I was made the head o'Patrol. The horse is a symbol o'strength and nobility." Finally, he pointed to the sun wheel. "And this I get when I become chief. The sun wheel represents the sun. Has great impact on life, its powerful and it preserves."

"Deep," she commented realizing how much thought had gone into everything in Majesty. There was the shape of the fire that everyone was obsessed with. There were the four cities dividing the species and maintaining the peace. Then there was the magic that went into making the Sui Generis'. There were twelve of them. That Hubable did some detailed work. Something clicking in her mind at that moment she posed another question.

"So the other two mirrors, we jus' have to wait until people come through it?"

"Yeah," he said.

"How long that could take?"

"Until the spirit find somebody suitable and they figure out the passage," he answered her. "Ever wonder why we have twelve guardians?"

"Nah," she said honestly. That thought had never crossed her once.

"Mass things in Majesty is based on superstition. The number twelve is considered to be whole. It have twelve hours in the day and twelve at night, twelve disciples, twelve zodiac signs, twelve months in the year, twelve tribes of Israel and so on. So we have twelve guardians. That was Hubable way of makin' Majesty whole as well." He explained.

"I never think about that before." She was impressed by this new information.

He smiled, happy to be the first to tell her this. "Anyway, go in the female room. It have somethin' in there for you and when you finish-hurry up please- we could go down to the celebration together."

"Doh rush me," she narrowed her eyes at him. She was practically rushing herself wondering what could possibly be waiting for her in the female room.

Entering the female room, she didn't know what she was looking for, but it wasn't hard to figure out. Stacked on the bed were two big brown boxes with gold covers. On the floor the same two boxes however, they were much smaller. She rushed over to it excitedly gazing in admiration. Sally's Perfect Seams was printed in a fancy font on the top. The cover was smooth to the touch and felt anything, but cheap. She wondered if Ecoli actually spent a large amount of points to get this, whatever it was, for her. Tossing the cover of the first to the side, a thin white paper was the only thing between her and this mysterious gift now. With forced steady hands and an eager smile dug into her features she peeled back the paper. In there she found a brand-new pair of common pants, black shirt and jacket; the same thing Marko and Scout wore the day they left for their mission. She breathed heavily out of joy through her mouth. Ecoli got her the official guardian mission uniform.

She wasn't going to be in that silly jumpsuit anymore. That was significant to her. She felt as though she was closer to becoming someone important, someone great, someone useful. Unable to find patience, she pulled out the jacket and shoved her arms through the sleeves relishing in the comfort off the cold material.

So busy enjoying her brand new clothes she had almost forgotten there were other boxes. Opening the second with the same amount of hungriness as she did the first, she peeled back the protective paper. Giselle wasn't sure if it was possible for her smile to broaden wider than it already was, but her lips were surely testing the boundaries. In the box, as crisp and new as anything could possibly look, was a guardian uniform. The official, recognized uniform exact to the one Ecoli wore. On top of it there was a card that had hand writing on it.

Congratulations! Feel free to put this on and meet me outside.

From: Ecoli

Pulling the jacket off she'd never done as she was told so fast in her life. The shirt was a light polyester material- short sleeved and collared. It was white with the crest on her just a bit higher due to the fact that she wasn't flat chested. The pants like Ecoli's, holding a business person's reputation. It fit so well as though it was specifically made for her. Judging by the name on the box it surely had to be. The only thing missing was the pallium regale. She wrote that off as something probably only the chief wore. All in all, everything was perfect. She saw now it was a waste to wonder what she was going to wear to the celebration as she'd have had to change anyway. The only thing she needed now was a nice pair of shoes to top off the look. Her high-tops weren't going to cut it anymore. This brought her attention to the two boxes at the foot of the bed. Lifting them to the mattress and uncovering she found exactly what she needed. One pair of boots which had to go with the mission uniform and a very classy, polished, covered, sensible shoe for the current outfit she wore. Those came from Sally's Perfect Seams as well.

She rubbed her palm against the wall revealing the route to the bathroom. Busy, she steeped in front of the mirror. Her hair was pulled neatly into a bun that Marcel had done earlier that day. She looked small. She couldn't help, but picture herself among the others, all wearing the same thing, yet she'd be the smallest. That didn't discourage her. It only made her more proud of herself that Ecoli felt she was ready to wear this uniform. Somewhere in between her crowded thoughts of how astonishing she was she wished Ruby and Grace could see her. She wanted desperately to know what they'd say to her. She kind of had an idea for Ruby's words. It would be along the lines of how proud she was and how much like her Giselle was turning out to be. Grace though, she didn't know her mother well enough to know what she'd say. Secretly she always wished she did. This was something she never told even Amron.

Finding Ecoli on the precipitous she was beaming bright as the sun. She tried as hard as she could to hold back her plump cheeks from rising so high and keep her teeth from showing too much. Her feet were practically leaving the ground. Walking out of the female room to Ecoli was something that never happened. She floated the entire way.

"Ya catch a glad? Why so excited?" His face was blank as if he truly believed his own questions, but his eyes gave away a sparkle of humor.

"Nothin'," she couldn't get her feet on the ground at will.

"Ya change clothes or ya was wearin' that the whole time?" he pointed her.

Unable to contain herself anymore she flew forward and hugged him causing him to stumble. Knowing it was the thing people did, Ecoli gave her a weak hug. He looked down at her as though he feared people being this close to him. As if he thought he was some type of hazard and he was afraid he'd hurt her unintentionally. The intensity of his body heat becoming too much too quick she let him go, but it didn't change her mood.

"Ok, we have to go." He took to the stairs.

He didn't show interest in taking the tubes and she wasn't about to remind him that it was an option. She took off floating behind him barking words like a Chihuahua.

"Wait so I could wear this before you introduce me to the public?" She ran her hand over the shirt loving the feel of it.

"I never say that," he answered without turning around.

"Huh?" She scrounged her brows in question. "But you tell me to put it on?"

"Cause some people like to look the part when they bein' introduced," he shrugged.

"Oh!" She exclaimed and grinned even wider. She wrapped him in another unexpected hug from behind and he was jerked to a stop.

"Please stop huggin' me," he said as politely as he could. She let him go when she was good and ready.

"People know I have an announcement to make tonight. First announcement for the night too so let's not waste time. I get a car for us to go in," he informed her in such a mature way.

She kept on, the whole way there, chatting his ear off. For some things she said he smiled and engaged and for others he had no interest or just hadn't the energy to carry on anymore. Giselle didn't care though. She had energy burning inside of her as if fire met gasoline in her stomach. She could not keep calm. The eagerness to meet up with BJ and Amron and show off to them was over the roof. This made the twenty-minute car ride seem like years. Finally, the car pulled of the well-lit road to a grassy setting larger than any playing field she had ever seen. It had to be bigger than the stadium in Grenada. There was a flat pitch that was crowded with occupants of all shapes and sizes and colours. Then behind them, iron stands built from the ground up over ninety feet tall. She felt her heart beat pulsing all the way to her fingers as the car pulled up behind the tall stage. She came out after Ecoli realizing now how cold it was outside. Majesty didn't experience winter, but it did get cold to the point of seeing your breath as you exhaled. This being something Giselle never experienced before she felt extremely underdressed. Her own outfit from home was picked for this weather specifically, not this. Something about actually being there now was swirling butterflies in her stomach instead of a heated flame to which she'd have preferred.

Ecoli held conversation with a few people in headsets behind the scenes. The whole time he was talking to them they kept glancing at her unable to contain their curiosity. Once he was done talking and they finalized their plans for the night they were able to speak to her.

"Honor to mee'ya," the curly haired man bowed his head and kissed the back of her hand that he frontishly took hold off. "Sure ya'll do great things."

"Thank you," she said not knowing if it was the right response.

"A pleasure," the woman bowed too.

Ecoli looked down at the flustered Giselle and smiled.

"Thanks," she muttered again her breath like a puff of smoke.

"Will open the show and then the mic is yours chief sir," The man addressed Ecoli with as much respect as he did the first time.

The two scurried away.

"Ya want this?"

She could have sworn she heard Ecoli ask her something, but it was as if he was speaking from behind a wall. The music was loud; a colourful tune in a language she didn't understand. It didn't sound like a recording so maybe they had a live band performing until it was time. There was a light show dancing across the sky and a loud roar of thousands of people talking at the same time and singing along with the music.

"Giselle, ya want to sit down?" She heard Ecoli faintly again.

"Hm?" He flicked into view. "No, I…"

"Nervous?" He asked. She nodded.

"I could easily switch the announcement. It have a lot o'things I need to tell the public. I could save this for another day," he said to her seeing the horror creep into her face now.

This was what Marko had told her about. She was about to be taken on stage and introduced to the county. She was about to pledge to dedicate her life to making sure it stayed unharmed and discrete. She had a talk with Vrai about this. She had what it took to be a guardian. Plus she had come this far. Majesty stood for something great and she wanted to support that. She wanted to be a part of something Ruby and Grace stood for even if that meant endangering her own life. She did pledge to let her curiosity run free should she find herself in Majesty again, so this was her following through. And if being a part of it helped to bring her family closer along the way she'd be thankful. The nerves rose naturally. Her entire family was magical (with the exception of Andre). They were from the get-go. Even if her mother hadn't decided against bringing them to Majesty, even if she wasn't made Guardian she'd have been in there some way, somehow. She was born for this.

"Eco-leave-every-body-behind," a playful soul approached from behind.

She turned around to be greeted by the remaining eight Guardians. They apparently all drove there together. It was strange to see people dressed up when you weren't used to it. Her eyes had gotten so used to seeing them all scruffy and down to earth in their mission clothes. Now they all seemed spiffy and sophisticated. Marko got a haircut and Scout combed his tangled mess for once. Tegan's uniform worked better for him than the mission clothes did. He was a classy person. Trevor still had bandages on, but they were obviously new ones. They were only on his arm, not his face, which had a scar from his ear to his chin. Ming settled for a red hairclip in place of her usual wear. Hozen had a navy green cloak on instead of brown that did well to hide his face. He was the only one not in the pants and shirt. They looked the same. The only thing different was the fact that Giselle didn't have that green cloak and badges like everyone else did. She didn't care to dwell on it. Small insignificant details she needn't worry about.

"You look so nice!" Marcel gushed when she saw Giselle.

"Not as nice as me!" Marko posed.

"You only look good because you didn't choose the clothes," Ming chastised.

Marko had vengeful comeback to slap her with, but everyone could see that he held it in.

"Good bwoy," Trevor joked at the annoyance on his face.

"Ain't nobody got the time..." Marko sighed.

"Ready for your pinning?" Tegan asked her.

She assumed he was talking about the reveal so she nodded in response. They stayed back there talking for some time. The stage people that were scurrying back and forth walked on egg shells in the presence of the guardians. Some of them stumbled their words. Others needed the space they were in, but were obviously too afraid to ask them to move. The stage manager had to relate everything his workers were afraid to say to them. It was about ten minutes when Giselle heard a male voice take the mic greeting everyone.

"Majesty how ya feeling tonight!" He spoke with enthusiasm.

In the bountiful shouted responses, the name Aubrey stood out well. Was that the same Aubrey that bad mouthed Ecoli like a hobby on TV? He was here now hosting the celebration? Giselle had distaste for him. Looking at Ecoli, he didn't appear bothered at all talking quietly with Ariel. Aubrey went on to telling the crowd about the planned program for the night, highlighting that the Guardians were going to take up the first ten minutes of the show. The crowd sounded most pleased about that. After a few minutes of him hyping the crowd Ecoli took the reins on stage along with everyone else. She stayed back with the stage manager who had kissed her hand earlier and waited until it was 'her cue'.

"This year's Christmas Hunt was one o'the roughest for us," Ecoli outlined and there was wide spread agreement passing over the crowd.

"With the death o'the great, Ms. Ruby Thomas, things, I admit, have been out o'balance." He spoke professionally and not like he was only twenty years old. "However, the scales have tipped in our favor. The Guardians, with help from the patrol unit and many others, managed to successfully keep Weyden Empire from infiltratin'." He let the crowd carry on for some time before continuing. "Everyone o'ya must know of the incident that took place in Head Quarters on Christmas Eve by now. I made very clear that it was nothin' to panic over. The details o'what took place was left vague, but tonight ya learn o'the true events."

The crowd wasn't being negative now, but they were restless about this so-called incident. Giselle peeked on stage from the back, but Aubrey's position was blotching her view. He smelled strong of cologne and was just as cockily dressed there as he was on TV. This was her first time seeing someone from TV in person and she was not in the slightest excited about that. She could hear him saying to one of his colleagues, "o'boy. Another secret." Trying her best to see around him, she managed to grasp the image of Ecoli standing in the spot-light talking into the mic. Behind him, the other Guardian's sat like a civilized bunch in front of a band. She wanted laugh knowing that the way they were acting now wasn't the same as when they were in headquarters. Marko and Ming feuded like children behind the scenes, but here they were sitting next to each other comfortably. Scout who always had a joint in hand and a vague expression was attentive. Trevor and Hozen weren't carrying on like two old buddies in a rum shop and Ariel didn't look mean. Tegan and Marcel were the only ones that looked the same. The nerves building inside were what kept her from chuckling. They did make her smile though and that was calming even if only a little bit.

"A few months ago, I had the honor o'meetin' someone significant. She came through the Sui Generis with just as much vibrancy and boldness the first time as she did on Christmas Eve." There were a few hoots in the air. "The first time she entered she had to fight off a Songbird. The second time she came in, she couldn' get out."

Ecoli recounted Giselle's earlier days in Majesty. She didn't know he knew Vrai wouldn't let her out that time. Did he pretend like he didn't just try to keep her there? She half laughed now.

"Talkin' to her for the first time I realized she wasn' a shy, reserved person. I have come to realize she is one, when she makes up her mind, it cannot be changed. She sticks with her decisions despite persuasions."

"God knows he probably tried," Aubrey commented.

Blocking him out, Giselle found herself thinking about Ecoli's words more deeply. If someone was to ask her about herself she'd never say any of that. Just by the way she had introduced herself to Tegan would confirm that. Hearing about the kind of person she was from someone else's point of view was odd to her. She could agree that everything he said was true, but up until then she hadn't even considered any of that.

"She has constantly proved herself to be a suitable candidate for Majesty. She aided in the rescue of a young shaman before she really knew anything about Majesty and put her life on the line to protect non-magical civilians from a Weyden Empire vampire without considerin' the danger. Her heroics rolled on right up to Christmas Eve. She selflessly snuck out o'Majesty, knowin' that Weyden Empire was huntin' her, to protect her family. By the end o'the night she escaped with not a scratch and her family with nothin' more than a bruise. She is the most inquisitive person I have ever met. Very good at collectin' information she was never meant to know. And never, in all my time admirin' Patrollers and trainin' to be a Guardian myself, have I seen someone grasp precision control over weapons the way she has. Tonight Majesty, we have a new Guardian."

There was a roar overpowering the night as the excitement grew in the crowd. Everyone wanted to know who it was. Even Aubrey was intrigued, not turning around once to see who he was blocking.

"She is Grenadian. A flight Ersatz. Jus' fourteen years old, yet highly tolerant o'the situations she has found herself in. She's a marksman. Granddaughter of Ruby Thomas…"

More cheers.

"Giselle Thomas."

"Miss. Thomas," the stage manager gestured the stage. In his efforts to guide her he nearly pushed Aubrey out of his way. It didn't look like any accident. He apologized. It didn't sound sincere.

Counting every step she took she reminded herself that her name had been called and she had been seen. It was too late to bolt in the opposite direction. She had to step up to the front to be read by the crowd. Eyes of all colours and shapes boring into her bringing up a sweat; she wasn't cold anymore. Ecoli was waiting for her to join him patiently. The spotlight was blinding and she could see nothing for a long time. There was a ringing in her ear. She never thought she had stage fright, because she had never been on a stage before. Maybe this wasn't stage fright. Maybe this was her realizing the commitment she was about to make. The sound waves emitting from the crowd vibrated on her chest and she had to force a few breaths out of her to make sure she stayed conscious. She was sure that most of these people were cheering because she was related to Ruby. To relax herself she started wondering whether people knew BJ was related to Ruby. They didn't flock him when he took them to Majesty on Christmas Eve. Thinking about her brother made her search the crowd now trying to find his face. So many creatures… she couldn't find either of them. Contorted figures and snake like features and claws and elongated canines greeted her from all corners.

"Giselle Thomas, the new owner of the Sui Generis Vrai-The Truthful Spirit."

Some people gushed over the fact that she had Ruby's Sui Generis as well. They were practically losing their minds being in the presence of their new protector.

Blinking her sights back she regained the gift of seeing. Ecoli couldn't speak. It was too loud and no speaker could over power this noise. There was howling echoing from all directions. She hadn't noticed when, but Marcel and Trevor were standing beside Ecoli. Marcel had a well decorated box that had little drawings like the sun wheel sprawled around it in all the colours of the units in Majesty; blue, purple, green, orange, brown, grey, gold and black. Inside there was a white pillow carrying two badges. Trevor had something Green folded in his hand. Marcel smiled and radiated that warm comfort that Giselle needed. She glanced over the crowd again sill unable to find her brothers. She could try looking for Aibell, but if she couldn't find people she had seen her whole life then that would be useless. Asking them to pipe down with hand gestures Ecoli began again.

"We will be startin' the new year with ten Guardians. Two away from bein' whole again." He said.

"Yeaaahhhh!" They chanted.

Retrieving the badge from Marcel he handed it to Giselle instructing her to hold it near her heart. She followed, carefully placing the badge with Majesty's crest in her palm and holding it over her heart. Then she had to repeat after Ecoli. Before he began she did another sweeping of the crowd for her brothers. She was taking it in sections now- searching the back left then the back right and the stands. She was aware it was a hopeless search, but she couldn't stop herself. Ecoli began speaking and she forced to pay attention realizing the crowd had gone silent now.

"I promise for as long as I am a Guardian…" Ecoli spoke.

"I promise for as long as I am a Guardian…" her voice didn't sound like her own over the mic.

"…that I will put my all into protectin' Majesty…" he continued.

"…that I will put my all into protectin' Majesty… I promise to treat the cities… Floral Cove, Nocturn Niche and Heavenly Heights… as equals. I promise to remember… that it is not the smartest of the species that survives… nor the most intelligent… it is the one that is more adaptable to change. And I promise to live by that philosophy." She finished her pledge witnessed by the denizens.

Ecoli did the honor of pinning the badge on for her. Then he retrieved the other badge from Marcel. Giselle looked down on her chest admiring the light blue badge she could now call her own. She hardly even paid attention to Ecoli holding up the other badge and speaking to the crowd.

"Ladies and Gentlemen, tonight we have found our third member of Dispatch," her eyes raised to him now putting a second pin on her. She never thought she'd end up in dispatch. Tegan said they were the best. Was she qualified for that or was Ecoli just pulling her leg? Her head constantly dropped ninety degrees as she admired the black badge. There was a gold eagle engraved in it. She swept the front left of the crowd- no BJ, no Amron. Ecoli retrieved a navy green cloak from Trevor and it was fitted around her. She was grateful for it. It was heavier than it looked, but the weight was tolerable for the warmth and coverage that came with it. She wasn't feeling the bite of the night air like she was before because of her shock. Still, she could feel the difference when the material wrapped around her.

It was her time now. She had to face the crowd as a Guardian and speak to them for the first time. Whatever words she said now would be her own. No matter how silly, outrageous, polite or rude it was it would be something the denizens would be talking about for years to come. What was she to say? She wished she had been given more notice to prepare something. Her mind was clean out of everything she had come to know as a living human being. It was that bad. She had to find her brothers. She was carelessly finishing off her search of the front left now knowing that the crowd was waiting on her to speak. They all gazed up, a few chattering here and there, with expectant eyes and the words were not forth coming. She scoped the front right corner now. She couldn't find them, but at this point she would have to say something. She could feel something heavy sinking in her chest wondering if her brothers even saw what just happened. Then, as she raised the mic to her mouth, looking down at it as she did so, she saw them. They had been directly in front of her the whole time. Right near the foot of the stage. She had been looking beyond it the whole time. A new sense of gladness coursed in her veins seeing them there looking up her. BJ pumped his fist in the air when he realized she had seen him Amron following to suit. He must have been in high spirits to follow after BJ. A grin spreading over her face once more she gripped the mic tightly and pumped her fist in the air looking directly at them.

And the crowd cheered.

CHAPTER TWENTY-THREE

THE PRESENT

THEY HAD STUCK around for some of the show, but when it came to remembering the lost Guardians things got depressing. In spite of their feud, Giselle managed to get the boys together for a walk after her welcome ceremony. They weren't outwardly verbally attacking each other anymore. Things had died down. It was evident Amron was still upset, but not enough to say anything to BJ about it anymore. Giselle couldn't understand why he wouldn't just let it go. She did. Yes, BJ kept things from them. Considering his reasons, he had good intentions. Plus, Ruby made him keep quiet and he respected her as both a grandmother and a chief to do as he was told. It wasn't all on BJ's shoulders; this she grasped.

They stood in the guardians' graveyard in solitude. It was New Year's Eve, and they wanted to officially pay their respects to their grandmother; the one that ruled over Majesty and gained the respect of allied nations and humbled Weyden Empire. They wanted to say good bye to that version of her even though BJ was the only who really knew that side. They had to let her know that they'd be alright embarking upon their new life and that they'd make her proud. They had to let her know they would stick together and take care of each other no matter what…

They were surrounded by the unique torches of Ecoli's unshaped fire and headstones of past guardians. To Giselle and BJ they were alone, but to Amron the grave yard seemed to be in the full swing of life under the purple of the sky.

"You come in a bad time," BJ broke the solace of the atmosphere.

"I didn' realize," Giselle hummed sarcastically.

"No," he snorted softly. "I mean Weyden Empire. I not gettin' a good vibe from them."

"You ever get a good vibe from them before?" She asked in a manner that said she already knew his response.

"Am an Emissary. I know all messages goin' in and out of Majesty and I know who send them and who it goin' to," he paused. "Somethin' don' seem right lately."

"How so?" Giselle was more attentive and less judgmental now.

"Bokamoso. More messages between them and people closely related to Roscoe. You might of heard of him. He get arrested. He is bad news and so was his sister Beth. Why we should trust anybody else related to them? As it is now recon have nothin' against them so we can' stop them from doin' anything."

"Maybe you should put Bokamoso under surveillance then. They need us more than we need them so they might comply. Majesty is the bread. Either that or put more conditions on the alliance." Giselle spoke rather business like.

"Well look at you," BJ had the proud glow about him. "Official guardian for ten minutes and already talkin' sense."

She joked and pushed his shoulder, "I mean, you should tell Ecoli that."

BJ raised his brow, "Me? Am jus' an Emissary. Maybe you should do that. Am older, but you have more power."

"Oh yeah," she gasped.

She did have more say in the affairs of Majesty now didn't she? She had the right to fix things if she didn't like it. She had the right to investigate things she found suspicious and the biggest one of all, she had the responsibility of looking over everyone in there. She had to do her best because all this meant was if anything went wrong it would be on her shoulders and could cost some lives. She was in dispatch now. That was an intense unit. Unlike the other units that maintained Majesty and made it a working country, her unit was like the great wall that had to keep all the bad things out. She had to do well. She had to be able to smoothly map out problems and find solutions.

…adaptable to change…

Amron stood up and joined them. From the time they had arrived, he started talking to their grandmother's grave quietly. He said he couldn't see her, but he just had a lot of things to say. BJ and Giselle left him to it.

"Anyway," BJ clapped his hand together. "Is five minutes until 2014 and I doh want to start the New Year fightin' with my brother." He stared hopefully at Amron who slowly glanced at him.

"Let we fix it here for gran'mom to see. Start the new year fresh," BJ continued pleasantly.

"She not here," Amron informed dryly.

"You know what I mean?" BJ responded to which Amron rolled his eyes.

"That mean somethin' different to me," Amron said.

"Amron, you can' still be mad. Sorry, but you have to understand why I didn' say anything," BJ approached him with a begging tone.

"I understand," Amron cleared up.

"So what then? You forgive me? You doh forgive me? You need more time? What?" BJ was as lost as Giselle was.

With barely any movement or change in Amron's face he said, "BJ I say I understand."

"Then we good?"

BJ's face was light again, but Giselle felt he was still uncertain. Playfully, like the likable person he was, he tried to hug Amron. With one swift motion, weaseling away from BJ before he could even be grasped. Amron glared.

"What?" BJ asked not as shocked as one would think. He knew Amron would try to get away from him. It was what siblings did. If BJ ever tried to hug Andre he'd get the same reaction. Giselle was the only one that accepted his hugs… on certain occasions.

"BJ!" Amron's voice was frightening. "Stop. You keep askin' me if I understand. Do you understand?"

"Understand what?" BJ narrowed his eyes.

"If you think about it then maybe you would!" Amron yelled at him. "You know the whole time I was seein' things and you act like it wasn' happenin'."

"We already established that."

Amron suddenly had an outburst so great it was quite plausible the dead would rise and ask him to be quiet.

"See, you doh understand because you not thinkin' about it from a different point of view. I get why you keep the secret. If I was you I probably might of keep quiet too. Eventually I would have tell Gizzy, but for the most part I wouldn' say anything," he argued. "But am not you. I thought I was goin' crazy. I thought I was just like mom. Imagine walkin' in a class with your friend and tellin' him you want to leave because it too crowded and he say he doh see anybody! Every day, everywhere I go, for as long as I could remember I was seein' spirits. People that was on the death news the night before was tryin' to talk to me the next day and I not supposed to think I crazy? You know haw scary that was? I didn' say anything because I thought dad was goin' to put me in the pink house and I was goin' to lose my mind and die just like mom!"

He was shaking animatedly and his eyes never left BJ who was deeply entrapped in his confession. Giselle felt as though her heart had stopped after hearing that. Turned out she didn't know her family as well as she thought she did. BJ, Ruby, Grace and Amron all magical and all fighting inner demons just like Andre and their dad was. She almost felt shallow. While they were all being deeply affected by inner conflictions surrounding their identity and personality all she wanted was to be treated like a grown up. All she wanted was to have a good family with money and to be able to partake in teenage activities without being questioned or stopped. She was still young and those were the things that were important to her, but she felt like it shouldn't have been now. She felt transparent.

"I thought what she had was genetic and all the time you know about it and you could of say somethin', but you leave me thinkin' it was only time before I die in the pink house. That's why I upset BJ! Am not mad! Am upset." He got quiet now, his voice cracking on the last words. He invited a strong breath of air into his lungs. "My whole life I was paranoid... and you could of help me just by sayin' *I know you could see things*, but you didn' do that for me. I didn' have to know about Majesty or Gran'mom or even mom. I jus' had to know I wasn' crazy and imaginin' things. But you didn' say anything."

Something so foreign made its way from Amron's eyes and down his cheeks. It didn't belong there. That wet streak of hurt. That substance that flowed out of one's body when one was filled to the brim with emotion and couldn't hold things in anymore. That liquid pain; something she didn't know Amron could produce. She didn't think he knew the formula until now. Not even when he was physically hurt did he produce this substance. He blinked his eyes trying to hide it away. She didn't know what to say. Her foul mouthed, fearless, troublesome brother who she thought couldn't feel these types of emotions was crying. And she could see BJ was at loss for a reaction too. Seeing Amron like that brought on the worst pain she'd ever felt in her life. Loosing loved ones hurt yes, but she knew that, that was inevitable. Seeing her brother, who was supposed to be invincible, falling through the cracks; she never imagined this happening. Trying to comfort him she wiped his tears and patted his back fearing that if she embraced him he'd push her away too.

"I didn' know-" BJ began, eyes like pre-cooled jello.

"-you would of know if you said somethin'."

Amron gently moved Giselle's hand away from him and tracked back to the arch way through which they came. He was leaving things like that. He opened up a whole can of emotions, spilled it all over the floor and didn't even try to clean it up. He simply wasn't ready to be ok with BJ and his motive was reasonable. His whole life he had been seeing things. That must have been terrifying as a child and having a mother like theirs didn't help him. Just like Andre was paranoid about his perfection he was paranoid about his imperfection. It explained why he was the way he was; hardened. He couldn't be a crybaby with a power like that; especially when he was trying to keep it a secret. He couldn't flinch every time a spirit came into the room or else he'd have to explain himself or he might have given his dad ideas. Being a Necromancer made him super aware of his surroundings and un-scarable. It made sense now. And having Isaac with him was why he always knew everything. He embraced the power enough to keep him sane, but not enough to be proud of it.

Giselle turned longingly to BJ as though begging him to go after Amron.

"You know it wouldn' make a difference," he shook his head.

He was right. Maybe in time, since he opened up now, he'd feel better. Although his words were cold, she could see and respected why Amron was upset. Now that it was out in the open she was hoping that the healing process would begin. Giselle couldn't help, but think again that all this could have been avoided if they had known about Majesty from the beginning. Isaac would be alive. Andre wouldn't feel the need to suck up to adults. Amron wouldn't have gone through what he did and maybe their mom and grandmother would still be alive. Dreaming of what her life could have been like could easily become her new obsession. They all could have been different. This feud would have never happened. She wouldn't have gone through what she did just to be trained as a Guardian. Not to mention she might have been older when she became a guardian; not a lost fourteen-year-old who had no clue what she was in for. All this because Ruby respected Grace too much to bring Giselle and her brothers into Majesty. All this for her mother, who she barely knew.

"BJ..." she started tearing up on her new shirt. She couldn't even get the words out.

"Shhhh," he comforted. "I go fix it."

And hot with tears and emotion she held onto her brother's words as though they were some sort of prophecy for the future. They had to get home soon to welcome the New Year with their family next. Soon they'd be saying 'remember when that happened last year?' Soon everything that had happened would be left in the year before and they'd have a blank calendar to fill with memories. So what did she want for this New Year? What did she want to fill it with? Last year she had made it her personal quest to save as much money as she could and to be treated like a bigger person. This year that didn't seem as important anymore. This year she didn't know what she wanted. She couldn't possibly predict what she was going to fill the days in her calendar with. She knew that she didn't want her family to be hurt anymore. She also knew that she didn't want to leave Majesty; either way Vrai wouldn't let her. So, what did she want? Was a new year's resolution even plausible right now? The conclusion was to forget the past, it had already happened and they couldn't change it. Forget the 'what if's' because worrying about what could have been would only hinder what is to come. She just had to worry about the present and know that somewhere in the future her family is whole again.

To Be Continued...

About the Author

Krystal Cyrus is the twenty-one-year-old author of The Enigmatics, a teen thriller set in her home island of Grenada. She is also the CEO of her own publishing company, OOTW Publishing & Media. Krystal enjoys telling stories and exploring the world of 'what if's'. Follow her online for great content and to learn more about the 'In The Mirror' series. She can be found online at www.ootwonline.com, Facebook as Krystal Cyrus and Instagram as @cyruskrys21.